In the Dark

Lina Areklew was born in Stockholm in 1979 and grew up on the High Coast. Today she divides her time between a house northwest of Stockholm and a croft outside Örnsköldsvik. After a career as a project manager within telecommunications, she studied literature and now works as a freelance copy editor. Her debut novel is set in Stockholm and on the island Ulvön outside Örnsköldsvik.

Also by Lina Areklew

Death in Summer
In the Dark

IN THE DARK

LINA AREKLEW

First published in the United Kingdom in 2026 by

Canelo Crime, an imprint of
Canelo Digital Publishing Limited,
20 Vauxhall Bridge Road,
London SW1V 2SA
United Kingdom

A Penguin Random House Company
The authorised representative in the EEA is Dorling Kindersley Verlag GmbH. Arnulfstr. 124,
80636 Munich, Germany

Copyright © Lina Areklew 2026

The moral right of Lina Areklew to be identified as the creator of this work has been asserted in accordance with the Copyright, Designs and Patents Act, 1988.
All rights reserved. No part of this publication may be reproduced or transmitted in any form or by any means, electronic or mechanical, including photocopy, recording, or any information storage and retrieval system, without permission in writing from the publisher.
No part of this book may be used or reproduced in any manner for the purpose of training artificial intelligence technologies or systems. In accordance with Article 4(3) of the DSM Directive 2019/790, Canelo expressly reserves this work from the text and data mining exception.

A CIP catalogue record for this book is available from the British Library.

Print ISBN 978 1 83598 388 1
Ebook ISBN 978 1 83598 389 8

This book is a work of fiction. Names, characters, businesses, organizations, places and events are either the product of the author's imagination or are used fictitiously. Any resemblance to actual persons, living or dead, events or locales is entirely coincidental.

Cover design by Andrew Smith

Cover images © Shutterstock

Printed and bound in Great Britain by Clays Ltd, Elcograf S.p.A.

Look for more great books at
www.canelo.co | www.dk.com

Prologue

The smell of urine hits her. Her eyes sting.

Her thoughts are clouded from the dream. It's summer and the sun caresses her naked body as if with a warm paintbrush. She is lying on the narrow, sandy beach down by the lake. No towel, just hot sand burning under her back. Her feet in the water. Cold lake water starts slowly creeping up her shins, over her thighs and stomach. The heat is gone. There is only cold now.

There it is again. The smell of urine. She opens her eyes but sees nothing. The first wave of fear is related only to her eyesight. Something is wrong. She runs through her training in her head. Sudden blindness. What could cause that? A blood clot? Something is wrong with her breathing, too. Each breath coming spasmodically, it burns just below her heart. Her whole torso hurts, but the pain is worst in the back of her head. Around the level of her ear it's throbbing.

Then her memory catches up.

The house, the snow, someone is suddenly standing in the living room. Cable ties chafing her wrists. She presses her arms to her sides and discovers that they're still tied behind her back.

Images from her memory come in rapid succession. The rear door of a car, swirling snow and the terrible cold. The parade of images freezes, and she understands. She isn't blind. There just isn't any light to see by.

The pain in her side must be from broken ribs. She is almost sure of it. The pain reminds her of when she fell off the wall bars in the gym in middle school. Her ragged breaths are also problematic. Could she have punctured a lung?

Still, she feels some satisfaction at having sorted everything into the right box. No loose ends that cannot be tied together into a rational, medical explanation. She has diagnosed her own hopeless situation.

She tries to move her hands around inside the zip ties to check her own pulse. Her heart is beating fast, too fast. With effort she gets up onto her knees. There is a flash of lightning inside her eyelids, but she manages to get to her feet.

It's impossible to say how many hours or days have passed. She sees and feels only the jet blackness around her. There is no way to tell if it's the middle of the night or the middle of the day.

Despite the fear surging through her and her body aching, her mind feels sharp. Her best weapon to get out of here. She knows that. How long can you go without? *The rule of threes.*

Three minutes without air.

Three weeks without food.

And only three days without water.

Thursday, 20 February, 2020

1

Fredrik looked down at his plate and noted with gratitude that Inga, who over the years had become something of a second mother to him, was once again doing her utmost to meet all his needs. Potato and Jerusalem artichoke puree with moose sirloin steak. Fredrik's slices were already pre-cut into thin strips, and then again on the diagonal to form easy to chew pieces, even though his jaw injury had long since healed. It was hardly visible anymore from the outside. A vague scar below his ear, but otherwise he could hardly feel it. She ignored the fact that he had given up eating all meat, anything that walked on four legs, many years ago, and firmly maintained that a grown man needed more protein than just beans and some measly fish every now and then.

They sat in the kitchen on Ålstensgatan, a stone's throw from the house he had grown up in with his mother, father and Niklas. Another family lived there now. The small yard in front was full of sleds. Somehow that felt good, as if the happiness he had felt when he lived there had been passed on to the next family.

He had gone over to his best friend Philip's flat in Bromma to pick up the car, but neither Philip nor the car had been there when Fredrik arrived. When he had stopped by Philip's parents' place to see if Philip was there, Hans and Inga had immediately trapped him. Inga never missed an opportunity to offer him food. Dinner was already ready, she had asserted, and he needed to eat anyway, so here he sat.

Hans nodded knowingly at Fredrik's plate and then put his fork into his own moose steak.

'You should give hunting a try, Fredrik,' he advised, his whole face lighting up. 'There isn't a feeling in the world that compares with the thrill of sitting in a blind early in the morning. The fog lies like a low, milky cloud over the meadows, all the forest sounds are crystal clear through the trees, and at any moment…'

Hans raised his fork over the dining table, a far-away look in his eyes. He was lost in his own poetic description of the glory of the hunt.

'At any moment, a 300-kilogram wild animal might step out of the trees on its long, majestic legs.'

Inga reached awkwardly across the table to clean up a few drops of chanterelle sauce that had dripped from Hans's fork.

'I don't think Fredrik has any interest in hunting,' she chided with a gentle edge to her voice to summon Hans back from his mental forest romp.

'No, it's not for everyone, I suppose. I'll give you that. You can't lose your nerve when you're sitting in the blind, no, you cannot.'

'Well, I didn't mean it like that,' Inga said, looking at Fredrik. 'I mean, I know you wouldn't lose your nerve, but given what you've been through, well… maybe guns aren't so appealing?'

Fredrik laughed joylessly and scratched his dark stubble. His dark brown hair was freshly cut, but he had forgotten to shave that morning.

'No, Hans. Guns don't appeal to me.'

Guns were the last thing he was interested in after the previous summer's commotion. Sure, the gunshot wound to his abdomen had healed as nicely as his jaw, but the psychological scars would be there forever. He had trouble sleeping and most nights he didn't sleep at all. He he had already suffered from nightmares, from before, but now those nightmares were kept company by recurrent replays of the gunshot that had hit him just above his appendix. If he hadn't been airlifted to Örnsköldsvik Hospital by helicopter for surgery, he would have died. Fredrik's mind just grazed the thought of Sofia Hjortén. She was one of the people who had been there to take care of him. Without her, he wouldn't have made it.

'How are things going with Ida?'

'Fine.'

Inga raised her eyebrows, and he realised she was waiting for him to go on.

Ida Niemi, the speech language pathologist, who had helped him with his speech rehab therapy after the hammer blow to the jaw, had worked wonders. He could chew and laugh, and his stiff facial muscles and slurred speech had eased after an abundance of articulation and jaw exercises. He would tire after only a couple of repetitions, but Ida had urged him on. A motivated patient had the best chances of success was her motto, and she had done everything in her power to motivate him. He was basically fully recovered now. All that remained was a clicking sound in his jaw when he yawned.

Ida had been there for him as an emotional support throughout his whole long road back. They had become friends, and once he was no longer her patient, their friendship had developed into something more, to Inga's and Hans's unconcealed delight.

Hans held his fork up suggestively, which resulted in more drips on the tablecloth.

'She's beautiful, Ida is, a real gem. You should take care of her.' He stuffed the piece of potato on his fork into his mouth and continued talking without biting into it.

'Grandchildren, Fredrik. We want grandchildren. And our own son doesn't seem like he's going to give us any.'

Inga frowned disapprovingly but then turned towards Fredrik and smiled. The grandchild conversation was not new, and Fredrik knew that this was high on Inga's wish list. Even so, the thought made him uncomfortable. He and Ida hadn't even had sex yet. They hugged and put their arms around each other on the couch, but they hadn't taken that next step towards the complete intimacy that he knew she longed for. He wasn't ready, physically or emotionally.

He was grateful that Ida wasn't rushing him. She was a warm, welcoming person. Uncomplicated. She had made it her life's work to make sure he did his exercises and was doing all right. Whenever she had a spare minute at work, she usually called or texted to find out how he was. Fredrik appreciated the distraction. The silence in his flat had started to get on his nerves a long time ago, and any opportunity to turn off his thoughts was welcome.

'Have you heard anything from work?' Inga continued, pouring herself some more wine. Hans, who seemed like he had had some before Fredrik arrived, set his now empty glass out for her to refill as well. She didn't even offer Fredrik any wine.

'Yes, we've been in touch some,' he replied evasively, but Inga was not so easily deterred.

'And?'

The doctors hadn't been stingy with the length of his medical leave. He didn't need to worry about getting back to work. But what was there to look forward to anyway? Day after day behind a pane of glass. *Step forward, place your feet on the yellow marks, look into the camera, sign here. You can pick your passport up in a week.* Sure, it paid the bills, but after just barely managing to escape death for a second time, Fredrik was starting to think that he owed it to himself to at least try to live, not merely exist.

He changed the subject.

'Are you going skiing this year?'

But Inga didn't take the bait.

'Are you going to get your old position back?'

Hans, who had just swallowed the last bite of his food, chimed in.

'Let him be, Inga! He's a grown man, for God's sake. He can look after himself.'

Inga smiled and nodded, but gave Fredrik a look that conveyed they would revisit the subject.

'Speaking of which,' Hans said and burped discreetly into his napkin. 'Have you heard anything from our son?'

Philip opened the hood and stared at the plastic cover over the engine. *Volvo*. Five familiar letters, but not even a hint about how to open it as far as he could see. How was he supposed to figure out what was wrong without being able to look at the engine? There was a worrisome hiss coming from underneath the plastic. He wished he was one of those men who could get down onto his knees and peer under the car and immediately determine which of all the parts wasn't working. But he wasn't. He needed a mechanic or, in a worst-case scenario, a rental car.

As luck would have it, he had made it almost all the way to the gas station in the middle of the small town. Philip had left the car in a snowdrift on the side of the road and now struggled his way across the unploughed crosswalk.

It was snowing so hard that he could barely see. He thought about Emil and Alfred's trip through the heavy snow to Mariannelund in Astrid Lindgren's Emil books. He was frustrated to have to stop now when it was only an hour and a half away.

He hoped she would be happy and that they would get back together. That she would see the gesture as romantic, even though he was only planning to stay two nights. He wanted to be gone before her father showed up on Saturday in any case. They would still get to spend two nice days together. They could go snowmobiling and trudge through the deep snow. Although he was hardly equipped for winter activities, either in terms of his clothes or psychologically. Philip looked down at his suede shoes. They looked like winter shoes, but they were undoubtedly made for a Stockholm city winter, not real winter. After only a few steps in the snow, they had already started to let in water, and his feet were ice cubes before he even reached the door of the gas station. He was glad he had chosen a proper down jacket at any rate.

'Wow, it's really dumping down out there!' The gas station attendant laughed as he stepped through the door. The floor was covered with melted snow and Philip cautiously shuffled over to the cash register through one of the gritty puddles.

'The ploughs can't even keep up with it, it's coming down so fast,' the woman continued, pulling her blue cardigan with the gas station's logo around her more tightly.

'My car broke down,' Philip stated awkwardly, pointing to the stranded car across the street.

The woman looked at him, waiting for him to go on.

'I… kind of need a mechanic. Or a rental car.'

A new customer walked through the door and stepped over the water, heading for the restrooms. The attendant raised her hand in recognition at the man who waved back before he went around the corner where the wiper blades and ice scrapers were hanging.

'There's no mechanic here today. Mikael, who usually works in the shop next door there,' she pointed with her thumb, 'is out ploughing. And we don't have a rental car place in town. The closest one is probably in Sundsvall.'

Philip pulled off his hat and rubbed his damp, ash-coloured hair. He tried not to let the panic take hold of him. He had already made it so far. This time last year he had been living in his parents' basement, cut off from the outside world. He could program and maintain the code for various companies' IT systems from his desk at home in the safety of Ålsten without any trouble, a seemingly endless job that was always in demand. He kept in touch with his customers via email and messaging apps. Many people thought he was strange, he knew that, but even so his one-man consulting firm was still highly sought after. Social situations made him nervous and uncomfortable. No one ever seemed to understand him, and he definitely did not understand other people. It had been that way ever since his early teens. Every forced attempt by his parents to get him to re-enter the world had been followed by severe panic attacks and an even greater need for seclusion. But after everything that had happened to Fredrik the previous summer, something had changed. Philip had been forced out of his shell. His friend had needed him, and he had very quickly discovered that he could actually handle seeing other people as long as he could do it on his own terms. In the last six months, he hadn't merely left the house. He had found himself a flat and taken an intensive course in Dalarna to get his driver's license. And now he had a girlfriend. Someone who saw him and appreciated him for who he was. Someone who, just like him, had a hard time understanding other people, but seemed to understand him like no one else. He intensely longed to see her. She would be so surprised that he had come, and their argument would be forgotten. Philip was determined not to be sucked into a pit of anxiety due to the mishap with the car. He would persevere.

The gas station attendant cleared her throat.

'Don't you have a roadside assistance plan?' she suggested.

He gave her a blank look. Try as he might, he could not think what that might be.

'You know, like AAA or Falck or something?' she continued.

Philip shook his head silently.

'It's not my car,' he mumbled.

'If you have roadside assistance, they can arrange for towing and a rental car. In a worst-case scenario, you could take a taxi to the nearest rental car company. If it's really bad, I mean.'

Philip thanked her for the advice and bought an obligatory coffee and a pack of cigarettes before he walked back to his now snow-covered car.

Fredrik pushed open the front door a few centimetres and looked up at the sky. It was cold and frost had started to form, but there wasn't a snowflake to be seen. The sky was clear and if it hadn't been for all the streetlights, the stars would surely have been visible. Hans and Inga stood in the front hall and kept him company while he put on his jacket.

'Here, take a pair of gloves. It's cold out.' Inga handed him a pair of leather gloves from the basket by the door. 'Are you going home now or over to Ida's?'

Hans and Inga couldn't have been more overprotective if they had been his real parents. They had been there for him ever since that night on the Baltic Sea that had decimated his own family. Along with his grandmother, they had had to act as his parents in the absence of his real mother and father.

Inga tried to take back the container of food Fredrik was holding. It was wrapped in a plastic bag, and she tugged cautiously at the handle, which was sticking out from under his arm.

'Wait, I'll add some more so there's enough for Ida, too.'

Fredrik held onto the food and shook his head.

'No need. She doesn't eat meat either.' He winked at Hans, but Hans didn't seem to get the joke. 'And I'm too tired to go over to her place now.' He glanced at the old alarm clock on the table in the front hall. It was already after ten. 'It'll be home and straight to bed for me.'

Inga nodded reluctantly and let go of the plastic bag.

'Did you bring your car?'

'No, I'm taking the tram. Philip borrowed my car. He was going to buy a new desk.'

They hugged goodbye in turns and Fredrik promised to come back again soon.

–

The tram stop was two blocks away. Fredrik set the bag with the food in it on the platform, pulled out his cell phone and read the two text messages that Ida had sent where she told him that she got off work at six o'clock today if he wanted to come over and watch a movie or something. Her tone had grown increasingly urgent lately. Even so, he was reluctant to take the next step.

It would mean a definitive end to what he had had with Sofia over the summer. Deep down, he knew that was already over, and yet something made him resist. But Ida's impatience was growing by the day and soon he would be forced to decide.

Just as he was about to text her back that he was too tired to get together, his phone rang. It was Philip.

'So, how did it go?' Fredrik asked. 'Did you get trampled by mums with strollers and a bunch of newlyweds in the sofa section?'

'Not exactly,' Philip muttered. 'Your car died.'

'What do you mean?' Fredrik asked and picked up the bag of food as the tram pulled up to the stop. He climbed in and sat down in a window seat.

'What's wrong with it?'

'How should I know?' Philip snarled. He sounded stressed out. Situations like this were just the sort of thing that usually pushed him over the edge.

Late the previous summer and over the fall, Philip had started leaving his parents' house more often. He had even visited Fredrik at Sundsvall Hospital, where he had had his jaw surgery, even though that was more than five hours away by train. Right before Christmas, Hans and Inga had rented a flat for Philip just a few blocks from their place. A studio with a kitchenette. It was a nice change from the basement of his parents' house.

'Just calm down,' Fredrik said. 'Leave the car in a parking lot and take a taxi home. I'll go look at it in the morning. Are you at the Ikea in Kungens Kurva or the one in Barkarby?'

Philip cleared his throat on the other end of the line, sounding strained.

'That won't work. I'm not at Ikea. I'm not even in Stockholm.'

Fredrik laughed.

'What do you mean?'

'What the hell do you think I mean? Do you have a roadside assistance plan?'

Fredrik could clearly hear that Philip was near the breaking point. Arguing about his location would only stress him out even more.

'Yes. There's a sticker on the inside of the driver's door. Call them and they'll help you. Philip, I'm a little concerned...'

But he had already hung up.

2

The baby would not stop kicking. While it was nice to know that it was in there and moving around, Sofia felt a growing irritation at not being able to settle down. It had been more than an hour since they had gone to bed, and even though she was incredibly tired, she could not fall asleep. No matter what position she was in, there was something pushing or pulling. When she tried to lie on her back, it was hard to breathe. If she rolled onto her side, the baby started kicking and protesting. The only thing that worked was sitting in the rocking chair she had dragged inside from the deck and putting her feet up on a footstool in front of her. For the last two months, this had been her permanent sleeping arrangement.

But the living room was occupied right now, so she had had to drag herself upstairs to the hard, wooden queen bed. It was her parents' old one and she had never gotten around to replacing it. The house had sat empty for so many years after her father's death that once she had moved back in, she hadn't had the heart to change anything. Everything exuded calm and patience and even though it reminded her of her mother, Claire, it was Sten's essence that dwelled in the walls. There was nowhere on earth where Sofia felt as comfortable as she did here. Her flat in the city was cosy and close to work, but most of the time she chose to stay out here on Ulvön Island. Even if that meant long commutes across the water in her father's Riva Ariston, a sleek, Italian wooden-hulled speedboat, to get to the police station in Örnsköldsvik in the mornings. Now the ice had come and the whole island was covered in snow. A soft, white blanket that muffled all sound and beautifully tucked the houses in for their winter hibernation. This lovely silence more than made up for the hectic summer months when tourists overran the island. There was a calm here that the tourists could never understand. Kick sled trips down to the village, grilling sausages over an open fire on the beach. Yet, Sofia missed the feeling of freedom of being out on the water. Although even if the waterways had been clear of ice, she wouldn't have been able to get into the boat with her unwieldy body. If she wanted to go to the mainland now, she had to catch the ferry from either Ulvöhamn or Fjären, which was closer. But if the ice was thick and the icebreaker hadn't been through, then there was only the hovercraft from Fjären.

Sometimes she worried about how things would go with her impending childbirth. But her decision had already been made, and she wouldn't be the first island-dweller to give birth in her own home. Sure, there were risks, but she was healthy and there hadn't been anything in her check-ups so far to indicate that childbirth would be any more dangerous for her than for anyone else. The fact that she was already thirty-nine didn't seem to concern the midwife at the maternity centre.

The baby had already turned and dropped. Margit, her nearest neighbour, had been a midwife for her whole professional career. She was retired now, but she had delivered many babies on the island over the years without any complications. Women have been doing this since time immemorial, she usually said. You don't need a hospital if the baby is healthy. Everything can be handled at home with a few clean instruments, a needle, some thread and primal female strength. Although Sofia appreciated Margit's grit and can-do attitude, she was not prepared to go quite that far. After the birth, she would go to the mainland and get both herself and the baby evaluated by the hospital personnel.

She adjusted her position again in the uncomfortable bed. Even though she didn't have any maternal role model from her own family, she felt strong and unafraid. She was going to give birth and raise this baby herself. She could handle that, no problem. And Tord, her godfather, would be by her side the whole time. And Kaj. Whether she wanted him there or not. Over the autumn and winter, he had taken on a series of lectures at the police academy in Umeå. Since they were expecting a child together, Kaj seemed think that gave him the right to stop by unannounced and stay for a few days whenever he wanted.

This particular week, the investigations group Sofia was a member of had in-house training in Police Competencies, or POLCOM, as her uniformed colleagues called it. The same group somewhat jokingly called the detectives' version POLCOM Light. But regardless of which division your belonged to within the police, there was annual training. This week it was plainclothes shooting, which it was assumed that Sofia, heavily pregnant as she was, would not participate in. However much it bothered her, she would have been lying if she said it wasn't nice to sit in her rocking chair in her house out on Ulvön with a cup of tea and her computer on what was left of her lap and work in peace and quiet.

The extreme nausea she had suffered during the first few months of her pregnancy had prevented her from doing the work she loved. There had been a series of hospital stays with IV drips until finally the head of the investigative division, Chief Inspector Vera Nordlund, had suggested that she should cut back on her hours. Sofia had of course refused. She had missed her job every second she was out sick. Her role as a police officer had grown from an idea into a calling, and it was as much an obvious part of her life now as walking, standing and breathing. So, she kept working. Of course, Kaj thought she should have gone on maternity leave a long time ago, but his authority as the baby's father did not extend that far. She made the decisions about her body and her life, and neither he nor Mette could change that.

The love affair, or whatever it had been, between her and Kaj had ended a long time ago. What remained now was mutual respect and a strong friendship. Kaj would make a good, stable father, a choice that, for the most part, she felt at peace with.

Sometimes she almost imagined that she was happy. The baby would have a loving home with a mother who had never thought she would get to experience the joy of becoming a parent. Tord would adore the baby and teach it everything there was to know about the woods, the countryside and fishing. He had already started talking about making the baby his heir, but Sofia had shushed him then. She didn't want to think about the day when Tord moved on. But of course it was reassuring that the baby would be taken care of financially. Tord was a wealthy man. Many people had him to thank for their land and houses. For generations, the Grändberg family had sold off what they owned at well below market value to provide a roof over the heads of the families who chose to stay on the island. And still there was more to be had. For his part, Tord lived in a modest little red cabin with a green door in the heart of Ulvöhamn, the small village that formed the island's urban centre. His cabin was a former mill building of about 550 square feet. The adjacent manor home with the traditional enclosed veranda and the tile stoves had been sold ages ago. Wealth and land did not appeal to him. A bustling village and a sense of kinship among the island-dwellers was far more important.

There was so much love in their odd little family that the baby could drown in it, but even so Sofia couldn't fully feel the rosy happiness that people expected of her. From the outside, she could probably fool some people. Her long blonde hair was glossier than ever and her pale, freckled skin glowed. But she was missing something. A baby should have two present parents. That was how it should be. Kaj would be a good role model, a strong and responsible man to look up to and who would walk through fire to protect his child, but he wasn't a father in the sense that Sofia had wanted. However happy she was for her child, she longed for a real family, the family she herself had never had. At the same time, she was embarrassed. Not because she was a single, unwed mother. That didn't bother her. But because she was lying here in her inherited house, which was surely worth several million kronor by this point, with a healthy baby in her belly, and wishing for something more.

Her thoughts were interrupted by someone moving around downstairs. The floorboards creaked right next to the stairs. The noises in the house were so familiar that they formed a map in her mind. Each new motion was revealed through sound, and now someone was coming up the stairs. Sofia pulled the blanket up higher over her shoulders and closed her eyes. It was quiet for a second, then the footsteps turned around and disappeared back down to the bathroom.

She exhaled.

Sure, she had chosen him as her baby's father, but she was not prepared to go as far as sharing her bed in order to play house.

3

Anders Svensson looked down at his jeans. They were far too tight and had holes in the knees. The sneakers weren't his style either. Big, black Philipp Pleins with a gold-coloured buckle on the side. The dark-blue bomber jacket hanging on the hook inside the modular office door was almost laughable for a man his age. He was aware of that, yet his American Express card ran hot in the expensive shops around the Stureplan public square. For a second, each new purchase quieted the feeling that everything was getting away from him. He was turning fifty next year. Amanda had planned a trip to Dubai for the whole family. He would have to foot the bill for it, of course. They were going to drive dune buggies in the desert and earn scuba diving certifications. He would have preferred to stay home and have a calm dinner with a few of his closest friends, but Amanda had insisted. And he wanted to make her happy.

The age difference between them provoked the jealousy of many of the men around him, but it didn't come without its difficulties. He loved to show off his beautiful, young wife, but had been forced to realise that he wasn't going to be able to keep up with her pace for much longer. In the beginning, his euphoria over their amazing sex life and the enormous self-esteem boost he got from her unabashed appreciation smoothed over his fatigue, but now, six years later, it was starting to catch up with him.

Anders looked out the modular office's barred windows at the building that stretched to the sky. The weather forecast had promised snow, but no flakes had fallen yet over the magnificent residential complex in the middle of Rosenlund Park. *Ready for Occupancy in Autumn 2022.* He wondered if that would actually be true. This was the most expensive building he had ever taken on, and they were behind schedule, way behind. He was going to present a revised schedule to the clients next week, and he wasn't looking forward to delivering the bad news. And as if that weren't enough, they were being inundated with calls from the Swedish Tax Agency and SWEA, the government office responsible for worksite inspections and worker safety, who had gotten wind of the lack of employment contracts and wanted to pay a visit. Plus, he was behind on his mortgage payments for the house. He hadn't dared to tell Amanda yet that the Enforcement Agency had begun sending letters. He didn't imagine for a second that she would stay with him if they were forced to move out of their 3,000-square-foot home in Djursholm, Sweden's wealthiest community, into a studio flat in Rågsved, notorious for housing immigrant labourers and widespread drug use. No, he was well aware that Amanda's interest in him was intimately tied to the lifestyle he could provide her with. And in order to partake in what he could offer her, she had treated him like a king for the first few years. Then Ellie had come along, and their sex life had gone from feral to non-existent. Amanda's care and attention was now directed exclusively at their daughter, and he basically served as their ATM machine.

It was too much. It was all too much right now. Anders glanced at the bottom drawer of his desk. He was such a fucking cliché, a hidden bottle of booze. But his thirst trumped his shame, and he reached for the key, unlocked it, and pulled out a bottle of Ichiro's Malt. His new favourite whiskey since his last trip to Asia. He poured himself three fingers and downed them. Then he immediately poured three more, but as he brought the glass to his mouth someone knocked on the office door. Construction site manager Jerzy Nowak stepped in without waiting for an answer. Anders didn't have time to hide the glass and the short man with the dark stubble didn't even try to hide his disappointed look.

'We're behind with the pay checks. I've tried to calm them down as best I can, but...'

Anders waved dismissively at Jerzy. He couldn't face thinking about that. They would have to wait for their pay checks. The important thing now was making up the lost time.

'Half of the workers here don't have ID06 cards,' Jerzy said.

'So?' Anders felt his first glass burning in his stomach, fuelling the anger that smouldered within him. It wasn't entirely his fault that things had turned out this way, was it? Jerzy had become a rich man by bringing his compatriots to Sweden to work under the table. From the first construction site out in the suburbs, where no one checked on employment contracts or how the workers were being paid, the number of undeclared workers in their crews had grown from two to more than half of the people working for SveAnd AB in and around Stockholm. A few had brought over their wives or sisters, who now worked for Jerzy in one of the various cleaning companies he had started on the side. As long as the site manager made sure that the workers who didn't have ID06 cards weren't there during inspections, Anders looked the other way. But obviously someone had tipped SWEA off.

'What do you mean, *so*?' Jerzy flung up his hands. 'Is that all you have to say? Don't you understand that this is all going to fall apart if you don't produce paperwork for all of them right away?'

Anders raised his glass and drained it as he looked at his site manager.

'So what are you standing around here for? It sounds like you've got your work cut out for you.'

'Not this time, Anders,' Jerzy said, shaking his head. 'This is your problem.'

'My problem?' Anders laughed. 'Don't you see that if I'm going down, you're going down with me?'

His tone was confident, although he was painfully aware that the one who fell first and hardest would be him.

'Look, I'm just an employee,' Jerzy said. 'No one can prove that I handled the hiring, and you don't really think I'm going to cover for you if it comes down to a choice between you or me? Sure, I'll lose one source of income, but I can always find a new one. What are you going to do if you lose your company?'

When Anders didn't respond, Jerzy zipped up his jacket and turned around.

'You need to deal with this,' Jerzy said, his voice resigned.

Anders opened his mouth to say something, but Jerzy had already disappeared out the site office's door.

4

My grandmother used to say, the greedy are always poor. I was only eleven when I began to understand what that meant for the first time.

I was going to work the opening shift at the corner shop, earn my own money. Finally I would be able to buy something that I wanted, the sorts of things my family never wasted money on, soda, candy, comic books. Maybe I could save up for a bicycle.

Dad knew the owner and I had gotten the keys so that I could go down there early in the morning and sweep the floor and set out the displays. A heavy bundle of keys, with keys for the shop and the back room where the safe was. If I had known what a beating would accompany that bundle of keys, I'd have chucked them in the river that very first day. But at that moment, I felt like they really trusted me, like I was one of the grownups.

When the day came for me to receive my first pay check, the owner decided that I hadn't been performing my job duties the way I should. I would receive another chance the following month. If everything was done to his satisfaction then I would be paid for both months. And it kept on like that.

I thought it would be different when I grew up, that working hard and being a good person would finally be rewarded. That if you deserved it all your dreams would come true.

I was so wrong.

5

Ida was quiet on the other end of the phone line, waiting patiently for Fredrik to say something. He could picture her sitting cross-legged with her long, dark hair down loose over her shoulders. It was already 10:30 p.m., but she always seemed to be around and answer when he called.

'It's late and I'm a little tired,' he said, trying the most disarming tone he could muster.

'I'm off tomorrow. You can sleep here if you want.'

'Couldn't we watch a movie another night?'

'Definitely, but… I just want to be with you.'

Fredrik looked around the empty tram car.

'I really like you, Ida, but you know what I've been through. I'm not ready for a relationship. You've been amazing these last few months, and I hope you want to keep getting together, but…'

Through the phone he heard Ida take a shaky breath.

Suddenly Fredrik wished he had never brought this subject up. His friendship with Ida was the only real relationship he had had with anyone outside the Lindén family. Ida was carefree, in every sense. She was compassionate to everything and everyone. The very opposite of Sofia, who mostly seemed to find fault in other people. When they had run into each other again the previous summer, he had thought they would have another chance. But he had never been good enough for Sofia. She had visited him in the hospital after he got shot, sat by his bed and held his hand. They hadn't said much. He, because his injured jaw prevented him. She, because… well, what was there to say, actually? What had happened to him was so absurd that it was impossible to take in. But Sofia had recovered from the shock fairly quickly. She went from being nurturing to looking up and starting to look towards the future. Part of her job as a police officer was dealing with difficult situations, looking at them in an organised and rational way, but he was stuck thinking about what could have happened if she and her boss, Vera Nordlund, had not shown up in time.

Fredrik had not been able to stop fretting about his little brother, either, even though he had promised himself several times he would give that up. Had Niklas actually survived the ferry disaster in the Baltic Sea that had claimed their parents' lives? Fredrik had missed his chance to find out what had happened and since then everything had taken a dramatic turn. He had tried to air his thoughts with Sofia, but her tone had changed when he did. She had started questioning him. She had said it was about time for him to give up his fruitless attempt to find his brother, who was most likely dead and had been for almost twenty-six years. That had set Fredrik off, even though he knew that what she was saying was logical. Eventually each of her visits had started to take on the same pattern. *Hi, how are you feeling? What does the doctor say about your progress? How are you planning to proceed? What's your plan for the rest of your life, Fredrik?* Her constant pressuring had drained him. Didn't he have the right to stop and think for a fraction of a second after he had almost died for a second time?

After a while, her visits had petered out. They did not look at life the same way. She had brushed herself off and moved on. He was bogged down in the past. The last time he had seen her was when Hans came to pick him up from the hospital. They had run into each other at the front door, but neither of them had made any attempt to speak to the other. She had disappeared into the building, and he had gotten into the car and left Örnsköldsvik.

But did that mean that he had to live alone for the rest of his life? He was almost forty. He might not get any more chances. Just because he wasn't good enough for Sofia didn't mean that he wouldn't be good enough for someone else, did it? Ida apparently thought he was good enough to love. Waiting for someone who would inspire the same irrepressible emotions that Sofia did was probably pointless. Maybe people made do with more lukewarm feelings plus some sort of attraction? A sense of community and belonging.

Fredrik scratched at the backs of his hands, feeling the familiar anxiety coming on. He didn't want to think about his life and all he had lost. He actively tried to block those thoughts as soon as they came, but it had been difficult this last fall. Last September had marked twenty-five years since the shipwreck that had claimed his whole family and nearly cost him his life. In addition to the anniversary and all that had brought with it, there were new diving expeditions and rumours about a new documentary in the works about the sinking of the MS Estonia forming new wounds in his soul the whole time he was trying to heal. As if that weren't enough, articles about the events on Ulvön Island kept popping up in the press. The commotion afterwards had been impossible to avoid. He was still getting friend requests from people he didn't know on Facebook and calls from journalists who wanted him to come on various shows and podcasts. It didn't matter how persistently he maintained that he had put it all behind him and didn't want to talk about it. He was like the walking wounded, and people stood in line to poke at his open wound. Plus each time Sofia's name popped up, it created another tear in his heart.

'Are you still there?' Ida sounded impatient on the phone.

'I'm still here.'

Fredrik thought about his empty flat and all the thoughts that dwelled there.

'All right, I'll come over.'

6

Ida was sitting on the sofa when Fredrik walked in the door. Her place in Stora Mossen wasn't far from Hans and Inga's townhouse. Ida had candles lit on the table, but the TV was off. The one-bedroom flat was just like her, warm and playful. A pink blanket that matched the throw pillows hung over the armrest of the sofa. The lampshades, curtains, and rugs were all in shades of light grey or light pink. Flea market finds were mixed in with expensive designer furniture and on a sideboard by one wall there was a framed cross-stich that read, 'A big cock is small comfort in a poor home'. Fredrik smiled. Ida was not only considerate and beautiful. She had a funny, spontaneous side as well. Something that neither he nor Sofia had. Maybe that was exactly what he needed? Someone to draw him out of his shell and teach him to appreciate life again.

'Hi.' Ida patted the sofa next to her. 'Come have a seat.'

Fredrik pulled off his sneakers and set them on carpet in the entryway. She watched him from the sofa.

'How did it go with Inga and Hans?'

'Moose steaks,' he said, lifting up the bag with the food from the hall carpet. 'Something you were craving, perhaps?'

Ida shook her head and laughed.

'How are you feeling today?' she asked as he sat down beside her. Her tone of voice sounded like the one she used in her professional role, but she quickly switched over to friend voice again once he gave her the thumbs-up rubbing his jaw as he opened and closed his mouth a few times.

'And what about in here?' Ida asked, running her thumb across his forehead. 'How does it feel in here?'

Fredrik made an effort not to pull away from her touch. He wanted her to touch him and yet he didn't. He had told her everything. Not just about Sofia and the events on Ulvön Island, but also about Niklas, the M.S. Estonia, and the horrors he had lived through that night. He had told Ida more than anyone else, more than Sofia or his psychiatrist, Torsten Bredh. Including that he still refused to believe that his brother had died. Ida had listened without judgment, asked questions, and reasoned with him. If Nikas had survived, then where would he have gone? Why hadn't he come looking for Fredrik? Why wasn't he mentioned in any of the official information or medical records? Fredrik had no answers. Neither did Ida, but she let him continue. Evening after evening, night after night on the phone. Without ever questioning what he said. Although it was liberating to talk openly about his thoughts, he sometimes wondered if it was really healthy or if she was just feeding his sick delusions.

Ida continued caressing his forehead with her thumb and let her fingers move down the back of his head to the nape of his neck. Her touch was not unpleasant. He turned and looked into her big, brown eyes. The only time Inga had met Ida, she said Ida had the kind of eyes you could marry. He was inclined to agree. He and Ida both had olive complexions and almost black eyes. He didn't know what Ida's parents looked like, but his own father had been blond and blue-eyed. His mother had claimed that it was her Belgian ancestors' genes coming through. The Walloon heritage, she usually said.

Ida's eyes were bright and pleading as she looked at him. She really was beautiful. He stroked her glossy hair. What did it matter if he let himself be seduced, actually? As if she could hear his thoughts, she leaned forward, allowing her lips to touch his. Her mouth was warm, she tasted like mint tea.

Philip folded up the lengthy contract from the twenty-four-hour car rental company and slid it in his inside pocket. He looked at the time. Almost half an hour after midnight.

'So, I can just drive it away then?' Philip asked.

The man facing him in the garage nodded.

'You're sure it's not going to be a problem for me to drive a stick shift?'

The man glanced anxiously at the freshly washed car parked behind them, probably quietly calculating in his head what it would cost to replace a transmission destroyed by some idiot in summer clothes who could only drive an automatic. And clearly couldn't even do that very well since he had fried the engine in his previous car even though it was below freezing outside.

Philip resolutely accepted the keys and thanked him again before walking over to the rental car. His driver's license clearly stated that it was only valid for automatic transmissions, and he had no idea how he was going to manage the last leg of his trip in a stick shift. In a snowstorm, no less. Plus, the drive was going to take more than an hour longer now since he had been forced to hitch a ride back to Sundsvall in the tow truck to pick up this new car. The man stood there and made sure he was able to start the car and pull out of the garage without bringing the whole building down with him. Philip said a short prayer that he would succeed without stalling and smiled triumphantly at the man as he drove out the garage doors.

He didn't know why the man's obvious anxiety bothered him so much. It was perfectly understandable that the man distrusted him. The utter confusion Philip was feeling must have been radiating out of him like a stoplight. He wouldn't want to loan himself a car either. He was still surprised that Fredrik had agreed to loan him his brand-new Volvo. Although of course Fredrik had thought Philip was only going to drive it within the metro Stockholm area.

Philip hadn't dared to ask where the car had come from. Fredrik had sold his grandmother's old Skoda that fall, and then one day he had just shown up at Philip's parents' place in the Volvo. Philip suspected Fredrik must have received some kind of payout for having been accidentally shot by the police, but he didn't ask.

After he had managed to get out of Sundsvall and was once again on the right course on the E4, he pulled his cell phone out of his pocket, but he quickly realised that the combination of text messages, snowstorm and manual transmission was not optimal. He didn't want to call. They had talked via chat originally before exchanging phone numbers and switching to texting each other. She had called him a couple of times, but their conversations had been halting and awkward, so they had gone back to communication forms they were both comfortable with. After two months, she had suggested that they meet. She was studying in Umeå but was home in Stockholm for the weekend. She was fully aware of his difficulties, seemed to understand them better than anyone he had ever met before. She had offered to come to his place, even though it was somewhat unconventional to have your first date under your parents' roof when you were a grown man. Philip had weighed the pros and cons of her offer and had ultimately decided that it was better if they met somewhere else. Hans and Inga would never stop interrogating him if a woman they didn't know suddenly turned up. It wasn't just the fact that he had met someone that felt awkward. It was also the twelve-year age difference. She was only twenty-seven and an undergrad at the university. They decided to meet at a café by Alvik's Torg shopping centre. That way, Philip would be close to home if he had a panic attack.

The date had gone well. They already knew each other so well that they didn't need to dance around with pointless questions about this and that. They had sat down, held each other's hands over their coffee cups and immediately started discussing the latest episode of a TV show they had both been watching. Afterwards he had felt lyrical, floating home without his feet even touching the ground. Hans and Inga had noticed of course that something was different, but he had consistently refused to invite them into his new world. And it really was a new world. With her at his side, he managed not only to leave the house, but to be out among people. To a reasonable extent.

They had taken it easy. The emotions were there, and the curiosity, but for Philip it had been an enormous step to shift his sexuality from a screen in the privacy of his own bedroom to a flesh-and-blood woman. He was constantly afraid of disappointing her. He had only been with a girl once, when he was fourteen, and his fumbling attempts to copy the sex acts he had seen in old porn videos had resulted in his coming after one minute, the girl lying motionless and silent beside him, not daring to say anything.

He had started withdrawing from the world even then, feeling like he was different. The things that interested other people did not interest him. One by one his friends had grown tired and eventually only Fredrik remained. Only then did the word disability start to come up. He had been allowed to attend school remotely and with that his opportunity to meet anyone his own age disappeared. Strangely enough, he had been content with his on-screen girlfriends all these years not missing the touch of another person.

Until now.

It snowed harder and harder the farther north he got. As Philip crossed the High Coast Bridge, the wind was so strong that he thought the car might slide off the road. The thought of the cold water below made his head spin, but he focused on the road and tried not to look to the sides. On the long hill past Skuleskogen National Park, he could see that several cars in the oncoming lane had gone off the road. He cast a grateful glance at the yellow vehicle with the orange flashing light on its roof, which was a few cars ahead of him. A freshly ploughed road improved the odds that he wouldn't get stuck in a snowdrift somewhere. His suede shoes could not withstand very many minutes of walking in this snowstorm.

According to the GPS on the dashboard, there would be a town coming up in only a few more miles, Bjästa. The symbol on the screen showed that both food and gas were available there. From Bjästa it was only ten kilometres to Sunnansjö. Philip fiddled with the lever on the left side of the steering wheel to see how far he could go on the gas he had left. 150 kilometres. He pictured how Madde would light up when he knocked on the door, even if it was the middle of the night. She would throw her arms around his neck. All would be forgiven, and they would sleep right up against each other. He felt himself blush in expectation at the thought.

He got off the E4 and continued towards Sunnansjö. As soon as he left the big, ploughed highway, the driving became more difficult. The deep wheel ruts caused the car to swerve and sway as if it were on rails. It was still snowing heavily, and visibility was lousy. The streetlights ended after the first exit and all he could see outside was forest.

Philip crawled along for the last kilometre, searching for the old schoolhouse she had described, but none of the few buildings scattered along the roadside matched her description. He stopped and pulled up their most recent chat on his phone. Narrow turnoff to the right after the mailboxes. Then there was a long string of angry messages after he had written that he had changed his mind and didn't want to come up.

At first they had decided he would stay for two nights. At the time that had felt doable. Then she had wanted him to stay longer and meet her father, who was arriving on Saturday. She wanted to show him off, she said. But Philip didn't feel ready to be shown off to a parent. Let alone in an unfamiliar place way up north where he didn't have anywhere safe to escape to. But he had changed his mind. Not about meeting her father, but about driving up to see her. He had decided to bite the bullet for her sake. And now he was here. Honestly, he felt proud.

Philip scanned the road and sure enough there was a row of snow-covered mailboxes. He put on his turn indicator even though he was the only one around and turned. A few hundred meters into the woods, up a steep hill, he saw the house. He pulled into the driveway and turned off the engine but sat there for a few seconds to compose himself. He should have bought flowers, he realised, but it was too late now.

Philip got out and smoothed his clothes. His heart was pounding, and his hands were getting sweaty, but it wasn't as unpleasant as it used to be. He felt excited.

He wondered if he should call first so he didn't scare her. It was late, already past three in the morning. But when he saw that there was a light on, he knocked cautiously on the front door. When no one opened and he didn't hear any noise from inside, he put his hand on the handle. The door was unlocked.

'Hello?'

The house was freezing. He walked through the downstairs without taking off his shoes. The enormous kitchen was empty, the guest rooms as well. A few logs were stacked in the open fireplace in the living room, ready to be lit. He knocked hesitantly on the bathroom door, but it was unlocked and there was no one in there.

'Madde?' Philip called again.

No response. Finally, he pulled out his phone and tried calling. The call went through; he heard her phone ring nearby. He stopped, trying to pinpoint the sound. It was coming from the closet.

7

I hear him out there. Uncertain footsteps out in the living room and then in the kitchen and then back again. He stops outside the closet door.

I press myself harder against the wall. Smell lavender and cedar. Little sachets to keep the moths from eating the expensive clothing while the family is away. The fur collar on one of the down coats grazes the back of my neck and I flinch. It itches, but I don't dare move from my hiding spot between the jackets and coats for fear that the hangers will make a noise.

Then the phone rings again. A muffled melody reminiscent of piano music. Slowly, the door opens. He stands there on the threshold without turning on the light.

We stand that way for a while. Him in the doorway and me against the wall only five steps away. He'll see me any second. I tense my body, ready to throw myself forward. His silhouette is thin against the hall light. I think that I'm probably stronger.

My heart is pounding.

Everything has gone to hell. Everything.

8

It was dark inside the closet. The light switch by the door frame didn't work. Even so, he tried turning it on and off a few times.

'Madde?'

The phone kept ringing. In the light from the front hall, Philip saw row after row of winter clothes, bags, skis and ice skates. He had time to reflect on the fact that this closet was as big as his whole flat before he spotted Madeleine's jacket on a hook and grabbed it. Sure enough, her phone was in the pocket.

He hung the jacket back up with the cell phone in it and closed the door. He stood there in the front hall, bewildered, and looked at the pool of melted snow that was starting to form around his shoes.

A sound from upstairs made him turn around towards the stairs. The entire old wooden house creaked and groaned in the wind. Reluctance creeped into him. The stairs were covered in thick carpeting and his shoes left wet footprints as he began to climb. The upstairs consisted of an open area with sofas and a large chaise longue with animal skins on it. The wall at the short end of the room was covered in wood panelling with two doors. One was ajar and he could make out a faint light from within.

'Madde,' Philip whispered into the darkness, 'are you awake?'

The storm lashed outside and tugged at the windows. Philip stood as if frozen on the stairs, not knowing what to do. Something felt wrong. Silently he creeped through the large common room, put his hand on the door handle and cautiously pushed the door open. It was cold in the room. The window was closed, but chilly air was pouring in from the air vent. Despite his jacket, he shivered.

'Hello? It's Philip.'

To the left there was a double bed with a dark wooden nightstand beside it. To the right, two chests of drawers made of the same type of wood side by side next to each other. Above them hung paintings with surrealist motifs in yellows and reds. He took it all in, registering the colour of the bedding, curtains and carpets. But he couldn't detect any trace of Madde anywhere.

The silence in the house seemed to be amplified by the howling of the snowstorm outside.

He looked out the large window, which faced the lake below. It was barely visible in the darkness, but the light on the boathouse next to the snow-covered dock revealed that it was there.

She wasn't here. Madde was not still in this house. Philip knew it. His pulse sped up, throbbing louder and louder until it sounded like a fire alarm in his ears.

'Madde?'

The sound of his own pathetic voice scared him even more.

Calm down. Surely she just went out for a minute. Maybe she's getting more firewood or going for a walk. Both alternatives seemed equally ridiculous. Madde wouldn't go a metre without her phone, not even to the bathroom. And no one took a walk in the middle of a snowstorm, especially not several hours after midnight.

His breathing had started to follow the rhythm of his heartbeat now. Hard, short breaths that made his head spin. He steadied himself against one of the dressers and leaned forward, trying to stave off the panic attack that was inexorably on its way. Everything started flickering in front of his eyes. He straightened, put his hand on his chest and tried to calm down, but it didn't work. Everything inside him screamed that something was wrong, that he should get out of here.

A sudden bang from downstairs made him jump. He ran across the room and lunged for the stairs. As he leaned over the railing, he saw that the front door had blown open and snow was swirling into the front hall. He had to get out of here. With every second, the flashes of lighting in front of his eyes seemed to cover more and more of his field of vision and soon he would black out.

Philip stumbled down the stairs and out to the car. The engine started right away but stalled when he tried to put it into reverse. On his third attempt he succeeded and turned around as fast as the snow-covered driveway would allow. With a jerky flying start, he set off down the hill, managing to miss the mailboxes down by the road by a hair's breadth. Everything inside him was screaming and his skin felt like it was vibrating. He tried to breathe and keep his eyes on the roadway as he fought with the gear shift. The soles of his shoes were covered in snow and kept slipping off as he tried to press in the clutch pedal. He bent down to try to scape some snow off the bottom of his shoes with his hand and took his eyes off the road for a second.

That was enough for the car to veer off onto the shoulder.

9

Anders woke up as his reclining desk chair came up off the floor and he flailed for the edge of the desk to keep from tipping over backwards. The whiskey bottle was still on his desk. Empty. He reached for his cell phone. Amanda had called five times. Anders scrolled through to find the taxi app, knowing better than to try to drive through the city in the middle of the night with a blood alcohol level far above the legal limit.

Outside, the bright floodlights still lit up the skeleton of what would become the Rosenlund Tower building. He leaned to the side to see the sky out the window. Still no snow.

He jumped as a shadow passed by outside and nearly lost his balance in his chair again. Was someone still here at the construction site? He fumbled around for the baseball bat he had acquired a few weeks earlier, found it leaning against the wall behind him and got ready. His adrenaline was pumping. Footsteps approached the door of the modular site office. Anders stood up, gripping the baseball bat tightly. He would not give in without a fight. Whoever came, he would fight for his life.

A quick knock, then the door opened.

'Hey.' The Securitas guard's belt rattled as he stepped into the site office. 'Are you working late?'

Anders dropped the baseball bat and sat back down heavily in the chair again. He rubbed his face, aware of the blood coursing through his body.

'What, did I scare you?' The guard chuckled and stuck both thumbs in his belt.

'A little.' Anders tried to smile.

'I was just going to tell you there's a taxi out here. Is it yours?'

Anders had stopped shaking by the time he got into the taxi. The fatigue hit him now instead, not just physically but also mentally. He was fully aware that the army of workers Jerzy had smuggled into the country were far from any type of choir boys. They were desperate men who were doing everything they could to support their wives and children back home in some corner of Eastern Europe. Jerzy was right. He needed to solve this payroll situation as soon as possible. The only question was where he would get the money from.

He was so incredibly sick of worrying. The company's financial problems took up all his working hours. But despite his worry that everything would be snatched away from him, he knew that he would survive this. He had worked his way up from nothing before and he could do it again. But Amanda would never accept the defeat. If things fell apart now, their marriage wouldn't survive.

At night, the really dark thoughts crept in. Usually, he fell asleep on the hard Chesterfield sofa in the living room with a glass of whiskey in front of him on the coffee table while Amanda and Ellie were curled up under the thick down comforter upstairs. He used to long to go up and join them, but he wasn't welcome anymore. Not when he'd been drinking. Not after what he had done.

Amanda had tried to forgive him, come downstairs and fetched him when he fell asleep on the sofa and led him up to the bedroom. They had climbed into the warm bed with Ellie between them and held hands, listening to their daughter's loud snores, laughing together in the darkness. Their love for Ellie bound them together even though their love had died, and their marriage was more than fraying around the edges.

He wished he could have been more like Amanda when it came to their daughter. Always enthusiastically engaged in all her adventures at preschool, drawing, doing crafts, going to the woods and the swimming pool. For him, he was happy if he managed to sit on the sofa with her for a few minutes each evening and watch a children's show. He often came home after she was already asleep and left before she woke up. It irked him that his job kept him from being part of her childhood.

That had been different the first time he became a father. His older daughter had been born with a heart defect and had had an operation even before her first birthday. Worrying about her had brought him and Jeanette together and the joy he felt once she recovered had been like winning the lottery. She was the apple of his eye. He had carried her in his arms day and night during those first months and then had just never stopped carrying her. Metaphorically, of course, but he didn't shy away from admitting to himself that she was his favourite child. She was grown now, independent and on her way to an amazing career. The only thing he worried about with her now was her sometimes impaired social skills. She had never been like the other children, had preferred to keep to herself.

As a teenager the differences had started to become increasingly obvious. When the girls in her class started wearing makeup and short skirts, she had dressed in bulky sweaters featuring the names of British punk bands. She never wore makeup, nor did she do her hair or nails. She spent all her time with her nose in various books about history and politics and lectured him and Jeanette at the dinner table about the environment and socioeconomic inequality. Within the four walls of their home, she was eloquent and confident, but outside she receded into her shell. After the divorce, their relationship had grown strained to say the least and even though he missed her every day, he didn't do anything to improve it. He had enough to handle with his own issues.

Anders sighed and looked out the window at the Stockholm night.

Oh, how he wished it had all been different.

Friday, 21 February

10

The darkness had still only gently begun to fade outside. There was at least an hour until the sun would be fully up.

Kaj was snoring on the sofa next to her, but she just hadn't been able to keep lying in that uncomfortable bed upstairs any longer. She did not plan to rearrange her whole life just because he insisted on visiting all the time and occupying her living room.

Sofia leaned back in the rocking chair and rested her teacup on her belly as she gazed out at the misty dawn and tried to predict what the weather would be like. She was not like Tord, who could smell snow coming.

So far, there had been a noticeable absence of sparkling winter days. The sky lay like a constant, grey lid over the sea and the wind stubbornly squeezed its way in the cracks in the house. Last night she had thought it would blow away. Ragg wool socks and a fire in the fireplace were a must to keep warm. Even so, the electric meter was on overdrive. She needed to install an air-source heat pump by summer, Tord had told her. She had promised but suspected it wouldn't happen, like the sewer replacement or adding a sunroom. Or updating the furnishings. Every piece of furniture was in exactly the same place it had been when her father died. Even his wooden clogs were still in the shoe rack just inside the door, even though it had been nineteen years. Claire hadn't bothered to clean the house out, leaving it for Sofia just as it was. When Sofia had finally dared to start living in it again, letting everything remain the way it had always been had made her feel safe.

A hard kick to her ribs told her that someone was awake in there. Sofia put her hand on her belly and felt the baby's feet under her palm. It was so strange to think about. Another person was living in there, inside her own body. Her baby.

She caressed her belly and quietly hummed the only lullaby she knew, 'The Wolf Song' from her favourite movie, *Ronja the Robber's Daughter*. Sten had always said she was like Ronja when she was little. More wild than tame as she ran around Ulvön's forests without the slightest fear. And that had continued. Instead of dance and horseback riding like the other girls her age enjoyed, Sofia had taken up orienteering. As an adult, she had gotten into competitive pike fishing.

The kicking subsided, but she kept humming. The midwife at the maternity centre had calculated that she had just over four weeks to go. Sofia wished the time would pass faster. She was already tired of not being able to move and had not expected this physical transformation to bother her as much as it did. Her legs were still slim, but in addition to her belly growing, her breasts had also ballooned and were now almost twice as big as they had been before. A good sign, the midwife had said. And as if it weren't enough that her body had changed shape, embarrassingly enough she now also had a constant desire for sex. It didn't feel at all consistent with her growing maternal body. Even if she had had a husband, she couldn't imagine anyone wanting to touch her. She was a housing unit for an unborn child. It felt scandalous to have such thoughts. And yet she woke up sweaty at night, remembering Fredrik's brown eyes, his strong hands and lithe, sinewy body. She could feel it in her fingers, what it felt like caressing his olive skin. She missed him so much her soul ached, but her pride forbade her from calling.

Her love for Fredrik had been frightening and overwhelming. It had not been like that with Kaj. Sure, there had been passion, but nothing like what she had experienced with Fredrik, whom she had met at a criminology summer course she had taken while waiting to be admitted to the police academy. A few weeks later, they had wound up sitting next to each other at a meeting for the Force where they had realised that student life did not suit either of them and had gone to a nearby pub for beer instead. Fredrik had not given any indication that he was interested in her, whereas she was nearly falling apart just from being close to him. She had had to stop herself from staring at him, fiddling nervously with her ponytail and laughing unnecessarily at his dry sense of humour. When the evening ended, they had hugged each other and gone their separate ways, without exchanging phone numbers. She had tried to forget him, but found herself walking more and more often through the hallways where she knew Fredrik usually went for his classes. One day he had turned up and they had gone home together, five stops in the wrong direction from where Sofia lived, and he had invited her up. She had left his flat forty-eight hours later, dazed, her whole body tender from lovemaking, and completely infatuated. Only to then never hear from him again. She had called and sent text messages. She had even gone to his place, but she hadn't heard a peep from Fredrik again. Right up until he had shown up on Ulvön Island last summer.

After the dramatic events in Ulvöhamn, she had visited him in the hospital in Örnsköldsvik. She had tried to support him while at the same time concealing how sick she was feeling due to the pregnancy. Sofia had sat on his bed, and they had talked. Or mostly she had talked. His jaw injury had caused him to slur his speech at first, but she had understood what needed to be understood. What had happened on Ulvön was not going to change Fredrik's life. He was going to carry on unchanged, without taking charge of his problems, with no ambition of getting his life squared away, always searching for a ghost. The risk that he would relapse into his pill addiction did not make anything any easier. They had eventually argued. She felt ashamed for being so hard on him. He had just survived an attempted murder and narrowly avoided death for the second time in his life, and there she was going on and on about getting an education and finding a more rewarding job. Their relationship had fizzled out. Mostly because of her, and yet not a day went by without her thinking about him.

His name and photo still appeared in the newspapers sometimes. She tried not to read the articles, tried to keep her mind off of him as much as she could and focus on the child growing inside her. Fredrik Fröding was a closed chapter.

11

Through the window he saw the plough's flashing lights pass by like a blurry, yellowish-orange disco ball. Philip rubbed the windshield with his jacket sleeve to create a peep hole. The plough stopped next to the car and a man in reflective clothing hopped out of the cab and walked towards him. He rapped on the window. Gently at first and then a little harder.

'Hello?'

Philip groped around for the button to lower the window but couldn't find it. So he opened the door instead which immediately crunched into a snowdrift outside. The man on the other side had a friendly face and a thick, northern Swedish accent.

'Are you all right? Have you been sitting here long?'

Philip looked at the clock. It was almost three-thirty in the morning. His body was stiff from the cold and his head was pounding.

He brought his hand up to his forehead just as the plough driver gasped.

'Oh no, you're injured. Should I call an ambulance?'

Philip ran his hand under the edge of his hat and saw that there was blood on his light-brown leather glove.

He shook his head.

'Yeah, I think it might be best,' the plough driver objected, pulling out his phone.

'There's no need,' Philip said, holding up his hand.

He looked at his fuel gauge and the man followed his gaze. Reluctantly, the man stuck his phone back in the chest pocket of his reflective jacket and took a step back to inspect the car.

'I'll tow you.'

After he towed Philip to the gas station, helped him get gas and offered multiple times to give him a lift to the hospital to get the cut on his forehead looked at, the plough driver finally gave up and set back out to continue his battle against the falling snow. But before he left, he suggested that Philip park his car outside the newsstand by the bus stop. They would open soon, and he could get himself a cup of coffee and a sandwich there before he headed home.

Philip sat in the front seat shivering even though the car was idling with the heat on max. He felt in his body that something unpleasant had happened, something far more frightening than his having driven off the road, but no matter how hard he tried he couldn't remember what it was. He couldn't even work out where he was. Not in Stockholm, that much he had grasped. Snow whirled through the air and lay like a fluffy blanket, covering all the buildings around him.

Why was he in the car? He had been sleeping or had dozed off. He didn't know which, but he sensed that he had been sitting in the car for a long time. If nothing else, his stiff hands and feet suggested that. It was six in the morning, but there was no indication from the sky of it starting to get light out yet.

Where was his cell phone? Philip felt each of his pockets but couldn't find it. Had he lost it or forgotten it? He looked around the car and discovered it on the floor in front of the passenger's seat. The car. Philip looked at the dashboard in surprise and remembered that he had borrowed Fredrik's car, but this wasn't Fredrik's Volvo. There was a sticker on the glove compartment with the car's registration number and a rental company logo. A rental car? Where had he gotten it from? Had he been sitting here all night? Where had he been before that? His head felt muddled, and he was colder than he had ever been in his life.

The thermometer said it was minus fifteen centigrade outside. He reached for the door handle to get out of the car, but stopped when he realised that he didn't know where to go.

Should he go knock at one of the nearby houses? Introduce himself, try to explain, let people gather around him, ask him how he is, invade him. No, that would not do. He had to be alone, totally alone. His chest felt tight, and he started to have trouble breathing. Everything around him shrank, the bus stop, the car, the world. He was not built for this. He wanted to go home to his flat, his computer and his safe space.

He had experienced this before, being more or less paralysed by his agoraphobia, but he had always had someone with him then, Mum or Dad or Fredde, someone who could talk to him, make sure that he didn't hyperventilate and pass out, bring him back home again to safety. Philip fumbled for his phone and looked at it for a few seconds. His head was spinning. He couldn't breathe.

He just had to close his eyes for a moment.

Shut everything out.

12

Sofia stood in the kitchen, her hand leaning on the counter. She had been awake more than she had slept overnight. She stretched and a jolt shot down her spine to her abdomen. She didn't know what to expect from labour but suspected that this was just a preview of what was to come. She rubbed her lower back with one hand, feeling the pain fade away. The baby could not come now, there were still several weeks to go. This must just be one of those practice Braxton Hicks contractions. Sofia wondered if she should call her neighbour, Margit, and ask, but decided not to. She didn't want to be the kind of person who called at all hours every time she felt the slightest twinge. Besides, she had other things to do today.

It upset her that she would have to temporarily give up her spot on the investigation team. Of course she was looking forward to the baby, but her job was her whole identity. And since the pregnancy, the way her coworkers treated her had changed. Her closest colleague, Karim Jansson, an Iranian gentleman who had fallen in love with a Finland-Swedish midwife and ended up settling in Örnsköldsvik, had always been pleasant and polite to her, but that was far more than could be said of the other police officers at the station. Her years in the Stockholm Police and her relationship with legendary criminal profiler Kaj Marklund hadn't exactly made it easier for her to be accepted. Sofia had handled it by distancing herself from her coworkers, even though that had played into their sense that she looked down on them. Even so, after she got pregnant, more and more doors had opened to her. Maybe they saw her more as a person now than before.

There was a quiet knock on the front door. The lock turned, and Tord came in.

'Oh, you're up already?' He stepped out of his worn winter boots and came over to her in the kitchen with a bag in his hand. Aside from the scar behind his ear that ran down to the back of his neck, Tord had nearly recovered from last year's assault. This guy must be northern Europe's fastest healer, his surgeon had said, and Sofia did not doubt it. Tord had spent his whole life outdoors – in the fishing boat, on the cross-country ski trails, in the woods. He was health incarnate, even though he was over seventy-five.

'Breakfast,' Tord announced, holding up the bag and pulling out bread and juice.

The last few months, food had mostly been a necessary evil. Sofia had to force herself to eat for the baby's sake.

'And how's the little lady doing?' Tord patted her belly. He was the only one, aside from Kaj, she permitted to do that.

'Have you ever considered that it might be a boy?' she asked.

He snorted and sat down at the kitchen table.

'I've seen enough bellies in my lifetime to know what's hiding in there. What you've got there is a girl belly. No question.'

'I see. I had no idea that you were such an expert on the female body.'

Tord grinned and pulled a snuff tin out of his pocket.

'Well, there are varying degrees of being an expert, but certainly I'm not completely clueless.'

Sofia put the juice in the fridge and started filling the coffee maker. Coffee was a vice that she continued to indulge in, even though both Margit and the midwife on the mainland had expressed a desire for her to give it up or to at least cut back on the amount.

'Have you heard anything more about the house next door?' she asked and sat down with some difficulty on the kitchen chair across from Tord.

He clouded over and looked down at his hand intently and the tin of snuff in it.

'There's been a lot of coming and going.'

'Buyers?'

'Nah, curious bastards who are just coming by for a looksee. There's never a moment's peace.'

Tord's place in Ulvöhamn had been overrun with tourists who wanted to see the spot where all the drama had unfolded last summer. So he often came to visit her, since not very many people made it out to Norrbysbodarna farther north on the island. He worked on the house, caulking the windows and readying the small room next to the master bedroom for the new family member to be.

Sofia could understand that there was a certain amount of interest, but it was hard to fathom that people were still stopping to gawk.

'The sister came by to pick up some furniture and paintings last fall, but I don't think they're going to find a buyer. It would have to be some poor idiot from Stockholm who doesn't know what happened there.'

Sofia smiled at Tord's feigned disgust for city-dwellers.

'I'm thinking about selling,' Tord said.

The coffee had finished brewing and she tried to stand up to pour it, but Tord beat her to it.

'I feel uncomfortable staying there,' he said with his back to her, taking two mugs off the hooks they hung from underneath the shelf next to the stove.

'You could live here if you want.' Sofia really meant that. Tord was like a father to her, and she was going to need both help and company once the baby came.

He turned around and smiled at her.

'That's sweet, but you're going to have your hands full between the little girl and him in there.' Tord nodded towards the living room.

'He is not going to live here,' Sofia assured Tord.

'Who's not going to live where?' they heard from the doorway.

'Well, good morning, Kaj,' Tord said, turning around. 'Would your police officership care for a cup of coffee?'

13

Fredrik stretched quickly and felt his neck tightening. It took a second before he realised that he was lying with his head on the sofa's hard armrest. Ida was lying on his arm. He wasn't wearing any clothes, just a soft blanket that Ida had knit herself out of an unusually thick yarn. The memory of the kiss, the stroking hands, came over him. He gently tried to coax his arm free, but that woke Ida up and she began to move. She pressed herself backwards against his body and pulled his free arm around her.

'Good morning.' She opened her eyes and put his hand around her breast. 'I guess we fell asleep.'

Fredrik cautiously pulled his hand away and sat up. He tried to look relaxed, but Ida was clearly offended that he didn't want to hold her.

'What is it?' she asked.

He shook his head.

'Nothing, I just…' He smiled and awkwardly patted her on the leg. Just then his phone rang on the coffee table, and he reached for it.

'You know what?' Ida asked and pouted when she realised he was thinking of answering it.

'Fredrik Fröding,' he said into his phone.

Ida eyed him for a second and then stood up, threw the blanket on the sofa and headed for the bathroom.

'Yes, hello. This is Gudrun Wahlström. I work at the convenience store at the gas station in Bjästa. Am I speaking to Fredrik?'

Bjästa. That felt familiar somehow.

'What is this in regard to?'

'The thing is, we have a man here, a Philip Lindén. He would really like to speak to you.'

Fredrik heard a faint murmur in the background before the phone was passed to someone else.

'Fredde.' Philip's voice was so weak that it was barely audible.

'What's up?'

'You have to come up here.'

'First tell me what happened.'

The phone was passed back and then Gudrun came on again. She lowered her voice before continuing.

'He's not in good shape, your friend. We've tried to call an ambulance, but he doesn't want that.'

'Is he hurt?'

'We found him sitting in a car here this morning,' Gudrun whispered. 'He has a laceration on his forehead and seems disoriented. He's very cold. He's sitting indoors with me now in the convenience store. I've given him a blanket and some coffee, but you are probably going to need to come and pick him up.'

'Bjästa, where is that?'

'Twenty kilometres south of Örnsköldsvik.'

Why the hell was Philip in Örnsköldsvik? The backs of Fredrik's hands felt vaguely itchy. The room started to contract. There was no way he could ever go back there, never. The last time he had been up there he had been one millimetre away, literally, from losing his life.

With his phone pressed to his ear, he leaned forward over his knees. This was not the right time for the panic attacks he had worked so hard to get rid of for the last six months to return. He tried to exhale calmly, to figure the situation out. Gudrun at the convenience store, Philip in Örnsköldsvik, Ida in the bathroom. Breathe.

'What happened, Fredrik?' Ida asked. She had emerged and stood in front of him in only her underwear, covering her breasts with her hands.

A sudden craving for the pills came over him. He thought about the bag he had at home. The doctors had prescribed him bags full of medications since the attack and the accidental shooting. Sleeping pills, muscle relaxants, sedatives, anti-anxiety medications and strong painkillers. He had tried talking to the doctors. He had explained his history of panic attacks and his addiction to pills, but no one had been interested in listening. Out of sheer defiance, he had begun filling the prescriptions and at each follow-up visit he would sit in the visitor's chair and amenably confirm that the medications were working. But instead of taking the pills he had been saving them up. What in the beginning had filled a small paper bag from the pharmacy now filled a large grocery bag to the brim. It sat on his kitchen table at home in his flat, like a suicide art installation.

His thoughts simultaneously stood still and raced.

Philip was in Örnsköldsvik, and he was obviously in bad shape. Fredrik didn't need to guess to understand what this was about. This was familiar territory for them both, something they had struggled with their whole adult lives, something they could even laugh about sometimes. One of them had PTSD and the other autism and agoraphobia. Sometimes Fredrik wondered if people with fragile mental health clung to each other like life jackets, even though the risk was so much higher of drowning since neither of them could swim. Was that why he and Sofia had become so intimate? She was the daughter of an alcoholic, and they were both orphans, alone and childless, broken together. Fredrik looked at Ida where she stood in the doorway. Her soul was not broken the way his was. She came from a nuclear family and seemed never to have experienced real grief. He reached his hand out to her, and she came over to him and took it.

He rotated the hand that held hers to look at his watch. It was nearly seven-thirty in the morning. Even if he got a car in the next five minutes, he wouldn't be in Bjästa until the afternoon. Should he call the police? Or Hans and Inga? He rejected that last idea right away. There was no point in worrying them. They would call in the National Guard without a second thought and that was the last thing Philip needed.

Suddenly anger bubbled up inside Fredrik. Philip couldn't ask him to drive 500 kilometres after lying about where he was going and on top of all that trashing *his* car on the way up there. And to Örnsköldsvik of all places.

'No way. I…'

He heard Philip ask Gudrun in the background, 'Is he coming?'

He sounded so helpless that something inside Fredrik broke. His legs stood up all their own. He threw on his clothes and headed for the door. His wallet and keys were already in his jacket. Ida had a car. This was just how it had to be.

14

Sofia waved to Tord from the front stoop. He had stayed after breakfast. He had swept the deck and sanded the front walk, but it was already lunchtime now and Sofia knew that Tord's patience for putting up with Kaj was limited. Despite the cold and a pale grey sky that revealed more snow would be arriving that day, he wore only a thin jacket and no hat. He never wore a helmet on his cargo moped and Sofia had stopped nagging him about it ages ago. 'When it's my time, it's my time,' he usually said, ending the conversation. Sofia wished she could have gone with him, hefted her big, clumsy body onto the flat cargo bed on the front of the moped and bumped away into the distance. She wished she didn't have to look into those eyes at the kitchen table, filled with longing and accusations. She had long since tired of all the discussions about preventative medicine and organic vegetables and not allowing plastic toys. Kaj had turned from one of the most experienced members of Sweden's nationwide criminal profiling group into some kind of cooing, soon-to-be hipster dad who was ploughing through books on childrearing as if they were on a conveyor belt.

Sofia went back inside, shut the front door and pulled her cardigan around her more tightly. Kaj's work bag sat in the front hall, already packed, even though there were several hours until the hovercraft left for the mainland. As if it weren't enough that he showed up at Sofia's place whenever he came north to give lectures, he had also recently arranged with the Örnsköldsvik police chief to use an office there at the station until the baby arrived. Sofia had objected at first, but Kaj had worn her down, arguing that he needed to be nearby before the birth and that he didn't want to keep making the trip back and forth. Mette didn't mind him spending time with Sofia, and no one had asked Sofia what she thought.

She sat down at the kitchen table and opened her laptop.

'How long are you planning to keep working?' Kaj asked, pointing slightly disapprovingly at her computer. 'Shouldn't you be taking it easy and thinking about the baby? You only have a few weeks to go. Surely Vera would understand if you handed the investigation over to someone else?'

Sofia hid her sigh behind her coffee cup. There had never been any question about whether she was keeping the baby. Kaj was welcome to be as involved as he wanted, but she had also made it clear to him that she wasn't going to demand anything of him. He was married and she had been aware of that when they had resumed their relationship the previous spring. And the baby definitely did not mean that they would be getting back together again, the way they had been during the years when Sofia worked in Stockholm, even if Kaj had at first seemed to push for that.

It had been a turbulent fall. Not so much for Sofia. She had tried to turn off all her emotions and just focus on feeling good for the baby's sake. Kaj, on the other hand, had gone through a very public separation from his extremely famous actress wife, Mette Severin Marklund. The headlines had screamed out the news in big, black letters from the front page of every gossip rag. 'Star's Husband Cheats on Her with Woman Twenty-Three Years Younger.' Luckily they hadn't written about the pregnancy, and Sofia had not been mentioned by name except in one gossip thread on the Flashback Forum website that she found when she googled Kaj's name in a moment of weakness.

Even though Kaj and Mette were in an open relationship, the baby seemed to have been the last straw for them. They were both in their sixties and Mette hadn't had any problem with Sofia and Kaj spending time together, but a baby was different. That required a commitment that she was not initially interested in. After seeing a counsellor several times, they had tried to patch up their marriage, and Mette had slowly begun to accept that Kaj was going to be a father. You could say a lot of things about Mette, but she didn't hold grudges. By the time the bump started to show and Kaj travelled up to Örnsköldsvik to attend the first ultrasound, she was ready to become a second mother and sent along tiny, yellow baby clothes and books on motherhood and childbirth. Sofia didn't know what to think about it. Just then, she wasn't up to thinking anything.

The baby kicked her ribs hard in reaction to the hot coffee Sofia had just gulped down. She set the cup down and shut her computer with a bang.

'Kaj, I need to work. I can't just sit in this house and stare out the window. If the baby comes late, it could be up to a month and a half until the baby's born.'

Kaj drained his coffee cup and got up to pour himself some more.

'But that doesn't necessarily need to mean that you need to keep working. I mean, you could go for walks, right? Come outside and get some exercise?' He stopped himself right away when he saw the look on her face.

Sofia took a deep breath and prepared to start ranting about how complicated it was to tie the laces of her winter boots, how tight her winter coat was and that she could hardly get her gloves on because her hands were swollen, but Kaj cut her off before she got going. He gave her a fatherly kiss on the forehead and opened the lid of her laptop back up to appease her.

'You work. I understand that it's too hard for you to get around out there in the snow. I'll go for a walk on my own.'

He didn't wait for her to respond, just left the room and went to the front hall. Sofia sat there with her computer in front of her, seething.

You work. As if she needed his approval to do her job. And obviously she was capable of going outside for a walk even though she was pregnant. Sure, her clothes were tight and all the extra weight she was carrying made it tough going, but still. It wasn't like she was sick. She tried to shake off her anger, thinking it was just the pregnancy hormones acting up. As soon as this baby was out, she would go back to being the calm, reserved person she otherwise was. It had to be that way.

Sofia put her hands on her keyboard. A few hours of reading the investigation materials would clear her mind. She glanced at the shoes by the front door.

Did Kaj really think she couldn't handle going for a walk?

15

The tires splashed through the slush as Fredrik pulled into the small town. The speed of the cars and the heat of the early spring sunshine had started to melt the snow on the roads, but the thick snow on the roofs would not melt anytime soon.

Fredrik had talked to Gudrun, who owned the convenience store, several times on his way north to Bjästa. He had confirmed that Philip was both harmless and physically healthy and he had tried to explain Philip's phobia of the outside world. In the end, she had agreed not to call an ambulance, and Fredrik had promised to pick Philip up as soon as possible. He had driven way too fast and had arrived more than an hour before the time estimated by the GPS.

He parked the car outside the entrance and went inside. Philip sat wrapped in a blanket at a table just inside the door. His face was grey and his eyes vacant. The woman at the counter, who he understood to be Gudrun, came right over to him and shook his hand. She was plump and had a friendly smile and short hair in three different shades of grey. The layer on the bottom had been dyed purple.

'He's had both breakfast and lunch, but you probably ought to go to a hospital anyway. He hasn't said more than five words since he got here.'

Fredrik squatted down in front of Philip as if he were a child. He put his hand on Philip's knee and a sob immediately ran through Philip's body.

'I'm here now,' Fredrik said. 'We have to go home.'

Philip shook his head.

A customer rang the bell by the cash register.

'Let me know if you need any help.' Gudrun gave Philip a comforting pat on the shoulder and turned away again.

Fredrik took Philip by the arm and stood him up. He took the blanket off him, folded it up and set it on the table.

'Philip, we can't stay here.'

'I can't drive home,' Philip replied quietly.

'That's okay. We'll sort everything with the cars out later. I'll drive.'

'I'm going to stay.'

'What do you mean? Here at the gas station?'

Philip looked around in confusion, as if he had forgotten where he was.

'I can't go home,' he said loudly. A couple of men who were filling out lottery tickets turned around to see what was going on.

'We can't stay here. If you don't want to go home, we need to at least find a hotel where you can take a shower and put on some warm clothes. And my car, where is it?'

Philip stared out the dirty window of the convenience store.

'No hotel.'

'Then what are we going to do? We can't sit here for the rest of our lives. I want to help you, Philip, but then you're going to need to help me. Why don't you want to leave?'

'Madde,' Philip replied without taking his eyes off the window. 'We got in an argument. We were going to get together, but we got in an argument. And then she wasn't there.'

'Who are you talking about?' Fredrik asked. 'What happened?'

Philip looked at him, resigned, and his lower lip started trembling.

'I don't know.'

Sofia stomped to knock the snow off her shoes and took off her scarf. Kaj had been right. It was too hard. The twelve-kilometre walk around Valberget Peak had nearly done her in, although she would rather die than admit that to him. Kaj had suggested that they turn back several times, but she had pressed on in the snow, determined to prove she could do it.

She went into the living room, which was adjacent to the kitchen, and sat down in the rocking chair while Kaj made coffee. She watched him through the wide pass-through window over the dining room table. Sten had wanted to remove the wall between the kitchen and the living room to create an open floor plan but Claire had not.

Kaj struggled to pull the lid off the coffee percolator. He made a big show of stretching and rubbing his back. He was no spring chicken, but if she could stay on her feet, he shouldn't be complaining. And yet, he was.

'You should get a better bed for the guest room. You know my back can't handle those hard wooden slats and I can't sleep on the sofa forever.'

'There's a bed upstairs.'

He came back into the living room and set two cups of coffee down on the coffee table.

'That bed is even harder.'

Sofia didn't respond, just reached for her computer which was charging on the armrest of the sofa.

'Maybe a double bed, so there will be room for Mette, too, when she comes to visit?'

She shot him a look, but he was prepared for it. He parried her look in a flash, a protective smile spreading across his face. Shielding oneself from the rage of a heavily pregnant woman was apparently a skill he had mastered quickly.

Sofia snorted and looked back down at her screen. Kaj took a few steps closer to her and cautiously set his hand on her shoulder.

'We can't have it be this way, Sofia.' His voice was gentle, almost patronising. 'This is Mette's and my baby, too. You must try to include us a little more.'

Sofia moved slightly to elude Kaj's hand. She didn't want to argue now. He would return to the mainland and then she would have her house to herself. Still, the anger seethed within her. *Mette's and my baby.* How on earth had they gotten the idea that this baby was somehow Mette's? If Mette wanted a baby, why didn't she squeeze one out of her own shrivelled, old uterus? Sofia bit her tongue to keep from blurting out the comment and turned to Kaj.

'It's my baby. It's my body and I'm the one who decides what's going to happen. Just because you and Mette have a bunch of opinions about to handle things, that doesn't mean that I need to stand with my hat in my hand and say thank you and amen.'

Kaj sighed.

'And nor are we asking you to do that, either, but it would be good if you could try to include her a little more. She really just wants to help. You haven't even answered about whether she can come up next weekend. Or how we're going to handle the christening.'

Just the thought of having both Kaj and Mette under her roof made Sofia's skin crawl. What if the baby came early? Was she supposed to lie there in labour in front of them while they cheered her on and giving her advice? No thank you. She would rather give birth in a snowdrift.

'We'll have to see,' she replied briefly and went back to her interrogation. 'I need to focus on this now. I'll drive you down to the hovercraft after the coffee.'

16

Philip's teeth chattered even though he was clenching them in the crowded cabin. Fredrik couldn't decide which would have been worse. The ferry or this disconcerting hybrid vehicle they were sitting in now. He had never seen anything like this in his life. It reminded him of those airboats they used in TV shows from Miami, with a big fan on the back. There was only room for a handful of passengers and their breath had already fogged up all the windows in the plasticky cabin. Every now and then Philip shivered, and Fredrik put his arm around him.

'Philip, this is all going to be fine. I talked to the skipper, and he said this is safer and faster than the ferry, okay?' Fredrik didn't know if he was trying to convince Philip or himself. The last time he had traversed these waters he had been chock-full of pills. Now he was forced to cope with his anxiety on his own, ideally without scaring Philip even more. Fredrik had called the rental car company in Sundsvall, received confirmation that his own car was in the shop there, and gotten permission to keep the rental car for a few more days. It was parked outside the gas station convenience store. Gudrun had promised to keep an eye on it while he and Philip continued their journey in Ida's car. Ida, right, he would have to get a hold of her later. She had loaned him her car without hesitation when he had explained that a friend of his needed help. She had even offered to take time off work to go with him, but he had declined. He had given her an obligatory kiss on the forehead and promised to be back that evening. Unfortunately, it now looked like he would have to break that promise. Philip was still refusing to go to the hospital, nor was he willing to leave Örnsköldsvik or go to a hotel. Fredrik had tried asking him what had happened, but he just shook his head, unwilling or unable to answer. Something had scared him, Fredrik understood that much, but in Philip's case that could mean anything. Some woman looked at him weird in the grocery store, a Salvation Army employee asked him for money, or he saw a protest march go by. At the wrong time, the slightest deviation from Philip's routine could have devastating consequences for him.

Despite Fredrik's attempts to convince him otherwise, Philip remained adamant that he would rather sit in the car outside the convenience store in Bjästa and freeze to death than go home to Stockholm. Frustration at not being able to get through to his friend was now mixing with desperation. Fredrik could not physically force Philip to leave Örnsköldsvik. That would only have made him dig his heels in further, but they also couldn't sit there in the car or inside the convenience store until Philip reemerged from his fugue state. Nor could Fredrik drive two cars home. In the end, he had made a decision. Here went nothing.

Sofia hadn't answered her cell phone. He still had Tord's number from last summer, and the old man had informed him that she was out at her house on the island.

Fredrik shivered and curled up even more in the seat. Once again he was trapped on the water between the ferry terminal in Köpanholmen and Ulvön Island. The only difference was that now the water was frozen. It was mindboggling that he was on his way out to the place he had promised himself he would never return to.

The engines started. The noise was deafening. A whir ran through the whole cabin. Even the ferry would have been better than this, Fredrik quickly concluded.

That was all he had time to think before the vessel roared off over the ice.

It took less than thirty minutes to reach Ulvön Island by hovercraft. It swooped along as if it were the easiest thing in the world. The idea of flying along in a vessel over the frozen water felt absurd, but after a few minutes Fredrik had gotten used to the whistling sound and the snow-covered world whizzing by outside the fogged-up plastic window. Philip sat with his head leaning on the window and his eyes closed. Every now and then Fredrik nudged him in the side to make sure he was awake. Philip grunted but then disappeared back into his own thoughts again.

Fredrik wondered what he would do when he got there. Sofia would probably insist that they needed to turn around and got to a hospital. How was he going to explain that that wouldn't help? When Philip got like this, it didn't work to try to force anything. It was simply a matter of waiting for him to come around. Fredrik had seen this hundreds of times over the years. As soon as Philip got scared, he withdrew into his shell. He worked through his feelings in there until he got everything put back together again and only then would he slowly begin to crawl back out. Many people who were like Philip had trouble coping when other people acting out emotionally, but for Philip it seemed like his own emotions were what scared him the most. And open spaces. And large crowds. And a bunch of other things that no one else would have paid any attention to.

But Philip was his best friend. When Fredrik came home from Turku University Hospital as a child, he had slept on a mattress in Philip's room for the first several months before he moved back home into his grandmother's place. Only thirteen years old and an orphan. They hadn't spoken. Not about Estonia. Not about Fredrik's family. Not about anything as far as he could remember, but Philip had sat with him on the mattress on countless nights and held him while he cried. Without moving or saying anything, with his arms loosely wrapped around his shoulders.

Most of his other friends had pulled away. The adults, too. People just didn't know how to deal with the horrifying ordeal he had been through or his paralysing grief. Some people wanted to know what it had felt like as the ferry capsized. Others were downright rude and angry, questioning how he had managed to survive when so many others had not. Who had he sacrificed to get out? Others just wanted to poke around in the open wound out of sheer curiosity. But most of them receded off into the periphery in the end.

Even though Fredrik had survived the ferry disaster, his journey had been far from easy. Years of addiction to pills and anxiety had isolated him. He had sacrificed many relationships and opportunities to bring himself back – his studies, his friends, and most of all Sofia. But after cheating death once again, it was as if something had happened inside him. Instead of completely falling apart from the feelings of guilt and panic attacks, he had decided to get back up. He had almost entirely stopped craving the anti-anxiety pills. What he craved now was a real life. If it wasn't too late.

Philip moved uneasily next to him. They were approaching the harbour on the north side of the island. He recognised the sign for the village of Fjären. Sofia's house in Norrbysbodarna was only a kilometre away.

The hovercraft began to slow down. They had arrived.

17

'Do we have to discuss this again? I don't want to sit in the car for six hours.' Amanda stood with Ellie on her hip even though her daughter was actually too big to be carried like a baby. Anders looked at her. She had changed. Her facial features had hardened. The softness and suppleness were no longer there. It was clear that he was not wanted, that he was disturbing her and Ellie's existence just by being there.

In the beginning, everything had been wonderful. But after Amanda got pregnant, everything changed. Then they had to run around to stroller shops and read books about childbirth instead. He went along with it for a while to make her happy, but to be honest he had been done with all that for twenty years. He loved Ellie with all his heart, and he wanted to spoil her as much as Amanda did. But he just didn't have it in him anymore. When his first daughter had been born, it had been simultaneously exciting and terrifying. Now it was just tiresome. Pretty soon, he had checked out, letting Amanda handle everything. Instead, he had devoted himself to the buildings he was working on and a few women on the side. Nothing serious, mostly to satisfy the needs that Amanda no longer seemed interested in. His construction projects around Örnsköldsvik had also given him a reason to go up to the vacation house, which gave him something akin to peace of mind. The latest project was a contract to build ten houses on the west side of Dekarsön Island southeast of the city centre with an amazing view of Örnsköldsvik Fjard. He hoped that selling the houses would help cover the company's out-of-control debts.

Amanda shifted Ellie from one hip to the other and looked at him tiredly.

'I really don't want to, Anders.'

'I want you two to come with me.' He pulled his hands through his hair. His nerves were jittery, and he just wanted to get going, to leave Stockholm, Jerzy, the late pay checks, and the half-finished building in Södermalm behind.

'Please, Amanda. Just for a few days.'

He needed to get them to get them to come without a fuss. Anders took a few steps towards the window and pulled aside the thick velvet curtains to look out at the yard. He was almost sure he had seen a car following his taxi on his way home from the city last night. Now every shadow in the neatly maintained yard seemed to move. He squinted into the setting afternoon sunlight. Wasn't there someone standing down there by the pool house?

'Why can't you just go by yourself?' Her tone was whiney. Amanda set Ellie down on the floor and walked over to him with their daughter in tow. She put her arm around him and leaned her head against his shoulder.

'Hey...? Can't we take a rain check? It's such a long drive.' She knew that usually worked.

Anders shook his head.

'No, we leave tomorrow, all of us. I want to be on the road before seven.'

Amanda took a step back and pursed her bee-stung lips. Her nostrils flared as she looked at him.

'When did you get home last night? Are you hungover?'

Anders kept the biting retort on his tongue to himself. He just wanted to get away, pretend like nothing had changed, and not have to look over his shoulder all the time. He stroked Amanda's cheek.

'Please. Can't you just pack Ellie's things? I think it will be good for us to get away together.'

Amanda held the eye contact, looking deep into his eyes.

'Has something happened, Anders?' Her concern sounded almost genuine.

'I just want my darlings to come with me for a few days.'

When he thought about the old schoolhouse, it warmed his heart. As soon as he had seen it, he knew they should buy it. Amanda had grumbled at first. A dilapidated old shack in the middle of nowhere was not high on her wish list. She had been lobbying for them to get a flat in the ski resort town of Åre but had eventually given in. Getting to decorate the house had amused her for several months, but soon she had tired of the place. Not Anders, though. He went there whenever he got the chance. He could be himself there, get away from all his problems, just walk around the yard and take in the fresh air and feel the joy of being alive. In the evenings he usually took the ATV down to the lake to fish. Completely alone, no one around as far as the eye could see. There were people nearby, of course, but none of the neighbouring houses could be seen from theirs or from their dock down on the lake. Sometimes he wished he could retreat and move up to the house full-time. Get rid of the Djursholm house, the construction company, the outrageously expensive slip for the boat, and the two cars. Buy an old, four-wheel-drive pickup and live out the rest of his life with a fishing rod in one hand and a beer in the other. But obviously Amanda would never accept that. There were no full-inclusion preschools or vegan food, no yoga studios, Gucci stores or beauty salons that offered Botox injections or lip augmentation. Just clean air and peace of mind, but unfortunately he was the only one in his family who valued that.

Amanda lifted Ellie back onto her hip.

'You're right. I'm sure it will be lovely. It's been ages since we were at the cabin.'

Anders smiled. You could say what you liked about his young wife, but she did not hold grudges. And he loved her, even if she called their 500-square-metre vacation home 'the cabin'.

He poked his daughter in the belly, and she laughed.

'Won't that be fun, Ellie? Going sledding and building a snowman?'

Ellie laughed and nodded.

Anders took her out of Amanda's arms and tossed her up into the air so her soft curls danced around her round face. Ellie squealed with laughter.

'Going fast down the hills, right Ellie?'

'Yes, Daddy. Really fast!'

18

Kaj was already standing in the kitchen as Sofia struggled her way out of the rocking chair.

'The hovercraft will be here any minute,' he said.

'Yeah, yeah, hold your horses.' Sofia forced herself to smile and tried to adjust her attitude. 'Sorry, I kind of lost track of the time.'

'Interesting investigation?' Kaj nodded to the stack of papers on the coffee table.

Sofia shook her head.

'Not really, but anything that keeps my mind off this is welcome right now.' She patted her belly and Kaj immediately reached out his hands to do the same. Sofia had to resist the impulse to pull away and stand still and let herself be petted like a horse.

There were so many aspects to pregnancy that she could never have imagined, having complete strangers come up to her and touch her body, for example. Kaj was not a complete stranger, of course, but acquaintances and coworkers were all so excited about the unwieldy bump, which now resembled a hard ball. They meant well, of course, but the pawing and petting made her feel uncomfortable. Not to mention all the good advice they shared. Mette more than anyone, even though she had never been pregnant. There were creams for haemorrhoids and exercises for the pelvic floor. She had even had the never to suggest some sex positions that were good for pregnant women. Just in case the mood struck her. As if Sofia and Kaj were still a couple. Sofia studied Kaj in his bulky down jacket and silly knit hat in the Hammarby soccer team's colours. What she had ever found attractive about this man was a mystery to her now, not just because of the age difference. That had actually made him more appealing. No, it was the whole package. Everything about him irritated her now. His heavy Stockholm accent, his silly attitude about the pregnancy, and all his cooing at her belly. And as if that weren't enough, he had revealed that he was planning to retire. Kaj Marklund, an institution, one of the most experienced criminal profilers and murder investigators in the country, was planning to leave the police presumably because it was time. He had reached retirement age, but Sofia couldn't picture him as anything other than a cop. What would he fill his days with? An unpleasant thought occurred to her. Was Kaj planning to retire to spend time with the baby? Did he think she was just going to politely step aside and let him and Mette take care of the baby while she went back to her investigation work? If so, he could forget that.

'Are you ready?' Kaj looked at her and then leaned over and talked to her belly in a baby voice. 'And what about you, you little apple core, are you ready?' He finished by kissing Sofia on her fleece jacket just above her belly button and the baby immediately kicked back. In protest, Sofia wanted to believe.

'Let's go,' she said. She couldn't stand another second of this.

—

Sofia pulled up to the ferry dock in Fjären and stayed in the car while Kaj got out of the passenger's side. He looked like the Michelin Tire Man. Why did he stubbornly insist on dressing for a polar expedition? It was barely fifteen below, a perfectly normal winter.

Kaj opened the trunk and took out his overnight bag before walking around to the driver's side. She rolled down her window.

'I'll see you tomorrow then.'

Sofia nodded reluctantly. Kaj was going to Umeå to give an evening lecture and would be back tomorrow. As far as she was concerned, it would have been nice if he could have stayed up there longer.

'You should give some thought to the stuff with Mette. She would really like to be there for the birth. If not in the room, then at least in some way.'

In the room? Sofia shook her head. What world was Mette living in? Did she think she was somehow going to be involved in the birth of this baby? It was obvious that Kaj still had not grasped that *he* was not going to be there. Tord, on the other hand, would not leave her side whether she wanted that or not. When Sofia didn't respond, Kaj stuck his hand in the window and patted her first on the cheek and then on the belly again through her fleece jacket.

The hovercraft docked just then and the first passengers started climbing up out of the hatch on its side.

'I'll call you when I get there.'

Sofia nodded without looking at him. As soon as Kaj left her, she closed her window and started the motor. She watched the father of her baby as he slipped and slid his way over the icy dock and enthusiastically greeted the skipper.

Then her gaze stopped on one of the passengers stepping out of the hovercraft. A sinewy man in a blue down jacket and jeans with dark hair and olive skin. He turned around and half lifted, half dragged out someone wearing a grey knit cap pulled well down over his forehead. Ash-blonde hair stuck out from under the cap. Her windshield had started fogging up again and Sofia was forced to open her car door to see properly. A cold wind swept into the car bringing some snow from the roof in with it. She wiped her cheek off with her mitten.

She had time to put one foot on the ground before she realised who she was looking at.

Fredrik Fröding.

19

I walk around in the house and look. Everything looks fine. There are no traces of what happened.

I run my hands along the leather spines in the bookshelves in the living room. Just there for decoration. I stop and pull out one book, August Strindberg. I find it hard to imagine that the people who live in the house read him or anything at all for that matter. No, this is a place for casual fun and entertaining guests. A freshly painted façade and an oversized deck, with a water view, barbecue grill, hot tub, and outdoor seating for at least ten people.

A house that screams prosperity. Not at all like the surrounding rural homes. Old, dilapidated bachelor houses and yards full of junk. No, here they want to say that they have money, that they have power, that they buy whatever they want — house, cars, people.

They'll be here tomorrow. And I will finally make things right.

Allow everything to trade places.

20

Philip recoiled when he saw the frozen sea, as if he had not noticed where they were until now. Fredrik pulled him by the arm and finally got him out of the crowded hovercraft and out onto the dock.

'Stay here,' Fredrik instructed and stepped back down into the cabin to get Philip's luggage. In the trunk of the rental car Fredrik had found a black bag with clothes and toiletries. If he had counted correctly, Philip had planned to be away for two nights. The bag contained two pairs of boxer shorts, two T-shirts, a dress shirt, and a pair of jeans. And condoms. He had even found a flat package wrapped in lavender paper.

Fredrik didn't have any overnight items for himself. His plan had been to drive north, fetch Philip, and return right away. He didn't even have a cell phone charger with him.

When Fredrik came back out onto the dock, he discovered that Philip had walked a short distance away and sat down on a bench. A woman stood beside him, leaning forward with her hand on his shoulder. A bunch of blonde hair stuck out from under the green hat. He didn't need to look twice.

Sofia Hjortén.

She was only a few steps away now and for a second he stood and watched her. He could walk over to her, hug her, and say that he missed her. It would be so easy. He lost himself briefly in fantasies of an emotional reunion where everything was forgiven, but then he remembered why he was there and what he was about to ask from her.

'Fredrik.' Sofia smiled but made no move to hug him. 'What in the world are you doing back on the island?' It was clear that she was not aware that he had called her earlier. Her fragile tone gave away the nervousness vibrating underneath. He was also having a hard time keeping his voice steady.

The hovercraft started up behind them. The big fan whipped up a small snowstorm and Sofia pulled her hat down farther over her ears. It was intensely cold out. Fredrik saw Kaj Marklund stick his head out to wave before the hatch was closed but then freeze. Fredrik waved awkwardly back. Kaj looked as if he were about to get out of the hovercraft but had to sit back down again nicely since they were pulling away.

Fredrik turned to Sofia. She was wearing an unbuttoned, dark blue, down jacket with a light blue fleece underneath. It was ridiculously obvious what state she was in. Her belly was as big as a beach ball, and he could clearly see her belly button poking out underneath the fleece.

Sofia was extremely pregnant.

-

Fredrik took a cautious sip from the coffee cup. He could hear Sofia speaking quietly in the guest room. Her tone was gentle and authoritative at the same time. She seemed to have an easy time stepping into the police role. It seemed to be a natural part of her.

He looked around at the kitchen in Norrbysbodarna. There was a large pass-through window over the kitchen table, which let you see into the living room. On the other side of the opening there was a dining room table and a little farther away an old cathode-ray TV. He could see the upholstered grey sofa facing it. Aside from the partially plastic wrapped baby carriage in the middle of the room, everything looked like the last time he had been here.

The outdoor furniture on the deck was covered with a tarp with several decimetres of snow on top. That's where they had sat last summer, sharing secrets, opening up to each other. How many times had he been thrown back into that moment? Sofia's hand on his knee. Genuinely sharing his grief about his lost family as if for the first time. The tears. She had held him and for a while there had just been the two of them in the whole world.

In retrospect, it felt like a silly, romantic movie with a laughable ending. Fredrik leaned farther out on the kitchen chair and turned his head. The guest room was across the hall. The door was open, and he saw Philip sit down on the edge of the bed. Soon he leaned back on the bed and Sofia pulled a blanket over him. She shut the door behind her before waddling into the kitchen with her enormous belly swaying in the air.

Fredrik couldn't help but do the math in his head. His biology skills might not be razor sharp, but he was smart enough to realise that there was a chance. The itching on his hands came creeping back and he was about to give in to it when Sofia pulled out the chair facing him.

'He's resting. I bandaged the cut on his head. What happened?'

'I don't know. He drove off the road, but there's something else, too, and he doesn't want to or won't say what.'

All Philip had said when Fredrik had repeatedly asked why they couldn't go home was: *I'm waiting until Madde comes back.*

Sofia sat down and put her feet up on the chair in front of her. Fredrik didn't dare look her in the eye.

'Sofia, I have to ask...'

The answer came like the crack of a whip.

'It's not yours.'

Fredrik nodded, feeling a sting of disappointment all the same.

'Who...?'

'Not that it's any of your business, but Kaj is the baby's father.'

'Well, I suppose I can congratulate you then.'

'Thank you.' Sofia's voice softened and to his surprise, she smiled. 'Thirty-six weeks. Only four weeks to go now.' She unzipped her fleece jacket and scooped up some papers that were lying on the kitchen table. Fredrik had time to see the police logo on several of them.

'Are you still working?'

She looked at him for a long time.

'What do you actually want, Fredrik? Why are you here?'

'I don't know anyone else near Örnsköldsvik. Ulvön Island was the only place I could think to come.'

Sofia eyed him sceptically.

'I'm sorry,' he said. 'I realise that this seems really odd. But Philip's not doing very well.'

'I can see that, but why didn't you take him to the hospital?'

Fredrik shook his head.

'It's not possible and it wouldn't help, either. He refuses to go home, and he refuses to stay in a hotel. He has kind of a hard time when he gets overwhelmed.'

Sofia eyed him incredulously.

'Is there any chance we could stay here for a few days?' he asked.

She shook her head.

'Do you understand what you're asking of me? We haven't had any contact with each other in over eight months and then you show up here all of the sudden with a man who is in obvious need of medical attention.'

Fredrik looked down at the table. She was right, of course.

'I have to work,' she continued.

'I understand that.'

Her fingers played irritably across the tabletop.

'And Kaj will be back tomorrow.'

Fredrik nodded.

'We won't be in the way, I promise.'

Sofia sighed loudly, but did not express any other objections.

21

It was dark out. Sofia sat in the rocking chair with her feet on the stool in front of her. The baby was asleep and for once her body felt relaxed. Even so, she couldn't sleep. There was a strange man lying in the guest room not far from her. Fredrik's closest childhood friend, he had explained to her over dinner, who had autism as well as agoraphobia. As far as she knew, Sofia had never met anyone with severe phobias. It was hard to fully understand what that entailed. According to Fredrik, Philip functioned just like anyone else as long as he could be in his own, secure environment. He had a job that paid well, a good education, but no friends other than Fredrik and no family of his own.

Sofia had been in to check on Philip a few times, but he didn't react when she adjusted the blanket over him. She should have objected when Fredrik asked to stay with her, but it was as if Philip had awakened some sort of maternal instinct in her. It was extremely obvious that he needed medical care, possibly inpatient psychiatric care. His condition wasn't drug related at any rate. That thought had occurred to her, of course, but she had encountered enough addicts in her line of work that she felt she could tell that much. Otherwise she wouldn't even have considered letting them stay.

Kaj must have called twenty-five times over the course of the evening, but explaining the situation to him was more than she was up to. She had sent a brief message back saying that Fredrik and his friend were going to stay for a few days, and had received a flood of texts back with questions she couldn't answer. She was grateful that Kaj was sleeping somewhere else tonight so she could put off dealing with that problem.

In addition to Kaj's stubbornly insistent attempts to contact her, Mette had texted twice to remind Sofia that they needed to set a date for the christening so she could start planning. Mette had also reminded her that she had packed some massage oils in Kaj's bag that would be good for leg cramps, since she knew Sofia had been having those during her pregnancy.

Fredrik and Sofia had eaten dinner in the living room while Philip slept. Pasta with pesto from a jar, that was all there had been in the house. Fredrik's jaw seemed to have healed well, and he didn't appear to have any trouble chewing anymore. She hadn't wanted to ask about the gunshot wound. The internal investigation was closed, but the whole thing was simultaneously both embarrassing and unpleasant. Their bullets could have cost him his life.

There was a creak on the floor in the guest room. Philip was up. She tried to get up out of the rocking chair, but by the time she had turned around, he was already standing in the doorway between the kitchen and living room. He rubbed his eyes, still half asleep. His movements were more intentional now. The sleep had obviously done him good. He sat down on the sofa across from her.

'How are you feeling?'

He shrugged.

'Have I been asleep for long?' he asked.

She nodded.

'Would you like something to eat or drink?'

He shook his head and then stretched his neck and looked out at the ice beyond the deck.

'We're on Ulvön Island, right?'

Sofia nodded.

'And you're Sofia?'

She smiled and nodded again.

'Nice to meet you, Philip.'

He nodded back.

'Fredrik has told me about you. That you were in love.'

Philip seemed to lack any sense for what you could and couldn't say to a stranger. Sofia looked down, embarrassed by the unfiltered conversation.

What little energy Philip had seemed to drain out of him again almost immediately. He yawned into his elbow.

'What time is it?'

She looked at her watch.

'2:30 a.m. Go lie back down, you who can,' she tried to joke. 'For my part, I'm tied to this chair here.'

Wobbling, Philip got up from the sofa and looked at her.

'Tied?'

She patted her belly, and Philip gave a wry grin when he understood what she meant. He gave a quick wave of his hand and then disappeared back into the guest room.

Sofia sat there and stared out into the night.

Saturday, 22 February

22

The picture of them on the front page of the newspaper makes the pit of my stomach burn with anger. I want to rip it out and tear it into a thousand pieces, watch their ripped faces raining down onto the floor, but of course that won't do. What would my coworkers say? I look up and around. Everyone looks just like they always do. It's a dizzying feeling. Someone is eating, someone else is fiddling with their cell phone. No one knows what is going to happen. No one knows what I'm planning.

I read the front page.

'SveAnd AB is building luxury homes on Dekarsön Island. The EPA worries about bird life on the island.'

Bird life? As if Anders Svensson was going to care about birds. Please, if you can throw people away like garbage, it's not like you're going to care about that sort of thing. I open the paper and encounter the family's fake smiles again. 'Anders Svensson with wife Amanda and daughter Ellie,' it says under a photo where the girl is holding a shovel and trying to dig by the barriers around the new building.

Ellie. I taste the name. Ellie Svensson.

23

'Is that everything?'

Amanda nodded, her eyes locked on the closed gates in front of the Range Rover. She would be driving anyway. They had split a bottle of wine with dinner, talked about the house up in Norrland. Everything had been almost normal. Ellie had fallen asleep on the sofa after they watched *The Lion King* together. Amanda had carried her upstairs and he had half expected her to come back down, but she hadn't. That feeling of being forgotten had come over him again, like he barely mattered in his own family. But he was well aware that he was the one who had gotten himself into this situation. The step to the whiskey bottle had been a short one after that, and he had ended the evening lost in his own musings in the living room without turning on the TV or the fire in the fireplace.

His career had looked so promising. He had been praised by industry colleagues for his quick deliveries and impressive construction projects. He had gone from four employees to over fifty in just a few years. He didn't even know when things had started to go awry. He had trusted Jerzy and had let him handle the hiring decisions. When there suddenly started not to be any employment contracts, he had looked the other way. He had deflected the tax authorities, the union, and the employees' complaints with his fancy dribbling moves, like a pro basketball player. He had dodged accusations about shoddy construction and terrible working conditions to bask in the glory of all the media attention. It had all happened so fast. Suddenly he was richer than he had ever been and with that money had come women. Only a few years after everything had started looking up, he had met Amanda and divorced Jeanette. Amanda was studying to be a real estate agent and had been at the opening of a hotel, which SveAnd AB had built near Arlanda. Her unbridled interest had flattered him. They had snuck around for a few months, but eventually Jeanette had realised what was going on and made an ultimatum – end the relationship or get a divorce. He had chosen divorce. Four months later, he had gotten down on one knee and proposed to Amanda with a one-and-a-half carat diamond ring. After the wedding and their honeymoon in the Maldives, Anders had looked forward to a quiet life with his young wife but had instead found himself dressed up like a Ken doll going to all sorts of night clubs and events. He had accepted it for a while, content to have his way when they got home late at night or early in the morning. Amanda was like a nymphomaniac compared to Jeanette who had never wanted to or never had the energy or the time. With Amanda at his side and a never-ending cash flow, he was king of his own kingdom.

But just a year into their relationship, everything had changed. They needed to buy a home in Djursholm, attend dinner events for couples with annoying people born in the nineties and live a fast-paced, healthy lifestyle. His toasted breakfast sandwiches were replaced with green glop and cold oats that were supposed to sit overnight in the fridge. Amanda forced him to play padel tennis and take a course to earn a green card so he could play golf. And then Ellie came along, permanently toppling him from his throne. He had found his solace in whiskey. And his work, even though it no longer gave him the same satisfaction. They had lost several contracts, and the money had stopped rolling in. He had started having trouble making payroll, both for the above-board employees and for the under-the-table employees. Jerzy had had to intervene and pay some of the workers who were threatening to go to the press, and soon the destructive snowball was rolling.

Anders felt his stomach rumbling. He was hungry but he didn't dare eat anything else. He got carsick and the hangover wouldn't help. Amanda had had to wake him up this morning. He was sitting on the sofa in his bathrobe with the glass still in his hand. She had packed his things without a peep, buckled Ellie into her car seat, and set the alarm on the house. He had taken a long shower, but it hadn't had the effect he had hoped. The hangover was still throbbing in his skull, and he had nearly thrown up when he tried to choke down some of the smoothie Amanda had made for him. But he was determined to make the most of their days up north.

'Snow!'

Anders turned around and looked at his daughter, seated in her car seat. He was filled with an overwhelming love for her.

'Yes, my dear. Soon we'll get to see the snow.'

24

Fredrik handed the cheese slicer to Sofia. She reached over as far as she could, but her belly was in the way, so he had to get up out of his seat to hand it to her. She smiled shyly. The kitchen smelled like coffee and the radio was playing a musical quiz show. If anyone had peeked in the window, they could have been mistaken for a perfect little family expecting their first child.

'That must be tiring, that there.' Fredrik gestured towards her belly.

She nodded and rubbed the small of her back.

'But it looks good on you.'

He instantly regretted saying that. This was hardly the time to flatter her now. Sofia was extremely pregnant, and the baby's father was on his way back to the island. Angry as a bee, he could guess.

'And Kaj, what does he say?'

'About what?'

'About becoming a father.'

Sofia took a bite of her toast and was quiet for longer than was necessary.

'I suppose he was shocked at first, but now he's happy.'

Fredrik took a sip of the black coffee. He had missed the percolator. No one he knew in Stockholm had one.

'And how about you?' she asked. 'Are you seeing anyone?'

He nodded. He felt obligated to make her aware of Ida's existence.

Their eyes met across the table. He felt a fire burning inside him. Her narrow green eyes watched him. There was a new calmness about her that had not been there before.

'Why are you actually here, Fredrik?'

He looked at her questioningly.

'Philip...' he began.

She shook her head.

'Why did you come specifically here?'

He understood what she was getting at, and he immediately felt the anger flare up inside him.

'You think I came because of you?'

She shrugged.

'Are you serious?'

'Yes.' Her tone was terse and condescending, which made him even madder. She was the one who had been pining after him from the beginning, not the other way around. How could she sit here with her belly jutting out and her legendary policeman boyfriend and look down on him?

'Do you really think I staged my friend's breakdown to give me an excuse to visit you?' He realised he was raising his voice, but he couldn't stop himself.

'Yes.'

Sofia's calmness fired him up even more.

'After you turned your back on me? I trusted you. I opened myself up to you, told you things I have never told anyone before. And you abandoned me.'

Sofia looked down into her coffee cup.

'I know that, Fredrik, but...'

'But what? Was I not as nice as your fucking Kaj?' He flung his arms up in the air. 'We had something, you and me. We had something last summer. You can't deny that.'

'I'm not, but...'

'But you'd rather have a sixty-year-old, married man?'

Sofia looked up at him.

'Yeah,' he said, 'I read the papers, too, you know. He's married to someone else and you're expecting his baby. Do you know what that makes you?'

He stood up and gathered up his cup, plate, and silverware and put them in the sink with a clatter. Sofia hadn't moved and didn't say anything. When he turned back around, her eyes were ice cold.

'At least he hasn't spent half his life looking for a ghost.'

25

The cold bit into her cheeks and Sofia pulled her hat down farther over her ears. Snowflakes swirled over the frozen sea like sparkling confetti. They were beautiful to look at but they stung when they hit your face. She closed her eyes and tried to feel the warmth from the sun, but it blew away before the rays reached her. She just wanted to stand here and let the wind carry her off to some other place. Somewhere where Fredrik wasn't waiting in her kitchen and where Kaj wouldn't be getting off the hovercraft soon. Why the hell had Fredrik shown up here again? Everything had fallen into place. Even though it was a strange situation, it was one she had control over. Now everything was upside down again.

She had gone too far during their argument. She had crossed a line by bringing up his dead brother and she should never have crossed it. It was both mean and insensitive, but she had wanted to hurt him, cut him down a notch for his arrogant attitude when he insinuated that she was a homewrecker.

She put her hand on her belly and tried to calm down. She thought about the long-awaited baby who was in there. Becoming a mother was a blessing she had never thought she would get to experience. The miscarriage and the removal of her ovary a few years ago had reduced her chances of getting pregnant but obviously hadn't completely robbed her of the opportunity.

He would be here soon. Despite Tord's insistence that she was carrying a girl, Sofia was convinced it was a boy in there. She had chosen not to find out the sex, but every time she dreamed about the baby, it was always a boy. It was hard to imagine what it would be like if she ended up having a daughter, what a mother-daughter relationship would look like. What did she have to teach a girl and later a young woman? Nothing. Her relationship with Claire had been an emotional trainwreck. She couldn't remember a single occasion when her mother had shown her genuine love. Sofia didn't doubt that her mother loved her, in her own way, but there had never been any tenderness between them. Even from a young age, Sofia had made a decision not to speak Claire's native language. Claire had continued to insist, picking up utensils, clothes, and toys, and asking Sofia to repeat the French words, but she had never complied. If Claire asked in French, Sofia answered in Swedish, the language that she and her father, Sten, had in common. As an adult, Sofia understood that she had completely shut her mother out of her and her father's world, but honestly, she didn't feel guilty about it. Claire had chosen wine bottles over them.

After Sten died of cancer, one day Claire packed up her clothes and her beloved porcelain figurines from the bookshelf in the living room and left Ulvön Island. Sofia had only been twenty-three at the time and had just started at the police academy in Stockholm. With the help of a lawyer, Claire had transferred the house and the flat in downtown Örnsköldsvik to Sofia. Claire had taken with her the money Sten had set aside for his dream trip to Alaska, but she had left the pricey Riva Ariston for Sofia. It was completely useless as a fishing boat, but Sofia enjoyed getting to look after the apple of her father's eye. She missed him and wished that they had had more years together. For her part, Claire was just relieved to part with the boat. Sofia had no idea where Claire was, if she was even still alive, but she really didn't care, either.

It had taken many years before she felt like she wanted to stay in the house. When she was on vacation from the police academy, she had gone home to Örnsköldsvik, but always staying in the flat in town and taking on as many extra shifts as she could like monitoring the holding cells at the police station. Christmas Eve had been rough, as had her first few birthdays, but she had very quickly adjusted to living on her own. And for the most part, she was quite content. She had had some fleeting friendships during college, but she hadn't stayed in touch with any of them.

Her relationship with Kaj had ended up replacing all social interaction. She no longer knew if it had been about love. It was sooner a tender friendship spiced up with a passionate sex life. And a childish pride at having snared the hotly coveted older teacher. Sometimes she wondered if she would even have been with Kaj if it hadn't been for Fredrik leaving her without any explanation.

Sofia straightened up. She tried again to pull her hat down to protect herself from the cold. The hovercraft was approaching the dock now. She pulled her jacket around her more tightly as Kaj stepped out and came towards her.

'You're standing out here freezing?'

Sofia gave him a strained smile and nodded her head towards the red Golf which was parked about ten meters away. He swept his glove under his nose to wipe away a drop hanging from the tip of his nose.

'Shall we go then?'

26

The snow had broken the branch Ellie's swing was attached to, but otherwise the place looked just like the last time they had been there. Anders had bought the old schoolhouse for a pittance. Aside from the tile stoves and the big woodstove in the corner of the kitchen, they had gutted the place. Amanda had brought an army of interior designers up from Stockholm with her and spent a week marching through the building like a heavily pregnant general with an entourage of yes-men, telling them what she wanted. There would be a cedar sauna imported from Brazil, an Italian marble kitchen island, Moroccan tiles in the bathrooms. Not the sort of thing you could buy at the hardware store, obviously. It all had to be imported. He had let her have her way and enjoyed seeing her engage with something besides yoga and her various social events.

Early in their relationship, he had envisioned a future for them consisting of travel, nice dinners, and a steady flow of money coming in. It had never occurred to him that Amanda would want children. But he had figured it out quickly enough when she simply started furnishing a nursery next to their bedroom at home in the Djursholm house, without even asking him first. When he questioned it, she had just laughed, as if it was a given that they would have children. Obviously he didn't regret having Ellie, but he also hadn't planned on spending his middle-aged years changing diapers and dashing off to infant swimming lessons.

'We're here, sweetie.'

Amanda leaned back from the driver's seat and stroked Ellie's leg. Her daughter grunted in her sleep but quickly woke up when she saw where they were.

Anders smiled. The sun had just managed to rise halfway into the sky over Kornsjö Lake down below their house. Soon it would sink behind the hill on the other side.

They had been driving all day but had had a nice time of it. He had fallen asleep when they passed Uppsala and slept for an hour. When he woke up he was sober and in a good mood and had offered to drive so Amanda could sleep. She had declined without sulking and had driven the whole way up to Örnsköldsvik. He ran his hand over her hair gratefully. On the way up, he had decided he would deal with everything. He would try to solve his problems at work and get a handle on his drinking. Amanda deserved a considerate, loving husband, and Ellie deserved a father who was present and could provide for them.

'I'll unload the car,' he said, and Amanda nodded and got out to unbuckle Ellie's seatbelt. The trunk was packed full of winter clothes, wine, meat that Amanda had brought up from the freezer at home, and two bottles of his favourite whiskey.

He promised himself that at least one of them would still be full when they returned home.

27

I'm so cold, my teeth are chattering. I've been standing at the edge of the woods for hours, watching them through the binoculars. They've been playing all afternoon. They shovelled the snow and pulled the little girl in the sled. So carefree, so unaware of the world outside their little bubble. I almost feel sorry for them. These clueless creatures who move through life without seeing the people they trample to get to the top.

There's smoke coming out of the chimney now. It's dark and I can see them through the living room window. They ate dinner in the main room. I didn't see what they ate, but I did see Anders drink several glasses of wine. That's going to make everything so much easier.

The girl is watching TV. The colourful flicker from the screen competes with the soft glow from the fireplace. She's so pretty. Curly, dark hair and fair skin. She's curled up in the corner of the sofa with a blanket over her pulled-up legs. I wonder how it will feel to touch such a little body. I wonder if she's warm, if her skin is soft.

I shiver a little at the thought.

28

'You're kidding?' Kaj's voice sounded upset.

Sofia's response was inaudible. Fredrik lay on a thin mattress on the floor of the guest room. He propped himself up on his elbows to hear better, but the thick wooden door only let in every other word.

He had been avoiding Sofia the whole day. He had only emerged from the guest room to help set the table and clear it again at mealtimes. The rest of the time he had lain on his back and stared at the yellowy-orange pine ceiling wondering how in the world he had ended up here again. Could Sofia have been right? Had he used Philip as an excuse to come to Ulvön Island and try to make things work with her? Was he that stupid?

'How irresponsible is this? You're going to be a mother soon, Sofia. How can you let someone mentally ill into our home?' It sounded like Kaj was pacing around in the kitchen as he spoke.

'This is my home, and I'll let in whoever I please. He's not mentally ill. He's...' The rest disappeared into mumbling that Fredrik couldn't make out. He listened for a while to Sofia's and Kaj's angry voices. Philip was still asleep. He had been asleep all day and had only gotten out of bed to go to the bathroom. Both Fredrik and Sofia had tried to persuade him to eat something, but he didn't want to. It wasn't unusual for that to happen. Philip's 'spells', as Inga so old-fashionedly called them, were often followed by tremendous fatigue which could take him several days to recover from. Fredrik hoped to God that he would be feeling better soon so they could go home.

The phone blinked. He pulled out the charger he had borrowed from Sofia and rolled over to face the other way on the mattress so the light from the screen wouldn't bother Philip.

> How's your friend doing? I'm thinking about you. I can't wait for you to come back.

Ida had sent several messages since Fredrik had left yesterday morning. But she hadn't been critical or seemed annoyed, just been genuinely empathetic. He thought about the clash between Sofia and him earlier in the day. It had been a much needed if belated discussion, but even so, he had felt empty afterwards. Her emotional coldness had hurt him. That judging voice. *Searching for a ghost.* Ida would never say that. Never. She had listened for hours while he talked about Niklas, without judging or looking down on him. A great tenderness filled him when he thought of her. Maybe she was exactly the sort of person he should be with? Ida was everything Sofia wasn't, soft, warm, nurturing. Why had he kept her at a distance for a chance with someone who obviously saw him as a nobody? Someone who had moved on and was expecting a baby with another man?

It was times like this when he missed his anti-anxiety pills. It had been so easy, never needing to feel anything, always having a chemical refuge accessible in his pocket whenever life got too tough. But he had managed to recover from his addiction, and he was proud of that. Torsten Bredh, the psychiatrist who treated him over the years, had warned him that it was going to be tough, but he hadn't imagined how tough. No doctor recommended quitting cold turkey, and yet he had done the previous summer. He remembered those first awful weeks of sweating, vomiting, heart palpitations, and pain all over his body. He had hidden it as best he could from Sofia. He had tried to replace the lost feeling of security with what he had thought at the time was the beginning of their rekindled relationship. It would have been easy to relapse after the assault and the abrupt ending of their love story, but he was determined to learn to manage his anxiety in a different way. The pills were the reason he had been caught in a situation that had almost cost him his life. He had taken painkillers after his operations, but no more than necessary and he had stopped as soon as he could. He had come to appreciate brutal reality for what it was. At least he felt something and that was a thousand times better than wasting his life in a paralysing drug-fog.

Someone slammed the bathroom door and Fredrik assumed that was the end of Sofia's and Kaj's argument. He responded to Ida's text.

> Philip is doing well. I'll be home by tomorrow night at the latest.

Short. Informative.
Then he deleted the whole thing and started over.

> Coming home tomorrow evening. Can't wait to give you a hug. XOXO.

29

It's snowing outside. The flakes land silently on the already half-metre-high snowbanks alongside the road. I turn the key in the lock and step into the front hall. The big fireplace in the living room is still glowing, but there are no lights on.

I pause for a moment, stand still and listen for any noises. When I don't hear anything, I make my way upwards. The old staircase cooperates and doesn't give away my footsteps. I navigate familiarly through the large great room despite the darkness, avoiding the sofas, the low coffee tables, and the pouffes.

The door to the bedroom is open, but the one to the child's room is closed. I put my hand on the handle and carefully push it down. The door swings open without making a sound. I squint into the darkness searching for the contours of the little child's body in the bed, but it's empty. A sound makes me jump. I hear a voice from the bedroom.

'Daddy, where's my Snuffie?'

She lisps the way little kids do. Her voice is high pitched. I feel strangely warm inside when I hear it.

No one answers her. I stand there, pressed against the wall of the child's room.

'Daddy, Snuffie's downstairs!'

The voice is louder now, demanding a response.

The covers rustle and Anders replies sleepily, 'Go down and get him, sweetie. I'm right here, awake. I'll wait for you.'

'No, you go.'

No response.

Soon, the sound of a small child's feet can be heard on the cold wood floor. I stand there inside the doorway of the next room. I realise that this is my chance.

She takes a few steps out into the main room. I see her through the crack in the doorway from the child's room. Her dark curls are tousled around her little head.

'Promise you won't fall back asleep,' she said, turning around towards her parents' bedroom. But no one answers her this time either. The girl stands still, hesitating. It's dark. It will take her many steps to run to the stairs that lead down.

She hesitates another moment, then she takes a breath and darts out across the soft carpets, reaches the landing at the top of the stairs, and starts quickly descending with her hand on the railing. The light downstairs comes on.

I sneak after her.

Sunday, 23 February

30

When Anders woke up, the sun was already up. The window had no blinds, and he could see that it had stopped snowing. Yesterday they had shovelled until their backs ached, but as soon as they had managed to expose the deck and had gone inside to eat dinner, it had started snowing again. A heavy snowfall that would require further efforts with the snow shovel today. But first he would play with Ellie for a long time. It was going to be a fantastic day of sledding and hot chocolate. He was going to dig a snow cave they could sit in and maybe light a fire in the fire pit.

Anders stretched in the bed and looked up at the exposed ceiling beams. He really loved this house, its old-fashioned charm with the tile stoves and the woodstove, and the large, open kitchen that Amanda had designed to perfection with a combination of polished marble and custom candlesticks and retro-style furniture. Anders had installed an air source heat pump but had left the original windows in place. The paned windows gave the house character. They let the cold in like a sieve, but he could afford to counteract that by beefing up the heat and running the tile stoves whenever they were up. Half the charm of the house was coming in the winter, feeling the cold, seeing the dust and the flies that gathered on the windowsills and feeling how time had stood still in their absence.

If he could only get rid of his headache, he would get up. After Amanda and Ellie had fallen asleep, he had gone downstairs and sat in the living room in front of the fire with a whiskey, staring into the flames and trying to contemplate his life. It would be hard to correct all the mistakes he had made but not impossible. He would become a better man, look after Amanda and Ellie. His idiotic decisions had put both his marriage and his company in a precarious position. The whole time he had had Jerzy by his side, a man who was respected by the workers and spoke their language, things had been under control. But now Jerzy had grown tired of everything as well. Anders promised himself he would deal with it all when he got back to Stockholm. For real. This time, he would come clean when he met with the clients. Maybe they would accept the delay. He would cut back on his drinking, too, and sit down with Jerzy and address his concerns. He would try to convince his site manager to calm the workers down. If they dragged the union into this, all the company's secrets would be exposed faster than he could say 'economic crimes'. Hopefully it would not come to that.

He rolled onto his side and tugged irritably on the blanket which he had wrapped himself up in like a cocoon. It was stuck and he tugged hard to get it to come loose.

'What are you doing?' Amanda's half-asleep face poked up from her side of the bed and she rubbed herself where his elbow had hit her shoulder.

'Sorry, honey. I'm stuck.' Anders wriggled free of the blanket to put his arms around her. She immediately stiffened. 'It looks like great weather,' he tried.

Even though she was wearing long-sleeved thermal underwear, she was the sexiest thing he had ever seen. His morning wood only hardened further as he looked at her. She never wore a bra. The new breasts he had bought her were round and firm. He was about to slide his hand in under her shirt when she sat up.

'Where's Ellie?'

'She probably just went downstairs to start unpacking her stuffed animals,' Anders tried, letting his hand slip in over her flat stomach.

'Ellie?' Amanda's shrill voice made him immediately go soft. There was no point in even thinking about it now. 'Come upstairs to me and Papa! Ellie, honey?'

When she didn't get any response, she swung her feet over the edge of the bed and buried them in a pair of sheepskin slippers. She rubbed her arms.

'Brr, it's so cold. We need to replace the windows next year, Anders.' He nodded and pulled the blanket up higher to cover his neck. The pain from his headache was getting sharper.

'Ellie?' Amanda was already halfway out into the upstairs family room. Anders closed his eyes. If she was in a good mood, he might get to go back to sleep for a while and get out of having to mess with the juicer, the oatmeal, and the toaster. Maybe he could get up to breakfast already on the table.

A few minutes later, Amanda stood in the bedroom doorway. Her face was ashen. In her hand she held Ellie's Snuffie, which they had left on the sofa yesterday.

'I can't find Ellie.'

Anders sat up, his headache pounding.

'What do you mean? Did you look downstairs? Maybe she…'

'I've looked everywhere,' Amanda interrupted.

Suddenly Anders was worried.

'But…?'

'She's gone, Anders.'

31

The clatter of silverware against plates was the only thing that broke the silence in the kitchen in Norrbysbodarna. Sofia looked out at the water beyond Kaj's shoulder, imagining some way to escape. She could row to the mainland. Anything to get away from this oppressive atmosphere. That would have been a good plan if it hadn't been for her pregnant belly, and the ice, and the fact that the idea was completely preposterous.

Kaj gave a strained smile and watched Fredrik stuff a bite of salmon and potatoes into his mouth.

'So, how's your friend doing? Philip, is it?'

'Not very well. He mostly sleeps.' Fredrik took a deep breath. 'I realise that it's difficult for you to have us here, but we're going to try to get out of here today.'

He sought out Sofia's eyes, but she was looking down at her plate. She still felt ashamed about what she had said during their argument.

'Yes, well, as you see, it's rather a bad time for a visit.' Kaj set down his utensils and proudly patted Sofia's belly the way you would pat a child on the head, she thought.

It required all the restraint she could muster not to knock his hand away. She opened her mouth to say that it wasn't at all a problem for Fredrik and Philip to stay for several days but was interrupted by Fredrik.

'Like I said, I understand that you don't want us here, what with the pregnancy and all, but Philip will be feeling better soon. And then you have my word that we'll leave right away.'

His resigned tone melted Sofia. She looked up and then into his eyes, feeling the familiar, almost pleasurable pain inside. The only man she had loved in her whole life was sitting in her kitchen and she couldn't touch him, couldn't tell him how she felt about him. He looked at her and smiled dejectedly. They both remembered their argument. She nodded, returning his smile, an unspoken confirmation of a reconciliation between them.

'It's no problem. You can stay.'

But Kaj immediately broke in.

'I have all the sympathy in the world for your friend's difficulties. My cousin has Asperger's.'

Sofia looked at Kaj in surprise. It felt unfamiliar that he would have any awareness of disabilities.

'Or ASD they call it now, right?' Kaj looked at Sofia, as if she could confirm this for him.

Fredrik set his utensils on his plate.

'Yeah, but it's not just that. He also has severe agoraphobia. That makes it so much worse when he shuts down. If I uproot him now and force him to proceed...'

'It doesn't matter,' Kaj interrupted. 'He needs professional help.'

The cockfight atmosphere seemed to escalate with every second and Kaj had begun to raise his voice. Sofia rubbed her temples exaggeratedly, but no one paid any attention to her. The baby kicked hard inside her belly.

'He doesn't need a hospital. He needs to rest, pull himself together, and...'

'We're expecting a baby here,' Kaj began.

Suddenly they heard footsteps out on the front stoop. The front door was abruptly flung open. The wind grabbed it and threw it against the wall with a bang. Tord's figure filled the doorway, his grey hair standing on end like a halo around his backlit head. Like a Messiah come to save me, Sofia thought.

He took off his shoes and sat down in the empty chair at the kitchen table.

Kaj looked down at his place and continued eating while Fredrik pointedly drank from his water glass. They were like two boys who had been caught bickering by the teacher.

'Well, well, it's certainly cheerful in here.'

Tord reached for the ladle and fished a hot potato out of the pot, which he tossed back and forth between his hands a few times before taking a bite of it.

'Well, what do you know? Fredrik Fröding in the flesh.' He smiled and pointed at him with the potato. 'You look pretty good for a youngster who got shot in the stomach and had his jaw bashed in.'

Fredrik looked up at Tord and a smile spread across his face. Kaj stared petulantly down at his plate as he pushed his salmon around without eating.

'Tord!' Sofia's eyes widened as she gave him a scolding look, but she also couldn't help but smile. Tord's frankness filled the room like a breath of fresh air.

Tord shrugged.

'I can't complain,' Fredrik said.

Kaj looked up and then made a strained smile.

'Would you like a plate, Tord?'

He shook his head and, amused, fished another potato out and took a bite out of it.

Then he grew serious and looked at Sofia.

'Have you talked to the station?'

'No, why?'

'Vikman's son over in Sörbyn. He belongs to that Missing People group or whatever it's called, the nonprofit that organises search volunteers. He got a call this morning. Apparently, there's a big hoopla over on the mainland. Up in Sunnansjö.'

'Why?' Kaj asked.

Tord kept looking at Sofia, even though Kaj had asked him a question.

'A four-year-old has gone missing.'

Sofia couldn't stop her hands from settling protectively around her belly.

'What do you mean missing?'

'She just got up and walked out the front door, no jacket and no shoes, no trace of her. Half the village is out looking for her.'

Kaj shook his head.

'That doesn't sound very likely. In this weather? She can't have gotten far. How does a four-year-old get around in a half meter of snow without leaving any traces?'

Tord shrugged again, swallowed the last of the potato, and then pulled his snuff tin out of the chest pocket of his red plaid flannel shirt.

'If they haven't found her by now, there's a risk that she's frozen to death.'

Sofia stood up and started scraping the remnants off her plate into the trash can.

'You don't need to go in.' Kaj also stood up and started loading the glasses and silverware into the dishwasher.

'Yes, I do.'

Just then Sofia's cell phone rang.

It was Vera Nordlund, her boss.

32

Amanda was hysterical. So much so that Anders's own worries seemed to fade into the periphery. She had turned the entire house upside down, throwing clothing, skis, and ice skates out of every closet as she yelled over and over again for Ellie in a loud, piercing voice. Alternately threatening and cajoling for their daughter to come out of her hiding place. They had searched the car, the garage, the guest cabins, the basement, and the root cellar out in the yard. Ellie was nowhere to be found. One of the neighbours further away in the village had been out on a long dog walk and had heard the commotion from the road. He had immediately offered to stay and help look. He had taken his dog and trudged through the snow around the eight thousand square meter plot to search. Amanda had followed right on his heels, wearing only her long johns and down jacket.

It felt like time was standing still, even so it couldn't have taken more than half an hour before they realised they needed to give up. He had called the police, who had decided to call in a full emergency response. They in turn had contacted Missing People Sweden and the military reserves, the Home Guard. In just a few hours, the courtyard in front of the house had filled with people. They all had the same goal, to find the missing four-year-old.

Anders could not take in what was happening. How could Ellie have gotten out? Had she just gotten up and wandered off without a jacket or shoes? Her pacifier, which Anders had asked Amanda in vain to wean her from, was still lying in the bed.

Now there was a police car and a blue Volvo in the driveway. A plainclothes officer was talking to the neighbour who had helped search. A younger woman in uniform sat with Amanda in the kitchen. There were another two police cars down by the foot of the driveway with a canine officer with a German Shepherd, which was walking with its nose pressed to the ground. The courtyard in front of the house had been cordoned off, but Anders had seen enough crime shows to know that any potential traces had long since been snowed over or trampled by him or Amanda or the neighbour. He shivered in his pyjama pants and down jacket. He hadn't even put on a T-shirt underneath.

'What time did you wake up?' The tall woman with the plum-coloured hair had introduced herself as Chief Inspector Vera Nordlund. She was as wide as a barndoor and her red Fjällräven jacket was stretched taut across her bosom. She pushed her eyeglasses up onto the top of her head, but they got caught on her grey knit hat, so she took them off and put them in her pocket. Anders could see the sticker with the magnification strength still on them.

'Nine, maybe. We were up really late yesterday, all three of us. Then I was up for a while longer after Amanda and Ellie went to bed.' Anders pulled his jacket around himself more tightly and looked over at the neighbour who was pointing in various directions to show the police where they had looked. Amanda came out of the house with the uniformed officer. She had put a cardigan on under her jacket but no hat. It had started snowing again. Light, noiseless flakes that stuck in her long, chestnut hair.

'And you didn't hear anything before this? No one coming into the house or moving around outside?'

'No.' Amanda immediately took over.

'Is anything missing?'

'No.'

'Ellie's jacket?'

'No, nothing is missing.'

'Does Ellie usually sleepwalk?'

'She has,' Amanda nodded, 'but never like this. She's never gone outside.'

'And you didn't see any tracks in the snow when you went outside this morning?' Vera Nordlund asked, scratching her forehead.

It was Anders's turn to shake his head now.

'What did you do after your wife and your daughter went to bed?'

Amanda's gaze burned into him.

'Uh, I don't know... I might have had a whisky, sat in front of the fireplace.'

'Was the front door locked this morning when you got up?'

Amanda shook her head.

'No, and we usually always lock it.' Her voice went up, almost into a falsetto.

'Can Ellie open the door?'

'No,' Amanda immediately replied, looking at the officer with desperation in her eyes. 'She can't reach the deadbolt.'

They stood in silence for a second, then the chief inspector turned to Anders.

'Were you drunk when you went to bed?'

'Huh?' He blushed.

'If you were drunk, maybe you forgot to lock the door.'

Amanda took a breath beside him and Anders was filled with a chilling fear.

Was it his fault Ellie was missing?

33

When Sofia arrived at the house in Sunnansjö on the mainland, the air was thick with snow. The sun had been out earlier in the day, but it had gradually grown overcast and the sky was now once again thoroughly grey. The police cars' bright blue lights stood out in harsh contrast to the white winter landscape. In the distance she heard the police helicopter moving over the area with thermal imaging cameras in search of the missing girl. A little farther up the hill towards the property's two guest cabins, a UAS pilot stood with a remote control in his hands, looking up at the sky where his drone was making sweeps over the village of Sunnansjö.

The people searching around the house had little piles of snow on their shoulders and their knit hats. Even so, she didn't feel cold when she got out of the car. If you dressed properly, staying warm in the dry winter cold was no problem. The man who met her in the driveway was anything but appropriately dressed. His long legs were covered only by a pair of thin, plaid cotton pyjama pants and underneath his thick down jacket, she caught a glimpse of his bare chest. He nodded in greeting to avoid having to remove his arms from the hug he was giving himself to stay warm.

Sofia closed her car door behind her, walked up to the man, and nodded towards Vera as she walked up from behind him. Karim was talking to one of the canine officers. It was clear that the intensive preliminary searches had slowed. A sense of despondency hung over those at the scene.

'Let's go inside.' Vera put her arm around the man's shoulders and pointed towards the double cedar doors finished with a dark stain. Sofia followed without trying to make conversation. They stepped into a front hall that was open all the way up to the ridge of the roof. The entrance led into a similarly open living room with panoramic windows and a round fireplace in the middle. On a white, horseshoe-shaped sofa drowning in fluffy throw blankets and sheepskins, sat a slim woman dressed in grey and neon pink long underwear with her hands over her face. Kicki Bjurvall, a short, uniformed colleague who had an almost completely round face, sat beside her. Kicki's short, dark-brown hair reinforced the shape of her face even more and made her look like a cartoon character. Sofia liked Kicki. They had coffee together in the cafeteria at the police station sometimes, and in late summer she had even been invited to Kicki's summer place for a crayfish party. But then her morning sickness had put an end to all her socialising plans. Kicki had extensive experience working on missing persons cases. Along with Vera, who had special expertise in MSO – the police methodology used to investigate missing persons – she was the first called in in cases like this, especially to handle communications with the family. That was an area where Vera's skills left a fair amount to be desired. Although she formally held the role of rescue operation lead, Kicki acted as her right-hand, coordinating the search efforts with Missing People and the Home Guard. In addition to that, she was interested in game hunting and knew the county's forests better than any of the others.

As Sofia and Vera entered the living room with the man between them, the woman in her long underwear looked up. Her face was red from crying and there was a dark look in her eyes.

'This is all your fault, Anders! Do you understand that?' She spat the words out. Kicki put her arm around her, and she began sobbing loudly.

Everyone except for Vera sat down on the sofa.

'This is Sofia Hjortén,' she said.

The man in the down jacket and pyjama pants nodded without making eye contact with Sofia.

'Ellie disappeared from the house sometime between midnight and 9:00 a.m. this morning. No clothes are missing, and we haven't found any footprints or tracks because of the snowfall.' Vera cleared her throat and looked at Sofia. 'It has come to light that the front door may have been left unlocked.'

Amanda hugged a pillow in her arms so hard that her knuckles turned white. Anders kept staring down at his knees.

'What do we do now?' His voice was higher pitched than usual and full of self-recrimination.

'We expand the search,' Vera said. 'But we've also filed a report of a suspected kidnapping.'

A whimper could be heard from Amanda.

'Sofia will reach out to you about the disappearance. Kicki and I will continue to coordinate the search.'

Vera nodded for Sofia to take over.

'I want to start by expressing how sorry I am...' She didn't have a chance to say any more than that before Amanda interrupted.

'She's dead, right? Is that why you're saying that? You think she's dead?'

Sofia shook her head and tried to find a comfortable position on the sofa.

'We don't know anything at this point. I just want to express how sorry I am that you find yourselves in this situation. We're all going to do everything we can to find Ellie.'

Anders looked into her eyes. The profound fear she saw in his eyes frightened her.

34

The cold snow stings his eyes. Every flake that hits him feels like the tip of a knife. They poke into his skin and burn holes. He looks down at his body and realises he's naked. Snowflakes are stuck all over his exposed chest. He desperately brushes over the burning holes, but nothing happens, it keeps hurting. He's freezing. His legs are numb. A woman is lying next to him on the ground. He sees that it's Madde. Somewhere deep inside him his consciousness makes itself known and Philip realises that this is a dream. It's a dream, but he doesn't want to wake up. He must not wake up. He needs to find her first. It's important. He must not go back into his desensitised state.

When Philip woke up, he didn't know where he was at first. The pine-wood bed had green sheets with leaves on them. He was only wearing underwear and a T-shirt. The covers were thin, and he was cold. He heard a voice out in the kitchen and remembered that he was at Sofia's house on Ulvön Island. But that wasn't her or Fredrik's voice. A man with a heavy Stockholm accent was talking to someone on the phone.

'It's her baby, too, Mette.'

The person on the other end of the call seemed to talk for a long time.

'Sole custody? On what grounds?'

More silence, waiting for another long explanation.

'Mette, we can deal with this after the baby is born. Right now...'

The conversation stopped and Philip heard Fredrik open the bathroom door in the hallway. Then he was standing in the doorway to the guest room with a towel around his hips.

'Good afternoon,' Fredrik said. 'How are you feeling?'

Philip sat up in bed with the covers still wrapped around him while Fredrik dug through his bag for one of the T-shirts.

'I'm borrowing this.'

Philip nodded.

Fredrik lingered by the bag and took out the package containing the necklace Philip had bought for Madde. Philip was staring at it when Fredrik came and sat down next to him on the bed.

'Who is this for?'

Philip took the package with the hand that wasn't holding his blanket.

'Madde.'

Fredrik looked at him, waiting for him to go on.

'Who's that?'

Philip set the package down on the bed next to him and pulled the blanket around him more tightly.

'My girlfriend.'

Fredrik didn't even try to feign indifference. He grinned and gave Philip a manly pat on the back.

'All right! So, when do I get to meet her?'

Philip looked down at his hands and burst into tears.

Fredrik was sitting in the kitchen when Sofia and Kaj walked in the door. He and Kaj had been avoiding each other all day while Sofia had been gone. Kaj had sat upstairs working while he had wandered around like a lost soul waiting for Philip to wake up so they could catch the last hovercraft.

When Philip did wake up, he was definitely in much better shape than he had been when they had arrived, but he was still refusing to go home. Fredrik didn't know what to do. He wanted nothing more than to leave Ulvön Island, but he didn't know how to get Philip to go with him and he needed to talk to Sofia. Kaj had gone over to the dock at Fjären to pick her up and then they had lost their chance to make the last hovercraft. Philip had gone back to bed, but his bag was packed in the guest room at any rate.

Kaj helped Sofia take her jacket off as she tried to get her winter boots off. It was still snowing outside and the doormat in the front hall was soaked from their shoes.

'How is Philip doing?' she asked and came and sat down across from Fredrik at the kitchen table. Kaj walked over to the counter to put the kettle on. He held up the jar of tea bags with a questioning look and Fredrik nodded.

'Better. He was up for a while. I hope we'll be able to leave tomorrow.'

'Good to hear,' Kaj said. 'That's he's feeling better, I mean,' he added.

The kettle boiled and Kaj set a cup and tea bag out for each of them and poured the water. Fredrik didn't want to talk to Sofia while he was around. Thankfully, Kaj didn't seem particularly keen on being in the same room with him either. He poured himself a cup and then took it into the living room with him. Soon they heard the theme song for the TV4 news. Fredrik and Sofia sat quietly while the news about the missing four-year-old girl was presented.

'Damn,' Fredrik sighed when the reporter moved on to talk about the upcoming US election.

'It's terrible,' Sofia said with a nod.

'The parents are beside themselves with worry.'

She moved her hand over her belly. They drank their tea without saying anything more, and Fredrik wondered how he should begin.

'Well, I talked to Philip a little. It seems like he came up here to see his girlfriend.'

Sofia raised her eyebrows.

Fredrik smiled.

'I was surprised, too, but it appears that Philip has actually met someone. She's studying in Umeå, so they were supposed to meet here at her family's vacation home.'

'Here in Örnsköldsvik?'

Fredrik nodded.

'But when he got there, she wasn't there.'

Sofia drank some of her tea.

'She wasn't?'

'He waited for a while but felt uncomfortable being in the house by himself. On his way out, he drove into the ditch. The cut on his forehead came from when he hit the steering wheel.'

Sofia put her cup down.

'But they had arranged to meet each other there?'

'Yes, or maybe no. They had had an argument. She went on ahead and he decided to drive up there anyway and surprise her.'

'I don't understand. That was all it took to put him in the state he's been in?' She nodded towards the guest room. 'That they got in an argument, and she didn't want to see him?'

Fredrik pursed his lips and breathed in through his nose before he continued.

'Philip hasn't really been out moving around in public for more than twenty years. Anything out of the ordinary could put him into the *state he's been in*.'

His tone caused Sofia to lean back in her seat, away from the conversation.

'He thinks something happened.'

Sofia crossed her hands over her big belly.

'Based on what?'

Fredrik didn't have any answer to that.

'It'll probably work itself you, you'll see.' Sofia stifled a yawn behind her hand. 'If you only knew how many "disappearances",' she put air quotes around the word, 'we've investigated that turn out to be due to a fight between a couple.'

Fredrik looked at her.

'So you're not going to do anything about it?'

'Like what?'

'Send someone over there to check it out.'

Sofia stood up awkwardly and put her empty teacup in the sink. Before leaving the kitchen, she turned around to look at him.

'We have enough to do with one missing child. If Philip is having lady problems, he can probably solve them without police assistance.'

35

The girl is sound asleep with her head leaning on the sofa cushion. A wet stain from her saliva covers one of the yellow flowers in the colourful pattern. Her dark hair curls up on her sweaty forehead. She moves her mouth in her sleep, making little smacking sounds. Sometimes she feels around her with her hands. I think she's searching for a pacifier.

It wasn't hard to get her to get her to come along. She screamed when I gave her the injection, but by then my hand was already over her mouth so no noise could escape. I had to hold onto her tightly for almost half a minute before she went limp in my arms. I stood there for a long time with her limp body in my arms, listening to see if anyone upstairs would wake up. But no one came.

She has slept heavily all day since I put her on the sofa. Every four hours I give her another dose of the sedating nasal spray, but first I shake her away and give her a bottle of formula to cover her nutritional and fluid needs. She eats greedily and then goes back to sleep.

I sit down on the armrest of the sofa. Raise my hand, thinking I want to touch her, gently stroke her soft legs. My hand looks enormous compared to her small body. I change my mind at the last second, don't want to risk waking her up.

If she wakes up, she's not worth anything to me anymore.

Monday, 24 February

36

Kaj pointed to the butter and Fredrik passed it to him without looking up. Sofia sat at the end of the table watching her two former boyfriends as they ate breakfast together in tense silence.

It was still dark out, and the wind howled around the corners of the house. It had stopped snowing and the sky was clear, but she still wasn't looking forward to going out into the cold. She had slept poorly and mostly just wanted to crawl back into bed again and pull the covers over her head. But a child was missing. There was no room for her own needs right now.

'So you're leaving today?' Kaj couldn't conceal his cheerfulness.

Fredrik nodded.

'On the eight o'clock hovercraft.'

'Then we'll be on the same one,' Sofia said.

Kaj pouted.

'Do you have to go in again today?'

'Yes, we start searching again as soon as it gets light out.'

'You shouldn't be outside trudging around in the snow and searching in your condition.'

'No, and I wasn't planning to, either, but...'

She stopped short when she heard the sound of an engine approaching outside. The glass in the front door vibrated as someone stomped the snow off their shoes on the front stoop. Tord's face immediately appeared in the doorway between the kitchen and the front hall. It had become a routine for him to stop by every morning and have a cup of coffee and check in on her. She appreciated it. Now more than ever.

'Come in, Tord. There's eggs and coffee.'

'Coffee will do it for me, but you sit down,' he said, waving impatiently at her as she tried to get up to serve him. He poured himself a cup of coffee and sat down on the metal stepping stool next to the fridge.

'How's the case?'

Sofia shook her head.

'Nothing yet. Both the Home Guard and Missing People are helping search. But in this cold, you can't survive long outdoors if you're not dressed for it.'

Tord murmured his agreement.

'I heard it's that construction guy's daughter?'

Sofia nodded.

'SveAnd AB.' That was already out in the newspapers, so she didn't see any reason to keep it secret.

Tord snorted.

'Not that I wish him ill, but my guess is that they probably just can't fucking stop the construction.'

'What construction?' Kaj asked.

'Those new houses out on Dekarsön Island.' Tord pulled his snuff tin out of his shirt's chest pocket and helped himself to a good-sized pinch.

'Waterfront homes each one with its own dock and pool,' he quoted. 'There will probably be a few Stockholm folks who snap those up because no one up in these parts will be able to afford to buy them.'

Thank goodness Kaj did not start a debate about Stockholm people and their purchasing habits when it came to waterfront homes in the county.

Someone quietly cleared their throat, making everyone turn to the kitchen doorway the led to the front hall. Sofia discovered Philip standing there watching them. His face was deathly pale.

Tord nodded hello and introduced himself. When he got no response, he looked at Sofia. She pulled out the chair next to her and lifted off her swollen legs, which had been resting there.

'Would you like some breakfast, Philip?'

He still didn't answer, so Fredrik got up and walked over to him.

'Philip, how are you doing?'

He looked worriedly into Fredrik's eyes.

'Who are you talking about?' Philip asked.

'It's a girl who disappeared over on the mainland,' Tord said.

'Who?'

Fredrik put a hand on Philip's shoulder.

'A little girl, she's four years old. We need to leave soon. Would you like to at least have some coffee?'

'I'll go out warm up the car,' Kaj said. He finished the last of his coffee, got up, and went out to the front hall without clearing the table after himself. Philip didn't move as Kaj pushed his way past him.

'I heard you say SveAnd.' Philip's voice was as frail as rice paper.

Kaj came into view again behind him in the opening between the front hall and the kitchen, with his scarf half wrapped around his neck.

'Is the girl's name Ellie?' Philip asked.

'Yes,' Sofia said, looking at him, 'Ellie Svensson. Why?'

'That's Madde's little sister.'

—

'There isn't necessarily any connection at all, Kaj.'

'You don't think it's strange that that psycho turns up right when the kid goes missing? How do we know Mr Philip Lindén didn't kidnap her himself?'

'Because he was lying in my guest room asleep when she disappeared,' Sofia replied sharply. It wasn't at all like Kaj to behave unprofessionally like this.

Kaj shook his head, annoyed, and flung his hand out to gesture in the direction of the house over in Norrbysbodarna. His nose glowed an angry red from the cold, but his forehead was sweaty even so. He pulled his gloved hand over his temple and adjusted his knit hat. His grey hair curled out from under the edge of the hat.

'And that Fredrik.' He pointed towards Norrbysbodarna again. 'Yet again he has succeeded in worming his way in somewhere where he doesn't belong.'

Sofia was smart enough to know that Kaj's statement stemmed as much from jealousy as concern about what this might mean for the current case. He had called Vera and informed her of the circumstances the second they realised that there was a connection between the missing girl and Philip Lindén's girlfriend. Vera had ordered Sofia to report to the police station immediately. Kaj had offered to go along and support the investigation if needed.

By this point, the hovercraft Sofia, Philip, and Fredrik were supposed to have taken at eight had already left for the mainland, but Vera had asked the hovercraft to go back and pick up Sofia and Kaj and drop off a police officer to question Philip. Neither Philip nor Fredrik would be able to go home today. Sofia didn't know if that made her happy or embarrassed. But she was going to do everything by the book this time. She would let someone else handle the questioning and not interfere, not withhold anything from Vera.

Sofia was about to say something about it to Kaj when their phones both rang at the same time.

'What the hell is going on?' Chief Inspector Vera Nordlund began her phone call without any words of greeting, as usual. 'What has that fucking youngster done now?' Youngster, the same word choice that Tord used. It struck Sofia that Vera and Tord would have made an excellent couple if Vera hadn't preferred women.

'Fredrik doesn't have anything to do with this. He came here to pick up his friend. Then it turned out that he, Philip that is, knows the older sister of the missing girl. They're dating.'

Sofia heard how messy that sounded.

'And he's at your place right now?'

'Yes. They had some sort of disagreement and he went up to her family's vacation house to smooth things over, but she wasn't there. It's a long story. I only just found out that he knows her,' Sofia hurried to add.

Kaj covered one of his ears so he could hear his own phone call better and turned away from her.

'Well, I'll be damned,' Vera grunted.

Sofia took a deep breath.

'We're standing on the dock at Fjären now. The hovercraft ought to be here any minute. We can sort this out when we get there.'

Three short tones indicated that Vera had hung up. Sofia put her mittens back on and stamped her feet.

Kaj was still on the phone, but nodded to her that the hovercraft was on its way in. She waved to the skipper and pulled her jacket around her as he pulled up to the dock.

Per Persson stepped out of the cabin. The new investigator had replaced the station's poster-boy police officer, Mattias Wikström, who had left them for a more exciting job in the communications department in Umeå. From what Sofia had heard, his behaviour was just as snooty there as it had been in the Örnsköldsvik police station.

The colleague approaching them now, on the other hand, was always cheerful and pleasant. In addition to his unlucky combination of first and last names, Per had been endowed with a short, compact build and a head of unruly red curls. Most of the time, though, his hair was covered by a well-worn cap from Örnsköldsvik's MoDo ice hockey team. Per never missed an opportunity to show his dedication to his team. Sofia hadn't had time to get to know him very well yet, since he had started in his position while she was out on sick leave. But she liked him already. He was in his early thirties, and had experience as both an investigator and a street cop. He aimed to undergo further training to become a crime scene investigator, and he knew his way around a crime scene, which made him a favourite of the two crime scene investigators they currently had at the station.

'Sofia!' Per held out his arms towards her and she realised to her horror that he was planning to hug her. Which, sure enough, he did before he gave her belly a friendly pat, as if they had known each other for years. Kaj, who was finally done with his call, took a few steps towards them and reached out his hand.

'Kaj Marklund. I don't believe we've met. I'm normally with the CP group, but I've been working remotely these days while awaiting...' He nodded proudly towards Sofia's belly.

'Marklund, what the hell? Of course I know who you are.' Per made no attempt to conceal how impressed he was. 'Shoot, that was impressive work, catching that guy in Vagnhärad.'

Kaj's most recent case had involved a serial rapist who had been ravaging the area around Trosa the previous fall. The Criminal Profiling group had worked up a profile of a young, socially gifted man who moved easily among young people and somehow anonymously managed to persuade a number of young women to pose naked. He had then threated to distribute the images if the women didn't agree to have sex with him. An approach that, unfortunately, wasn't all that unusual, but which had come to an end when the man was arrested and convicted, among other crimes, of child rape. He had later committed suicide in his cell by hanging himself with his T-shirt. Even though it was clearly wrong for a police officer to think this way, Sofia was secretly grateful for the outcome. There were other things society's resources could be devoted too besides trying to rehabilitate a paedophile.

The skipper gestured for them to hop aboard and Sofia pointed to her red Golf in the parking lot.

'The keys are on the left front tire. Fredrik and Philip are waiting for you at the house.'

37

The loud knock on the door made Philip jump on the sofa beside him. Fredrik patted his leg reassuringly and got up to go answer it. Outside stood a short man a few years younger than himself. His curly, reddish orange hair was evenly clipped around his head and resembled a very short afro. Instead of a hat, he wore black leather earmuffs. His complexion was pale and freckly. He flashed Fredrik a big smile, held up his ID with one hand, and reached out with his other.

'Per Persson. I'm here to speak to Philip Lindén.'

Philip stood behind Fredrik in the doorway and lethargically reached his hand out to Per.

'Come in.' Fredrik admitted the policeman, who politely took off his shoes and set them in the shoe cubby before he pulled the front door shut behind him.

'Would you like some tea?' Fredrik didn't dare attempt the percolator. It felt strange to play host in Sofia's house, but he felt forced to offer the visibly freezing man something hot to drink. Per accepted and sat down at the kitchen table. Philip sat down across from him without saying anything.

'She has a nice place, Sofia does.' Per stretched and gazed out the window. 'What a view!'

Fredrik nodded and smiled. He instinctively liked the redheaded man who was obviously trying to get both him and Philip to relax.

'Do you know her? I couldn't really work out how you know each other.' He looked at Philip, but when he didn't get any response, he turned to Fredrik.

'We went to school together a million years ago,' Fredrik said.

Per lit up.

'Ah, so are you a policeman?'

Fredrik shook his head.

Nearly, but he had stumbled at the finish line. That he had even finished high school was entirely thanks to his grandmother. Greta Fröding had been a tough woman, but fair and gentle when it was necessary. She had used both the carrot and the stick along with plenty of nagging to get him through his studies until he stood there on the school steps with his high school diploma in hand. The police academy had been his way of giving back to all the people who had helped him on his way from a broken-hearted, orphaned thirteen-year-old to something approximating a whole person. He wanted to be like them. Help other people and give them new chances in life. His cadet position with the Solna police had been his final step towards getting out into the community and working as a policeman. But everything had fallen apart when the tenth anniversary of the MS Estonia's sinking had been blazoned across all the media and the journalists has started chasing him. He had just been starting to find his way back into living again after his grandmother Greta has passed away. One morning he had found her cold in bed after a massive stroke. He was already so fragile and hadn't been able to handle the memories and all the fuss the anniversary entailed. Soon he had fallen into a deep, black hole and was hooked on the anti-anxiety pills. Fredrik dropped out of his cadet position and the years that followed were a jumble of sessions with psychologists, treatment homes, and medical leaves. Finally, he had landed a job that he almost liked at the passport office in Solna. It was the closest to the police he could get.

'I dropped out as a cadet,' he said.

'I suppose it's not too late to pick it up again?' Per said. 'If you wanted to, I mean. We always need more police officers.'

The thought had crossed Fredrik's mind more than once during the last six months. The events of the previous summer, despite their nearly fatal consequences, had given him more zeal for life than he could remember having had since everything happened to his mother, father, and Niklas that awful autumn night more than two decades ago.

His dream of getting to work as a police officer had begun to grow in him again, but his doubts always got in the way. Would he make it through the years as a beat cop? He was nearing forty. Who would want him? Was it even possible to jump back into the training, just like that? He would probably be forced to do it all over again. He had half-heartedly tried to get in touch with several of his old classmates to ask, but no one had responded and then he had forgotten about it.

'Hmm, maybe not.' Fredrik set the kettle on the table along with three cups with teabags in them. The hammered copper sugar bowl was already out on the blue checkered tablecloth and Per stirred three cubes into his cup.

'So, Philip, let's hear it. I understand that you know the missing girl's older sister and that you're up here to visit her?'

Philip nodded.

'She's my girlfriend.'

'How long have you been together?'

'A couple months. We've mostly talked online.'

Per took out a small notebook, which he leaned on his knee.

'And you were supposed to meet at the house in Sunnansjö, outside Bjästa?'

Philip nodded again.

'Madde wanted to surprise her dad. She wanted me to meet him. It's his vacation place and he was going to come on Saturday, but we were going to go up already on Thursday.'

'Did he know that you were going to be at the house?'

'I don't know.'

It got quiet in the kitchen, but no one said anything to hurry Philip up.

'I chickened out,' Philip said. 'I have... well, I don't like to be around new people. I don't know, it just got to be too much. I said that I didn't want to go, and we argued. And, well... then I changed my mind. I thought I would surprise her, but then the car broke down and...'

Per and Fredrik exchanged a glance over Philip's head.

'Take your time.'

'I got there, but she wasn't there.'

'And then?'

'She wasn't there,' Philip repeated.

Per nodded.

'What did you do then?'

'I called her. Her phone was in her jacket, which was hanging in the closet.'

Per took noted, biting his lower lip.

'What happened then?'

'I heard a sound upstairs, so I went up there. But there wasn't anyone there.'

'And then you left?'

'Yes.'

'But you didn't go home?'

Philip looked down at the table.

'I was going to drive to Umeå where she goes to college, but I couldn't decide, and then...'

'What happened then?'

'It was slippery. I drove off the road.' Philip's hand went up to the cut on his forehead. 'Then that guy with the plough came, pulled the car up, and towed me to a gas station.'

'And you called Fredrik from there?' Per asked, looking over at Fredrik again.

'No, the lady in the convenience store at the gas station in Bjästa did that,' Fredrik broke in.

'And then you drove up there?'

Fredrik nodded.

'Does this kind of thing happen often?'

Fredrik was about to answer with something evasive when Philip interrupted him.

'Yes, it happens a lot,' Philip said. 'I have autism. And agoraphobia. And panic disorder.'

Per nodded at Philip's list of diagnoses but showed no sign of finding the whole thing remarkable. Philip's insight into his own situation had always impressed Fredrik. He accepted the state of things without shame or putting any emotional value on it, something that Fredrik himself and so many other people never managed to do. Maybe people would feel better if they just accepted their difference and limitations in the straightforward way Philip did, Fredrik thought.

'What happened then?'

'Fredde came up and I didn't want to go home until I had gotten hold of Madde. I was feeling like shit, so we came out here, to Sofia's place.'

Per wrote a bit in his notebook.

'Have you talked to her family?'

'I don't know them,' Philip said, shaking his head.

'Do you usually argue, you and Madeleine?'

'No, we've never argued before.'

Per looked at Fredrik.

'I'd like you to stay here, Philip, until we've sorted everything out.'

Fredrik nodded on Philip's behalf.

'You'll see. It will work out,' Per continued. 'Maybe she just needs a little time to think things over and calm down. We're going to try to get hold of her. This probably has nothing to do with the little girl.'

Everyone in the room realised that that last part was probably not true.

38

Sofia looked at Kaj, Vera, and Karim who were sitting around the oval table in the library. Kicki Bjurvall was also there to attend the afternoon meeting, even though she was not part of the investigative group. The furniture had been replaced since the summer and the new blue armchairs were far more comfortable than the old ones. It didn't make any difference to Sofia, though. All chairs were uncomfortable right now. She could feel the baby's head pressing downwards, as if a bowling ball were lodged in her pelvis. The thought of what it was going to feel like when the baby came out popped into her head, but she put it out of her mind again just as quickly. A woman she had met at the maternity centre, who was expecting her fifth child, had kindly informed her that it felt pretty much like you were dying. *But don't worry. You don't! It just feels that way for a while.*

The taxidermised brown bear stood in one corner of the library, the one that had been in the lobby for so many years. Its paws hung limply, its eyes glassy.

Vera, who loved analog police work, had rolled a whiteboard in and put up a picture of the missing Ellie Svensson. Arrows were drawn to Anders and Amanda Svensson as well as Madeleine Svensson. Everyone's pictures had been printed out from Facebook. That was just one of the many digital forums that had made their work easier over the last decade. Another arrow pointed to SveAnd AB and another to a picture of the construction site on Dekarsön Island. Underneath it all, Vera had drawn a timeline.

'The girl is believed to have disappeared between midnight and nine o'clock Sunday morning. The door was unlocked when the family woke up and neither her shoes not her jacket were missing.'

'When did it start snowing?' Karim asked.

'According to SMHI, the snowfall picked up again around 9:00 p.m. Saturday night. We haven't been able to find any tracks or prints around the house. Everything had been covered by fresh snow or trampled.' Vera pushed her glasses up on top of her head. 'We should have found her by this point if she went out on her own. You can't last long in this cold without the right clothes. It's possible that her body has been covered by snow, but then the dogs should have found the body.' The chief inspector's blunt statement made Sofia shiver.

'But if we instead assume that she did not disappear voluntarily,' Karim said, 'but rather that someone took her, then there's a chance that she's still alive.'

'We're running a rescue operation and then in parallel also investigating a suspected kidnapping,' Vera said, nodding. 'The search for Ellie will continue for the rest of the day today and tomorrow.'

'And Madeleine Svensson?' Karim asked, looking at Per.

'As I said,' Per replied, 'I went out and talked to the boyfriend, but he doesn't know where she is. I have tried to reach both Anders and Madeleine's mother, Jeanette, but haven't managed to connect with either of them.'

'Anders is probably out with the search party,' Kicki commented.

'I did however reach several classmates and a teacher,' Per continued. 'The last time anyone had contact with Madeleine was on Thursday afternoon when she left Umeå. We've tried tracing the cell phone that Philip Lindén claimed was left in her jacket in the closet, but it's turned off. The area has already been searched in the hunt for Ellie and there was no trace of Madeleine either.'

Vera took a deep breath.

'And we're sure she wasn't in the house when Lindén got there?'

'That's what he claims anyway.' Kaj pursed his lips. 'But it wouldn't be the first time a boyfriend said the woman in his life disappeared only for us to later discover that he had killed her. Like in the Äppelbo case, for example.'

'We'll see what the forensics team finds inside the house,' Vera said.

As a preliminary investigation into the kidnapping was opened due to Ellie's disappearance, the family had been forced to temporarily move into one of the guest cabins while the forensic investigation was conducted.

'I suppose,' Karim began, tugging at a few hairs that stuck out of his otherwise perfectly trimmed black beard, 'that the big question is if the disappearances are connected? And if so, who would stand to gain by abducting Anders Svensson's daughters.'

'The first people you look at in these sorts of cases are always those who are closest,' Kaj said.

Vera nodded in agreement.

'Although we shouldn't put too much stock in this before we know what's going on. It has happened before that people have disappeared after an argument only to turn back up again after they have calmed down.'

'Has Madeleine Svensson been reported missing?' Per asked.

Vera shook her head.

'First we need to figure out if she's staying away voluntarily.'

'I can also try contacting Anders again after our meeting and see if I can get ahold of Jeanette Svensson, too,' Sofia said. Per nodded.

'But proceed with caution,' Vera said. 'We don't want to frighten the parents any more than necessary. They're going through enough hell already.'

It was unusual for Vera to comment to the group about the family's emotions at all. Sofia knew she was an empathetic person, but she didn't usually show it. Sofia couldn't help but wonder if it was the divorce that had changed her. The previous year, Vera had surprisingly confided in her that not only was she married to a woman, but she was also in the process of divorcing her after more than twenty-five years of living together. Vera's wife, Lillemor, had given her an ultimatum: retire or I divorce you. Vera had chosen her job and had been living by herself in a flat in Domsjö ever since. Clearly it had affected her mood. The colourful swear words and the routine scoldings that had been a part of her leadership style before had been replaced with a more understanding approach. Which was not to say that Vera Nordlund was a dependably charitable person. Quite the contrary.

'If the parents haven't heard anything from Madeleine, I'll file a report.'

'Who did we get as the prosecutor for Ellie's case?' Per asked, practically cringing in anticipation of the answer. Although he was new to their investigative group, he had already acclimated enough that he understood that there were some people who would help their work and others who would hinder it.

'Anna Sondell.'

Per looked pleased. Anna was new but very experienced. She had worked as a police officer in her youth and then gone back to school to study the law. She was smart, familiar with their work methods, and most of all, she was always on their side. She would rather make one decision too many to use coercive measures than one too few, which was unusual in the Swedish Prosecution Authority.

'Good. Can we request call logs and cell tower dumps right away?'

'I'll call her right after we finish here,' Vera said, jotting a reminder in her notebook. 'We'll go through the preliminary investigation with Ann tomorrow afternoon. She's already warmed up, but I thought that would be a good opportunity to brief Marie at the same time.'

Vera's voice had assumed a strident tone. Investigations of serious crimes in Örnsköldsvik and the surrounding area were always led by someone from Sundsvall. In most cases, it was Marie Fransson. Chief Inspector Vera Nordlund did not appreciate being taken off an investigation, although she was fully aware of the hierarchy. Marie Fransson was not one of Vera's favourite people. No human beings were actually Vera's favourite people, but Marie less so than most. The 155-centimetre-short preliminary investigation chief wasn't only deeply religious but was also gentler than Jesus and had a burning passion for geraniums. At each visit, new plants and cuttings were deposited at the police station, to Vera's and several other colleagues' chagrin. One year, Marie had tried to use the police station garage to over-winter the few flowers that had survived their neglect, but Vera had put a stop to that.

'I've started looking into SveAnd AB,' Karim told Vera. 'I'll stop by Economic Crimes after this meeting and ask around some more.'

'Good,' Vera said. Sofia studied the whiteboard again. The company had stood out even at first glance. Without really knowing why, it left a bad taste in her mouth. The newspapers had devoted a lot of space to the construction project on Dekarsön Island and how it would disrupt the environment in general and bird habitat in particular. The motive could be revenge, blackmail or maybe someone wanted to scare Anders into dropping that whole construction project.

Vera looked around the room.

'Per, will you make sure that one of the crime scene investigators attends the morning meeting tomorrow if they've finished going through the house?'

Per murmured in response and Vera continued.

'Kaj and Sofia, I'd also like you two to take a closer look at Anders Svensson, the man. Find out what his personal finances look like, if he's involved in any family feuds or has any sort of addiction to gambling, sex or drugs. The same with his wife.'

She put her glasses back on.

'How is the search for Ellie going?'

Kicki opened up a map that showed Sunnansjö and Kornsjö Lake.

'There aren't very many homes along these roads here. Immediately around the Svenssons' house, there are only four other families and they all live there year-round. Three of them took part in the search for the girl. The fourth is a lady in her eighties, who didn't take part for natural reasons. We've been inside all their houses with the homeowners' permission and we've interviewed witnesses and knocked on doors. There's one memo per address in the investigation materials. In addition to those houses, there are a few old barns and some outbuildings that no one uses. They've all be checked.'

'What about the lake?' Per asked.

'It's frozen over, so there's really no way she could have gone down into it. We've searched the entire surrounding area.'

Kicki looked glumly at Vera.

'We have several people who have offered to lend us snow scooters and it's no problem to expand the search. Obviously we'll keep going as long as you want, but the chances of Ellie having survived outdoors at this point are, as we've said, minimal.'

Vera took off her glasses, set them on the table, and rubbed her face.

'It's more likely,' Kicki continued, 'that someone broke into the house and kidnapped the girl during the night without the parents noticing.'

Vera's gaze moved out the window to the snow-covered pink Elim Church building across the street.

'Yes, but how the hell is that possible? The child must have woken up? And how is it that the parents didn't hear anything?'

None of them had an answer.

39

It was only half past three in the afternoon, but the sun was already setting over the bare, rocky islets across the water from Sofia's house. Philip had gone back to bed. Fredrik walked restlessly around the house. He thought about what Philip had said about Madeleine, his girlfriend. How could he have kept her a secret? It had completely escaped Fredrik's notice that Philip even wanted to meet someone. Sure, they had talked about girls when they were younger, but over the years that had faded and for the last two decades neither he nor Philip had had any steady girlfriend. There were periods when Fredrik had dated women, when he was feeling better, but none of the relationships had lasted more than a few months. Either they got tired of him not wanting to take the relationship to the next level or he got tired of... well, what did he get tired of, actually? That they weren't Sofia?

He knew that Philip hung out in various online forums where he talked to women, but he couldn't say if that had ever led to Philip getting together with anyone before. Could you even have a relationship with someone you hadn't met in real life? But now he was in a relationship with Madeleine. He assumed they had met online, but Philip hadn't wanted to tell him about it. Fredrik wondered if Inga and Hans knew about it and realised at the same time that he needed to get in touch with them and tell them that he was with Philip, and everything was okay.

Fredrik pulled his phone out of his jeans pocket and opened the messaging app. Ida had sent two texts. Both with worried questions about how he was feeling and how Philip was doing. He replied briefly that things were fine, but that they would be staying a couple more days and he wondered if it was okay if they borrowed her car for a little while longer. She replied almost immediately.

> That's no problem. I can't wait to see you.

He looked out at the ice and the setting sun.

It's always sunny on Ulvön Island, Sofia had once said. He remembered when he had mowed the lawn here last summer with the big, unwieldy lawn mower, when they had made love upstairs with the balcony door open to the sea. He had thought that someday this could become his and Sofia's home. That all felt far away now. The area around his heart stung when he thought about the lives that had been lost. Not just his and Sofia's, but also his mother's, father's and Niklas's.

40

At twenty to five, Eva, the station's administrative assistant, called to announce that Anders Svensson was in the lobby. Sofia reluctantly let Kaj go down and get him so she didn't have to deal with the stairs. In the meantime, she filled three disposable cups with coffee from the machine and set out a few pyramid-shaped tetrapaks of milk in the library.

When Anders stepped into the room, he was hollow-eyed and pale. You could read the worry from his face, just like the lack of sleep.

'We could have come to you,' Sofia said but appreciated not having to make that trip.

'I had to get away from the house. I... Amanda...' Nothing became of his sentence.

Kaj indicated where he should sit.

Anders sat down without taking off his gloves or hat.

'Have you heard anything?'

Sofia shook her head.

'Unfortunately not. We're looking into all the possibilities right now. We've requested cell tower dumps to see who was in the area around your house when Ellie disappeared. Missing People and the Home Guard are continuing their search efforts, but...'

'But if Ellie disappeared of her own accord, the chances of her surviving outside in the cold are slim,' Kaj finished for her.

Anders nodded, his eyes on his lap, clearly unwilling to accept that thought.

'Would you like a cup of coffee?'

Kaj held out the cup without waiting for an answer. Anders pulled off his gloves and took it.

'I have to ask you, Anders, do you or your wife take any drugs?'

'How so?'

'We're a little puzzled about how a potential abduction could have occurred. How could someone have gotten into the house without your hearing it?' Kaj leaned back in his chair with his own coffee mug in his hand.

Anders shook his head.

'No, no drugs. Amanda takes sleeping pills, but they were prescribed by a doctor.'

'How about alcohol then?'

'I drink a fair amount.'

'And you had been drinking Saturday night?'

He nodded.

'Amanda, had she taken sleeping pills?'

'She does that every night.'

That could explain why neither Amanda nor Anders noticed someone entering the house in the night, Sofia thought. She looked at Kaj. Reined herself in so as not to add to the poor man's worries by telling him that they feared another of his family members might be missing.

'How much contact do you have with Madeleine, your other daughter?' she asked.

'I suppose we're in touch, but it's not like it was before the divorce. Why do you ask?'

Kaj cleared his throat.

'We've received information that she was at the house in Sunnansjö a few days ago. Is that true?'

Anders looked surprised.

'No, I don't think so. I talked to her on the phone last week and told her I would be coming up. I asked if she wanted to come down from Umeå, but she said she was going to be studying. It was the middle of exams.'

Kaj set his coffee mug down.

'Had you and your family been planning to come up here that weekend for a long time?'

'No,' Anders shook his head, 'just me. It was a last-minute decision for Amanda and Ellie to join me.'

'Did Madeleine know about that?'

'No. Or, actually, she did. I texted her and said I was going to try to get Ellie and Amanda to come up with me and asked if she was interested in studying for her exams in Sunnansjö so we could all see each other. But I didn't get any response. She's not so fond of my new family,' he added and peered resignedly down into his coffee cup.

'When was that?'

'Last Thursday night. I had worked late and took a taxi home. It was probably around three in the morning.'

Who works until three in the morning? Sofia thought. Although maybe that was normal in the construction industry, what did she know?

'Did you see any of Madeleine's things in the house when you got here? Clothing, luggage, her cell phone? Was her jacket hanging in the closet?'

'No. But I don't understand... what does it have to do with Ellie if Madde was in the house?'

Kaj ignored the question.

'We've been trying to reach your ex-wife, Jeanette, but can't get a hold of her. Do you know where she is?'

'In Thailand,' Anders replied. 'She's coming home today. Why do you want to reach her?'

Sofia leaned forward as far as her belly would permit and put her hand on Anders's arm.

'I'm sorry, but we're worried that something might have happened to Madeleine.'

Anders pulled his arm back and looked from Sofia to Kaj.

'Do you know if anyone has had any contact with her since Thursday?'

He shook his head.

'Madde's in Umeå,' he said, sounding stressed. 'Of course she is. I was going to call her and tell her what happened to Ellie and everything, but it slipped my mind with all the chaos.' He looked down at his lap and then up at Sofia again.

'I'm afraid she's not in Umeå, not according to her friends.' Sofia tried again to put her hand on his arm.

Without saying anything, he leaned back and reached for his cell phone, which was in the pocket of his jeans. It was a reflex Sofia recognised from many people she had met in her role as a police officer. In crisis situations, the phone served as an electronic lifeline.

Anders entered his passcode and dialled Madeleine's number. He looked at them with the phone to his ear. The call went straight to voicemail with the sound leaking out into the room of a high voice asking him to leave a message after the beep.

'It's Dad. I'm at the police station. Ellie is…' His voice broke and he took a deep breath, tilted his head back and looked up at the ceiling before continuing. 'Ellie is missing. I'm worried about you. Call me as soon as you get this.'

'She's not answering,' Anders said unnecessarily after he hung up and set his phone on the table. His gaze dated back and forth between Sofia and Kaj.

Kaj cleared his throat.

'Are you aware that Madeleine has a boyfriend?'

'No, she's never mentioned anything about that.'

'Well, she does,' Kaj said. 'She was also in the house.'

Sofia could not bring herself to look into Anders's lost eyes.

'What the hell is going on?'

The words came out as a blend of part whisper and part scream.

41

The last rays of sunlight make the hard crust of snow out in the field sparkle like crystals. The cold bites the cheeks.

I'm sitting in one of the chairs on the deck behind the house. I need a break from the constant noise. I can hardly think straight, let alone sleep at night.

The deck looks really rundown. Ice and snow have overtaken all the outdoor furniture and sprouts are sticking out of the cracks in the terra cotta pots of snow-covered geraniums. It's been many years since anyone has looked after this place. It's better inside the house. With a little paint and new wallpaper, it could be almost nice.

It's cold sitting in the chair without a cushion. My pants let the wetness from the seat seep through.

I get up and go in the patio door, closing my eyes when I hear the sound that gains strength as I move through the house. I stop outside the basement door.

Why won't she stop screaming?

42

On his way back from the police station in Örnsköldsvik, Anders had called everyone he could think of who might know where Madde was. He didn't really know who she was hanging out with these days, and most of the people he talked to hadn't been in touch with her for several years. He got ahold of Jeanette less than a half hour after she stepped off her plane from Thailand. She had taken the news in stride at first. 'You know how she is, Anders. She just wants to be left alone for a few days.' But when he explained about Ellie and what had happened, she had grown alarmed. They had considered all the options, trying to convince each other that there must be some natural explanation. Madde had disappeared before, not for long, but for a few days when she needed a little time away from the surrounding world. Usually she had just turned off her phone and buried herself in a Netflix series, but this was different. Ander could sense it.

When he got to Sunnansjö, Amanda was finally asleep. Her breathing was shallow and her eyelashes danced against her cheeks with worry, but she was asleep. It was only seven o'clock in the evening, but they had both been awake for far too long. Neither of them had wanted to go upstairs to bed yesterday, so they had brought the blankets and pillows downstairs and lain down in opposite corners of the sofa staring into the guest cabin's fireplace. The main house was still being investigated by two crime scene investigators. Anders could see their white outfits moving past the windows now and then, illuminated by big construction lamps. It felt macabre and unreal at the same time. He had asked what they were looking for, but they wouldn't answer. He was smart enough to understand that they were looking for traces of anyone who could have taken his daughters – fingerprints, DNA, maybe blood. He shuddered.

Amanda had refused to speak to him for the whole day. They were both helpless in the face of the situation, but completely unable to seek comfort in each other. She accused him of leaving the front door unlocked. He accused himself of the same thing.

His body was weary from all the worry. He hadn't eaten anything since yesterday morning. As soon as he closed his eyes, he saw Ellie. In her pyjamas with frightened eyes, trapped, locked up. His thoughts flew back and forth through his head. One second he felt hope, the next, profound grief. But he did nothing, just kept staring into the fire and waiting for someone to call and say they had found her alive. Unharmed. What had happened to Madde was beyond his comprehension. Were the disappearances connected? Was he the cause of both?

Anders rubbed his face. The last two days had been one long nightmare. An army of local village residents had turned out to help search for Ellie, but to no avail. Long after darkness fell yesterday, he had seen the beams of light from their flashlights moving across the big meadow down towards the lake.

He had listened to what the police said, but hadn't been able to take it all in. Missing People, canine units on loan, Home Guard, hypothermia, drones, thermal imaging, helicopters. Now they were talking about an expanded search radius as well.

He had remained at the police station for a long time with Kaj Marklund and the pregnant officer whose name he couldn't remember. They had asked him the same questions over and over again. Was there anyone who wanted to harm them? Did they have any enemies? Who would have a reason to kidnap your daughters? They had asked about his company, his current construction projects, and his finances. He had answered as best he could, weighing every word on a gold-weighing scale. Nothing would be improved by the company's secrets coming out. If a potential kidnapper were to send a ransom demand, he needed to be able to quickly access whatever company assets remained. That wouldn't work if the authorities froze the entire business. He would empty every account he had, sell everything of value. If he could only get his daughters back.

He got up and walked through the guest cabin, trying to suppress the sobs that threatened to explode out of him. He wanted to scream, smash things. Someone had taken his children away from him. His cute little Ellie with her chubby cheeks and curly hair. Ellie, who had barely gotten to experience anything of life. And his beautiful, intelligent firstborn, who always made him so proud. How would they ever get over this and be able to live a normal life? If they came back at all.

Now it came. The tears poured out of him. His sobs were so intense that he couldn't breathe. He slid down onto the kitchen floor and cried until there were no tears left.

43

Sitting down had never felt so wonderful. Sofia leaned back on the red Ikea sofa and closed her eyes. It was too late to go back out to Ulvön, so she would have to stay in the flat in Örnsköldsvik tonight.

She had her shoes and jacket on. Her boots had left puddles of melted snow all the way from the front door into the living room. She made a few fumbling attempts to take off the big, lined Sorel boots, but gave up with one hanging halfway off her foot. Instead, she lifted her legs up one by one onto the coffee table. The colourful mosaic that Claire had covered the tabletop with felt cold through her jeans. It was like a dream to her cramping calves. She was so tired she could have fallen asleep on the spot.

But she would never admit that to Kaj. Or Vera.

Sofia had just dozed off when she heard the front door of the building bang shut down on the ground floor. She slid her legs down onto the floor and grabbed the sofa's armrest. With strength she didn't actually have, she got back onto her feet. She grabbed a blanket that was lying over the armchair in the corner, tossed it on the floor and used her boot to drag it along and wipe up the wetness from the melted snow. She heard footsteps approaching in the stairwell. She shoved the blanket into the closet, managed with some effort to get her boots off, and then tossed her jacket onto the coat rack. When Kaj poked his head in the door, she was standing at the sink hand-washing a clean cup she had grabbed from the dish drainer.

'You're doing the dishes? Sit down and rest instead. I brought Thai food.' Kaj held up a square cardboard box with a grin.

'Thanks, but I'm not hungry.'

Kaj remained undaunted.

'Of course you'll eat.'

Fifteen minutes later, Sofia was sitting at the kitchen table. It was already after eight thirty. Her body was screaming for energy.

The search had been called off several hours ago. Nothing could be seen in the pitch blackness. The odds of Ellie Svensson being found alive out there were vanishingly small. Their best chance right now was that someone had kidnapped her and would make a ransom demand, which would mean she was indoors somewhere warm, however horrible the thought was.

The question of where Madeleine, the older sister, remained. No one has seen her since Thursday afternoon, and after having spoken with Jeanette and Anders, Sofia had now reported her missing. Anders hadn't known anything about Madeleine planning to be at the house when he came up, let alone hoping to introduce her boyfriend. On the other hand, they had been in touch with a classmate who knew about both the boyfriend and the trip to Sunnansjö. According to her, the relationship was good. As far as she knew, they had never argued before, and Philip absolutely had not been violent towards Madeleine. Jeanette Svensson seemed even more out of the loop than Anders. She had just come home after three weeks in Thailand with her new boyfriend and hadn't had any contact with her daughter during her trip. She had explained that Madeleine wasn't all that good at staying in touch and that she had occasionally disappeared in the past for a few days at a time, but in light of what had happened to Ellie, she was naturally extremely concerned.

Sofia didn't really know what to think at the moment. Kaj seemed completely convinced that Philip had something to do with the disappearance. For her part, she had trouble believing that Philip was the kind of person who would be prone to violence. But personal opinions had no place in a police investigation. She knew that very well, and yet it seemed impossible to completely separate out her own thoughts and feelings from this particular case.

Kaj set utensils down next to her. He had lit candles and dished the take-out food up onto plates. He poured cola out of a can that had come with the food and got up to grab a beer out of the fridge for himself. She ignored the utensils and reached for the chopsticks.

'So what do you think about the investigation?'

He took a bite of pad Thai and looked at her. His lightblue eyes twinkled. Sofia knew that Kaj loved this, working and living together. This was how it had been when they were a couple in Stockholm. The conversations with Kaj, his insights and his experience, had made her into a better police officer. She knew that. It had given her an advantage but also sowed discontent among some of her colleagues. She wondered what it would be like when they were no longer colleagues but the mother and father of a child. And what would happen when he retired? His whole identity was wrapped up in his being a police officer. Who would he be then? A father? A husband?

They had not discussed at all what their living situation would look like after the baby was born. She had no plans to move to Stockholm and she doubted that Mette would agree to move up to Örnsköldsvik with Kaj. Sofia had assumed he would come up some weekends now and then to see the baby, but all his talk of retirement had made her uneasy. Was he expecting to play a larger role in the baby's life than that?

'What do you think happened to the little girl?' Kaj attempted to get the conversation going again.

'She didn't just get up, walk out, and disappear. That much is clear.'

Kaj drank a swig of his beer and looked at her over the top of the glass.

'If the parents aren't behind it, then something else must have happened. Maybe she snuck out and a wild animal got her? A lynx? A bear? A lynx that was big enough could probably carry away a four-year-old without any problem.'

Kaj stroked his grey hair back and drank more beer. In his youth, he had been a flaxen blond, and the transition from blond to fully grey had been almost imperceptible. His skin was still fair and smooth, and if you didn't know how old he was you might think he was at least ten years younger. He was kind, considerate, and one hundred percent prepared to be a father. And yet he annoyed her. A lynx? What the hell kind of theory was that?

'So then what about Madeleine? Did a wild animal get her, too?'

Kaj smiled and shovelled more food onto his fork. Obviously pleased that she was participating in the deliberations, even if he surely hadn't missed her sarcastic tone. The more tired she was, the harder it was for her to hide.

'No, for that we're going to need to have another chat with your friend Philip.'

She opened her mouth to say that Philip wasn't her friend but decided against it. That wouldn't get them anywhere. She realised they were going to need to question Philip again.

She went back to poking at her chicken and rice noodles with her chopsticks. Her stomach was rumbling with hunger, and yet she found it hard to eat anything. Finally, she gave up and set her chopsticks on the plate. All her body wanted was sleep.

Tuesday, 25 February

44

When Sofia woke up, Kaj was already up. Outside, the sky was grey and heavy with snow, but no flakes had started falling yet. It was almost 8:30 and the morning meeting would start at nine. Luckily the flat was so close that she could see the police station from the kitchen window. It took exactly three minutes to walk from the front door of her building to the police station entrance if you got green lights the whole way. Although in her current condition it took three times as long.

Kaj had made a breakfast sandwich and set a silver mug with a lid out on the counter for her to take her coffee in. She ignored the sandwich but filled the mug to the brim and screwed the lid on. She didn't have the energy to shower, but quickly ran a brush through her long, blonde hair a couple of times, brushed her teeth and was standing by the front door ready to go before Kaj.

'Wow, you're in a hurry to get to work.' He smiled and leaned down to her belly.

'And what about you, my little apple core, are you...'

Sofia felt the anger bubbling up inside her. She pulled her jacket closed right in front of Kaj's nose.

'We don't have time for that,' she snapped and clomped with all the dignity she could muster down the three flights of stairs to the front door.

'Have you heard anything?' Per looked worried as he stirred sugar into his cup with the MoDo ice hockey team logo on it.

They had all gathered in the library and Vera had rolled the whiteboard in from her office as usual. It didn't really serve any actual purpose anymore. Everything was digital and the investigators could follow everything from their laptops. Still, the whiteboard was a simple depiction of their thinking. At the beginning of the investigation it was empty, but little by little it filled up with pictures, names, and locations, which were then erased and replaced with others until the day it all became clear. Sofia had happened upon Vera many times, sitting in her chair in front of the whiteboard and just looking at it, as if to discover whatever it was that the others had missed. And often she succeeded.

Vera shook her head.

'I have nothing new to report since last night. I talked to Kicki ten minutes ago. No bodies have been found.' She paused and removed her eyeglasses, setting them on the table. 'At this point, we can assume that neither Ellie nor Madeleine Svensson disappeared voluntarily. It's not possible for a small child to travel father on her own in a snowstorm than the area that has already been searched. Naturally Madeleine could have made it farther, but no trace of either of them has been found and it doesn't seem very likely that they both independently went out into the snow and froze to death.'

Per finally stopped stirring his coffee, set his spoon right on the table, and took a big gulp.

'So we stop searching?'

'We'll see what the prosecutor says this afternoon.'

'What a nightmare for the parents,' Karim said, rubbing his beard.

Everyone nodded except for Kaj. Sofia realised that he was having a hard time letting go of idea that a close relative was the perpetrator.

'Have you received the cell tower dumps?' Vera asked.

'No, but when they come, I need to prioritise them,' Per replied. 'And the press release has gone out. Hopefully some tips will come in during the day.'

'I've requested surveillance video from both of the gas stations in Bjästa and the gas station at Docksta Baren,' Karim said. 'We've also requested footage from the two gas stations in downtown Örnsköldsvik and the one by the northern highway exit. I'm also waiting on one from Husum. If either of the daughters was abducted by car, the perpetrator may have been caught on the footage from one of them. We're also checking store security cameras and traffic cameras, but coverage from those isn't great out in the countryside.'

'I've been in touch with Örntaxi, Örnsköldsvik Airport, the local bus service, and the travel desk at the certain train station,' Per said. 'Everyone has been instructed to contact us if they see anything unusual.'

Vera got up and walked over to the whiteboard. She turned around and looked at the group.

'Where's Johan?'

Sofia hadn't met the new crime scene investigator, but she had heard through the grapevine that he had made a few of her younger coworkers' hearts beat a little faster.

'They're not done yet,' Per said. 'It's a large house. He'll come to the afternoon meeting and go through any findings.'

'I've looked into SveAnd's finances,' Karim said, holding up a stack of paper. 'Apparently things are not going anywhere near as well for the company as Anders Svensson would like us to believe.' Everyone looked up and took one of the printouts he passed around. 'He's got two different government agencies after him, the tax authorities and the Kronofogden, who as you know are responsible for debt collections.'

Vera quickly skimmed through her copy.

'That's not very cheerful reading. It looks like SveAnd AB is nearly bankrupt.'

'This could be about blackmail,' Karim said. 'Maybe someone who hasn't been paid decided to play hardball to get their money?'

Vera nodded and jotted down what Karim had said under 'Motive' on the whiteboard. She took a step back and looked at the jumble of names and theories.

'Or someone who wants revenge.'

45

She screams again. I put my hands over my ears and try to focus on the TV. Soon, I won't be able to listen to her anymore.

The first days, she negotiated. Begged, pleaded. She wanted food and water. She wanted to go to the bathroom. She wanted me to release her. She wanted me to turn on the light.

If she would just stop screaming, I would try. Put a pitcher of water and some sandwiches in there. The light is broken, but I could give her a flashlight. But she is so angry and loud that I don't dare go down there. What if she attacks me again, hurts me? Then the whole plan could be ruined. And what about the little girl?

I sat outside the door for a while and listened to her earlier today. When she stops screaming, she cries.

I almost feel sorry for her.

46

Philip sat in the living room watching the TV. All morning he had wandered back and forth between the deck, where he smoked a couple of cigarettes, and the sofa. The show was about moose and how they migrate across the Ångerman River. No talking, no facts, just moose. Fredrik sat next to him and spent more time looking at Philip than at the actual show.

'Have you heard anything?'

Philip didn't respond, just kept staring at the screen. Fredrik poked him in the side.

'Have you heard anything about Madeleine?'

The girl's name got a reaction out of Philip. He reached for his cell phone and looked at its screen but then shook his head and went back to the moose.

Fredrik was restless. Wind gusts blew across the ice and cracks were beginning to open up in the grey blanket of clouds, letting some blue sky and rays of sunlight through. Every now and then a few thin, weightless snowflakes fell, which immediately blew away before they landed on the ground.

They were trapped on an island, not knowing when they would be able to leave. He so terribly regretted having brought Philip here. Why in the world had he thought that was a good idea?

Sofia and Kaj hadn't come back last night, and she hadn't answered any of his text messages either. He was happy to be rid of Kaj, but he wished Sofia were here. Something told him this was the last time they would ever be under the same roof. Then the baby would come and she and Kaj would live happily ever after with their newborn infant. The backs of his hands started to itch, and his thoughts went to the grocery bag on his kitchen table back home in his flat. In his mind's eye, he could hear the sound it made when you opened the box of anti-anxiety pills, could picture himself coaxing the patient information leaflet out, turning the box over and letting the foil backed plastic blister pack of tablets drop into his hand. Oval, half centimetre large gateways to a world where nothing hurt anymore, a refuge that had long been his only survival strategy.

He got up off the sofa again. No, he did not want to go back there to an existence where the pursuit of mental numbness was the only thing holding him upright. An existence of constant itching, anxiety, insomnia and emotional shutdown. It wasn't worth it. He had decided to face the rest of his life clean. If it was going to hurt, let it hurt.

Fredrik went into the kitchen to put some coffee on but got distracted when he remembered that the percolator coffee, which he loved so much, seemed impossible for him to get right. He poured himself a glass of water and asked Philip if he wanted anything, but didn't get any response. He sat down at the kitchen table with his glass of water and picked up his phone. The news about Anders Svensson's missing daughters was all over the media and their pictures had been shared so many times on Facebook that they were showing up in his feed, too. Fredrik looked at the cute little girl with the big brown eyes and curly hair. How could anyone kidnap a child? It had to be a really sick or extremely desperate person to do such a thing.

He was just about to put his phone away when Ida's number appeared on the screen. At first he thought about not taking the call, but he resisted that impulse and answered.

'How's it going?' Ida's voice sounded strained. The warmth he expected to hear in her voice wasn't there at all.

'The police want us to stay until they've figured out if Philip's girlfriend is also missing or if it just has to do with their argument. The whole thing is a big mess.'

'So they haven't found her or the little girl yet?'

'No.'

'Ugh, those poor parents.'

Fredrik combed the fringe on the blue and white checked tablecloth and tried to think of something to say, but he was empty inside. After his argument with Sofia, he had felt only love for Ida. He had missed her. But no matter how hard he tried, he couldn't get her voice to elicit that emotion in him now.

'I miss you,' she said hesitantly.

For some reason, that irritated him. Did she have to be so clingy? Was he going to need to put up with this his whole life? Someone who constantly needed him and checked up on him. He understood how unreasonable his thoughts were, but that didn't help. He pictured Sofia, Kaj, and the baby. And himself, returning to an empty flat and a woman he was trying to force himself to fall in love with.

'Do you need your car?' he asked, instead of commenting on what she had said.

'No.' Her answer came out harshly, but she softened again immediately. 'I know I'm being childish right now, but…'

Silence.

'But what?'

'Are you staying there because of Sofia?'

He looked up from the tablecloth.

'What do you mean?' he replied. It came out sounding ruder than necessary. Philip, who had just come in from yet another trip to the deck, shot him a look through the serving window. Fredrik shook his head to assure him that everything was OK.

'I mean, you were together and… I was just thinking…'

'Are you serious?'

Fredrik could hear that he was overreacting, but he couldn't stop himself. All his disappointment at the situation exploded out of him.

'A four-year-old is missing, my best friend's girlfriend is gone, and his mental health is in a very delicate place, and you think I'm choosing to stay here to put the moves on my ex?'

'No, I just…'

'And even if I were…' *Stop right now, Fredrik.* 'What does that have to do with you? Are you trying to monitor me? Do you want to keep me like some kind of pet to feed and take care of? Are you really that fucking pathetic?'

Ida started crying on the other end of the line, but he couldn't stop. She had picked at a wound and now the blood was gushing out.

'You'll get your car back, don't worry. And then this here, whatever it is, will be over.'

'Please, Fredrik,' Ida sniffled. 'I love you.'

He felt something inside him clench like a fist, white-knuckled.

'That's too bad, because I don't love you.'

Then he hung up.

47

At exactly one o'clock they gathered in the library. Marie Fransson, who was in charge of the criminal investigation, sat with Vera at the far end of the table. The whiteboard was to their right. As was her usual habit, Marie sat cross-legged. Next to Vera's big, sturdy body, she looked like a child. She waved to Sofia and then gave her pregnant belly a thumbs-up. Marie didn't have a mean bone in her body. Her congratulations about the baby were as genuine as they could be, and Sofia accepted them gratefully.

Prosecutor Anna Sondell sat in the chair on the long side of the table closest to Vera. The two women were about the same age, but Anna was significantly more concerned about her appearance and today she was wearing a matching grey jacket and skirt set with a light-grey blouse underneath and red lipstick. Her blonde hair was cut in a modern but practical short style. She nodded to Sofia as well, but didn't comment on her belly, which she had already seen several times that fall. Without offering her congratulations then, either.

The last to enter the room was the new crime scene investigator, who had been out at the Svensson family's house conducting the forensic investigation. He was younger than most of the group, thirty at most. His blond hair was long, and he had it up in a bun at the back of his neck, and he was unnaturally tan considering that it was the middle of winter. He wore a thick bracelet of what looked like seashells around one wrist.

Karim lit up when he walked in.

'Johan! I've hardly spoken to you since you got back. How was Bali?'

Johan Nyström raised his hand to everyone around the table and Sofia nodded in return. The gossip was true. He was an attractive man. His intense blue eyes met hers and he leaned forward over the table.

'We haven't met.'

He squeezed her hand. His was warm and dry, and even though her fingers felt like stubby, swollen, little sausages, they seemed to disappear in his large fist. Her eyes were drawn to his muscular forearms. Kaj was just about to reach out his hand as well when Johan leaned back in his chair.

'Yeah, Bali was nice, but we had to come home earlier than planned. Half of Asia is shutting down because of that virus in China.'

'Yeah,' Karim nodded, concerned. 'Makes you wonder when it will get here. I have family coming from Tehran in a week. We haven't seen each other for two years and they're so excited to get to see snow.'

'We'll probably be okay,' Johan said, clasping his hands together behind his head. 'It was the same with the swine flu and the bird flu and all those other ones. It's not like this one is going to be any worse than any of them.'

Vera cleared her throat, leaned in over the table, and pushed aside one of the evening papers, whose headlines screamed out the news about the missing four-year-old girl and her older sister.

'Should we talk about Bali or the investigation?'

Johan held his hands up apologetically.

'Who'd like to start?'

Per raised his hand.

'I've been promised that I'll receive the information from the cell tower dumps this afternoon. Thank you, Anna, for your quick action there.'

The prosecutor gave Per a noncommittal smile.

'That will give us a picture of who was in the area around the house at the times when Ellie and Madeleine Svensson disappeared,' Vera clarified. 'And show what incoming and outgoing calls were made from Philip Lindén's, Madeleine's, Anders's, and Amanda's phones.'

Anna Sondell nodded wearily. She was well aware of what the procedure looked like.

'Do you suspect that the parents were involved in Ellie's disappearance?'

'It's much more common than people think for the perpetrator to be someone closely related,' Kaj replied. 'I have investigated many cases where a parent killed their child and then pretended there had been an accident or that the child had gone missing. But if I've learned anything in all my years in the police, it's that children don't just disappear.'

They quietly mulled over what he had said, but the prosecutor did not look especially impressed.

'Thank you, I'm familiar with the statistics, too. However, I think that sounds like a far-fetched theory. Sure, an accident could have happened that the parents are trying to conceal, but how does that fit in with the older daughter's disappearance?'

'We don't know if it does,' Kaj said, looking at her, 'but we need to at least consider the possibility.'

Marie pulled one leg out of her cross-legged position and leaned forward over the table.

'Do they have an alibi?'

'For Thursday when Madeleine disappeared, yes,' Sofia said.

'But not for Saturday night and early Sunday morning?'

'Only each other's testimonies.'

Marie nodded and then straightened out her other leg as well.

'Of course that doesn't necessarily mean that there's not some sort of connection.' Vera stood up and walked over to the whiteboard. Unwilling to break her routines even though Anna was sitting in the room expecting a quick, general run-through.

The prosecutor did not seem to mind, though. Maybe as a former investigator she appreciated a little honest policework as a change from the courtroom. She turned her chair to face the whiteboard and clasped her hands in her lap.

'If we start with the little girl. Do you have a working theory about how she might have disappeared?'

'We talked to Anders Svensson yesterday.' Sofia tried changing her position in the chair so the baby would stop pressing against her lungs. 'He told us that his wife takes sleeping pills every night. He already admitted earlier that he had been drinking before he went to bed the night Ellie disappeared. That could be why they didn't notice if someone entered the house.'

'Or maybe that's the reason why they deliberately or accidentally killed their own daughter,' Kaj interjected.

'They don't really strike me as an abusive family. Not the classic kind anyway,' Karim said. Sofia agreed. They were aware that abuse could occur in all types of families in all strata of society, but in this particular case it seemed far-fetched that the parents would have been so intoxicated that they caused their daughter's death.

'So in other words, it doesn't seem likely that the family was involved in Ellie's disappearance,' Anna summarised.

Kaj opened his mouth to reiterate one more time what the statistics said, but the prosecutor continued without paying any attention to him. 'And the older daughter?'

'Madeleine's phone is turned off and no one has had any contact with her since Thursday afternoon,' Vera said. 'However, we did receive confirmation that she was planning to go up to the vacation home and meet her boyfriend, Philip Lindén. But we don't really know any more than that, apart from what Lindén himself has said.'

'And he's the only suspect right now?'

Kaj answered in the affirmative. Sofia did not feel comfortable at all with Philip being identified as a potential kidnapper but realised that she didn't have any evidence at all to the contrary.

Anna frowned.

'I assume that you have scheduled further questioning with him? Has he been swabbed? Fingerprinted?'

'We'll take care of that tonight.' Kaj nodded to Sofia, as if it were a given that they would conduct the questioning together.

Vera wrote something on the whiteboard.

'Is he still at your place on Ulvön?' she asked.

'Yes.'

'You can come out with us, but Kaj will handle the questioning.'

'But...' Sofia began.

'No buts.' Vera turned around and narrowed her eyes at her. 'It would be highly inappropriate if you were personally involved with someone involved in a criminal investigation.'

None of the others said anything. Only Vera and Kaj knew about what had happened last summer and the official misconduct Sofia had committed by withholding information from her boss and her colleagues. It had almost cost her her job. Had it not been for Kaj's contacts combined with the fact that it didn't look very good to fire a pregnant officer, she would probably have been unemployed today.

'And the forensic investigation?' Marie looked to Johan.

'We found fingerprints on the exterior door and on the banister of the staircase to the upper floor that we can't match to anyone in the family,' Johan said. 'We also found fingerprints downstairs, including on the door to the closet where Madeleine's jacket and cell phone were reportedly found. We've also found DNA. But a lot of people had time to run around in the house before we got there. We're working as fast as we can to map out everyone who has been there. But we haven't found any evidence suggesting that the girl was taken by force. No signs of someone being dragged, blood or anything else.'

'And Madeleine?' Marie asked, scratching her chin. 'Any traces of her?'

Johan shook his head.

'None that we can connect directly to her or her disappearance. The jacket with the phone in the pocket is not in the closet anymore as you know, and we haven't found anything in the guest room she usually used the few times she had been there. The guest cabins were completely snowed in, so we know that no one was in them before Anders and Amanda move into the one.'

'You haven't found anything at all?' Vera sounded impatient.

'Nothing other than what I just mentioned. We've been focusing mostly on ingress and egress points as well as where the little girl slept and the guest room.'

Marie looked at Vera.

'And there still hasn't been any ransom demand or any sort of communication with a possible kidnapper?'

Vera shook her head.

The room was silent. Everyone was well aware that time was not on their side. Sofia tried to put out of her mind all the images of the world's young women and children who had been kidnapped, abused, and then sold on or killed.

She wondered if those images were in Anders's head, too. They surely were. It must be a punishment worse than death to know that your child was out there and suffering but not be able to do anything.

Just the thought made her feel sick.

48

She's been asleep for a long time now. She's so pretty lying there. Sucking with her mouth and sometimes whimpering in her sleep. The pale pink pyjama pants and the top have an ice cream pattern. Colourful ice cream cones with eyes and smiles. Even on that first day I discovered that she had diapers on under her pyjama pants. Maybe she's younger than I thought, but diapers are still good. I change her several times a day.

I was planning to let her keep lying on the sofa, but I couldn't stop thinking about her. That soft baby skin and the curly hair.

Ultimately, I couldn't help myself and went and got her and lay her down next to me in the bed. She's still lying there. Completely unaware of everything that's happening.

49

The wind whined outside the house and Fredrik felt uneasy. An exterior light shone down by the boathouse, but beyond that it was just black ice that couldn't be distinguished from the equally black sky. Philip was still sitting in front of the TV, but at least he had eaten a grilled sandwich that Fredrik had made him. He seemed to be feeling better. He had been outside to smoke on the deck a few more times during the evening and had answered some work emails from his phone. Fredrik had called Inga and Hans and said they were visiting a mutual acquaintance and would be home again soon. He had also called the rental car company in Sundsvall to let them know that they would be returning their rental car soon and would pick up his Volvo which was now repaired and was still at the garage. He wanted to leave but had not received any information about when the police would let them go.

He went into the kitchen and opened the fridge even though he knew it was more or less empty. Tord had come over around lunch time with a bag from the little grocery store down in Ulvöhamn. A few pierogies, two cans of pea soup, a loaf of bread, and two litres of milk. He took two pierogies out of the freezer and put them in the microwave.

Fredrik glanced at his phone. Ida still hadn't responded. He had regretted his outburst as soon as he hung up and had tried to call her to apologise, but she hadn't returned his calls or texts. Now the whole day had passed. It had never taken this long before he heard back from her. He sent yet another message. His guilty conscience was bothering him, but it was more than that. His behaviour had been terrible. What if she never forgave him? The thought was unexpectedly painful.

Philip ambled into the kitchen when he smelled the pierogies.

'Can you get out the silverware?' Fredrik asked, pointing to the drawer next to the sink.

Philip got out knives, forks, and plates, and poured two glasses of water. They were about to sit down to eat when Fredrik's phone rang.

He had time to think it was Ida but then saw that it was Sofia and strangely enough he was relieved to realise that he felt disappointed.

'How are you guys doing?'

'Good,' he answered succinctly.

Sofia cleared her throat.

'We need to talk to Philip.'

'Again? Is that really necessary?'

'We suspect kidnapping. He needs to be swabbed.'

Fredrik looked at Philip who was opening the packaging around one of the pierogies.

'Oh, my God.' He went into the living room.

'We'll be out on the last hovercraft. Kaj is going to question Philip.'

He whispered back to her, 'You can't really believe that he has anything to do with this! Philip would never hurt a person.'

'That's not for you to judge.' Sofia's voice was harsh.

Fredrik stood there holding the phone in his hand and staring out the window after Sofia had hung up. He ran his hand through his hair. How the hell could everything have gotten so complicated? They couldn't seriously believe that Philip was involved in this? What had actually happened to Ellie and Madeleine?

He collected himself for a moment and then went back into the kitchen. He was just about to stuff his phone into his jeans pocket and tell Philip that Sofia and Kaj were on their way out when it rang again.

Ida.

Fredrik had time to feel happy but quickly discovered that the voice on the other end did not belong to Ida.

'Hi, this is Jonna. I'm Ida's sister.'

He accepted the plate Philip handed him.

'Has something happened?' His stomach began to churn. He always expected bad news, almost regardless of who was calling. Maybe that was because of everything that had happened in his life. Even so, he was not prepared for what he heard.

'Ida tried to kill herself.'

Fredrik dropped the plate onto the counter.

'What are you saying?'

'They found her unconscious in your flat.'

His head was spinning, and he was forced to lean over forwards so the dizziness wouldn't take over.

'In my flat?'

'She called me and said she had taken pills. I called the ambulance.'

Fredrik straightened up, looking into his own reflection in the kitchen window. He shook his head even though she couldn't see him through the phone. It couldn't be because of what he said? No, that was completely impossible. Ida was strong. She wouldn't let a thing like that drive her to something like this.

'I don't understand…'

Jonna took a breath on the other end of the line, and he could hear the anger in her voice through her tears.

'We're at Söder Hospital. If you have any spine at all, come here.'

Then she hung up.

50

When they pulled into the driveway next to the house in Norrbysbodarna, Philip was standing out on the deck smoking. He raised his hand in a wave.

They got out of the car and made their way through the snow towards the front door. Philip put out his cigarette and vanished from the deck back in the side entrance, the door at the gable end of the house that her dad Sten had always referred to as the 'fancy entrance', to distinguish it from the front door, which was on the shady side of the house and was the one Sten had used whenever he came inside wearing dirty boots or with grass clippings between his toes. The only times Claire had truly seemed to enjoy the house on Ulvön Island was when they had guests over. The guests would always be shown in the 'fancy entrance' and then ushered through the living room to admire her collection of porcelain figurines. From there, they would be led back outside again through the deck door on the long side, where the magnificent view of the water and a table filled with wineglasses awaited them.

Sofia and Kaj rounded the corner of the house, and she noticed that the steps to the front stoop had been both swept and sanded. She had asked Tord to check on Fredrik and Philip, and as usual you could count on him.

Philip met them in the front hall when they came inside. They hung up their jackets, left their snowy shoes on the hall carpet, and proceeded into the kitchen.

'Come,' Sofia said. 'Let's sit down.'

Philip did as he was asked. There was no sign of Fredrik. Maybe he was sleeping.

Kaj sat down across the table, rummaged through his bag, and pulled out a small tape recorder, which he turned on. It felt beyond strange to conduct a formal questioning session in her own kitchen, Sofia thought.

'Questioning Philip Lindén on 25 February, 2020. Present: Detective Sofia Hjortén and Detective Superintendent Kaj Marklund.'

He turned to Philip.

'We still don't have any leads on Madeleine.'

Philip looked down at the table.

'What do you think could have happened to her?'

Philip shrugged but did not look up.

'You don't think it's strange that she said she was going to be at the house and then wasn't there when you came, but had left her phone there?'

'Yeah.' Philip looked up, but avoided making eye contact with Kaj, choosing to look into Sofia's eyes instead. She empathised with him. It was obvious that he was not comfortable with the situation.

'Do you know if anyone has threatened Madeleine or her family?'

Philip shook his head.

'When did you last see Madeleine?'

'Six weeks ago. She's a student at the University of Umeå, so we don't see each other in person very often.'

'And when was the last time you spoke to her on the phone?'

'On Wednesday.'

'What did you say to each other then?'

'We didn't say anything,' Philip replied. 'We wrote.'

'What did you write then?' Kaj asked, sounding strained.

'We had an argument when I didn't want to stay longer than we had decided to meet her father, so I backed out of the whole trip. She wrote that she was going to go to Sunnansjö anyway. Then I drove up Thursday evening to surprise her.'

'Describe what happened when you got to the house.'

It was as if the air went out of Philip and he leaned forward over his arms, which were resting on the table.

'I've already done that,' he said with his forehead on his forearms. The gesture made him look like a child.

'Describe it again.'

He lifted his head and leaned back in his chair. He looked tired.

'I went inside, and she wasn't there. I called her. Her phone was in her jacket pocket in the hall closet. I went upstairs and looked. She wasn't there either. I left and then drove off the road.'

His description was short and without details.

'And you're sure that she wasn't in the house when you got there?'

'Why are you asking the same thing over and over again?'

'Because we want to know that you're telling the truth,' Kaj replied.

'I am.'

Philip looked at Sofia and she nodded that he should answer the question.

'No, I didn't see her at any rate, and I looked in all the rooms.'

'Was there anyone else in the house?'

'Not that I could see.'

'Did you see anything strange when you were there? Dirt on the floor? Signs that the front door had been jimmied open?'

'The door was unlocked, and the key was in it on the outside.'

Kaj looked at Sofia.

'You didn't say anything about that when our colleague questioned you.'

Philip looked at Kaj for a moment before briefly noting that his colleague had not asked anything about the door. Sofia could see Kaj struggling not to lose his patience. Obviously, it was hard for Philip to describe an event without being asked direct questions.

'Did you see anything strange in the front entryway?'

'No.'

'Blood anywhere in the house?'

'No.'

'Was anything a mess or in the wrong place?'

'I don't know. I've never been there before.'

Kaj took a deep breath.

'Was any object lying in an unusual location? A sofa cushion on the floor, a painting that was crooked, any cupboards or drawers that were left open?'

Philip thought for quite a while.

'The fire extinguisher in the living room was not in its holder on the wall.'

51

Fredrik was half frozen even though he had been driving with the heat on full blast for half an hour. He stopped at Docksta Baren and hopped out to fill up the gas tank. The convenience store was closed and the hot coffee he had been looking forward to, would have to wait. He had been the only passenger on the evening's last hovercraft trip to the mainland from Ulvön Island. Ida's car had been completely covered with snow, and he hadn't found a scraper, so he had had to sweep off the windshield with his jacket sleeve. It was still wet. The car door had been frozen shut and he had had to yank on it several times before it budged. He hated winter.

Jonna had not called back, nor had she answered the phone when he tried to reach her. He had no idea how seriously injured Ida was. He was racked with worry.

In a second, she had gone from being a person he didn't know how he felt about and who stifled him, to being the most important person in his life. He pounded his hands on the steering wheel in irritation. He had been completely blinded by his jealously of Sofia's and Kaj's perfect life and expected baby. Right now he hated Sofia. He never wanted to see her again. Her or her gigantic belly. Or super cop Kaj Marklund.

He wished Philip had come with him. It felt like a monumental betrayal leaving him there on Ulvön, handing him over for police questioning, to wait in suspense for them to find his girlfriend.

Fredrik had tried to get Philip to come with him.

'You don't need to stay here because the police say so. Come home with me. We'll sort this out on our home turf.'

But Philip had merely shaken his head, his eyes fixed on the TV, showing neither concern nor despair. He had disappeared into himself the way he always did when things got to be too much.

'I'll stay until Madde calls.'

There wouldn't have been any point to arguing with him. Reluctantly, he had left Philip there on the sofa, promising he would be back soon to pick him up. It pained him to leave his best friend there in a strange house with strange people, but he had no choice. He knew he should tell Sofia he was leaving, but he wasn't up to having that discussion right now. He just wanted to go home.

Home to Ida.

Sofia sat in the rocking chair and listened to Kaj snoring on the sofa next to her. They had both refused to sleep on the hard double bed upstairs and were now forced to share this room for the night. Something that hadn't happened in eight months. Kaj was not thrilled that Philip would be staying in the house with them, but had been content knowing that he could see Sofia.

She needed sleep, but it was like her emotions were boiling within her, mostly angry emotions. Her guest room had turned out to contain one fewer guest when they got out to Ulvön. At sonic speed, Fredrik had taken the few belongings he had arrived with, including the cell phone charger he had borrowed from her, and gone back home. He had used her as some sort of convalescent home and then left without a word. Again. Just like last summer. As if her house had revolving doors and people could come and go as they pleased. She had tried questioning Philip, but he didn't know why Fredrik had left. Fredrik had said something about a crisis and then caught the last hovercraft to the mainland. If she and Kaj hadn't been late getting down to the dock at Köpmanholm, they would surely have run into him there. What the hell kind of a friend was he to leave Philip here with a complete stranger, leave him to go through police questioning by himself? When Fredrik knew his support was really needed. She felt sorry for Philip. He must be beside himself with worry, but he didn't seem able to express that emotion. She had tried asking him how he was feeling and if he wanted to talk about anything, but he had just remained silent and eventually asked to go to the guest room and lie down.

Sofia poked at the coffee table with her foot to get the rocking chair moving a little. As she rocked, she thought about the investigation. They had swabbed Philip and taken fingerprints which would be brought to Johan on the first hovercraft the next morning. Philip had sat there, spinning the long swab against the inside of his cheek as he gazed at the floor in front of him. But there wasn't the least indication that he was lying to them. There wasn't anything in his story that didn't seem to be true. Sofia had seen lots of people try to lie their way out of situations. Experienced criminals were, of course, harder to detect. They had developed an indifferent attitude towards the police. Ordinary people, on the other hand, rarely succeeded in getting away even with a little white lie during police questioning. They fiddled with their hair, their eyes wandered, they changed position in the chair, sweated, blushed, and delivered utterly imaginative, detail-rich stories that Sofia and her colleagues could very quickly poke holes in. Philip was not exhibiting any of those behaviours. Her gut told her that he was being sincere with them.

She genuinely hoped she was right.

Wednesday, 26 February

52

The waiting room at Söder Hospital was empty when Fredrik arrived. It was 3:30 in the morning and he had had to ring a bell to be let in. Then he had had to wait for more than two and a half hours before anyone had time to take him into the ward. He had fallen asleep several times before a nurse in blue scrubs and white clogs came to get him. He had only stopped twice on his way south to Stockholm, first to fill up with gas and then to buy coffee. He hadn't dared to eat anything for fear that food would make him drowsy. Still, the drive had taken seven hours because of the slippery road conditions. He desperately needed some more coffee now and a sandwich.

'Are you the boyfriend?'

Fredrik nodded without any hesitation.

'How is she doing?'

'Good, all things considered.'

The nurse didn't say anything else as they walked side by side down the hallway, passing several rooms with open or half-open doors. Inside, in the darkness, he could make out beds and legs covered with hospital blankets. He shuddered. This was an environment he loathed. It all came back to him. The cold, the raft, the warm blankets, the hands, the smiling faces, and the mellow accents. He had been so well taken care of afterwards, but what good was that when his whole family was at the bottom of the Baltic Sea? Being forced to stay in a hospital again after his gunshot wound had been almost unbearable.

But this wasn't about him. He needed to be strong for Ida now.

They stopped outside a closed door. The nurse knocked and a faint 'come in' could be heard from within.

Fredrik didn't know what he had expected, but the sight that greeted him broke his heart. Ida lay on her back with her knees gently bent to one side. She wore a faded hospital-issue top and had a yellow blanket over her legs. The button of her top was open and there were wires on her chest that were connected to a machine displaying red and green numbers and several wave patterns. There was a needle in one of her hands held in place with surgical tape. It was red around her mouth and her lips were chapped and bluish. Her dark brown hair was in a braid, draped over one shoulder. A woman his own age sat next to the bed, holding Ida's hand. Her facial features immediately identified her as Ida's older sister.

The nurse left the room and Fredrik stood there in the middle of the floor. Jonna sat there with Ida's hand in her own, her eyes fixed on her sister's face, not saying anything. She didn't look like she had slept at all, and her eyes were red from crying.

'Can I sit down?' Fredrik pointed to the chair on his side of the bed. She didn't respond, so he pulled the chair over and sat down next to Ida.

'Have you been here all night?'

No answer.

'How's she doing?'

Jonna made no effort to look at him but opened her mouth to say something at least.

'They took tests to check her liver and kidney function. And blood tests. They put a catheter in, too.'

Every word out of Jonna's mouth was like a whiplash on his back.

'What did she take?'

He would never forget the look when their eyes met.

'What do you think?'

The bag. That's why Ida had called Jonna from his flat. She had keys. She knew what was in the bag.

Fredrik rubbed his face with his hands. How the hell could this have happened?

'Has she been awake at all?'

'No.'

Jonna was holding back, but Fredrik could see that soon the dam would break. She shook her head at him, her lips pressed tightly together.

'This is your fault.'

Her tears overflowed and Jonna wiped her nose with the back of her free hand.

'You don't know what she's been through. How she's fought to get back. Then you came along and ruined everything.'

Fredrik didn't understand what Jonna was talking about, but it was quite clear to him now that he was the reason Ida was lying here now.

'She told me what you said.'

He nodded again. There was nothing to say. His behaviour had been vile. But if he had only known Ida was capable of something like this, he wouldn't have…

Jonna sniffled and he handed her a tissue from the plastic pack sitting on the wheeled table next to the bed. To his surprise, she accepted it. Her red-rimmed eyes looked into his own.

'I'm sorry. I know you weren't the one who… it's not your fault. I'm just so angry, so scared.'

Fredrik's shoulders relaxed and he leaned forward and put his hand on Ida's leg. So close that he almost touched Jonna. Silent tears ran down her cheeks and Fredrik gently stroked Ida's leg through the blanket.

'It's going to be okay,' he whispered, mostly to himself.

53

Sofia yawned and arched her back, but the seatbelt in the black Volvo XC90 she used as her mainland car immediately locked. She didn't know how long she would be able to keep running around like this. Back and forth between the island and the mainland. What was she trying to prove?

Everything hurt – her feet, her thighs, her shoulders, and her calves. And there were still four weeks until the baby was due. How was she even going to be able to walk upright the last week?

The sun had fought its way up and was now peeking through the greyish white clouds above them. Sofia looked out the side window as they left the Köpmanholm ferry terminal behind them on their way to attend the morning meeting at the station in Örnsköldsvik. Her reflection mixed with the passing snow-covered landscape outside. She saw the crease between her eyebrows, her mouth a thin line.

God damned fucking Fredrik Fröding.

Sofia had half-heartedly tried to get Philip to come back to the mainland with them, but no matter how many times she had asked, his response had been the same: 'I'll wait until Madde comes back.'

—

When they walked into the station, only Vera and Marie were there. Johan, who had received the information about the fire extinguisher after their questioning session with Philip, had taken his team out to Sunnansjö to conduct another crime scene investigation in the house. Per had received the phone records late yesterday and he and Karim had spent much of the night pouring over them. They would be in a little later in the day.

Sofia, Kaj and Marie went into Vera's office and Kaj pulled out the guest chair so Sofia could sit down. She started to protest but then changed her mind and sat down. Her feet already felt like clumps of concrete even though it was still only morning.

'How did it go with Philip?' Vera asked.

'He's been swabbed and fingerprinted. Johan has received all that.'

'And? What did he say?'

'Same as before,' Sofia replied. 'That Madeleine wasn't in the house when he got there.'

Vera held out her hands, palms first, as if to say *whoa*.

'But how do we know that's the truth? How do we actually know that anything Philip Lindén says is true?'

'I agree,' Kaj said.

'Why would he lie?' Sofia could hear that she sounded overly defensive.

Vera and Kaj exchanged a look over her head. Was her judgment no longer reliable?

When Kaj didn't say anything, Vera continued.

'If I've understood correctly, he's a little...' Vera scratched her eyebrow. 'Well, a little...'

Sofia interrupted, 'he is on the autism spectrum and has agoraphobia.'

Vera made a gesture as if to concur, as if those were just the words she had been searching for. Then she leaned back in her chair, which was set almost to a reclining position.

'And you believe that would not make him a likely perpetrator?'

'I don't believe anything,' Sofia said. 'I'm just saying that his diagnoses don't make him any more prone to violence than anyone else, sooner the opposite. I find him to be an extremely passive person.'

Marie looked sceptical.

'Although is that something we're able to judge? Maybe we should talk to a psychiatric expert, investigate whether the ASD and phobia in tandem might not actually lead to an increased proclivity towards violence and aggression.'

What was it with everybody? Did no one trust her anymore? Sofia rubbed her winter-chapped lips to stop herself from saying the words that were actually on her tongue.

'Sure, we can definitely do that, but the question is how are we going to get Anna Sondell to decide to order a psychiatric evaluation? We don't have a shred of evidence that suggests Philip could be involved.'

Sofia took a childish satisfaction in her colleagues' disheartened expressions. She was right, and they knew it, too.

Vera nodded.

'Sofia is right, but I want him to stay within Örnsköldsvik's municipal boundaries until we have something more to go on. Right now, he's the only lead we have in Madeleine's disappearance.'

Kaj nodded reluctantly.

'And what about Ellie then?'

Vera leaned forward in her chair so quickly that her backrest bounced back and forth.

'Kicki thinks we should call off the search soon. There's no indication that she's in the Sunnansjö area.'

Marie pulled a yoghurt out of her Kånken backpack. She opened it and licked off the lid before setting it on a napkin on the desk.

'There's not much else we can do but go back out and talk to Anders Svensson again. Confront him with Karim's information about the company's poor financial situation.'

Sofia was about to say that she could stay at the station and help Per with the call logs, but Kaj beat her to it.

'Sofia and I will do that.'

54

By the time Sofia and Kaj reached the Svensson's vacation house in Sunnansjö, it had started snowing. The first search pass of the day was done, and everyone had gathered in the courtyard out front to gear up for the next one. An older woman in a purple ski suit and matching headband was handing out sandwiches and hot coffee. Several cars were parked along the forest road below the driveway and while Sofia and Kaj walked up to the house, another one arrived. This was one of the things Sofia loved about small towns and especially rural areas. People helped each other. When something happened, they came together. She wondered if Anders and Amanda had the presence of mind right now to appreciate that. Probably not.

The police were there again with their search dogs, along with about fifty volunteers. Everyone was properly dressed in boots, heavy winter jackets, and reflective vests with the Missing Peoples logo on the back. The Home Guard's men and women wore military attire. Many had orange snow poles in their hands to probe the snow with.

They walked past the group and nodded in greeting to Kicki, who stood in the middle, talking on her cell phone.

The main house was once again cordoned off and she could see Johan and the other crime scene investigators wearing white outfits inside the blue and white police tape. Sofia and Kaj stopped outside the markings and Johan came over to them with a large camera around his neck. The techs had left black charcoal powder stains on the frames around the tall double doors in the front entry.

'Hi.' Johan nodded to them but kept his eyes down on his camera screen as he browsed through photos.

'How's it going?' Kaj stretched and peered into the house.

'We're still working on the living room.' Johan nodded towards one of the guest cabins, obviously uninterested having his work interrupted. 'They're up there.' Then he pulled his mask back up over his mouth and nose and went back to what he had been doing. Kaj held out his hand so Sofia could support herself on him as they walked up towards the red, two-storey house which was one of the property's guest cabins.

Amanda stood just inside the front door with her coat on. The ceilings were low, and the small building was reminiscent of one of those old bakehouses that were found on many of the farm properties around there, although this one was obviously new construction. Lace curtains hung in the grid windows and the walls were decorated with watercolour paintings of northern Swedish summer themes. Amanda wore an all-white ski suit with a black sash around the waist and had a pair of big, black sunglasses perched atop her chestnut hair. She looked like she was going to an après-ski event at some ski resort in the French Alps. Only her eyes, red from crying, revealed that she wasn't heading out for a joyride.

'Could we sit down?'

Amanda shook her head and continued tightening the laces on her big winter boots.

'I'm going out to search,' she said.

'Is that really a good idea?' Sofia put a hand on Amanda's arm and immediately pulled it back again. Amanda lowered her eyes to look at Sofia's belly.

'Is this your first child?'

Sofia nodded.

'Then you don't know. You don't know *anything*.'

Sofia stood there in the front hall as if turned to stone. Amanda was right. She didn't know anything about what it was like to have a child. But she did know what it was like to lose one. And that experience was enough for her to be able to at least partly comprehend Amanda's emotional state right now.

'I don't have time to talk to you right now,' Amanda huffed, taking a step towards the door. But Kaj stopped her.

'This won't take long,' he reassured her.

Amanda stopped, annoyed.

'Well, get on with it then.'

She was acting very differently from before. When they were out at the house on Sunday, she had just sat apathetically on the sofa and cried. But Sofia had met enough worried parents to know that their emotions changed quickly, from grief to anger, from resignation to hope. The idea that soon she was going to become aware of how it felt to be responsible for a life terrified her. But it was too late to change her mind now.

'Your husband's financial dealings, how much do you know about them?'

'What does that have to do with Ellie and Madde?' Amanda looked puzzled.

'Just answer the question, please.'

Amanda sighed, annoyed.

'I suppose I know what I need to know. That things are going well, that the money rolls in every month, that we're in a good place. Why?'

Kaj and Sofia exchanged glances.

'It has come to our attention that it's not going anywhere near as well as he has made it seem. SveAnd AB is on the very of bankruptcy.'

Amanda snorted and adjusted her sunglasses on the top of her head.

'Anders would have told me if there were problems with the company.'

But the doubt was clear in Amanda's eyes. And something more. Sofia couldn't quite interpret what. She reminded herself that Amanda was much younger than she appeared in her

Chanel earrings and expensive ski clothes. She was born in the nineties. Oh good Lord, Sofia was in middle school then.

'If you'll excuse me, I'm going out to look for my daughter now. You can talk to my husband about that.' This time, Amanda did not allow herself to be impeded, just pushed past Kaj and left the guest cabin.

Anders came out into the front hall. There was a fire in the fireplace in the living room behind him. He had a blanket around his shoulders. His eyes stared vacantly.

He looked from Kaj to Sofia.

'Do you have any news?'

'Come on, let's sit down,' Kaj said, putting a hand on Anders's shoulder. He obediently led the way and sat down on the armrest of the white sofa. Sofia sat down heavily and Kaj remained standing.

Sofia handed over the folder full of papers she had in her lap. It contained all the information Karim had obtained from the authorities about the company's finances. He had also sought out the site managers for the construction projects SveAnd was currently working on. Jerzy Nowak, who was in charge of the Rosenlund Tower construction site in Stockholm, had had quite a bit to say, but apparently hadn't told them everything. He had not gotten ahold of the site manager for the new houses being built on Dekarsön Island yet. Anders took the folder without looking at it.

'Your construction projects.'

Anders pulled the blanket around himself more tightly with his free hand.

'Yeah?'

'Is there anything you'd like to tell us about them?'

He reluctantly looked at the printouts.

'What should I say?'

'Well, for example, that both the Tax Agency and the Enforcement Agency are after you. That the Building Workers' Union is involved and that the workplace safety folks have received multiple complaints against SveAnd AB regarding working conditions and multiple cases involving workers without ID06 cards.'

Anders took a wheezing breath and coughed into the hand that was holding the blanket around him.

'I was going to tell you…' The rest of his sentence disappeared into mumbling. He kept staring at the floor.

When he looked up again, he was crying.

55

The guy with the list comes up to me, asks for my name and social security number. I give him a name, not my own, of course. I tell him I forgot my driver's license at home. He hesitates and scrutinises me but then decides to let me take part. I promise I'll come by and show him my ID tomorrow. He writes down something own on the list and then moves on to the next person.

Soon he calls for our attention and we gather in a tight cluster around him. Everyone looks serious, but I can't help feeling excited. It's so close now.

I've been thinking all night about how to proceed, but you can't really predict anything. So far, everything has gone smoother than I could have imagined. I'll have to rely on an opportunity coming up this time, too.

Most people came by car, others on snowmobiles. I didn't dare steal a car to get here. That would have been an unnecessary risk. Luckily, I have come across one no one will miss for several days.

'Does everyone understand where we're meeting?'

Several people nod. I nod, too, and pull the lined cap with the earflaps farther down over my face. Along with the sunglasses, it probably makes me unrecognizable. Not that it matters. Anders hasn't put in an appearance out here all day.

A woman comes walking down the driveway. The coordinator greets her, puts an arm around her shoulders and gently pushes her towards the group.

'This is Amanda. As you can imagine, this is a very difficult situation for her, but she still wants to help search.'

Amanda nods to the group in greeting, but without looking anyone in the eye.

'Will someone bring Amanda to the next gathering spot?'

This is almost too easy. I hold up my hand.

Amanda and my eyes meet. A hint of a smile.

'You can ride with me, Amanda.'

56

Anders sat staring into the fire as he put on several logs. Just as he had done for the last two days, without letting go of the thought of what could have happened to Ellie and Madde for a second. It was more than warm enough in the cabin, but feeding the fire was all he could bring himself to do. It was already dinner time, but he wasn't hungry. He hadn't had lunch or breakfast, although normally he was starving when he woke up in the mornings. I couldn't even remember when he had last eaten. Coffee was the only thing he could get down. He didn't even want whiskey.

Concern for his children overshadowed all his own needs. He thought about what it had been like to become a father for the first time. Once Madde had recovered from her heart condition, everything had been so easy and uncomplicated. He and Jeanette had been young and had had unlimited energy. They had gone on bike rides, picnics, taken the train to Göteborg and spent a fortune on rides at Liseberg Amusement Park. They hadn't been anywhere near as well off as he was today, but they had been happy, and they had appreciated their little life. They had had a strong bond, done everything together. Sure, he had seen that Madde wasn't like other children, but that hadn't mattered. She was his and he loved her. The tears came again, and he wiped his nose with the back of his hand.

What had he done to deserve this?

At least he had told the police everything now. About the threat against his family. He should have done that right away, but he hadn't wanted to process it. Hadn't wanted to think that it could be his shady business dealings that were the cause of his daughters' disappearance. He thought about that evening four weeks ago when the young Polish guy had gotten past both the gates and the security intercom at home. Suddenly he had just been standing there in the pine branches that Amanda had laid out on their lit up front porch. Dressed in reflective clothing with the SveAnd logo on it. He looked like any old worker. Anders had opened the door, caught by the contrast between the look in the man's eye and the smell of tacos and the sound of laughter from Amanda and Ellie who were having a nice Friday evening on the sofa.

The rough looking face lit up by the strands of holiday lights wrapped around the pillars on either side of the wide front steps. Anders had recognised him. He had helped renovate the house up in Sunnansjö. One of the guys Jerzy had brought over. His English was bad, hardly intelligible, but his tone was unmistakable. He remembered every word of the conversation. It echoed in his head at night.

'Jerzy says we go home?'

'Yes, maybe so.'

'My money?'

'We'll have to see how it goes. I haven't worked out all the details yet. Worst case scenario, you'll have to wait for the money. You have to go now. I don't want you coming to my home. If you want something from me, we can talk about it during the day at the construction site.'

But he hadn't left.

'I family at home. Two children, baby on the way.'

Anders had lost his temper. Did the man not understand who he was talking to?

'I don't give a crap about your family. I have enough to think about. Now get out of here!'

But the man didn't move, with his arms hanging at his sides and his eyes locked on Anders's, looking past him into the house.

'You have family?' The tone had been mild, almost gentle.

'Little girl. Four years?' The man had gestured with his hand at about Ellie's height. She had visited the construction site a few weeks earlier. Walked around in a construction helmet and waved at everyone. 'You watch out and little girl. Understand?'

The seriousness of his eyes had frightened Anders to his soul.

'Are you threatening me?' It had taken everything he had in him to keep his voice steady. 'If you even come close to my family, I'll make sure you never see a lick of your money or get another job in Stockholm. How will you provide for your children then, eh?'

The man's threatening smile was etched into his retinas.

'You watch out, Anders.'

Then he had turned around, walked down the gravel path, past Anders and Amanda's cars, and disappeared out through the gate.

As if nothing had happened.

57

'This just gets more and more complicated.'

Kaj shook the plate off a few times over the sink and handed it to Sofia who sat at the kitchen table in the flat in Örnsköldsvik. She had put her feet up on the chair in front of her and had a red checked dishtowel in her lap.

'I mean, it must be a kidnapping, right?'

Sofia nodded absentmindedly and set the plate on the table. She could still see the hollow look in Anders Svensson's eyes and his pallid, greyish face. The case had grown from a missing four-year-old who was feared to have gotten lost in the snow and frozen to death into a nationwide alert for two missing people from the same family. Although Sofia would never admit this to Kaj or Vera, it was starting to feel overwhelming. Both physically and mentally. Her big, unwieldy body was no longer suited to slogging around in the snow and quickly hopping in and out of police cars. She wasn't as nimble mentally as she had been before, either. Maybe it would be more responsible to start her maternity leave now and let other people take over.

Kaj dried his hands and opened the fridge. He took out the leftovers from Monday night's dinner. They only had an hour for dinner and then they were meeting back at the station again. Sofia wasn't looking forward to a whole night in an uncomfortable office chair, bent over a never-ending stack of phone records, maps, and transcripts from questioning sessions. They had knocked on doors in half of Nätra parish and uniformed colleagues had interviewed witnesses who worked in all the grocery stores, gas stations, and shops in Bjästa and Sidensjö, which were the closest larger communities to Sunnansjö.

Kaj set the Thai food that he had heated in the microwave in front of her and handed her a napkin.

'I wonder how Philip is doing,' she said, poking at her noodles a little.

Kaj tilted his head sideways and looked at her.

'You don't know this Philip person and you have absolutely no responsibility for his well-being.'

Sofia didn't say any more, too tired to argue. Too tired for anything is how it felt. Kaj shook his head and put a forkful of chicken into his mouth.

'And you need to focus on is what's important here, the investigation and how you're feeling. Obviously not in that order.' He smiled and his tone softened when he saw the look on her face. 'You have to think about yourself now. And the baby.'

Sofia looked at Kaj and took a shaky breath. She felt for Philip, his fragility, his different way of being, and his sad, frightened eyes. He had awakened a protective instinct in her that she found hard to shake. She dabbed the corner of her eye, annoyed. All these fucking tears she couldn't stop. Her soul had somehow gone soft and as soon as she felt tired or worried or dejected, they came. Could hormones really affect an otherwise healthy body this way?

Kaj eyed her with pity.

'Aww.' He reached out his hand and placed it on hers. 'Are you really so worried about him?'

She shook her head.

'Yes. Or no. I don't know. I'm just tired.'

He stroked the back of her hand with his thumb.

'Should I talk to Vera? See if you can do something else? Maybe it would be better for you now anyway, given how close we are to the birth and the fact that Philip is living in our house and...'

Sofia dropped her chopsticks onto her plate and got up out of her chair.

'You will not do that! I am fully capable of taking care of myself.' She wiped her nose with her napkin and dropped it on her plate as well. 'And as for the house, it's mine, not ours!'

Then she stomped off to the bathroom.

58

Once Sofia had finally toiled her way up the stairs to the investigations department, she paused to catch her breath. Kaj had gone on ahead while she showered. Her anger had drained out of her once she was standing underneath the hot, running water. Now only the tiredness remained. Was it going to be like this now? Life in a constant fog and with a body that refused to cooperate. Sofia got a lump in her throat and the unwelcome tears returned. *Pull it together!*

Obviously she wouldn't feel like this all the time. Once the baby was born, she would be herself again. She and Kaj would find a way to resolve the practical details. They simply had to. Everything would be fine.

A loud laugh interrupted her musings, and she realised the sound had come from Vera's office. It was almost eight o'clock at night and yet the lights were on in every room in the hallway. It was going to be a long night, but no one was complaining. Two people's lives might be at stake. That trumped fatigue, family dinners, and down time. Even pregnancy.

Sofia strolled down to the open door and knocked on the doorframe.

Vera looked up with a big smile on her face, which she quickly adjusted when she spotted Sofia. Kicki Bjurvall was sitting on her desk. Extremely close to Vera.

'You're back?' Sofia said in surprise.

Kicki turned to her and smiled ingratiatingly.

'Yes, we're done for tonight.'

'We're discussing whether or not to keep going,' Vera interjected, as if her colleague's presence required further explanation.

Sofia nodded towards the library.

'Are you coming or what?'

—

'Four weeks ago, Anders was threatened by one of the Polish workers from the Rosenlund construction site.' Sofia glanced around at her colleagues' serious faces as she began the meeting with the new information she and Kaj had obtained. 'An undocumented worker who hasn't been paid. He said that he would hurt the family if he didn't get paid.'

'And it didn't occur to Anders to tell us that before now?' Vera shook her head from her seat by the whiteboard.

'He didn't dare,' Sofia said. 'He wanted the opportunity to drain the company of what money was left in case he needed to pay ransom.'

Vera tossed an empty disposable cup into the trash can next to the whiteboard. Coffee splashed onto the wall behind it.

'What the hell? Does he not understand that he has jeopardised his children's lives by keeping this from us?'

Sofia empathised with Anders Svensson. The realisation that he might be the cause of the hell he was going through now must have been dreadful.

'We need to take this threat very seriously. I'm trying to get some information from Jerzy Nowak, the construction site manager for the Rosenlund Tower project. I asked for the names and info on everyone who has worked without an employment contract for the last six months,' Kaj said. 'But the problem is just that. They don't have contracts. He didn't even have full names for half of them.'

Vera sat down at the conference table and looked at Per and Karim, who both had dark circles under their eyes.

'How did things go for you?'

'I'm reviewing the cell connections made to the towers closest to the Svensson's house,' Per said.

'And I'm checking the call logs from Anders's, Amanda's, Madeleine's, and Philip Lindén's phones,' Karim said, running his hands through his beard. 'It's going to take a while.'

Per held up a printed map with several red markings on it.

'I haven't been able to get the big picture yet, but I started with the night when Madeleine is supposed to have disappeared. Sure enough, her number did connect to the cell tower that covers the Svensson's house at around ten p.m. on Thursday night. So that confirms that she was there.'

'So Philip was telling the truth,' Sofia said.

Kaj clicked his pen.

'That just says that Madeleine's phone was still there when Philip arrived,' Kaj said. 'It doesn't say anything about whether it was also still there when he left.'

'Actually, it does.' Per flipped through the printouts. 'Philip's cell phone moved to the next tower at 3:20 a.m., but Madeleine's remained there. Her phone didn't start moving until 3:45 a.m. We have questioned Enar Gottfridsson, the snowplough driver. By that time, he had already gotten Philip out of the ditch and started towing him towards Bjästa.'

'Thank you, Per.' Kaj gave a strained smile and set his pen down on the table.

Sofia wondered what it would have been like to be a detective before the entire Swedish population carried a device that could tell you where they were, when they were there, and who they were in contact with. And much, much more.

Marie looked up.

'Then we can at least conclude that it wasn't Philip Lindén who moved Madeleine's phone. Does that mean we can also rule him out as the perpetrator?'

But Kaj didn't seem prepared to let it go.

'Philip could very well have had Madeleine with him in the car even if her phone stayed at the house.'

Vera shook her head.

'It's not reasonable that Philip would have had time to abduct or, in a worst-case scenario, kill Madeleine Svensson, hide her body, get rid of all the evidence in the house behind him, and then fake a car accident with a subsequent panic attack to give himself an alibi. Especially not in just twenty-five minutes. If he had had a body in the car, it would have been discovered.'

'He could have had Madeleine in the trunk,' Kaj suggested.

Vera took off her glasses and looked at him while she cleaned them on her sweater.

'No, he couldn't. Because Gottfridsson opened the trunk to secure the towlines.'

Kaj nodded and took a deep breath in through his nose and slowly exhaled. Even though he was clearly focused on the idea that Philip might be their perpetrator, at least in Madeleine's case, he wasn't one to turn a blind eye to evidence.

'Okay, then we rule him out.'

Sofia smiled to herself. She looked forward to telling Philip that they no longer suspected him of being involved. Although that was small consolation given that Madeleine was still missing.

Marie reached for Per's printout of the cell tower connections.

'I thought of something. Could Madeleine have been at the house without Philip discovering her?'

Per scratched at his red hair.

'That's possible. It's a large house. She could have waited for Philip to leave and then left, taking her phone with her. But at 3:53 a.m., just eight minutes after the phone started moving away from the Svensson's house, it was switched off. It has not been traceable since then. And why wouldn't she have made herself known when Philip was there only to then leave the house and turn off her phone?'

Thinking, Marie picked at the sticker on a banana sitting next to her laptop.

'Maybe because they had argued,' Marie suggested, 'and she didn't want to see him?'

Could it be that Madeleine was voluntarily staying away after all? Sofia thought that seemed pretty far-fetched.

'That doesn't explain why she hasn't been in contact with anyone since then, or why she didn't come forward after we went public with the APB.'

Karim continued in the same vein.

'On the other hand, if Madeleine was abducted against her will, the perpetrator must have returned to retrieve her phone after Philip left the house. Neither it nor the jacket were there when Anders and the family arrived. Why take the risk of going back for a phone?'

'Maybe there's something on it that couldn't be revealed?'

Kaj nodded to Per.

'Possibly. Or it was left behind and the perpetrator wanted to get rid of all the evidence.'

Marie handed the printouts back to Per and turned to Vera.

'We need to determine the identity of the Polish construction worker. He's our most likely perpetrator right now.'

'If that was the case,' Sofia said, leaning back in her chair and putting her arms around her belly, 'he must have known when the Svensson family would be in the house. But not even Anders himself knew that Madeleine and Philip were going to be there. Plus, according to Anders, they decided at the last minute that Amanda and Ellie would go. If someone planned to kidnap both daughters, he or she must have been incredibly lucky that they showed up almost at the same time at the same place.'

'What do you think?' Vera turned to Kaj.

'Hard to say with this little to go on. Kidnappings for ransom are unusual and complicated to carry out. Usually, the people behind them are professional criminals.'

'Not that I'm anti-immigrant,' Per said, 'but there are a lot of professional criminals among those who immigrate from the Eastern Bloc.'

'We could be dealing with multiple actors,' Kaj said, straightening up in his chair. 'Returning to the scene of the crime is a big risk. We can assume that this person or people are very good at not attracting attention to themselves or alternatively that they're not afraid of being discovered. Maybe they have reconnoitred the house and the area before.'

'I think we'll wrap it up here for now,' Marie broke in as Kaj took a breath before proceeding. 'We need to plough through the call logs more carefully and get the names of everyone who worked at SveAnd's construction site. There's no point in our sitting here and speculating.'

Marie Fransson did not seem to care that Kaj had worked in the criminal profiling group for many years, so he was hardly just sitting around and speculating, but he did not seem to take offence. The meeting was concluded with the sound of scraping chairs and everyone besides Vera and Sofia left the library.

Vera stood up and pushed the whiteboard into a corner.

'We need to talk,' Vera said. 'Shall we go into my office?'

59

Once they were in Vera's office, Vera sat down behind her desk and let Sofia drag out the chair intended for visitors, which had been pushed back against the far wall. Vera sat quietly while she moved the furniture around, huffing and puffing.

'That looks like a lot of work,' Vera remarked when Sofia finally sat down across the desk from her.

Sofia tried to smile. It felt like the baby had wedged itself in crosswise and she was having a hard time breathing. But the last thing she wanted was for Vera to see her pregnancy travails.

'It's fine. I'm just pregnant, not sick.'

Vera nodded slowly.

'I wanted to have a little chat with you about your future.'

Sofia recalled a similar conversation they had had the previous summer. That one had been about Sofia's chances of taking over Vera's position someday. She suspected that this one would not be about that.

'I've recommended that Kicki take over your job while you're on maternity leave.'

'Take over my job? What happens when I come back?'

Sofia didn't know if she should laugh or cry. Had Kaj gone behind her back after all and talked to Vera?

'Sofia, you know I think you're a good detective, but do you really think you'll be back fulltime? I mean, as a single parent with a child and with the hours we sometimes have to work?'

They didn't think she would come back. Sofia opened her mouth to respond, but her anger took over and she couldn't get a word out. Her cheeks blazed. Had it not been for the fact that she couldn't get up out of the chair fast enough, she would have stormed out of Vera's office and slammed the door behind her.

'I suppose you haven't even decided if you're going to keep living up here, have you?'

'Why would I not want to keep living here? Did Kaj say that?'

Vera looked down into her lap seeming almost ashamed.

'No, but I assumed that you would want to live closer to each other after the baby was born.'

'And so you assumed that I was going to go live with him?'

'Yes,' Vera replied succinctly.

Sofia wanted to tell her to go to hell, but all her energy had gone into getting angry. Instead, she felt the damn tears coming. They found their way up her throat, even though she fought to hold them back, and soon her eyes were faithlessly overflowing with tears. She was betrayed by her own body and her own fucking hormones. What had been anger was now despair and shame. She didn't want to be one of those women who cry their way through pregnancy or have mood swings every five minutes. That wasn't who she was. And yet, here she sat in her boss's office, sobbing with her nose running. Like a nobody.

Vera handed her a Subway napkin from next to a sandwich wrapper from the same restaurant. It had a dressing stain on it, but Sofia took it and blew her nose loudly.

'Sorry, I… it's all a little much right now.'

'Sofia, no one is trying to push you out of your job. We're all just worried that you won't be up to coming back fulltime and we need to plan for the future.'

Sofia nodded and folded up the napkin.

'I want to work.' Her voice was pitiful and pleading.

'Of course you're going to work, Sofia. Maybe just not on these types of cases. The plan was for you to take over from me. It's no secret that I wanted that, right? But now that might be hard, what with the baby and everything. That's all I'm saying.' Vera sounded genuinely worried about her.

On some level, Sofia grasped that Vera meant well. At the same time, she was quite certain that by law a boss was not allowed to say these things or act this way. Surely the Swedish Police did not have any right to interfere with how she planned on parenting. She had colleagues who were uniformed officers, working night shifts, day shifts, weekends and evenings, and who had a whole passel of kids at home. Was there something specific about her that made her unable to be both a parent and a cop?

'I can't stop you from working for the rest of the time until the birth, but my strong recommendation right now is that you devote yourself to internal investigation work. Maybe work from home part of the day? I don't want you to wear yourself out.'

Sofia nodded. Defeated both physically and mentally. And somewhere deep down inside, relieved at not needing to bustle back and forth between Ulvön Island, the police station, and all the search locations that were being processed now in the search for Ellie and Madeleine Svensson.

Vera pushed a folder full of paperwork across the desk.

'These are tips that have been called in. Go through them.'

Sofia accepted the folder, stood up with as much dignity as she could muster, and headed for the door.

—

When Sofia got home to the flat, all she wanted to do was cry. It was dark out and it was already after nine p.m., but she couldn't be bothered to turn on the lights. The shame of feeling so completely exhausted from work stung in her soul. In just this instant, she regretted having kept the baby. Would the career she had fought for her whole life burn to the ground now? Was she going to become one of all the thousands and thousands of women before her who had chosen family life over professional life? She was furious, but her anger was not enough to make her act. The sofa was so infinitely more enticing than starting to make calls to her union rep and the human resources department. And to be honest, Vera might be right. Was it even possible to combine the job of being a single mother with the job of being a detective?

She pulled off her winter boots but kept her down jacket on and wandered into the dark living room. Her calves felt like logs, and she wanted nothing more than to put them up on the coffee table. Just as she was about to sit down, her cell phone, which was still in her computer bag in the front hall, rang. She sighed and turned around. By the time she finally managed to fish the phone out of the bag, it had stopped ringing. She looked at the display. The police station switchboard. Eva answered after the second ring.

'You were looking for me?'

'How are you doing? I heard what happened with Vera.' Sofia should have been surprised, but she wasn't. Eva was on top of everything that happened at the station and anything she didn't know wasn't worth knowing.

'It's fine. I'm just tired and...' There they were again. The fucking tears that were constantly showing up. She swallowed and tried to sound composed. 'I'll be at home working the rest of the night.'

Eva cleared her throat.

'Not that it's any of my business,' she said then, 'but I don't think it's appropriate for our detectives here at the station to start romantic relationships with their superiors. It just doesn't feel quite right.'

Sofia couldn't believe her ears. Was Eva going to the trouble of calling her just to tell her what she thought of her and Kaj's relationship? And besides, they weren't even in a relationship anymore, so why would Eva even give a shit? True, they were expecting a baby together, but surely that wasn't illegal.

'What do you mean by that?'

Eva was quiet for a second. She seemed taken aback by Sofia's reaction.

'Oh, my God, Sofia! No, I didn't mean you and Kaj. For crying out loud, that is not what I was referring to.'

She laughed, an exaggerated, nervous laugh. Sofia knew that Eva had a soft spot for Kaj. She had made that abundantly clear last summer when he had helped investigate the murdered man who had been found below the Ulvö Hotel. The investigation team had never been offered so many sandwiches and homemade cakes. Eva had come up with a plethora of creative reasons why she needed to come into the library right when the investigative group was in there. Even more often, she had errands that took her into Kaj's makeshift office. After it came out that Sofia was expecting his child, she had backed off a little, but there was still a gleam in her eye every time Kaj walked by.

'I'm sorry, Eva, but I'm tired. My whole body aches and I need to sit down. What were you actually referring to?'

Eva lowered her voice to a whisper so Sofia had a hard time hearing what she was saying.

'Kicki and…'

'I can't hear what you're saying, Eva. Who's Kicki having a relationship with?'

Eva raised her voice from a whisper to a hiss.

'Vera. Kicki and Vera are sleeping together.'

60

Fredrik stopped just inside his front door and looked down at the mail lying on the carpet there, some window envelopes and a flyer from Rusta. He had sat in a chair next to Ida's bed all day long. Every now and then he had nodded off from lack of sleep. Brushing his teeth and falling into bed were his only goals now.

He set down a bag with bread and juice that he had bought on his way home and looked farther into his front hall. There was a pair of blue disposable gloves and a see-through package that seemed to have contained some kind of medical device. There were shoe prints on the floor from the paramedics' black boots.

He moved his gaze into the kitchen, but didn't dare look at the round kitchen table where the grocery store bag used to sit. Instead, he fixed his eyes on the floor underneath. Ida's purse was there. A patterned thing in black and grey with a red and green handle. She wasn't big into designer labels, but she had told him that she had treated herself to the Gucci purse when she earned her speech therapy degree. It had tipped over and he gathered up a bunch of keys, a pack of chewing gum, and a pen that had fallen out and put them back in. He couldn't resist the impulse to smell her purse. He thought he caught a faint whiff of Ida's perfume.

Suddenly he was overcome by such a terrible despair over what had happened to Ida that his legs wouldn't hold him up anymore. He sank down onto the floor with her purse in his lap. Kind, lovely Ida who had helped him back to life. What the hell had he done? Tears came and he didn't bother to stop them. He let them run freely over his stubble, sitting there with his back leaning against his kitchen cabinets.

With Ida, he had been safe. She had believed in him, supported him, and shown him love. And yet, it had only taken a few days without her for him to start fantasising about Sofia again. He hugged her purse closer to his body and sat there until the crying stopped. He pulled his cell phone out of his pants pocket to see if Jonna or anyone from the hospital had called, but the screen was empty. He didn't even know if they would make the effort to contact him. He understood that they blamed him for what had happened. He had provided Ida with both the justification for the suicide attempt and the method.

Fredrik stood up, hung his jacket over one of the chairs, and wiped his face with his sleeve. He needed to shower and sleep. Tomorrow he would get up early and go to the hospital again. Whether they wanted him there or not, he would be by Ida's side through this and when she woke up they would be together.

He opened the fridge and found it empty except for a litre of milk, a yoghurt that was past its expiration date, and a pack of vegetarian hot dogs. When Fredrik opened the cupboard under the sink to throw the yoghurt away, he saw that there were boxes in the trash bag. He pulled the trash can out and stuck his hand in and grabbed several medication boxes. All empty. Ida had had the presence of mind to clean up after herself so he wouldn't have to. Fredrik felt a lump in his throat again. He dropped the packaging and set the trash can down. He grabbed the grocery store bag from the kitchen table and aggressively crumpled it up and chucked it into the trash bag, pulled the bag out of the can and tied it closed. This shit was going to be thrown away now. He would never pick up a prescription again. Never. As he walked to the front door to go to the garbage chute, he noticed a thick A4-sized envelope sitting on the bench in his front hall.

To Fredrik.

Thursday, 27 February

61

The sun shone in the window and right onto Sofia's face. She had fallen asleep on the sofa with her clothes on. One leg hung down, resting on the floor, and her lower back ached worse than it ever had. She looked around for Kaj but remembered that he had come home late in the night and left again early in the morning. She had meant to get up when he left but had fallen back asleep.

Vera had sent an email last night that Sofia was now working remotely in the mornings and their morning meeting would be held digitally. Despite her protests yesterday, she was grateful not to need to rush over to the police station.

It took a good five minutes, with breaks, for Sofia to stretch enough that she could stand up. Hunger burned in her stomach, but her need to pee was even greater. She shuffled to the toilet and spotted her computer bag with the folder that Vera had sent with her. *Damn it, she should have looked through that last night.* Vera would be expecting an update on at least a couple of the tips. But instead she had slept from sometime after nine until, well, what time was it now? 8:53 a.m. Twelve hours. She hurried into the bathroom, peed, splashed a little water on her face, and pulled out her computer. She had just gotten settled on the sofa when she realised it needed to be plugged in. After yet another trip to the front hall, she was back and joined the morning meeting just as everyone else started logging in on their laptops. Everyone was sitting around the table in the library except Vera, who as usual sat by the whiteboard. All

Sofia could see of her was a pair of dark blue pants legs behind Marie's head.

'Sofia, can you hear me?' Vera asked loudly.

'Let's go around the table,' Marie said and took over the meeting in a much quieter voice. 'Johan?'

Everyone turned to Johan already seeming to have forgotten that Sofia was not in the room.

'The fire extinguisher that Philip Lindén claimed was on the floor when he was in the Svensson's house definitely was not there when we did our first investigation of the crime scene. I checked all the pictures we took. We conducted a new investigation yesterday and this time we focused on the area around the fireplace and the passage between the front hall and the living room where the fire extinguisher hangs.'

'You didn't examine everything the first time?' Vera asked grumpily from her spot by the whiteboard.

But Johan kept his cool.

'We went through the rooms we considered of interest.'

Vera knew as well as the others did that a complete crime scene investigation of every corner of a five-hundred-square-meter house could not be done in the short amount of time they had right now. With every passing day, their chances of finding Ellie and Madeleine alive decreased.

'Did you find anything?' Marie asked.

Johan adjusted the bun on the back of his head and nodded.

'We found skin scrapings and blood on the fire extinguisher, as well as fingerprints on the handle. We also found blood spatter on the wall by the sofa although not very much. It was all sent straight to NFC for analysis last night. They have determined that the blood is Madeleine Svensson's.'

Sofia leaned back on her sofa. Although she had never actually believed there was a chance, any hope that Madeleine was staying away voluntarily was now gone. How was she going to tell Philip this?

'Wait, we got the results back already?'

'Missing four-year-olds get priority at NFC.' Johan smiled sombrely at Marie.

'Have you found anything to suggest that Ellie was also subjected to violence in the house?' she asked.

Johan shook his head.

'Although we were able to establish that the fingerprints on the fire extinguisher were from the same person as the ones on the handrail on the stairs, in several places in Anders's and Amanda's bedroom, in the bathroom, and in the kitchen.'

'What does that mean?' Karim asked.

'I don't know, but it suggests that someone not only went into and out of the house but also moved around freely between rooms without wearing gloves.'

'Are you implying that it could be someone they know?'

Johan shrugged.

'I'm not implying anything. I'm just telling you want I observed. The fingerprints have been checked against the fingerprint and sketch registry,' he continued. 'No hits in Sweden or in any other EU country.'

Marie jotted down a note. The sound of clicking keys echoed in Sofia's computer speakers.

Kaj brushed back his silver-grey hair.

'With Philip ruled out, we have only one lead left to follow.'

Everyone nodded.

Vera's stomach and chest came into view on Sofia's screen as she sat down in the chair in front of her computer, still holding the whiteboard pen in her hand.

'We need to get hold of that damned construction worker and quickly. We need to talk to Anders again.'

62

Today I didn't even need to rely on luck. Amanda chose my car and my company for the search all on her own. Yesterday I didn't get a good opportunity, but today it will happen.

The countryside passes by outside the car. Snow and more snow. She sits slouched in the passenger's seat with her arms wrapped tightly around herself. Her resigned posture makes me almost feel guilty. Almost. Those eyes, red from crying, and the dark circles under them. Dry, chapped lips that tremble despite the heat being on in the car.

'How are you doing?'

Amanda doesn't react to my question, just keeps staring straight ahead at the road.

'Would you like some coffee? There's some in the thermos on the floor.'

She looks down at the bag by her feet and shakes her head almost imperceptibly.

I don't know why I say things like that. I don't care at all how she's doing or if she wants coffee. I don't care about her at all. She disgusts me. The way-too-tight ski suit, the ridiculous black sunglasses that look like big fly eyes, the lips that have been injected with God knows what. No respectable woman looks like that. I bet the money she paid for those white, lined winter boots would have been enough to support mother and father for a whole month. Maybe more.

I put my hand on her arm as she sits next to me.

'Try to rest a little, Amanda. All this will be over soon.'

63

Kaj pulled off the E4 at Bjästa. As they took the exit and headed towards Sunnansjö yet again, snow swirled around the car tires but this time the sun shone in a clear blue sky.

He drove up the driveway as far as he could and parked so that Sofia would be close to the guest cabin, which she appreciated. Even so, it was a struggle to get there. Someone had shovelled and sanded, but it was hard for her to keep her balance on the narrow path between the snow drifts.

Kicki Bjurvall met them at the guest cabin and held the door open as if she lived there herself. She looked amused as Sofia pushed past her in the doorway.

'Not far to go now?'

Sofia slipped away from Kicki's hand, which was moving towards her belly. The last person she wanted pawing her body was the woman who was sleeping with her boss and was apparently about to take her job away from her.

Kicki gave her a look, but didn't make a big deal out of it.

'Do you have children?' Kaj asked to try to smooth over Sofia's behaviour.

Kicki shook her head.

'No, children aren't for me. I had a golden hamster when I was ten. It wound up in the vacuum cleaner by mistake. After that I realised that I wasn't capable of looking after anything living. I don't even have potted plants at home.' She laughed dryly.

That surprised Sofia. She had imagined Kicki as the kind of woman who stood in the ice hockey rink cafeteria every weekend to support her five hockey-playing sons' various teams. Or lugging violins and recorders back and forth to music lessons and standing right up front with her camera at every end-of-the-school-year celebration. But given that she didn't seem to want a husband, maybe she wasn't planning on kids either.

'Are they here?' Kaj nodded towards the combined living and dining room.

'Anders is here. Amanda is out with the search group again today. We were planning to wrap up the whole search operation by lunch but got a tip about a man who was seen with a little girl Ellie's age.'

'When was that?'

'About an hour ago.'

It annoyed Sofia that they hadn't been informed about it.

'Where?'

'On the road that goes under the railroad bridge by Orrvik, not all that far from here.'

Kaj nodded and removed his winter boots. He paused, kneeling on one knee, and she realised he intended to try to help her off with her boots. Kicki was still standing there, watching them.

Sofia pulled her leg away with a jerk and started trying to use her right foot to help her get her left boot off.

'I can do it myself.'

Kicki and Kaj left her in the front hall and headed for the living room, but she had time to seem them exchange a look.

I can do it myself. Like a three-year-old.

Anders Svensson was sitting on the sofa with a cup of coffee in his hands when Sofia walked into the room. The fireplace was going, and he didn't look away from the red flames.

'You're here again.' It was a resigned statement of fact more than anything else.

Kicki sat down next to him and Sofia and Kaj remained standing.

'Yes, unfortunately.'

Sofia took a deep breath and began.

'I'm terribly sorry to have to tell you this, Anders, but we have found blood in the living room of the main house, Madeleine's blood.'

Anders looked up at her. His face crumpled and he broke into heaving sobs. They sat silently and waited out his crying fit while Kicki stroked his back.

'As you know, we suspect your two daughters' disappearances are connected.'

Anders clutched his cup spasmodically without wiping away the tears running down his cheeks.

'I've told you everything I know.'

Sofia shifted her weight to her other foot and snuck a glance at the empty seat next to Anders. She would have done anything to be able to sit down.

'Are you sure? We don't have very much to go on and still haven't identified the man who threatened you. The more time that passes, the lower the odds of getting Ellie and Madeleine back unharmed.'

Anders leaned forward and slammed his cup down so the coffee sloshed over onto the matte finish of the birch coffee table.

'Don't you think I get that?'

'They need to ask about everything.' Kicki, who had spent the most time with the family and had clearly won over Anders's trust, put her hand on his shoulder and he raised his hands apologetically to them.

'Sorry, I'm just so...' Anders broke into sobs again. 'I don't think we can take much more of this. Who would do something like this to us?'

Kicki's phone rang, and she excused herself, getting up and going into the kitchen.

Kaj and Sofia stood in silence and watched Anders, who was sniffling with one hand over his face. Sofia wanted to say something to comfort him, but what could you say to someone whose children might never come home again?

Kicki promptly returned. She nodded for them to follow her out, but Anders stopped them.

'What is it? If you've found something, I want to know.'

Sofia could see that Kicki was straining to maintain her profession composure. Her eyes were wide and her mouth a thin line.

'Both of the search groups have returned.'

'And?' Anders interrupted. 'Did they find anything?'

'No, but they're missing one person.'

Anders stared at her, open-mouthed.

'Amanda.'

64

Kaj set two coffee cups on the conference table, opened a milk and poured the contents into his cup, and handed her the other cup. She accepted it gratefully and leaned back in her chair. They were alone in the library, waiting for everyone else to arrive. Karim and Per were working on the call logs and the cell tower dumps and trying to find anything that could be connected to the Polish construction worker. So far, they had failed at every attempt to determine his identity. Vera and Marie were on the phone with prosecutor Anna Sondell.

Sofia was thinking about Anders Svensson. It was a wonder he was still functioning at all. A nurse had come out to the house and given him a sedative and something to help him sleep before they left. She hoped that he would get a few hours' rest before he woke up to the nightmare he found himself in.

On the way back from Sunnansjö, Kaj and Sofia had checked in with Magnus Söderström, who was leading Missing People's search operation. He told them that Amanda had left her search group to go back and search an abandoned barn not far from the railroad tracks out in Orrvik, where the man with the child had been seen. Magnus had informed Amanda that they had already searched there, but she had insisted. The others had kept going for about fifteen minutes before they realised that she was not behind them. That was the last they had seen of her.

A full mobilisation was underway again including helicopters, canine units, and thermal imaging cameras. The whole county felt like it was on emergency footing. Sofia felt like she could almost feel it as she drove through the empty winter streets. Worried locals were constantly calling the station to ask if they had heard anything and if they dared send their kids to school. Was there a paedophile ring running rampant? Was there a risk that this could happen to more people? Could they be dealing with a serial killer? These were questions that none of them could answer.

Vera appeared in the library doorway, flanked by Kicki Bjurvall. She stopped to let her colleague in first. Marie came in right behind them.

Per and Karim came in immediately afterward and closed the door behind them. Vera assumed her position by the whiteboard, took out a pen and wrote *Amanda* next to Ellie's and Madeleine's names.

'Oh, my God,' Per shook his head. 'What the hell is going on?'

Vera looked around dejectedly at her colleagues gathered around the table. They had never been involved in a situation like this before. And no matter how many resources Marie requested from the Northern Sweden Police – which covered an enormous area but had a small staff – the fact remained that they had no idea what had happened to Ellie, Madeleine or Amanda. The Stockholm Police were combing through the construction companies they knew of that hired undocumented workers, searching for the Polish worker who had threatened Anders Svensson, but without a name or a description or a clearer description than Anders could give, it was nearly impossible.

'Yeah, what the hell is going on?' Vera repeated. She set the whiteboard pen down and took a seat.

It had been five days since Ellie disappeared and it was almost a week since the last time anyone had heard from Madeleine. And now Amanda was missing, too. The newspapers were riddled with pictures of Ellie and Madeleine, with all sorts of speculation about what might have happened. And yet no relevant tips or sightings had come in. The communications department in Umeå was handling all contact with the media. Given his experience and local knowledge, Mattias Wikström made daily comments on the situation and occasionally took a swipe at his former colleagues in the Örnsköldsvik Police for their inability to find the missing girls. And starting tomorrow, Amanda's face would be on the front pages, too, Sofia thought.

'How did it go with the phone records?' Vera pointed at Per.

'I found five numbers that were moving around in the area on the day when Ellie and Madeleine disappeared.' Per flipped through a stack of papers. 'Three of them belong to Nätra Home-Help Services and one to a woman in Mellansel, but she was only there the night Madeleine disappeared. I'm going to call and talk to the home-help workers,' he continued. 'Karim, can you take the woman in Mellansel? She might not be involved, but maybe she saw something.'

Karim nodded.

'And the last number?' Marie asked.

'I haven't found any owner for it yet. It seems to belong to an unregistered prepaid phone account.'

'So that could be our perpetrator's number?'

Per murmured his agreement.

'Good, how do we proceed?'

Sofia said a silent prayer that Vera would not ask her about the list of tips she should have called her way through the previous evening. She promised herself she would get right on that after the meeting. But the thought of the pile of printouts made her clench her jaws. How could her attitude have changed so quickly? She loved her job. And yet she just wanted to throw her computer and papers into the trash and go to bed. Or better yet, go out to her house on Ulvön Island, lock the door, and sit in the rocking chair staring out at the sea. Not think about anything, not talk to anyone. Then she remembered Philip. He was still out at the house, alone and surely very worried. He didn't know yet that he was no longer a suspect. She had asked Vera if she could inform him, but Vera had asked Sofia to wait a little longer.

She needed to ask Tord to look in on him this evening. Should she tell Philip about the blood they had found? No, that would be both improper and official misconduct. It wouldn't do any good to share the information with him. She hoped to God that Fredrik would come and get him soon. He couldn't sit out there by himself, just waiting for Madeleine to be found.

Marie took the plastic wrap off a cheese sandwich. Despite being uncommonly short and weighing no more than a fifth grader, she ate constantly. There was always a Snickers bar, a banana or a sandwich on the desk next to her computer.

'We need to establish a motive if we're going to narrow in on a perpetrator. Someone has obviously gone to a lot of trouble to hurt Anders.' Vera started writing on the board. 'As I see it, we have two possible scenarios here. Either it's a kidnapping and the goal is to extort money from Anders. Or it's about revenge, possibly because of financial irregularities.'

'A kidnapper should have made a ransom demand by this point,' Kaj said and then leaned back in his chair, hands clasped behind his head. He looked tired. 'I think it's time we realise that this is about something else.'

65

The girl is waking up as I come upstairs.

I stop with the bottle of formula in my hand and look at her through the narrow opening where the door is ajar. She blinks her dark eyes and tightly hugs the teddy bear I found in the closet. She doesn't look scared, more confused.

When she turns her back to the door, I quickly walk over to the bed. She doesn't react. I pull the blanket up over her head so she won't see my face and hold her tight. I expect her to scream, but she doesn't.

Maybe she has gotten used to my touch? It is so hard to stop myself. Lying awake and looking at her. Caressing that soft skin. I have started to be afraid of my feelings. I want her to be mine.

'Hi, Ellie,' I whisper.

She doesn't answer.

'This will all be over soon. You don't need to be afraid.'

The body under the covers shakes now with a sob.

'I want my mom.'

I pat her through the covers. Feel her relax and go back to sleep. She won't remember any of this.

'Mom is sleeping. She's going to sleep for a very long time.'

66

By the time Fredrik woke up, it was already late afternoon. Even though he hadn't slept at all the night before, he had had trouble falling asleep. He had not dared to open the letter from Ida, terrified that it would be filled with anger and accusations that would further exacerbate his regrets and self-reproach. The last time he had looked at the clock, it had been 1:30 a.m. But in the end, the long drive and his worrying about Ida had taken their toll and he had fallen into a deep and dreamless sleep.

Now he was sitting beside Ida again in the hospital and gently stroking her hand. Her face was smooth and relaxed. The tubes were still connected to her chest, which slowly rose and fell. He could feel the warmth of her body under the blanket.

How could this happen? Ida who was so strong, so healthy. She who nagged him about how you couldn't live off of sandwiches, who sent along boxes of healthy food that he never ate, who suggested yoga and meditation and forced him to go to a spa where they wore kimonos and swam in outdoor pools even though it was snowing. How could she be one lying here now? If anyone should be lying there, it should be him. Fredrik thought about the bag of pills. She had asked him to throw it away. She had even packed it all up once and told him they should take it to the pharmacy and turn it in, but he had wriggled out of it. He wanted to hold onto it as a lifeline. Or as a sign that he had defeated the demons or as a challenge, he didn't know which. Seeing the bag, but not touching it, had been a small victory every day. One more day without needing anti-anxiety drugs. Philip had laughed at him but had also been proud. Fredrik's addiction to pills had always been a source of contention between them. Philip detested both alcohol and medications.

Once again, Fredrik was struck by how strange it was that broken people seemed to be drawn to each other. Talking and thinking about anti-anxiety pills and antidepressants was everyday life for him. The same for Philip, who had been through Lord knows how many doctors' visits trying to cure his phobia. Whereas Philip had consistently refused to take the pills, Fredrik had manically tried to obtain more. Their lives had been surrounded by chemical substances that had in no way helped either of them. It was beyond him how doctors believed people could medicate their way to happiness.

There was a knock on the hospital room door and a woman with a pierced eyebrow and unnaturally red hair entered. She smiled at him and then walked over to look at the curves being generated by the wires attached to Ida's chest.

'How is she doing?' he asked.

'Better.'

'Is it normal for her to sleep this much?'

The doctor smiled with compassion.

'It's rough on a body when it goes through something like this. But we haven't found anything abnormal in her tests, so we'll move her during the day tomorrow.'

Fredrik looked at Ida. Her eyes were still closed. She didn't seem to react to their talking right next to her.

'Where to?'

'To a psychiatric ward. They'll decided from there when she's stable enough to be discharged.' She put her hand on Fredrik's shoulder. 'She's probably asleep now for the night. Go home and rest.'

'I just got here,' he said apologetically.

'You can't do anything right now anyway. Better to save your strength.'

'I was the one who... It was my fault,' Fredrik blurted out.

She patted him cautiously on the shoulder.

'It's no one's fault when something like this happens. You can't control mental illness.'

Fredrik nodded in resignation.

He got up, stepped over to the head of the bed, bent down, and kissed Ida on the forehead.

'I'll be back.'

As he walked out of Ida's ward, his phone rang.

'Where are you?' Sofia asked curtly.

'I'm in Stockholm. Why?'

'Why? Well, your friend Philip is up here as you might recall?'

'I've been a little preoccupied. I...'

'And you mean I haven't been? Like I have all the time in the world to look after your friends?'

She had a point. It had been beyond self-centred to dump Philip in Sofia's lap and then disappear, but that hadn't been his choice.

'I apologise. Things have been a little...'

He fell silent.

'Did something happen?' Sofia asked.

Perhaps he should have been surprised that Philip hadn't told her anything, but he wasn't. Philip's emotional world was so quintessentially different from most other people's that there was no point in trying to understand how he thought. He had learned that a long time ago and thus saved himself a great deal of disappointment and frustration. He accepted Philip for who he was and vice versa.

'My... girlfriend tried to commit suicide.'

The phone went quiet for a second. Fredrik didn't know whether Sofia was reacting more to the word 'girlfriend' or 'suicide', but when she finally responded, she sounded composed and genuinely sorry for him.

'I'm sorry, Fredrik. That's really bad news.'

Fredrik nodded at the receiver and stepped into the elevator, which had stopped and opened its doors at his floor.

'How are things going for you? Have you found Madeleine and Ellie?'

'Don't you read the newspapers?' Sofia sounded more surprised than annoyed. As if it were a given that he would be following the case via the media. Maybe it was a given, but there hadn't been a second extra for anything other than pondering what he could have done differently so that Ida wouldn't have chosen such a drastic way out.

'Amanda Svensson is also missing,' Sofia continued.

'Wait, what?'

Sofia said mmhmm.

'Two, maybe three people's lives are at stake.'

'You can't seriously believe that Philip is capable of something like this?'

She was quiet again for a moment. Fredrik knew what that meant. She was considering whether she should share information about the investigation with him or not.

'We don't think that anymore,' she finally said. 'But he needs to go home. I know that he wants to stay here until we find Madeleine, but it doesn't look good that he's at my house after… well, after how things were last summer. I don't want to sound heartless, but he can't sit out there by himself, and the investigation is keeping me on the mainland so I can't look after him.'

Fredrik understood. Sofia had done both him and Philip a big favour by letting them stay there when Philip wasn't feeling well.

'I'll come as soon as I can.'

He lowered his voice as the elevator stopped to let on a middle-aged couple.

'What do you think happened to them?'

This time, Sofia didn't need to think.

'You know that I can't discuss that with you, Fredrik.'

Her cop voice turned right on, the one he both loved and hated.

'Anders Svensson seems to have plenty of money. Maybe they'll ask for ransom soon?'

Sofia didn't answer.

'Should I talk to Philip, try to figure out if he knows anything? It might be easier for him to talk to me than to you. He might...'

'You should not,' Sofia interrupted. 'Focus on your... girl-friend.'

Sofia's breathing was strained. Maybe it was her belly that made her sound so winded. 'Let us focus on the investigation. But come and get Philip as soon as possible.'

'I will.'

67

The stacks of paper on her coffee table felt like they were mocking her. *A white van driving slowly down a street, a man lifting a sleeping girl into a car, a girl standing by herself in H&M crying, although then her mother came.* Each one was less plausible than the next, still, someone had to go through them all, and she had been given the thankless job of doing it. When she made it to the last stack, where the top tip began and ended with *A stranger, a man with dark skin, drove by in a light-blue Volvo*, she set down the stack of paper. Who called the police to leave only this as a tip for someone who committed a crime?

Sofia leaned back on the sofa and stretched her legs and back. Everyone else was still at the police station, but Kaj had insisted that she go home and she hadn't protested. She was bleary-eyed with fatigue, but even so, she couldn't sleep. Something in her chest was bothering her, right around her heart. So much so that at first she thought it was a physical sensation. It wasn't until she got into the shower and let her thoughts about the investigation wash away for a second that she understood what it was. It was jealousy. Dark, painful, inconsolable jealousy. Fredrik had a girlfriend. A real girlfriend, not just someone he was seeing, as he had said before. Someone he cared about so much that he jumped in head over heels to rescue her when she needed him. Leaving Philip and Sofia behind in the hubbub. As the water ran over her unwieldy body, she let the tears come. Ashamed of the conflicting emotions her big belly gave her. She was going to be a mother, something she had never thought she would get to experience. She already loved her baby more than she could comprehend. Even so, she felt panicked. The baby was the end of her and Fredrik's relationship. She was stuck with Kaj and the family she herself decided would be the best for the baby. Fredrik would move on with his girlfriend. Maybe get married and have a family of his own. That thought made her want to lie down in a heap on the bathroom floor and scream.

But obviously that wouldn't do. Personal emotions had to be set aside for the moment. Amanda was still missing. Several hours had passed and the search party was out there even though it had been dark for a long time now. Everyone who had been part of Amanda's Missing People group had been questioned, but no one had seen or heard anything. They still hadn't received any ransom demand, nor had they received any new information. At this point, no one doubted that the disappearances were connected. The only question was how.

Sofia stepped out of the shower, dried herself thoroughly, and put on her favourite lotion from Rituals, but avoided her steamy reflection. When she entered the kitchen, she saw that Eva had called. She sat down on the kitchen chair, still in a towel, and called back.

'Hey, there,' Eva said. 'How are you doing?'

'Good, thanks. Are you working this late?'

'I'm just on my way home.' Sofia could hear the sound of the glass door by the reception desk closing.

'Listen, I wanted to apologise for being gossipy yesterday,' Eva said, not sounding the least bit apologetic. 'I just thought you should know. I hope you weren't upset?'

'Why would I be? Vera's entitled to…' She couldn't say *have sex with* when it related to her boss. 'See whoever she wants.'

'Of course, but don't you think that…'

'Was there anything in particular that you wanted?'

Eva did not seem discouraged by Sofia's reluctance to take part in the gossip. Surely there were many other people who would listen eagerly to this. The rumour had gotten around that Vera was a lesbian. Lillemor had come down to the police station in the fall and made a scene trying to get Vera to change her mind about the divorce. But Vera had stood her ground, and the divorce had gone through. The fact that the whole police station now knew that Vera had been married to a woman didn't seem to bother her anymore. The secret was out, but she was probably confident that no one would dare question her or comment on her private life. The only person in Vera's proximity who wasn't afraid of her was Marie Fransson, which Sofia guessed was one of the reasons why Vera disliked Marie. As preliminary investigation chief, it was Marie's job to question things, but many people before her had failed to put Vera in her place even when it was part of their job description. It was possible that Karim could qualify as one of the few people who wasn't afraid of Vera. But in his case, it was probably just a total inability to wind up in conflict with anyone. No one could provoke him to raise his voice.

Eva cleared her throat on the other end of the line.

'Yeah, I'm calling about a lady from Drömme who called in wanting to file a report. Her name is...' Sofia heard Eva moving her computer mouse in the background. 'Judith Nordin, age eighty-six. She says her neighbour's lights are on all the time. That's not exactly something you can file a police report for, but I promised we would be in touch.'

Sofia sighed.

'I'll call her tomorrow.'

'Good. And, hey, don't worry about Kicki and Vera. It will be over soon. I'm sure it's just a fling.'

'I don't care...' Sofia began to protest, but Eva had already hung up.

Friday, 28 February

68

It's time. I can't believe that everything lined up so easily. Now I just need to find a good place to leave the girl.

I lay awake all night thinking about how to do it. Everything was decided so quickly that I didn't think about how to finish it.

The woman is still in the basement. The little one will be easy to move, but I don't know what I'm going to do with the woman. She won't come willingly. Maybe I can force some of the nasal spray sedative into her, but I don't dare go downstairs.

She screams nonstop. Less now at the end, but even so, enough that someone might hear. I don't dare give her any food or even open the door.

Maybe it's best to just leave her there.

69

When Fredrik got off the subway at Medborgarplatsen to go to Söder Hospital, it was snowing. As he ate breakfast, he had gone through the newspapers on his cell phone and noted that what Sofia had said was true. You could read page after page about the Svensson family and the strange disappearances. He wondered how Philip was taking it. He had called him several times, but without getting an answer.

Jonna had sent a text and informed him that her and Ida's parents were on their way down from Övertorneå. They would arrive in the afternoon to be there when Ida was moved to the psychiatric ward on the other side of Ringvägen. He wasn't looking forward to meeting the mother and father of the woman he had disappointed and driven to attempt suicide.

Fredrik looked up at the sky, at the light flakes falling silently towards the ground and turning into grey slush the instant they landed. He had stopped and bought flowers for Ida. Pink tulips. Her favourite.

Before he left the hospital yesterday, the doctor with the eyebrow piercing had told him what he could expect now that Ida was being transferred to the psych ward, and what she had been through during her time in the intensive care unit. A wave of incomprehensible medical terms was hurled at him, but he hadn't dared to ask what it all meant. The important thing was that Ida had pulled through.

Fredrik wiped away some snowflakes that had stuck on his forehead, feeling their coldness burning. That damned grocery store bag. Why had he saved it, and why had he said what he said to Ida? The guilt was eating him up inside. If he had just kept his mouth shut, none of this would have happened.

He passed Rosenlund Park and saw some kids in reflective vests toddling around in the snow, closely monitored by preschool staff. He thought about Sofia and the baby. Soon she would be the mother of a little one like that, picking up and dropping off, packing mittens and lunches. Would he ever get to experience that himself? He looked away from the group of children. He tried to force the image of Sofia out of his head. How could he think about her now, when Ida lay injured in a bed only a few blocks away?

He stood there outside a high construction fence, with big sheets of plastic set up to reduce visibility and protect the construction workers from the wind and weather. Through the cracks he could see workers wearing blue helmets and yellow reflective vests. The half-finished skeleton of what according to a sign was going to be a residential building had been erected inside. One of the construction workers pushed his way through the fence and nodded to him as he walked by. Fredrik lowered his head. He felt like he was sneaking a peek. After the man passed, he continued reading the sign. The residential building would be done in the spring of 2022 and would contain eighteen two-storey flats. It looked expensive. The pictures showed big, glassed-in balconies and a terrace with lush plantings on the roof of the building. He wondered who could afford to buy a flat like that. His eyes stopped on a photo of a smiling man in a suit and a hardhat that looked out of place on his head. He stood with his arm around a younger man in a construction vest. The text over their heads read:

> Site of the future Rosenlund Tower! Come visit SveAnd AB's model unit. Entrance around the corner.

Fredrik stopped. *SveAnd AB*.

Anders Svensson's company.

70

Philip looked out at the sea. He was fascinated by how quickly the weather had changed. Only a few days earlier the snow had swirled around the house and the freezing cold had stung his skin when he had gone outside to smoke. Now the wind was almost gentle and early in the morning he had seen an icebreaker cut a wide groove through the ice between Sofia's boathouse and the island on the other side. Tord had told him its name was Ronön Island.

He liked the old man. Every day since he had arrived, Tord had come by with food and cigarettes. He was different from most of the people Philip met. He could easily sit for a half hour and drink coffee with him without needing to say anything. It was as if their personalities clicked somehow, even though they were so different. Philip didn't make sense to most people, who desperately tried to fill the silence with meaningless small talk, which was what Philip was worst at. He always seemed to say the wrong things, and more than once, he had upset people by pointing out something about their appearance or the way they behaved. Other people seemed to have a built-in ability to say the right things at the right times, and especially to refrain from saying the sorts of things that weren't socially acceptable to say. He was aware that he completely lacked that ability. What he thought, he said. If someone asked what he thought about a new hairdo, he answered. Even if the answer was that it was ugly. Hans and Inga had desperately tried to teach him what was appropriate to say when, but when it mattered he forgot and said what he was thinking. He wasn't trying to be mean. That was just the way he was.

In Madde he had found a kindred spirit. They had the same difficulties, and they had understood that right away. Both had high-functioning autism and neither of them had any problem completing a university class in half the time. They had both been valedictorians. He had done it via distance learning, while she had struggled through, trying to manage the social interactions with classmates and teachers. It had gone better for her than for him, but not well. Now she was studying to become a teacher. A job that would entail an awful lot of contact with people she didn't know, but she was determined to do it.

His heart ached when he thought about Madde. Where was she? Could it be as simple as her staying away because she was mad at him? No, that wasn't her style at all. When she was mad, she said so. Why hadn't she called him? The police didn't seem to think she had disappeared of her own free will either. That meant that something had happened to her.

That thought was worse than anything else. He couldn't lose her, the only person who understood him.

71

Vera looked extra serious when her face appeared on the screen. Sofia stared at her creased forehead, which was the only part of her that was visible, for a long time before the others joined the video meeting one by one. Prosecutor Anna Sondell also joined them from the Prosecutor's Office, which was unusual. Normally, Marie filled her in outside of their meetings.

Once Marie also logged in, Vera began. Sofia saw a hand with a seashell bracelet adjust the camera so that Vera's entire face was visible.

'We all know what happened during the night.'

There were murmurs and nods in people's windows on her screen. Sofia was puzzled. Kaj had already left when she woke up this morning, and she had no idea what they were talking about.

'The car that Amanda Svensson was found in is undergoing forensic examination.'

'Is she going to survive?' Marie asked.

'They don't know yet,' Kaj replied. 'Apparently it was really bad.'

Vera leaned forward over the table, letting her large breasts rest on her crossed arms. Her forehead came so close to the camera that Sofia could see the grey roots of her plum-coloured hair.

'And the home-help worker's phone number?'

Sofia didn't get a chance to break in and explain that she had no idea what they were talking about. After many days spent fumbling around in the dark, her colleagues' hackles were up now. Their hunting instincts had kicked in and the adrenaline was pumping.

'Still no response,' Per said.

'What the hell.' Vera pulled her hands through her hair.

'What about the car then?' Marie said.

'It's a dark green Volvo Amazon, and it belongs to Dagny Holmström. She's Svensson's nearest neighbour out in Sunnansjö.' Karim shrugged. 'Before anyone gets too excited, I need to add that Dagny has dementia and receives in-home help from a caregiver four times a day. In addition, the search parties searched her house twice. The same applies to her outbuilding and garage. The car hasn't been used in many years but has never been de-registered. It's extremely unlikely that Dagny would be our perpetrator.'

'How did Amanda get the car?' Vera snapped, as if it were somehow Karim's fault that Dagny could be ruled out as the perpetrator.

'They're neighbours, you know?' Marie said. 'It probably wouldn't have been very hard for her to get it out of the garage. It's less than five hundred meters to Dagny Holmström's house.'

'I understand that, but what the hell would she be doing in the car? What would she have it for?'

No one responded.

'I'm sorry, but what exactly happened?' Sofia's voice made everyone turn to their screens.

'Oh, my God, I'm sorry, Sofia.' Marie's hand flew up. 'We forgot to brief you.'

Sofia had never felt so neglected in her whole life. As if it wasn't enough that she had been stripped of her regular duties and a new person brought in to replace her. Now they had completely forgotten she existed.

'A dog owner found Amanda Svensson in the driver's seat of the car we're talking about. She had driven through the road closure gates and down a steep pond embankment near Drömme and crashed into a pile of stones a few kilometres from the place they were searching when she disappeared. She had several broken bones and a serious head injury. The car seemed to have rolled several times. In addition to that, she was severely hypothermic when she was found. If she hadn't been so appropriately dressed to participate in the search party, she would be dead.'

'That doesn't make any sense,' Sofia said, shaking her head. 'What happened?'

'Still unclear.' Johan leaned back in his chair and adjusted his man-bun. 'We're getting the car towed and we have people at the site, but the terrain is really awful and it's difficult to access. So far, it's impossible to say whether it was an accident or a deliberate attempt to crash the car. In other words, a suicide attempt.'

'But what do you think happened?' Sofia repeated. She was having a hard time taking in what she had just heard. Why had Amanda stolen or borrowed a car from a neighbour, only to then drive it down an embankment several kilometres away?

'As I said,' Kaj explained, 'we don't know yet. Amanda is being kept sedated following an operation. Even if she survives, it's going to be several days before we can talk to her.'

Marie pulled the silver cross back and forth on her necklace as she always did when she was thinking.

'We need to talk to Anders again,' Marie said.

Vera glared at her.

'Really, you think so? That we should talk to Anders?'

Anna Sondell exaggeratedly cleared her throat and then straightened up in her chair. Even if Marie had kicked in a wide-open door, Vera's sarcasm wasn't helping any of them.

Vera exhaled a deep sigh.

'I'm sorry,' she said. 'I'm just so frustrated.'

The silence that followed in the library was palpably uncomfortable, even by video. Vera had apologised to Marie. What in the world was going on? Had her boss's personality changed beyond recognition?

Kaj gave a strained smile and looked right into the camera.

'I have tried to get ahold of Anders Svensson several times but can't reach him. According to the doctor, he's had quite a shock and is not available for questioning right now. He's in the ICU with his wife. They have a policeman outside the door 24-hours a day.'

Sofia heard Vera grunt next to Kaj.

'God damn it.'

Well, she wasn't completely changed at any rate, Sofia thought.

'What makes the whole thing even stranger is this.' Johan held a piece of paper up in front of the camera. It was a copy of a sheet of paper from a spiral-bound notebook, but Sofia couldn't make out what it said on it.

'We're checking fingerprints and DNA, but it seems likely that Amanda wrote it. And if so, what the hell are we dealing with here?'

'What does it say?' Sofia asked, annoyed. She was trying to read the text on the piece of paper, which kept moving around as Johan moved his arm.

'*Sorry, Anders.*' Johan read out loud. '*I had to try. You didn't give me any choice. I will always love you. Until death do us part.*'

Sofia leaned back. What could that mean?

'Try what?'

Johan took down the piece of paper.

'No idea, but it certainly sounds ominous.'

72

Fredrik stepped into the model unit and found a lavish kitchen with a stainless-steel refrigerator and black granite countertops. A fancy, polished-copper lamp with bare bulbs on arms spreading out in different directions hung over the kitchen table. A bowl of cherries sat on the table and there were several bundles of informational brochures about the building. On the wall opposite the kitchen counter, you could see animated images of what the units would look like. The rooms were as unimaginatively furnished as the model kitchen, but the message was clear. Rosenlund Tower was for people with deep pockets.

He didn't know why he had gone in. But as soon as he realised where he recognised SveAnd AB from, his feet had started moving on their own.

Fredrik picked up one of the brochures and flipped through it. Planning for the SveAnd project in Rosenlund Park had begun in the fall of 2019, and the building was expected to be move-in ready within two years. The images showed a smiling Anders Svensson breaking ground, shaking hands with politicians, and making statements like, 'Luxury amenities in the heart of trendy Södermalm.' It was hard to connect him to the man whose family's faces were all over the front pages right now. He must be going through such hell. Fredrik sincerely hoped they would find his daughters and his wife. He continued flipping through the brochure. The Rosenlund Tower was apparently just the first stage of a major development in the area. Fredrik couldn't help but wonder if any green space in the city would remain untouched. Those preschool children were going to have to go somewhere else to play in the snow next year.

A blond man his own age in a tight blue jacket and light brown shoes approached him holding his hand out.

'Dan Möller, real estate agent.' Apparently, his job was to hang out in the model unit waiting for someone to waltz in out of the slippery snow and buy an eighteen million kronor flat. Fredrik guessed that he was the first visitor today. 'Nice, right?'

'Indeed.'

'Where do you live now?'

'Östermalm,' Fredrik replied confidently, and the real estate agent didn't even try to conceal his glee. Dan Möller didn't need to know that Fredrik lived in a two-room flat without a balcony that he had inherited from his grandmother.

'Are you interested?' The man handed him a glossy brochure. 'There are a few units left.'

Fredrik didn't answer, but flipped through the brochure, which showed options of all sorts for the hardware, fittings, tile, and range hoods. It seemed like more than just a few of the units were available. From what he could see of the floor plans, only two were marked as sold. The penthouse and one of the units on the floor below that. There was only one large plan for the ground floor, which would house several restaurants.

The agent read over his shoulder.

'The penthouse just became available again.'

'Really, how come?'

Dan dropped his cell phone into his jacket pocket and gave a secretive shrug.

'That particular sale has been a bit of a mess but, as I said, it's just come on the market again.'

Fredrik flipped through to the page that showed the penthouse. Two floors with decks looking out in three directions. You would be able to see all of Stockholm from here. The asking price was northward of thirty million kronor. The agent came closer and beamed.

'The developer himself was actually going to buy it, but he's pulled out. It's a once in a lifetime opportunity. What do you say? Are you interested?'

Fredrik nodded and something in Dan Möller's eyes lit up. He put his arm on Fredrik's shoulder and invited him to sit down.

'Would you care for an espresso or perhaps a latte?'

73

When Fredrik left agent Dan Möller, it was with a bag full of brochures and his head full of the promise of enormous profits from a potential future sale and, reading between the lines, the promise of a steady stream of women who would be impressed by the lavish pad. Fredrik had tried to fish for information about Anders Svensson and had concluded that Anders's moral compass left a lot to be desired. The agent hadn't exactly spelled it all out, but he did happen to let slip that the construction project was both behind schedule and significantly over budget.

Fredrik stood there outside the model unit gazing up into the snowy sky. The skeleton of the skyscraper almost made him dizzy. A shiver ran through him, and he pictured the huge sinking ferry in his mind, how enormous it seemed when you suddenly found yourself on the outside of it.

He thought about Niklas, his little brother, whose hand he had let go of on that night in the Baltic Sea and who was always in his thoughts. He had never given up hope. He pictured the other inflatable orange life rafts being tossed by the waves around them. Some of them battered, some of them filled with white bodies floating around inside. But they had been there, so close, when that big wave came, and Niklas was washed away by the masses of water. Fredrik just knew that Niklas had gotten into one of them. It simply had to be. Even though he was only a child, he was strong and a good swimmer and unlike so many of the other people that night he had not drunk any alcohol.

Two men in hardhats approached Fredrik, interrupting his thoughts.

'Are you looking for someone?' the older of the two asked. His voice sounded harsh and full of suspicion.

'No, I'm just looking. I'm thinking about buying a flat.' Fredrik held up the bag with the SveAnd logo on it and the man immediately softened.

'Oh, right. I'm sorry if I sounded rude. There's so many journalists running around right now we can hardly work. Jerzy Nowak, I'm the site manager here.' He shook Fredrik's hand, sounding genuinely sorry. Fredrik's fictional thirty-two million kronor would presumably be a welcome addition to the construction company's cash box. The other man stood silently at his side.

The site manager waved for Fredrik to tag along. 'Come in and have a look if you'd like.' His Swedish bore traces of some kind of Slavic accent, but his grammar was impeccable.

'Yes, I heard what happened to the developer's family. Super creepy. Is that why all the journalists are running around?' Fredrik asked Jerzy's back as he followed him in the gap through the perimeter fence around the site.

Jerzy nodded without saying anything more. Instead, he handed Fredrik a hard hat, which he put on.

'Which unit are you interested in?'

'The penthouse,' Fredrik lied, holding up the bag again as some sort proof that he was a genuine prospective buyer.

'Oh, it's available again?' Jerzy sounded both surprised and resigned at the same time. The phone in his pocket rang and he used his teeth to pull off his construction glove and then got the phone out. He exchanged a few brief words in what sounded like Polish and then waved to the younger man who had accompanied them.

'Show him around. I have to run over to the other gate and accept a delivery.'

The man nodded.

Jerzy raised his hand in farewell and trudged off across the snow-covered construction site. The younger man nodded for Fredrik to follow him.

'Tomasz.' He patted his chest. He looked around, seeming to wonder which direction they should go. 'The top?' He bent his neck and pointed to what would become the penthouse.

Fredrik nodded.

'I understand that the owners had planned to live there,' he tried, but Tomasz just shrugged as if that was news to him. Or maybe he didn't understand Fredrik's Swedish.

When they rounded the corner of the building, Tomasz turned to him and said under his breath, 'You write about Anders?'

Fredrik was just about to wave his bag of brochures around again when he realised that Tomasz was after something completely different. Tomasz looked around to make sure no one was around and then rubbed his thumb and middle finger together. Money. Tomasz wanted to be paid. He thought Fredrik was a journalist who had managed to trick his way into the construction site to snoop around. Fredrik deliberated with himself for a second. What did he actually stand to gain from bribing a construction worker for information about Anders Svensson? Didn't he have totally other things on his mind besides Sofia's investigation? Although on the other hand, what had happened did concern his best friend, too. Philip would have done this for his sake if the situation had been reversed. He had already done it the previous summer, helping Fredrik with information even though he would have gotten in trouble if that had gotten out. His hand moved to the inside pocket of his down jacket where he kept his wallet. Six hundred kronor was all he had in cash, but Tomasz seemed content with that amount. He indicated that Fredrik should follow him farther in among the construction office trailers and then leaned forward and whispered.

'They're getting divorced.'

'They were going to live there, in the penthouse? But now they're getting divorced?'

Tomasz nodded.

'Do you know why they're getting divorced?'

Tomasz grinned.

'Other women.' He shoved the bills he had received into his pants pocket. 'His wife. Not happy.'

74

When Sofia came up to the police station after lunch, Vera, Marie, and Kaj were still sitting in the library with their laptops. Containers of leftovers from a variety of take-out meals sat on the table. Kicki met her in the doorway with a downcast glance and then disappeared down the hallway. The search was over in Sunnansjö, and she didn't have anything to report to the investigation team at the moment. Sofia couldn't help but wonder what Kicki would come up with now so she could be near Vera while she waited to steal Sofia's job.

Karim and Per walked into the library right after Sofia.

'What are you doing here? I thought you were working from home?' Karim smiled and pulled out the chair for her.

'Only in the mornings,' Sofia replied, trying to sit down as graciously as she could. Kaj was on his way over to help her, but the look she gave him made him sit back down.

'What can I do?' Sofia opened her computer. 'I've called my way through almost all the tips,' she added when Vera glanced at her.

Kaj stretched out his long legs, leaned back, and clasped his hands behind the back of his head.

'I'll gladly take all the help I can get. Anders hasn't said a word since his wife was admitted to the ICU. If there's no change, the doctor wants to admit him to the psych ward.'

Vera pushed her reading glasses up onto the top of her head like a tiara and rubbed her face with her palms.

'I mean, it makes sense that the guy is not doing well, but it's fucking inconvenient that we are not allowed to question him. Without his and Amanda's testimony we're not going to get anywhere with this.' She pointed dejectedly to the copy of the letter that had been found in the car with Amanda. 'Kaj, I want you to talk to Anders as soon as the doctors say it's okay. And put a little pressure on them. We don't have all the time in the world to wait.'

'We can't get fixated on the car and the letter right now,' Marie said. 'That's not going to do any good anyway as long as we're unable to ask Amanda about it. Or Anders. It might not even have anything to do with Ellie's and Madeleine's disappearance,' she added. 'We have another lead that we need to make headway on: SveAnd's undocumented workers. Were the border police any help?'

'It was a dead end,' Per said, shaking his head. 'To be honest, I don't really know how we should proceed. We've accepted help from all the agencies we could. All we know is what Jerzy Nowak has told us. There were only a few of them in the beginning, friends of Jerzy's from Poland. But now it seems like batches of hundreds of people have been working for SveAnd and at other construction sites in the country. Most of them came to Sweden through people Jerzy didn't even have any direct contact with. The reason it was able to go on for so long is that they had a person on the inside who would tip them off about when to expect ID06 card inspections at the construction sites, a person whose name Jerzy absolutely did not want to reveal.'

'What's an ID06 card?' Sofia asked.

'It's an identification document that regulates employment, taxes, and so on. It's also used as a sort of timecard.'

'And the Polish man who threatened Anders didn't have one?'

'Jerzy couldn't answer that but probably not.'

Vera leaned over the table so she could see Per who was seated farthest from her.

'How did it go with the phone numbers from the cell tower dump?'

'I was finally able to reach the home-help services office. They have several cars that typically make the rounds around Sunnansjö at the same time. They have a large area to cover. There are a lot of old people who sit alone in their houses and need food and help with their clothes and hygiene. Each car has its own cell phone assigned to it, but I haven't been able to determine which people used which cars during the period in question.' Per took off his MoDo cap and bend towards the screen before putting it back on again. 'Only the unit manager and the group coordinators have access to the schedule. The unit manager is on long-term sick leave, and the two group coordinators were not available when I called. One of them was working half days and the other was out taking care of a client who had died and needed to be transported to the morgue. I've asked her to call back as soon as she can.'

'Is that all we have?' Marie was visibly stressed. Sofia knew that she needed to submit a report on their progress to prosecutor Anna Sondell by the end of the day, and they didn't have much to show for themselves yet.

'No, I've been in touch with the woman in Mellansel,' Karim said. 'Her name is Karin Vedin and she works for Jetpak.'

'Jetpak?' Marie asked, puzzled.

'A courier company. She had been to Bjästa to pick up a package that was supposed to be delivered the following day. She saw Madeleine Svensson walking along the road from the bus stop and stopped to ask her if she wanted a ride. It was snowing pretty hard, and it was at least a kilometre's walk from the bus stop.'

'Did she accept the ride?'

Karim nodded.

'Karin Vedin dropped Madeleine off at the driveway of the Svensson's house at just about exactly ten p.m.'

Marie nodded with satisfaction.

'And what about Karin Vedin herself?' Kaj asked.

'She went straight home. We checked with her husband, and he confirmed that she had come home at the time she said she did.'

'Then there's just that last phone number left,' Marie said. 'The burner phone.'

75

The coffee in the disposable cup had grown cold ages ago. The cafeteria on the ground floor of the hospital looked like an elementary school cafeteria. Bland, birch-veneer furniture and a long counter with trays where you could order various pre-packaged dishes that you then warmed up in a microwave in the room. A mother sat at the table next to Fredrik with her eight-year-old son, his leg in a cast from the hip down. They were each eating their own helping of storebought Karin's-brand lasagna. The yellow wrappers were still sitting on the table. The mother was picking at her food, but the son had a good appetite.

Fredrik had been upstairs with Ida for a while and had left her the now somewhat frozen tulips. At times she had been awake and had let him hold her hand, but they hadn't said anything to each other. The nurse had explained that they were gradually reducing the sedatives she had been on the first few days, which made her groggy. She had gone back to sleep almost immediately, and he had gone downstairs to get himself something hot to drink. And, to be honest, to be out of the way when Ida's parents and older sister came to be there for her move to the psychiatric ward.

His bag with the SveAnd AB logo on it, containing all the brochures for the Rosenlund Tower flats, sat on the table in front of Fredrik. He emptied it and spread them out across the table. He didn't actually know what he was looking for, or if Anders Svensson's missing family members had anything to do with the construction project. If they did, what would it be? He picked up his phone and googled SveAnd. A flood of pictures of Anders Svensson in front of various construction sites and buildings around Stockholm came up. A couple of pictures of him outside a church with tabloid headlines announcing his marriage to the much younger American-born Amanda Wilkins. Fredrik studied the photo. The age difference was obvious even to someone who didn't know the couple. Anders's thinning hair was combed back and the beginnings of a bald spot shone through as he leaned forward to kiss his bride. Amanda was thin as a reed with unnaturally large breasts and equally unnatural lips. The plunging neckline of her wedding dress evoked as sailor suit, but it was so low cut you could nearly see her nipples. Fredrik was no monk. Sure, he appreciated a pair of beautiful breasts just as much as any other man, but he had never understood men who were attracted to all that plastic. He thought about Ida. Her naturally tan face and long dark hair, which was also its natural colour. She was beautiful naked, both fit and curvy in all the right places.

He looked at the brochures again, trying to push the image of Ida out of his head. What had that construction worker said? That Anders Svensson's wife wanted to divorce him because he had been unfaithful. Fredrik looked at the picture on his phone again. Based on what he had read during the short time he had been sitting in the hospital café, Amanda Svensson had not come into the marriage with any fortune of her own, and it had recently been insinuated that Anders had been blinded by the young real estate student who had made a good match by replacing the wife he had been married to for almost thirty years. A Jeanette Svensson who had surely made a fortune in the divorce, but who clearly had drawn the short straw when Amanda had entered the scene. Could everything that was happening now be related to Amanda's and Anders's impending divorce?

Fredrik rubbed his face wearily. He reached for his cold coffee and drank up the last of it without tasting it. This was not his fight. He loved Philip like a brother. He should go get him and he should support him through all the terrible things that were happening, but he couldn't solve this for him no matter how much he wanted to. This was a job for the police, and he was painfully aware he was not a member of that profession.

76

Sofia sat in her office, flipping through the stack of tips, unable to focus. The sun shone in the window and the temperature had risen quickly. In just one day, the snow had started melting and dripping off the roofs. The investigation team had broken up from the library to continue working independently. She had called almost all of the remaining tips on the list but had been able to dismiss them right away. One person had realised it was actually a coworker's daughter they had seen, not Ellie. Another apologised and explained that her kids had called in a false tip to play a prank. Sofia had asked that last person to sit down and have a serious conversation with her kids. Making false tips to the police or prank calls to 911 was the beginning of the sort of disrespect for society that she had seen escalate several times into something much worse. She had worked as a youth engagement officer for a year during her time in Stockholm and was well aware that prevention work with children and teenagers could make the difference between a law-abiding life and a life in the clutches of the criminal justice system. Oddly enough, many parents refused to recognise this.

She still had a few numbers left to call, but she did not plan to stoop to contacting the person who reported seeing 'an unknown dark-skinned man'. Let Vera say whatever she wanted to later.

There were still fifteen minutes to go until the afternoon meeting. Despite the fatigue that felt like a sandbag over her eyes, she felt restless.

She picked up the phone and was about to call the next person who had left a tip when Fredrik's number appeared on her screen. She let it ring a couple of times before answering. Didn't want him to think she had been waiting for his call.

'Hjortén.'

'It's Fredrik.'

'I can hear that.' Her snippy tone was unnecessary, or maybe it was absolutely necessary. She couldn't decide. What had he actually done to her besides ask for help? At the same time, jealousy burned within her. Sofia had to remind herself of the situation Fredrik was in. His best friend's girlfriend was missing, and his own girlfriend was in the hospital after attempting suicide. The last thing he needed was her adolescent nonsense. She cleared her throat.

'How are you?'

'Terrible. Ida mostly sleeps, but I met her sister. Her parents are on their way, too. We're going to move her to the psych ward this afternoon.'

We. Fredrik and his new family. The thought that he was cherished by a new family who had welcomed him into their warmth made it hard to breathe. Not having any close family members was something they had in common, a unifying starting point. They had shared a pride in their solitude. Now he was abandoning that, becoming part of something else. Sofia pictured him having coffee with his in-laws, Christmas Eves with tons of children, charter vacations to celebrate milestone birthdays, and a rotating schedule of holiday celebrations with the relatives. All the things she had wished for growing up. A family without alcohol-addled fights at every holiday. She couldn't help but feel disappointed that Fredrik was abandoning her in her orphanhood.

Although, what did she think was going to happen? She was expecting a baby with another man. Fredrik was entirely free to go make a life with someone new. After all, she was the one who had ended their romance last summer.

'Don't be mad, but…' Fredrik sounded hesitant. 'I happened to stumble across a little information about Anders Svensson.'

The melancholy tenderness she had just been feeling evaporated.

'You happened to stumble across information?'

There was silence on the phone.

'Damn it, Fredrik. When will you get it? You're not a cop. You've never been a cop. Let us do our job. No good will come from you running around playing detective. Didn't you learn anything last summer? You nearly fucking died!' Her tirade was long and contained way too many swear words. Sofia realised to her horror that she sounded like Vera.

'I didn't do anything illegal, I swear. I just chatted a little with some people at the building Anders Svensson is building in Rosenlund Park.'

'Why?'

'I don't know. For Philip's sake, for the family's sake… for your sake. Do you want to know what I found out or not?'

Sofia gave an exaggerated sigh. Partially to convey her displeasure, partly to conceal the tears that were lurking, threatening to erupt from the lump in her throat. *For your sake.* He wanted to help her. The thought touched her and irritated her at the same time.

'Yes, let's hear it.'

77

Kicki was leaning over Vera, who sat at one end of the long conference table in the library. Sofia had to fight to keep from staring at them.

Vera Nordlund, who had preached to her about the importance of not mixing her personal and professional lives, and Kicki Bjurvall. Could it really be true, as Eva said, that they were seeing each other? Kicki had gone from being a valued colleague to a person who Sofia intensely disliked. Not only was Kicki going to take her job, she was also going to steal the mentor that Sofia imagined Vera had been to her over the years. Per followed her gaze and leaned in closer.

'So you know, too?'

Sofia jumped.

'Know what?'

Per grinned and was about to say something more when Marie took her seat at the other end of the table and began the meeting.

'I'm a little upset.' Her voice sounded stern. Sofia guessed that this was the closest Marie could come to sounding angry.

The others' eyes turned towards Marie, but Vera and Kicki hadn't heard her start the meeting and were still sitting at the far end of the table chatting.

A bang suddenly made everyone jump. Marie's palms smacked into the tabletop so hard that Johan's coffee cup sloshed over. Apparently when push came to shove, the mild-mannered Marie Fransson was not so mild after all.

Vera sat as if turned to stone.

'Do you two have anything you'd like to share with the rest of us about the investigation? Or does it somehow not matter to you that we're fumbling around in the dark and time is getting away from us?'

'I apologise…' Kicki began, but was immediately interrupted by Marie whose palms were still on the tabletop, her eyes locked on Vera.

'I do not want apologies. I want results.'

There was dead silence in the room.

Marie's eyes seemed like they might burn holes in Vera. Kicki slunk away out of the room and carefully closed the door behind her. Marie and Vera glared at each other for a moment before Marie sat down and continued in a calmer tone.

'We need to act faster, better, smarter. Ellie's and Madeleine's lives are on the line.'

Karim raised his hand to indicate that he had something to say.

'The burner phone is owned by Albin Nygren. He's sixteen years old and lives with his parents in Vik, not far from Sunnansjö. It turns out that young Albin sells Rohypnol in his free time and uses the burner phone for that.'

Marie took a deep breath in through her nose and closed her eyes.

'I've already called my way through all the tips,' Sofia added quickly, before Marie had another nuclear meltdown. She glanced over at Vera, who sat pouting, her cheeks flushed and her arms crossed. Everyone in the group was used to her leading the meeting rundowns and especially doing any yelling that needed doing. Normally, Sofia would have felt sorry for her, or at least taken her side, but right now she felt a smug sense of schadenfreude that Marie's sharp reprimand had affected Kicki, too. Although however satisfying it was, internal conflict didn't benefit anyone. Especially not the two people whose lives were in danger. If they were even still alive.

'The tips didn't lead to anything, but I have something else,' Sofia said. 'I have learned that Anders and Amanda Svensson's marriage was not at all as stable as Anders wants it to appear.' She avoided saying where she had obtained the information from, and to her relief no one asked. 'They were going to buy the penthouse in SveAnd's new building in Rosenlund Park in Stockholm, worth over thirty million kronor. Very recently, they changed their minds and no longer wanted it. It appears that they're getting divorced. The reason is reportedly that Anders was unfaithful.'

Her colleagues looked at her without saying anything. Everyone's thoughts kicked into high gear. Kaj was the first to find his tongue.

'So, Amanda could have a motive to want to harm Anders. Could she have arranged the kidnappings, but then something went wrong? Maybe that's why she wrote the letter and drove over the edge of the embankment?'

Maria clicked on her computer and then read aloud, '*Sorry, Anders. I had to try. You didn't give me any choice. I will always love you. Until death do us part.*' She fiddled with her silver cross with a faraway look in her eyes. 'That could be.'

Kaj leaned forward with his elbows on the table. This was his territory. In her whole police career, Sofia had never met anyone with as keen an ability to see motives and potential scenarios as he had. Kaj intertwined his fingers and looked at Marie as he continued.

'With Amanda as a potential perpetrator, we could be dealing with both a financial motive and a revenge motive. Suppose she finds out about the infidelity, wants to divorce Anders, but he refuses. Maybe they have a prenuptial agreement? Maybe he tried to take custody away from her? She stages a kidnapping of Ellie, plays the grieving mother who takes part in all the searches and then plans to disappear with her daughter. But then something goes wrong.'

Marie nodded enthusiastically.

'Just because Amanda claimed that she had no idea that the company was having financial difficulties doesn't necessarily mean that's true. Maybe she knew that SveAnd was going bankrupt and wanted to get her share out before it was too late? She may have needed the money to start a new life with her daughter.'

'Then why hasn't there been any ransom demand?' Karim looked sceptical. 'And Madeleine still doesn't fit into the picture. What reason would Amanda have to kidnap her?'

'Maybe she knew something about the plan and threatened to give Amanda away?' Marie suggested.

Karim bit his lower lip sceptically and shook his head.

'I haven't found any evidence in the phone records that Amanda called or texted Madeleine. Or vice versa. How would Madeleine have found out that Amanda was planning to kidnap her own daughter if they hardly ever socialised?'

'Maybe she was somehow in the way? Needed to be cleared out of the way for the plan to come together?' Marie continued and received a nod of encouragement from Kaj.

'Well, I don't know...' Karim looked at Sofia. She agreed with him. There was something off about that theory.

'Amanda has an alibi for the night Madeleine disappeared.'

'She could have had an accomplice,' Marie said.

That wasn't impossible. But Amanda had seemed genuinely upset the times they had talked to her, Sofia thought. Was it really possible to fake that level of anxiety?

'Although, would Amanda really risk anything happening to her daughter?' Karim said. 'I mean, if she's involved, someone else must be looking after Ellie. She can't have hidden her and left her alone without being able to check on her?'

'Maybe she didn't take any risks,' Per said. 'Someone she trusts completely could be taking care of Ellie.'

'But that still doesn't explain Madeleine's disappearance,' Sofia insisted.

'Not yet,' said Vera, who had been silent up to this point. 'But this is good, really good. We could have a credible motive here. Karim, find out everything you can about any prenuptial agreements or family law or social services documents. And check if anyone has filed for divorce. Kaj, can you assist?'

Kaj nodded.

'We absolutely need to keep it out of the press that the woman in the car was Amanda Svensson. If there is a possible accomplice, we don't want to scare them off.'

Sofia didn't want to think about what that would mean for Ellie and Madeleine.

'Per,' Vera continued, 'I want to know who uses those three home-help services phone numbers. Today.'

She looked at Sofia, whom she obviously did not intend to give any of the credit to, even though she was the one who had provided the information that led them down this new path.

'You continue with the tips as they come in.'

78

Fredrik was late. Afternoon had become evening. He had waited in the cafeteria for as long as possible, hoping Ida's parents would have time to help her move into the new ward and then leave. He didn't want to see them, not yet.

He left Söder Hospital behind him, crossed the Ring Road, and took the elevator up to Psychiatry. When it stopped on Ida's floor, his phone vibrated in his pocket, and he saw that it was Philip. He stepped out and answered.

'Hi, I've been trying to reach you. How are you doing?'

'Fredde…' His voice, which was usually more monotone than most people's, was now completely flat, almost hollow.

'Why haven't they found her?'

Fredrik closed his eyes. He didn't care if other people saw him standing there with his eyes closed in the middle of the hospital hallway. There was room here, if anywhere, to display feelings of sadness and dejection.

'I don't know.'

He wanted to comfort Philip but didn't know what to say. All the words felt empty and just like his friend he had no control over what was happening right now.

'I'm sure Sofia and her colleagues are doing everything they can.'

He pictured Sofia, her unnaturally large belly and slender body, the wrinkle between her eyebrows when she concentrated. He knew she would do everything in her power to find Madeleine and Ellie.

A powerlessness came over him. How could he be enough to support both Ida and Philip? He felt the familiar itching blossom over the backs of his hands. What did other people do when life fell apart around them? How could you survive when you couldn't drug away the feelings of total impotence and insufficiency? He realised that he didn't have anyone to ask about that. Ida was the only one he could talk to. She was strong. Wise in a way that made him believe it was possible to cope with life and everyday issues. But now she had succumbed, too. She had shown that she didn't know how to resist the seductive allure of getting rid of whatever was bothering her soul. During the years Fredrik had spent being shunted around in psychiatry, he had seen hundreds of examples of people falling apart from grief. They were all trying to run away from something that was impossible to get away from. Maybe that was the lesson life was meant to teach, how to deal with and survive adversity? The philosophical reasoning took him by surprise.

Suddenly he realised that he was disappointed in Ida. She was the one who had urged him to dare to face the world and his own feelings of loss and loneliness without pills. But then she herself had given up. Sofia, on the other hand, stood strong through it all. She had listened to him, let him tell her about his grief and his belief that Niklas had made it up into a different life raft, that he had survived. But unlike Ida, Sofia hadn't let him brood. She had listened but not participated. Like a rational person would. Like someone who knew that what he believed was impossible would, he realised. Maybe Ida had never believed that Niklas survived either. Maybe she had just wanted to make him happy, to give him a false sense of happiness that would end in an even bigger emotional crash than if he realised he had been wrong from the beginning. That was what Sofia was trying to give him. The truth, however horrific it might be. Maybe that was what he needed to move on with his life.

'Hello?'

Fredrik had forgotten that Philip was still on the other end of the line.

'I'll come and get you as soon as I can.'

'Okay.'

Philip mumbled something in closure. Didn't ask anything about Ida or how she was doing. Fully preoccupied with his own anxiety.

Fredrik hung up and stood there outside Ida's door.

He heard several voices from inside, forced laughter. Ida was awake. He was going to meet her family now. See their accusing looks and feel the snare of conscience tighten even harder around his neck. He didn't want to.

It would be so easy to just turn around and walk away, not have to deal with all the difficult stuff. Although Ida deserved more than that.

Fredrik stood for a moment with his hand on the door handle, urging himself to go in.

Then he turned around and walked back towards the elevators.

79

'Calm down.' Kaj tried putting his hands on her shoulders, but she backed away. He closed the door to the tiny room that served as his borrowed office. 'Lower your voice.'

The afternoon meeting had dragged on and it was already pitch black outside the window.

'But isn't it completely fucking unbelievable? I provide a tip that could mean a breakthrough in the investigation, but I'm not allowed to help investigate it.'

'It has nothing to do with your abilities as a detective. Vera probably just wants to keep you safe and doesn't want you running around questioning a bunch of people. You know, I think you should go home to the flat, run yourself a bath, and unwind for a while.'

'What the hell, Kaj! I'm pregnant, not sick.' She had repeated that sentence hundreds of times the last several months but had become increasingly less convinced of how true that was the more her belly grew. Maybe she wasn't sick, but her body was really exhausted. Everything in her cried out to lie down, close her eyes, and rest, but she wasn't planning on doing that just because Vera and Kaj told her to.

Kaj held up his hands to signal that he wasn't going to force anything.

'You do what you want. I promised I would help Karim investigate the Svensson's family situation.' He pointed to a sticky note on his desk. 'That's the 24-hour number for the social services office in Danderyd. You can start by calling them and finding out if they have anything on the family.'

Sofia looked dejectedly at the sticky note. All of the sudden that bath was starting to sound very tempting.

Kaj smiled and yanked the sticky note off his desktop.

'Oh, just go home.'

Sofia opened her mouth to protest, but exhaustion was already tugging at her eyelids and it didn't take much to let herself be persuaded. The draw of the sofa's red upholstery was so great that there was no resisting it.

–

Ten minutes later, Sofia sat sunken in among the sofa cushions, staring at the TV, which was not on. The remote control was too far away for her to reach. She thought about Anders. Unfaithful cheater or not, she felt monumentally sorry for the man who was sitting alone by a hospital bed waiting for word on whether his wife would survive or not and if his daughters would be found alive. And even worse, maybe he had come to the same conclusion they had, that the whole thing might have been staged by Amanda. No human being deserved that agony. It wasn't so hard to understand that Anders was on the verge of a mental breakdown.

She picked up her phone and dialled the number for the landline and then Philip's cell phone. No answer. She called Tord, who answered right away.

'How's it going?' she asked.

'Just fine. I went over with a little food and some smokes for him this afternoon. He still seems okay anyway, I must say.'

Sofia wondered how the hell Tord could tell if Philip was okay when he hardly talked to anyone, but Tord had a knack for reading people. She trusted his judgment.

'I don't know when I'll be able to make it over. The investigation is taking a lot of time right now.'

'No worries,' Tord reassured her. 'But promise me that you're taking care of yourself and the little girl.'

Sofia smiled.

'I promise.'

They hung up and she closed her eyes. Everything felt sore and achy. She pulled her hands over her stomach. Underneath her left breast she felt the bulge that was the baby's butt. Her touch caused the little one in there to move, and through her shirt she saw a foot bulging out on the opposite side. Purely theoretically, she knew the baby could come at any time since it had already dropped, but the midwife had explained that it was possible she might go past her due date since this was her first baby.

Sofia looked at her computer bag in the front hall. If she had had the energy, she would have felt angry again, but the energy was not there. Everyone had been put to work except her, even though she could help the investigation in a lot more ways than just going through meaningless tips. But Vera obviously didn't want her out in the field.

Her thoughts swirled around in her head like drunken teenagers at a music festival. Every blink of her eyes grew longer and longer.

By the time Kaj came home, she had been asleep for several hours on the sofa.

Saturday, 29 February

80

The morning meeting was cancelled, and Sofia had slept until nine. For once, she had been hungry when she woke up. After two grilled sandwiches, a big cup of coffee, and a long shower with scalding hot water she had felt so refreshed that she had even put on a little mascara before she left for work.

Sofia sat down at her desk and tried to find a comfortable position. She had just managed to get her feet up onto an adjustable highchair she had stolen from the play corner in the lobby, which functioned exceedingly well as a footstool, when Karim's face appeared in her doorway.

'The divorce petition was submitted at the end of January to Attunda District Court, but with only Amanda Svensson's signature.' He waved a piece of paper. 'It was withdrawn automatically when no administration fee was paid. There's a prenuptial agreement,' he continued. 'Amanda doesn't get anything in a divorce until after seven years of marriage. They have only been married for six years.'

'So it could have to do with money?' Sofia said, scratching her neck. 'Or maybe Anders threatened that he would take Ellie away from Amanda if she tried to go through with the divorce?'

Karim murmured his agreement.

'I'm trying to reach Amanda's parents to see if they were aware of the infidelity and the divorce plans.'

Sofia nodded and Karim attempted to proceed down the hallway but stopped and dutifully asked if she needed any help with the tips. Had it gotten to the point that even he, who had never made any distinction between men and women, thought she needed help just because she was pregnant? She thanked him but waved him away.

Sofia opened the investigation on her computer and clicked through the various memos and witness statements. Like everyone else in the investigation group, she was painfully aware that the clock was ticking. Madeleine and Ellie were still missing without a trace. Amanda was fighting for her life in a hospital bed and wasn't able to tell them anything. If she had an accomplice, there was a risk now that the accomplice was sitting around waiting for instructions that would not come.

Her cell phone vibrated on the desk. The switchboard number appeared on the screen.

'Hjortén.' She decided to keep the conversation brief in case Eva had called to gossip some more.

'There's a lady here looking for you. Judith Nordin, I'll put her on.'

The old woman in Drömme whom Eva had asked her to call. It had completely slipped her mind. There was a click on the phone.

'I apologise for not getting back to you,' Sofia began. 'We've been pretty busy here.'

'When do you think you can come out?' a surprisingly steady voice asked. 'I think something might have happened to my neighbour Ingegerd.'

Sophia squeezed the phone between her cheek and shoulder to look at her watch.

'Would it be all right if I come over now?'

If she left right away, she could get to Drömme and back before the afternoon meeting. She couldn't just sit here and stare like some bloated wallflower while everyone else was toiling away on the investigation. Even if this wasn't a priority task, it was real police work. It had happened that they had found people who had been dead for several weeks in their houses out in the countryside. Usually, the neighbours were the ones who first raised the alert about mail overflowing in the mailbox and such. Might as well deal with it.

Twenty-five minutes later, Sofia pulled in outside a neatly shovelled home in Drömme. The front steps had been swept and sanded and planter boxes hung on either side of the steps with heather and little angels in them. She climbed the stairs and rang the doorbell. She heard light footsteps inside immediately.

'Sofia Hjortén, Örnsköldsvik Police,' she said when the door opened. 'Are you Judith Nordin?' She held up her police ID so the old woman could see it. Judith leaned forward and put on a pair of reading glasses that hung on a rhinestone-studded chain around her neck to study the identification carefully. When she seemed satisfied with her scrutiny, she took a step back and showed Sofia into her front hall.

'Okay, dear child. You look like you're about to explode. She pointed to Sofia's down jacket, the zipper on which – sure enough – was no longer fully up to its task. They went into the kitchen and Judith gestured for Sofia to have a seat on the kitchen sofa bench. There were several plates of freshly baked cinnamon rolls on the table. The whole house smelled like the baked goods case in a Pressbyrå newsstand and to her surprise, Sofia felt the craving for a roll. Judith prepared the coffee in silence and then set a cup on a saucer next to Sofia on the sofa bench and held out a plate of rolls.

'Help yourself now. Both you and the baby need strength before the export. I'd say two days max, maybe three.'

'Until what?'

'Until she arrives, obviously.'

Sofia stared at Judith.

'Well, don't look at me like that,' Judith said with feigned indignation. 'I birthed five children myself. And that little girl,' she pointed to her belly. 'She'll be out before the week is over.'

Sofia couldn't help but smile at the old woman, who seemed more with it than she felt herself at the moment and apparently knew what she was talking about when it came to childbirth.

'My due date isn't until 18 March.'

Judith scoffed, took a bite of a roll, and then nodded, as if she were impressed with her own pastry. She took her time chewing and then drank a sip of the black coffee.

'You have that swelling in your face that means it's almost time.'

Sofia felt her stomach sink with worry. Obviously she had grasped that the baby was going to come out eventually, but the notion – according to self-proclaimed midwife facing her – that it might happen in only a few days made her nervous. She looked down at the coffee grounds that remained in the bottom of her cup. Would she really be a mother in only a couple of days? And how was it that she was only realising this now? She pushed aside those thoughts to focus on Judith.

'So, you were worried about your neighbour?'

Judith nodded and craned her neck a little so she could see out the window.

'Yes, Ingegerd. She lives in that white brick house down the hill there.' She pointed and Sofia began trying to get up from the bench to see, but Judith waved her hand impatiently for Sofia to sit back down again.

'There's only one white brick house. At the bottom of the hill down there. You can't miss it.'

Sofia stood up now and looked out the window. The house was so far away that she needed to squint to see it.

'How in the world can you see that from here?'

Judith pointed casually to a pair of binoculars on the windowsill.

'The lights are on all the time over there. The home-help person comes, but I don't see Ingegerd. Usually they wheel her out onto the front porch for a while when the weather is nice. Old people need fresh air, too, you know.' She glanced at Sofia as if this would be news to her.

Judith Nordin might not be so with it after all.

'But if the caregiver is there, then it's probably nothing. They probably just forgot to turn off the lights. Have you been down there and knocked on her door?'

Judith shook her head.

'We don't get along.' The statement was short and unemotional.

'And yet you called the police?'

The old woman scoffed.

'Yes, of course.'

Sofia tried to change her position on the kitchen bench. She set her coffee cup down next to her and looked around for the gloves and hat she had set down. It was more of a rule than an exception for neighbours to keep tabs on each other out in the countryside, but unfortunately it was common for the elderly to get it into their heads that something was wrong, but it would turn out that the neighbour had left them both their phone number and their keys because they were going to the Canary Islands for two weeks. Even so, every time the police needed to go and check.

'I'm sure your neighbour's fine, Judith, but I'll stop in on my way back to the station and knock.'

'You won't go in?'

'I can't just walk into someone's house just because I'm a police officer. We need a warrant or probable cause to believe that something has happened to the resident.'

'And my word isn't enough.' This time, Judith looked genuinely offended.

'I'm afraid not.'

Judith pursed her lips and shook her head.

'Well, then I suppose I'll have to go down there myself and break in.'

'You will not do that.' Sofia raised her index finger in warning.

Judith stared intently at her for so long that Sofia felt forced to look away.

'Do you know what, let's do this. I'll go down there and knock. If I don't get any answer, I promise I'll call the home-help service when I get back and ask them to come out and check. They have the key and are allowed to go in. Will that be all right?'

Judith nodded reluctantly.

—

Sofia parked her car in the driveway and sat there for a bit looking at the house. The single-storey house was made of white brick with dark brown wood panelling above that. The yard was not as well tended as Judith's. There were snow-covered geraniums in the window flower boxes and the walk from the mailbox to the front door had not been shovelled. Sofia got out of her car and cautiously shuffled to the front steps, being careful not to slip, and rang the bell. When no one came and opened the door, she rang again, this time for longer. There was no sound from inside. She knocked hard on the frosted windowpanes in the door and then put her ear to the wood. She imagined that she heard a whimper from the front hall. She knocked again hard and waited, but no one came to open the door. She felt her pulse speed up. Had Judith been right after all? Had something happened to the old woman?

81

I'm standing at the kitchen sink preparing a bottle of formula when the doorbell rings. I drop it in the sink and drop to the floor. The doorbell rings again and I hear a woman call out. Crouching down, I sneak out to the front hall and reach for the old competition pistol I found in the garage.

Through the frosted windowpane in the front door, I see her silhouette moving away. As she passes the kitchen window, I catch a glimpse of flaxen-blonde hair sticking out from underneath a green knit cap.

The police. It's that pregnant cop I saw outside Anders's house. Why the hell is she here?

Is she going to ruin the whole plan just as it's all about to go down?

From the room father down the hall, I hear Ingegerd's slurred whimpers. She is far too weak to yell for help. All is quiet from the basement, far too quiet. I should have gone down there and looked, but I don't want to.

My pulse pounds in my ears. I wait a second and then move through the house towards the back. I put my finger up in front of my mouth when I meet Ingegerd's terrified gaze from the bed.

I'm not planning to give up voluntarily. That much is clear.

If she comes in, she'll get a bullet in the head.

82

Sofia had climbed up on a pile of snow to peer in the kitchen window. Nothing looked unusual in there. The refrigerator and freezer were closed, and the chairs were neatly pushed in around a pine kitchen table. There was a porcelain sugar bowl with a hand-painted pattern of wild pansies sitting on a crocheted purple lace table runner on the table.

She walked around the house. Her feet sank down a good thirty centimetres through the hard crust on top of the snow and it was hard to keep her balance. The blinds were drawn in the last kitchen window, but there was a good view into the living room at the end of the house. There was a sofa upholstered in a fabric with big yellow flowers and a shiny glass coffee table. There was a basket of yarn and crochet hooks on the coffee table. Across the room, she saw a TV in a dark-stained wooden bookcase. The whimpering could be heard more clearly here, short, guttural sounds.

'Hello?' Her word bounced off the windowpane and her breath left a steamy ring behind when she leaned forward with her hands shielding her eyes to get a better view in.

'Is there anyone home? It's the police,' she hurried to add so she wouldn't frighten Ingegerd if she was there.

She made her way around the corner of the house and stepped up onto the deck. The snow had melted on the side of the house facing the sun leaving a watery ice rink. Sofia held onto the white brick façade as she walked over to the patio door. It was locked. She looked in through the glass and saw a dining room set and several bookshelves made of the same type of dark-stained wood as in the living room. She stood still and listened. Everything was quiet.

She was just about to turn around and go back around to the front of the house when a loud bang made her jump. Her foot slipped on the icy deck, and she fell with a hard thud straight down onto the ice-covered deck without any time to break her fall.

Sofia got up onto one elbow just in time to see a black cat's butt disappear, darting out onto the frozen crust of the snow in the field behind the house. The cat door's plastic flap was still swinging like a saloon door in a wild west movie.

'Stupid cat,' Sofia muttered and tried to get back up again without falling over forwards. She held her hand around her belly and got up onto her knees first and then onto her feet. Nothing was broken and the baby was kicking like crazy in there.

She stood there for a long time listening for noises inside the house before she left.

There wasn't a sound to be heard.

83

Sofia parked the car outside the hospital and tried to drag her bruised butt out of the driver's seat. The wind felt almost warm, and she had to shield her eyes with her hand against the bright sunlight. The rock-hard grip that winter had on Örnsköldsvik had eased up in only a few days. The gritty snow piles outside the hospital entrance had begun to melt. Spring was on its way.

She had talked to Kaj on her way home from Judith's house. Anders had been sedated yesterday and had slept through the night. The doctors felt they could question him briefly now.

A little farther away in the parking lot she saw Kaj get out of his car and walk towards her.

'What are you doing here? You were supposed to stay at the station.'

'I was out driving around anyway and since you said you were coming here I thought I would tag along.'

Kaj gave her a tired look, but did not protest.

They took the elevator up to the ward and stopped at the nurses' station to ask which room Amanda Svensson was in. They were shown to a room at the end of the corridor. Sofia nodded to the uniformed colleague who was stationed outside the door.

Anders was sitting in a chair at his wife's side and convulsively clutching her hand when they came in. It looked like he was praying. I would be doing the same thing in his position, Sofia thought.

The young woman's face was swollen and bruised. If it hadn't been for her unnaturally long eyelash extensions, it would have been hard to locate her eyes. She had a large bandage around her head and there was tape around her mouth holding a tube in place that went down her throat. Her long, chestnut-coloured hair seemed to have been shaved off due to the operation, Sofia could see short stubble sticking out from under the bandage. Blue stitches were visible by one ear and continued down the back of her head.

Kaj stepped forward and put his hand on Anders's shoulder. He jumped as if he hadn't heard them come in. His eyes were bright red when he turned to face them. He looked like he had lost several kilos in the last few days and his skin was an unhealthy grey. His blond hair lay limply on his head, which was starting to go bald.

'They say it's a miracle that she survived.'

Sofia looked at the woman who looked more dead than alive.

'She was so hypothermic that she almost didn't show any signs of life when she was found. If she hadn't been warmly dressed for the search, she would have died from the cold.' Anders reported his wife's condition impartially, but his voice wavered considerably.

Kaj sat down on the chair next to him. Sofia looked around for somewhere to sit but didn't find any, so remained standing. Kaj took a folded A4-size piece of paper out of his jacket pocket and put it on Anders's lap.

'This letter was found in the car with Amanda. Do you have any idea what it might mean?'

Anders leaned closer to read. When he was done, he looked up at them and shook his head.

'We think Amanda wrote it,' Kaj said. 'As you understand, that could mean that she's involved or at least has some knowledge of what happened to Ellie and Madeleine.' He took back the piece of paper Anders handed him. 'We understand that there was a bit of conflict between your new wife and your older daughter. Can you think of any reason that Amanda would have staged something like this?'

Anders shook his head.

'Amanda would never hurt anyone. From day one she has tried to build a relationship with Madeleine and get her to be more involved in our family. And it's totally inconceivable that she would put Ellie in any kind of danger. No, Amanda doesn't have anything to do with this.'

'But the fact that the letter was found with Amanda indicates that…'

'Amanda doesn't have anything to do with this!' Anders interrupted. 'Find the person who did this instead of standing here and insulting my wife. Find my daughters!' He clutched his wife's hand so hard that his knuckles turned white.

'Of course we're also investigating the lead about the man who threatened you and your family, but we don't have any more to go on than that he was from Poland and was working under the table at your construction site. Is there really nothing more you can tell us? A name, anything at all?'

Anders shook his head.

'Did Amanda want to leave you?'

The question seemed insensitive given that Anders's wife was lying in the bed next to them, but Sofia had to ask it.

At first he seemed to want to deny it, but then apparently didn't have the strength.

'Yes, she wanted a divorce.'

'Why?'

He stared down at the yellow hospital blanket for a long while without answering. When he finally did, his voice sounded defeated.

'She had walked in on me with others.'

Sofia shifted from foot to foot, trying to find a comfortable position. Kaj got up and offered her his chair and she sat down heavily next to Anders. She clasped her hands over her belly and intentionally sought out eye contact with him.

'But you didn't sign the divorce papers?'

'No, I wanted to try again, but it's been hard for her to get over the infidelity.'

'How long have you known that she wanted a divorce?'

He looked away. His free hand picked little fuzz balls off the blanket.

'Not long. Since before Christmas maybe.'

'Did you get mad when she filed the paperwork?'

He shrugged.

'Mostly sad. Disappointed in myself. After my divorce from Jeanette, I had promised myself that I wouldn't cheat again.'

'Was Amanda trying to get sole custody of Ellie?'

Anders looked up at Sofia. His face was composed, but his eyes screamed fear. Maybe he realised what she was really asking about. Understood that there was a risk that their theory was right. He leaned in so close that she could feel his breath. It smelled sour, as if he hadn't brushed his teeth in several days.

'Are you not hearing me? Amanda has nothing to do with this!'

Kaj took a step forward, but Sofia raised her hand to indicate that that wouldn't be necessary.

'Anders, both of your daughters are missing. Time is passing and we're not getting any closer to an answer about what happened to them. Is there really nothing you can tell us? About the divorce, about the threat, about your company? Anything that could help us move forward?'

He looked out at the blue sky, visible through the cracks between the slats in the window blinds. The only sound in the room came from the machines that were keeping Amanda alive.

'No, nothing.'

84

When they got back to the station, Kaj went straight to Vera and Marie to report on how the meeting with Anders had gone. Sofia fetched a cup of coffee and decided to call the home-help service about Judith Nordin's neighbour before she forgot. The rest of the group was busy trying to piece together the puzzle surrounding Amanda and her possible involvement in Ellie's and Madeleine's disappearances. Real police work. The kind that Vera seemed to think Sofia was too pregnant to take part in.

She sat down with her coffee and put her feet up on the highchair underneath her desk. Sofia had just turned on her computer and looked up the number for the home-help service in Nätra, when there was a knock on her door.

'Come in.'

Kicki's round face appeared in the doorway. Her short hair was pulled back with a zigzag plastic headband.

'Vera and Marie were busy, so I thought maybe you wanted these in here?' She seemed nervous in front of Sofia and couldn't bring herself to say what she wanted to say. Instead, she took two quick steps into the room, dropped a stack of papers onto the desk, and then backed away towards the door again.

'Those are the lists of everyone who helped out with the search efforts. I spoke with the group that went with Amanda Svensson earlier. There's a memo in the investigation materials.'

Sofia nodded in thanks.

Kicki nodded back but remained in the doorway.

Go now, we don't have any more to talk about, Sofia thought. Everything about her body language must be screaming that she didn't want Kicki to stay. But Kicki didn't seem to be able to read the room.

'Right. Hey, there was one thing I wanted to discuss with you.'

No, thank you.

Sofia did her best to smile and look indifferent. She sat quietly hoping that Kicki would change her mind and walk away, but she had no such luck.

'Vera and I are a couple,' Kicki blurted out. As if she would change her mind if she didn't. 'I know that you two are close, or as close as a person can be to Vera.' She laughed and tried to make eye contact with Sofia, but when Sofia didn't start laughing with her, she grew serious again. 'We've been dating for a few months. It's not ideal, since I'm going to start working in the group, but I… I just wanted you to know.' Kicki was obviously fishing for Sofia's formal approval, but when she got a brief nod in response instead, she took the hint and left the office without saying anything more.

Sofia stared at the open doorway. So, what Eva had said was true. She was as shocked by the news as she was by the fact that Kicki thought it had anything to do with her. She reached for her phone and dialled the number she had just located, and it was answered almost immediately.

'Nätra Home-Help Services, Jelena Hagelin speaking.'

'Hi, my name is Sofia Hjortén and I'm calling from the Örnsköldsvik Police. Do you have a moment?'

The woman on the phone sounded stressed.

'You'll have to make it quick. We have two people out sick and one home with a sick child and hardly any staff on site.'

'This is regarding Ingegerd Westin. She lives at…' Sofia looked at the address Judith had written, 'Drömme 440 in Sidensjö.'

'Has something happened to her?'

'Her neighbour is worried about her. Apparently, she hasn't seen her outside for a while and the lights are on upstairs.' Sofia realised that this didn't sound particularly concerning.

Jelena seemed relieved.

'Oh, no, everything's fine with Ingegerd. Her daughter is visiting. They paused their home-help visits for a few weeks. It's hard to transfer Ingegerd into the wheelchair if you're on your own. That's probably why she hasn't been outside.'

'Okay, the neighbour was concerned.'

'You know how it is with old people.' Jelena laughed.

Sofia knew. How many of their work hours over the years had been spent searching for confused old women who had wandered off into the woods or confused old men who had forgotten which way the E4 went.

'Was there anything else? If not, unfortunately, I've got to run. Like I said, we're short-staffed here today.'

'No, nothing else. Thanks for your help.'

85

Fredrik knocked cautiously on the door. He had been contemplating what to do all day, agonising over the fact that he had wimped out yesterday. Finally, he had pulled himself together and set off for the psychiatric ward. When he walked into Ida's room, Jonna was sitting in an armchair with her legs pulled up underneath her. Ida lay on her side in the bed, sleeping with her mouth open and her long hair over her cheek.

'How is she?' Fredrik asked in a quiet voice.

Jonna took a deep breath in through her nose and put away the cell phone in her hand.

'Better. She's been up and she ate dinner and showered. You don't need to whisper. They gave her something to make her sleep.'

Fredrik sat down by the foot of the bed and put his hand on Ida's leg. She didn't react.

This room was much cozier than the hospital one had been. There was a blue accent wall at the head of the bead. The furniture was white and from Ikea. There were summer-themed paintings hanging on the wall. But although the ward overall might be less sterile than the one she had been in before, the missing handles on the windows told Fredrik that this was a place for people who could not be trusted.

He looked at Ida where she lay in the bed. Her chest rose rhythmically up and down and he imagined that she had more colour in her cheeks. She had been asleep the majority of the time since her suicide attempt. Fredrik worried what would happen when she woke up for real and reflected. Would she be mad at him? Blame him for what had happened and never want to have anything to do with him again? That thought was surprisingly painful.

He had lain awake at night thinking, pondering. There was nothing more he could do to ensure that he and Sofia would have a future together. She had chosen another man and was expecting a child with him. What they had had between them was irretrievably gone. Their whole romance had been like a fire that had flared up quickly and then been extinguished with a pot lid before anyone had time to understand what had happened. The frustrating attempts at conversation they had had when he was in the hospital after the attack had only made things worse. It was over now. For real this time. He would never be whole if he was always looking backwards and thinking about what could have been.

Jonna looked at him.

'She asked about you yesterday. Why didn't you come?'

'Honestly?'

She nodded.

'I didn't dare.'

Jonna got up out of the armchair, hung her jacket over her arm and stuffed her cell phone away in her purse. She walked towards the door.

As she passed Fredrik, she stopped and their eyes met.

'If you're going to be part of this family, Fredrik Fröding, you're probably going to need to brave up a little.' She nudged his shoulder with her elbow and then left the room.

Fredrik sat there, looking at the closed door. What did that mean? She hadn't sounded angry. More teasing. Almost happy. A part of this family. A part of a family.

He felt something flutter inside his chest. Yes, that's what he would be. They would live together, he and Ida. He would bet on her with his whole heart. Whatever happened now, he promised himself that he would be the perfect boyfriend. He would care for her the way she had cared for him, show her his appreciation for the amazing person she was. They would move in together, have children, and live a happy life together. If only she would have him and forgive him. Suddenly a thought struck him. He would propose to Ida.

The sound of the door opening brutally yanked him out of his romantic fantasies and back into the sickroom with its smell of cleaner and anxiety. A janitor pushed a cart in and asked if it was okay to clean. Fredrik nodded, got up and gathered up his things and pulled on his jacket. Before he left, he leaned over and kissed Ida on the forehead. She mumbled something in her sleep, and he caressed her cheek.

'I'll be back tomorrow.'

86

Sofia hurried down the hallway to the library. The sun had set. The days still seemed far too short given that it was already the end of February.

Vera waved Sofia in when she opened the door. A slight curl at the corner of her mouth told her that Vera was displeased that she was not on time, even though the afternoon meeting had been pushed back.

'Right, as you've seen, the shit is out in the media now. It's fucking amazing how fast stuff like this can leak.'

Per shook his head and Marie sighed loudly. Sofia had seen the newspapers and understood that Vera was referring to the fact that it was Amanda who had been found in the crashed car.

'No one,' Vera said, shaking her index finger at the group, 'no one says a word about the letter until we know more. We in this room are the only ones who know about that.'

'And the NFC,' Johan interjected.

Vera muttered something inaudible and then opened her laptop.

'Have we gotten any results back from them?' Marie turned to Johan.

'No, not yet.'

Kaj's eyes were locked on the tabletop in front of him. Sofia could see the gears in his head spinning at full speed. Criminal profiling was a sport of experience, he used to say. And if anyone had experience at it, it was him.

'What are we really dealing with here?' He pulled his index finger over his lips without taking his eyes off the tabletop. 'The

MO suggests that the kidnapper knows exactly what he's doing. Or we're dealing with someone wo is completely unconcerned about being caught.'

Kaj reached for the copy of the letter and held it up as if to underline what he had just said.

'The latter could indicate a desperate person, or a person who is acting under a great deal of emotional stress. Somone related. The former could mean that we're dealing with someone who has done this before.'

Vera looked at the piece of paper Kaj set back down on the table.

'Or both.'

Kaj nodded enthusiastically.

'Exactly. Amanda could have hired someone to perform the kidnappings. Someone who knew exactly how to do it. The motive might have been to pay Anders back for his infidelity and suck the last of his assets out of him before she left him. Maybe she was worried about a custody battle.'

The situation was looking worse and worse for Amanda, Sofia thought. She must be involved in what had happened in some way. And yet, it didn't add up.

'Would an experienced professional criminal really leave fingerprints all over the house?'

Johan gave her a look that was hard to interpret.

'That's exactly what I was thinking.'

'Either way,' Per said, 'it doesn't explain why Amanda drove the car off the cliff.'

'Or why she wrote the letter,' Marie added.

Johan cleared his throat.

'We were out at the scene before they towed the car and there was no sign there suggesting a struggle or that anyone had pushed the car over the embankment. The barrier gate on the road from Drömme had been forced and as you know Amanda was sitting in the driver's seat. So we can establish that this was not a staged accident. However, we can't rule out the possibility that Amanda could have driven off the embankment by mistake.'

Vera shook her head.

'Why would she have gone there in the first place and in Dagny's car?'

John shrugged.

'Maybe she was meeting someone there?'

Kaj picked up the copy of the letter again and looked at it for a long time.

'Maybe the person Amanda hired to do the kidnapping wanted more money and was trying to blackmail her? Maybe everything had become so complicated that she didn't see any way out besides taking her own life?'

'Not impossible,' Sofia said. 'But if the scenario is the way you describe and she arranged the two kidnappings that went awry, then committing suicide could be the equivalent of signing both Madeleine's and her daughter's death sentence.'

Vera got up and stood there in front of the whiteboard without writing anything.

'The only person who can tell us how it all fits together is heavily sedated in the ICU. It's so damned frustrating.'

Kaj shook his head.

'I talked to Amanda's doctor earlier today. Her head injury is very serious. She won't necessarily be able to answer question even if they do wake her up from the medically induced coma. There is a significant risk that Amanda's functioning will be severely impaired for the rest of her life. If she even survives.'

Sofia's cell phone rang. She stood up with a great deal of effort and left the room to take the call, which had come in through Eva at the switchboard.

'It's Judith Nordin.'

'I'm a little busy right now. Can I call you back later?'

Judith paid no attention to Sofia's attempt to end the call.

'Did you talk to the home-help service?'

'Yes, I did. There's nothing to worry about. Ingegerd's daughter is visiting.'

'What did you say?'

Sofia raised her voice and spoke clearly.

'Yes, I said that Ingegerd's daughter is visiting. She's probably the one you saw.' More silence. Sofia looked towards the door. She wanted to get back to the meeting. 'Well, if there wasn't anything else, then…'

But Judith interrupted her.

'Ingegerd doesn't have a daughter, does she?'

87

How could she survive? She's ruined everything, absolutely everything. Why couldn't she just die? I saw the car flip several times.

And the girl. I don't know what I want to do with her anymore. She's so beautiful. She deserves better than to have all this happen to her.

In just a few days, she has awakened something in me that I didn't think was there. Something that I never thought I would get to experience. When she's not sleeping, she sits with the teddy bear in her lap and watches the movie I put on for her, her movements sleepy, her thumb finding its way into her mouth. With her other hand, she rubs the bear's ear. All I want is to be close to her. I can't think of anything else anymore. Not the plan, not Anders, not anything.

I've gone soft in the soul. Maybe it would be better to just get rid of her and disappear?

To stop feeling all these feelings.

88

Per and Karim, who had families, had gone home for the day. It was already nine o'clock on a Saturday night. Everyone was exhausted. Vera had shut herself in her office and Kaj was sitting in his. Marie was on the phone with the prosecutor.

Sofia would have been more than happy to go home to her flat and lie down on the sofa, but her conscience objected. Instead, she sat down and dialled the number for Nätra Home-Help Services for the second time today. She had promised to take on the task from Per. None of the group coordinators had gotten back to them about who had used the cars and the phone numbers associated with them which had been moving around in the area around the Svensson's house at the times when Madeleine and Ellie had disappeared, even though the information had been requested more than 24 hours ago. If someone at the home-help service didn't pull the names out of the computer this evening, Marie was going to get a search warrant. They didn't have time to wait.

'Nätra Home-Help Services. This is Maja Mäkelä.'

'My name is Sofia Hjortén and I'm calling from the Örnsköldsvik police station.'

'Hi.' The young woman on the other end of the line suddenly sounded unsure.

'We're still waiting on some information from you about which individuals used the cell phone numbers that we sent over.' Sofia's tone sounded much gruffer than it needed to.

'Okay. I don't know if I can help you. Jelena's not here and Gunnel is out somewhere...'

Sofia took a deep breath.

'This is a murder investigation! If you don't produce the information, we're going to dispatch a squad car over there to pick up both you and that damn computer.'

Oh, my God. She really had turned into Vera.

She heard Maja gasp through the phone. She heard keys jangling in the background.

'Hang on, Gunnel just arrived,' Maja said, relieved. 'She has the password.'

'Right, well go get Gunnel then.'

Maja disappeared but returned right away with Gunnel.

'I apologise that we haven't gotten back to you,' the group coordinator began. 'Things have been really chaotic here lately.'

She logged into the computer right away. Sofia read out the telephone numbers and the dates in question. She heard Gunnel clicking frenetically with the mouse.

'Samuel Eriksson drove the car with the phone number that ends in 73, Johanna Wikner had the one with the number ending in 08, and Nina Sandberg the one with the number ending in 19.'

'Can you see what hours they worked?'

'All three worked the night shift on both Thursday and Saturday last week. The night shift starts at ten p.m. and ends at seven a.m.'

'Can you take a picture of the schedule and send it to me?' Sofia read out her email address to Gunnel. 'And one more thing while I have you on the line. One of your clients, Ingegerd Westin in Drömme has paused her home-help visits.'

'Yes, her daughter is taking care of her.'

'According to Ingegerd's neighbour, Judith Nordin, Ingegerd doesn't have a daughter.'

'Really?' Gunnel sounded unsure.

'Do you know how long the visits have been paused for?'

Sofia heard Gunnel tapping on the keyboard.

'Unfortunately not, but I can check with Jelena.'

'Would it be possible for you to do that now and call me back this evening?'

Gunnel promised and then they hung up.

Sofia wrote down each name and phone number on a sticky note and stuck them to the top of her computer screen. For many of her colleagues, this was the beginning of the most boring part of the job, comparing numbers and matching people to the locations they had visited. But for her part, she loved this. Her eyes flew over the screen, sorting out information from the jumble of numbers, hunting for connections, although it was hard to read in the blue light from the screen. When she leaned closer, her belly hit the edge of her desk. She hit the print command and waddled to the printer room as quickly as she could. She waited impatiently while page after page emerged.

'Sofia, can you come in here?'

Vera's voice echoed down the hall.

She prayed to God that this wouldn't have anything to do with Vera's private life. A few years ago, she had longed to be a part of her boss's inner circle. Now she wanted nothing more than to escape it. Vera asked her to close the door when she came in, but Sofia deliberately remained in the doorway with the printouts in her hand to show that she was on her way somewhere.

'I know that Kicki talked to you,' Vera said quietly.

'That's none of my business…' Sofia began, but Vera interrupted her.

'We're a couple. We started seeing each other last fall. I realise that I was on your case for the same thing not that long ago and I apologise. I didn't realise then how hard it was to abstain from someone you were in love with for the sake of your job. I appreciate that this is not Okay, but I don't know how to end it. I'm in love. I hope you can keep it to yourself until we've figured out what we're going to do.'

Sofia stared intently at the floor, or rather the part of the floor she could see beyond her belly. In all the years she had worked at the Örnsköldsvik police station, she had never heard Vera apologise, and now this was the second time in only a few days. And in love? Was that what Vera had just said, that she was in love with Kicki?

'Anyway, I wanted to tell you since you're not only an esteemed coworker but also a friend.'

Sofia looked up and into Vera's eyes, and then realised her mouth was hanging open. Who was this person, actually? It certainly wasn't Chief Inspector Vera Nordlund, whom everyone in the building went out of their way to avoid so they wouldn't get scolded. She had been replaced by a gentle, almost cheerful person who expressed her emotions and appreciation. Sofia wasn't quite sure how she felt about the transformation.

'Thanks,' was all she got out before she was able to quickly leave the room and carefully close the door behind her.

She hurried back to her own office, sat down in her desk chair, and put her feet up on the highchair. What was going on? Was everything going to change now? Her job, her career, her life. Vera was in love. She tasted those words and discovered that they were bitter. The same way that Daddy Kaj and Bonus Mom Mette left a bad taste in her mouth.

Sofia tried to steer her thoughts back to her job and spread the printouts that she had just fetched out on her desk.

She put the night Madeleine disappeared in one pile and the night Ellie disappeared into another. Then she started with the highlighter.

Pretty soon, she was able to determine that Samuel Eriksson had been the first one to bring his home-help service car into the area around Sunnansjö, but that had been a full two hours before Karin Vedin from JetPak report dropping Madeleine off at the house. Johanna Wikner had not been there until seven in the morning the following day. But one person had been exactly below the cell tower that covered the Svensson's house just a half hour after Madeleine had been dropped off. Sofia dove into the second stack of papers and started reading. There was the phone number again. The same night that Ellie disappeared.

It was Nina Sandberg's number.

—

Sofia stared at the closed bathroom door. Outside, she could hear her coworkers coordinating their departure. Their footsteps were quick and their voices amped up with adrenaline. After she had told Marie that Nina Sandberg had been near the Svensson's house at the times of both Madeleine's and Ellie's disappearances, it hadn't taken long to plan an operation. Gunnel at Nätra Home-Help Services had explained that Nina had worked for them for many years and often on the route that went by the Svensson's house on the way up to Dagny Holmström's place. Maybe she and Amanda had run into each other in some context?

Sofia closed her eyes and tried to take deep breaths. She had been feeling contractions since the afternoon but had ignored them. While she was searching through the call logs, she had felt two more and now there was blood on the toilet paper. Margit, the midwife on Ulvön Island, had said that was perfectly normal. It was a sign that the cervix was softening or something like that. Sofia hadn't listened that carefully. If she asked Kaj, he could probably give a whole lecture. But she decided not to say anything. There was no point in getting all worked up.

She flushed, washed her hands, and returned to her office. She barely had time to sit down before Marie appeared in her doorway.

'We're going now.' As she spoke, she adjusted her service weapon inside her jacket and secured the Velcro clasps on her body armour. 'I talked to Sondell and we received a search warrant for the house. If she has the girls then...'

Vera and Kaj walked past in the corridor behind her. Marie nodded to them. 'See you in the garage.'

The regional SWAT team had been called in and they, along with the local police intervention group, had been tasked with bringing Nina in. For her part, Sofia wanted nothing more than to go home. The adrenaline rush she had felt as she compared the phone lists had drained back out of her again just as quickly. She hadn't even tried to join the SWAT team. In an earlier life she would have fought tooth and nail to deploy to a location where they expected to liberate two people who were being held captive and apprehend the kidnapper. Now she couldn't think of anything else besides getting her boots off, putting her feet up, and closing her eyes.

'While we're gone, I want you to find out everything you can about Nina Sandberg. The motive is the most important thing right now. We've already established that she had the opportunity. Look for links between her and Amanda Svensson. Has she had any contact with SveAnd AB? Check if she had financial problems. Amanda may have offered her money to carry out the kidnappings. Look into her bank accounts, find out who she has dealings with. Check old boyfriends, girlfriends, and relatives who might be in our records.'

'I know what to do.' Sofia tried not to sound as tired as she was. 'Get going now and bring her in!'

Marie gave her the thumbs-up and hurried away down the corridor. Just a few minutes later, Sofia heard the cars' sirens as they left the garage at high speed, heading north towards Arnäsvall and Nina Sandberg's flat.

89

When Kaj came home to the flat, Sofia had already been asleep on the sofa for a few hours. Kaj had promised to call her as soon as it was all over and she had waited up as long as she could, hoping for good news, hoping Anders Svensson would be reunited with his children and that they be, at least physically, in good shape.

She heard Kaj sneak in the front door, hang up his jacket, and then proceed into the kitchen and get something out of the fridge.

Sofia got up and went out to him. He was leaning on the counter and emptying a can of beer in long gulps. Everything about his body language signalled defeat.

'How did it go?'

He jumped and started coughing, spraying beer across the counter. Kaj pounded on his chest with his fist and coughed another few times.

'You scared me.'

Sofia sat down at the kitchen table while Kaj wiped the counter and spread toppings on a couple pieces of crispbread. When he sat down, she saw how tired he was. She was surprised at how guilty she suddenly felt. She hadn't looked at it that way before. She had just been sulking about how she wasn't getting the fun work assignments anymore. Hadn't even thought about how Kaj was working around the clock while she lazed around.

'How are you doing?' Kaj asked.

She didn't say anything about the bleeding, just gave him a thumbs-up.

'So, let's hear it,' Sofia urged. 'How did it go with Sandberg?'

Kaj shook his head.

'It did not go at all. When we got there, she and her boyfriend were watching TV. They were totally high and both really drunk. There was a quite a commotion. They had a dog, too, a big asshole of a dog. It probably took ten minutes before they got a leash on it so Marie and Vera could go in.'

He took a bite of his crisp bread.

'Were Ellie and Madeleine there?'

Kaj shook his head and rubbed his forehead.

'We have no idea where the hell they are.'

He usually never swore, but Sofia understood him. It had been almost a week and half since Madeleine disappeared and almost a week since they discovered Ellie was gone. The hope of finding them alive was beginning to fade.

'Did you find anything else?'

'Beer, booze, marijuana in the ashtray on the coffee table, but nothing else. Nothing that suggests that Nina Sandberg kidnapped Ellie and Madeleine. Or rather, no indication that she had them in her flat anyway. We went through her storage unit in the basement, and we checked the homeowners' association's rental flat, but there was no trace of them. We have people on the ground now knocking on doors, but I find it hard to believe that they could hide a four-year-old and an adult woman in a densely populated residential neighbourhood without one of the neighbours seeing or hearing something.'

Sofia nodded.

'How about you?' Kaj asked.

At first she thought he meant her belly again, but then she realised Kaj was asking about the work tasks she had been assigned.

'Nina Sandberg is squeaky clean. Not even a speeding ticket. She's worked for Nätra Home-Help Services since 2007. No children, has never been married.'

'Well, she's definitely not squeaky clean,' Kaj muttered.

'She hasn't done anything that has come to our attention anyway. Where are she and her boyfriend now?'

'In custody sleeping it off. There was no point trying to question them tonight. Vera wants us to talk to Nina Sandberg first thing in the morning.'

Sunday, 1 March

90

Fredrik woke up to the sound of his mail slot opening and some junk mail falling onto the doormat. In all the years he had lived alone in the flat since his grandmother had died, he had been planning to put up a note saying he didn't want any junk mail, but he had never gotten around to it. His grandmother had loved browsing through the advertising leaflets and dreaming about buying lawn furniture or planting boxes despite the fact that they didn't even have a balcony. For later, she would say, when we have a place in the country. But there never did end up being a place in the county.

Fredrik pulled the covers off and lay there for a moment, feeling the coldness of the room waking his body up. He grabbed his phone and sent Philip a text. Philip responded right away. No news about Madeleine. Fredrik replied that he would come as soon as he could and that he hoped Madeleine would be back soon.

It was only seven o'clock so he would have time for a long shower and to go down to the grocery store to buy a freshly baked roll and some juice before he went to the hospital. He thought about this business about proposing, how ecstatic he had gotten about it yesterday. He had expected the feeling to pass overnight when he slept on it for a night, but it was still there. He would propose to Ida and they would become a family. Would she take his last name, or he, hers? Fredrik Niemi. No, his grandmother would not have liked that. His own father had agreed to take his mother's name to keep the Fröding line going.

And Fredrik should start working again. It was time for him to get back to living and forget about what had happened last summer. According to his psychiatrist, Torsten Bredh, it was important to belong to a workplace and to participate in the community. He wondered what it would be like to go back to work without the pills, to see everything clearly, be a part of the comradery, maybe make friends. In his head, he pictured showing off his wedding ring, that he was a married man with a normal life and a nuclear family. The rosy fantasy he had been painting for himself over the last 24 hours, however, was tarnished by his choice of workplace. He didn't want to go back to the passport office. Endless days helping people stand in the right place for the photograph, sign their names in the right place, take the fingerprint in the right place. He thought about what the policeman who had questioned Philip had said. That it was never too late. Could he pick up his police training again after so many years? Would he get credit for anything? He had actually finished everything except for his cadet training. Although the training had probably changed so much that he wouldn't get much benefit from what he had learned back then. He reached for his cell phone and googled police training. It started in the fall, rolling admissions. He had all the grades and qualifications. Oh, my God, should he do it? The physical ability test would be an ordeal. He had been in significantly better shape the last time he had done it. But on the other hand, he had several months to work out. It should be fine. He had always been wiry and had good stamina. Despite the abuse his body had endured due to all the pills, he felt strong. Of course they would ask about his scars. They would definitely do a background check on him and see if he was in their records. Or maybe they would only check if he had a criminal record? He didn't. The psychological test would be worse. Could they request his medical records from Torsten? No, that didn't seem reasonable.

Fredrik pulled the covers around himself again and rolled over onto his side. He could treat himself to a little while longer in bed if he skipped breakfast. They sold sandwiches in the hospital cafeteria. His bedroom door was open, and his eyes fell on the kitchen table. The thick A4-size envelope from Ida was leaning against the salt and pepper grinders. He might as well go grab it. He would read Ida's final words to him and then throw the letter away. It would symbolise the start of their new life. Fredrik got up, wrapped in his covers, shuffled into the kitchen, sat down on one of the chairs, and reached for the envelope. He opened it and let the contents slide out onto the table. There was a handwritten letter on top. There was no sign of the anger and disappointment he had expected to find. Ida's tone was calm and loving, matter-of-fact, but resigned. In an old-fashioned writing style, she professed her eternal love for him. He read her words several times. He felt the tears coming on. She concluded her letter with *your Ida*. At the bottom of the pages she had added: *Do what you want with this. I've been working on it for a while.*

He set the letter aside and picked up the stack of papers that had been in the envelope but flinched immediately when he saw the sticky note attached to the first page. Ida's handwriting.

Final Report on the MV ESTONIA Disaster.

91

Sofia was already awake when she heard Kaj's alarm go off in the bedroom. The baby had lain still almost the whole night, and it felt like the hard pressure just below her ribcage had eased a little. The bleeding had stopped, and she felt calmer. She had made coffee and two cheese sandwiches for their breakfast. When she saw how overwhelmed Kaj was by that small gesture, she realised how self-absorbed she had been lately. She was in such a good mood that she even let Kaj talk directly to her belly in that ridiculous baby voice for a long time.

When he was done, she poured the last of the coffee into their silver-coloured travel mugs, and then they headed to the police station. It was a bright sunny March day and she was looking forward to the short walk.

–

Nina Sandberg had already been retrieved from the holding cell and moved into an interrogation room with her public defender by the time they got there. Nina was in her fifties. Her face was puffy and red, and she had a wide grey streak in her brown hair. She had large bags under her eyes, and it looked like she had been crying. Her urine test had been positive for marijuana. None had been found in the flat and the prosecutor had already announced the summary imposition of a fine since Nina had confessed. It would amount to a tic mark in the criminal record and a fine adjusted based on her income. She would probably also end up losing her job, but none of this was their focus right now.

After Kaj had recited the usual phrases to begin the questioning session, he pointed to the microphone so that Nina would understand what was expected of her.

'You were arrested for drug offenses last night.'

Nina nodded, which caused Kaj to point to the microphone again.

'Yes,' she stated clearly.

'Do you know why we were at your house?'

'No.'

They waited her out for a while to see if she was just playing clueless, but she seemed to have no idea. She didn't look like your usual pothead, but she also didn't seem with it enough to have questioned why the police would have shown up at her house for no reason.

'Do you take drugs often?'

Most people who were arrested usually claimed that this was the first time, but Nina admitted right away that she had been using an increasing amount of pot and alcohol over the last six months.

'I suffer from rheumatoid arthritis,' she added as if that might win their approval.

'Where were you the evening of Thursday, 20 February?'

Nina thought back.

'At work, I think. Why?'

'And the night of Saturday, 22 February?'

'I was working then, too,' Nina replied without thinking about it. 'What is this actually about?' There was a mixture of irritation and concern in her voice. The perfect starting point for an interrogation.

'Which clients do you usually visit?'

Nina thought that over.

'If I was working at night, then it was the area around Sunnansjö. Yes, it was probably Ingegerd Westin in Drömme, then Lars-Erik. He lives on the road into Sunnansjö. Then Dagny. She lives up on the hill, as they usually say. You know, near where the old school is…' What little colour Nina had had in her cheeks disappeared the instant her synapses started working.

'The missing people?' She put her hand over her mouth. 'That's why you're asking about this. That girl and her sister…'

Kaj nodded but didn't say anything. He let the silence drive the confession. Nina's defence attorney looked at her.

'But, I wasn't…' Her sentence died away and Nina seemed to consider which statement would result in which consequences. Meanwhile, Kaj broke in. His voice was sharp.

'Tell us where they are, Nina. It will be easier for you if you tell us right away.'

Nina looked at her defender. He nodded for her to answer.

'I didn't…' The tears began to run down Nina's cheeks and she hurriedly rubbed her eyes.

'Did you need money to buy drugs? Was that why you agreed to do it? How did Amanda contact you?'

Nina vigorously shook her head.

'Who's Amanda? I have no idea what you're talking about.'

'Where are the girls, Nina?'

'I didn't…'

'A four-year-old's life is at stake. Tell us where you're hiding them.'

Kaj's voice was loud now. Not even Sofia would have dared to contradict him. Nina pulled away, scooting to the back of her chair.

'I don't know! I haven't done anything. It wasn't me.'

Kaj quickly leaned forward over the table.

'Who was it then?'

Nina went quiet but maintained the eye contact with Kaj. The tears poured out of her red-rimmed eyes. She inhaled a snotty breath. Sofia felt her heart pounding in her chest. There it was again, that intensity that she loved about her police job. They were close now.

'I think it might have been Jelena.'

92

Fredrik flipped back and forth through the papers without truly grasping what he was looking at. Everything was so familiar. He had read the Joint Accident Investigation Commission's report many times but had never dared to do what Ida had obviously done now: taken action. He knew why. Because if he did, there was a risk that he would get an answer that he did not want. Instead he had fixated on it, blamed himself, been dragged down into a bottomless pit from which only the pills had been able to pull him back out. The first few years after the disaster, he had completely shut down, acted out at school, cut school, hung out with the wrong people, pretended that he was Okay. An orphaned teenager who was besieged by reporters and people who wanted to ask what it had been like, how he had survived, what he had seen that night, and how did he feel now. In hindsight, it was a miracle he had survived. Not just that night on the MS Estonia but also the period that followed. He had stood on the platform at the train station many times, wondering. Would it all go away if he just took that step out? But he never did. He convinced himself that it was that last spark of life that kept him from taking his own life those times, but he realised that it was fear. He simply hadn't dared to do it.

Without his grandmother, it would never have worked. She had guided him back to life with a strict and loving hand. If she hadn't been there to pick him back up when everything fell apart, it wouldn't have mattered if he dared to take his own life or not. The pills would have taken the choice away from him.

He had never overdosed. Not more than blacking out, anyway. Usually in combination with alcohol.

He ran his hand over the pages that had been torn out of a spiral notebook and that he had found at the bottom of the stack of papers. Page after page in Ida's handwriting. They went with the printouts she had made. In addition to the pages from the Joint Accident Investigation Commission's report, there were excerpts from various articles and interviews. They were all about the rescue operation after the Estonia sank. Fredrik found lists of the survivors and notes that Ida had made about which hospitals they had been taken to, and which rescue vessels had received them. He found his own name on the list of rescued people who had been taken to Turku University Hospital. He was mentioned as the youngest survivor. There was no mention of Niklas.

At first he didn't really understand what all of Ida's notes meant. There was a long list of Swedish, Finish, and Estonian names with either an email address, a phone number or the word Facebook noted next to them. It wasn't until he compared them to the people who had been on the ferries that had plucked people out of the Baltic Sea that he understood. Ida had methodically gone through everyone who had participated in the rescue operation or otherwise been involved in the subsequent hospital stays and found contact information for them. Some of the names had been crossed out, but he couldn't tell if any of them have been contacted yet. It was hard to take in everything she had done for his sake. He was deeply moved by her commitment and her belief in his story.

Ida had tried to find his brother.

93

Per and Karim still hadn't come in. They would join them in the afternoon and take over for Marie. Both Kaj and Vera had declined to be relieved.

The investigation had taken a dramatic turn. Sofia was sitting in Vera's office with Marie and Kaj and watching the recording of Nina Sandberg's interrogation.

Jelena Hagelin's registered address was a house in Gullänget, north of Örnsköldsvik. It was her ex-husband's previous address. He had emigrated to the Philippines, his new girlfriend's country of origin.

The regional SWAT team had been called back in again and a strike was planned the second Jelena's name was spoken. The police officers involved in the intervention operation were ready to take over and take her into custody, but to their great disappointment they had come back emptyhanded yet again. They could not locate her at her house or at her workplace. Jelena had not shown up for her shift that day.

Everyone was now working feverishly to try to find her and any connection to Amanda Svensson. An APB had been issued for Jelena and her name, passport picture, and personal details had already been spread to every police district in the country.

'Where the hell could they be?' Vera pushed her glasses up on top of her head and rubbed her eyes hard. 'And how the hell did Amanda come into contact with a home-help services worker and then convince her to kidnap Ellie and Madeleine?'

Kaj shook his head. It was beyond strange, but they had just received the information. They could work out the exact how and why of it later on. The important thing now was to find out where Jelena was holding Ellie and Madeleine before it was too late.

'Nina Sandberg says that she traded her work shifts on the nights when Madeleine and Ellie disappeared,' Kaj said. 'Apparently, that wasn't the first time Jelena had offered to take her shifts. At first, Nina thought it was because Jelena wanted to earn extra money because her old man had gotten tired of her and divorced her, as Nina so charmingly worded it.'

Vera pursed her lips.

'Anders Svensson's closest neighbour, Dagny Holmström – the woman who owns the Amazon car – received visits four times a day from the home-help service,' Kaj continued. 'Early morning, late morning, mid-afternoon, and evening, a route that Jelena generally handled herself. The two group coordinators shared responsibility for the scheduling. Whenever the other group coordinator prepared the schedule, Jelena would ask to trade with Nina. But she never took any pay for the hours she worked in Nina's place, and she never updated it on the schedule.'

'Why?'

Kaj pointed to the laptop and Vera pressed play again.

Nina appeared on the screen. She was moving anxiously in the chair. The camera was pointed at her, but you could see Kaj's hands on the table between them.

'What reason did Jelena give for wanting to take your work shifts?' Kaj asked in the recording.

'She said she was very fond of Dagny, and that Dagny only trusted her.'

'Was that true?'

Nina appeared to reflect for a moment.

'Dagny was quite troublesome and she like Jelena, but I don't know. The rest of us probably could have handled her.'

'And you never told your unit manager anything about swapping work shifts?'

'No.' Nina looked down at the table. 'Jelena knew that I… well, that I smoked weed. She threated to tell if I said anything. And I got paid anyway. Plus, I got out of having to work. It was basically a win-win for me.'

'Why do you think Jelena wanted to work your shift?'

She kept looking down at the table.

'To be honest…' Nina cut herself off.

'What?'

'Well, I don't know, but I had the sense that Jelena was meeting someone up there.'

'When did that start?'

'A few years ago.'

Sofia paused the video and looked at Vera.

'Anders and Amanda bought the house a little over four years ago. I suppose it can't be a coincidence that Jelena Hagelin started taking on extra work tasks around Sunnansjö around that same time?'

Vera took off her glasses and poked the one temple arm into her mouth for bit as she contemplated this.

'The house was completely renovated, right? If Anders used undocumented workers for his construction projects, then it's probably not so far-fetched to think that he did that in his personal life, too, right?'

Kaj nodded.

'Where is Jelena from?' Vera asked.

'What do you mean?'

'Nina said that she had been "imported".' She put angry air quotes around the word. Despite Vera's sometimes tough attitude towards her staff, prejudice and injustice really made her see red. She had zero tolerance for racism, homophobia or biases.

Sofia looked Vera in the eye. She realised what Vera was thinking.

'Poland.'

Marie, who had sat quietly through the whole meeting, her eyes glued to the screen, cleared her throat.

'Just like the worker who threatened Anders.'

Vera nodded.

'So, Jelena could have run into a fellow countryman at the house, one of Anders's construction workers. Maybe someone she knew from before?'

'That could explain how Amanda came to be in contact with her,' Kaj said. He picked up his coffee cup to take a sip but changed his mind and continued. 'Maybe that's how the whole plan was set in motion?'

'That's possible.'

'We need to talk to Anders again,' Sofia said.

'I've called several times,' Kaj said. 'He's not answering his cell phone. We'll have to go over to the hospital.'

94

Anders was sitting in the same place he had been the last time they were at Örnsköldsvik Hospital, his hand resting limply on Amanda's thin leg and his eyes closed. He looked cleaner today, dressed in light-coloured chinos and a grey, V-neck sweater that said Hugo Boss on it.

Kaj pulled out the chair that had now been moved around to the other side of Amanda, and Sofia sat down.

'We've been trying to reach you.'

'I set my cell phone to silent mode,' Anders said, looking from Sofia to Kaj. 'Have you heard something?'

'No, but we have received a tip that we're very interested in.'

'And?' Anders impatiently raised his hands from his wife's leg.

'We need to talk to you about something, about the house in Sunnansjö. When you remodelled it, did you use undocumented workers?'

Anders did not respond.

'We already know that you have people working illegally at your construction sites. There's no reason to be evasive about it, if that was the case for your remodel, too.'

'Okay, fine.' Anders crossed his arms in front of his chest. 'Yes, I did. But what does that have to do with this?'

'Did any of the workers live in the house?'

'Some did. Not all the time, but sometimes.'

'Do you know if one of them used to receive visits from his girlfriend?'

Anders scoffed.

'In my house? No, certainly not.'

'How many of them were there?'

Anders shrugged.

'May five to ten guys, in batches. Jerzy picked them. I didn't have any direct contact with them.'

'When was the house finished?'

Anders looked at Kaj.

'I was completely finished two years ago.'

'And since then you haven't had any construction workers there?'

'No.' Anders's answer seemed sincere.

So the house had been finished for two years, Sofia thought. And yet Jelena had continued swapping shifts with Nina Sandberg. All the undocumented Polish workers would have already gone home by then. So who was she going to all this trouble for? Suddenly it was all clear to Sofia. One by one the thoughts connected and quickly built a chain of evidence strong enough to withstand even Anna Sondell's exacting scrutiny. Kaj must have realised it at exactly the same instant, because their eyes met and he nodded.

'Have you been at the house often since then?' she asked.

Anders shrugged.

'I usually come up on the weekends sometimes.'

'Alone?'

'Yeah. Amanda thinks it's too far for Ellie to travel.'

'Do you have many friends up here?'

Anders snorted and managed to put on something that looked like a smile.

'No, that's half the point. To get to be alone.'

'Completely alone?'

He turned around and looked at Kaj, upset.

'What kinds of questions are these? Yes, completely alone. Is it illegal to be alone in your own vacation home or something?'

Kaj looked into Anders's eyes for a long time. The air in the room stood still and the only sound was the hissing, rhythmic noise of the machines controlling Amanda's breathing.

'Do you know someone named Jelena Hagelin?'

Anders stiffened, his mouth half open. He looked first at Kaj and then at Sofia. His face was deathly pale.

'Is it her? Did she do this?'

When no one answered, he got up from his chair and took a few steps towards the empty hospital bed on the other side of the room. He stopped at the foot of the bed and stood still for a few seconds before he shook the bed so that the head end slammed into the wall.

'God damn that fucking whore. I'm going to kill her.'

Kaj took a few steps towards Anders, who held up his hands.

'Don't touch me!'

The air went out of him, and he slid down onto the floor with his back against the bathroom door. He leaned his elbows on his knees and let his face fall into his hands. His back shook with sobs and they let him sit for a while before they said anything.

'It was you,' Kaj said, 'wasn't it?'

Anders wiped his nose on his expensive, brand-name sweater sleeve.

'You had a relationship with Jelena Hagelin,' Kaj repeated.

Anders nodded.

'Tell us about it,' Sofia encouraged him.

'She came by one evening and asked if she could see the house. She was working for the home-help service and said she had been driving by it for several years. It's an old school,' he added, as if that were somehow significant. 'She's from Warsaw and I've been there many times, so we talked quite a bit about that. Then I asked if she wanted a glass of wine. I was lonely, tired after a long day. One thing led to another.'

'When was this?'

'A few years ago.'

'And you kept seeing each other after that?'

Anders shrugged.

'Sometimes. She used to be with me on the weekends when I came up on my own to work on the house. One time we met at a hotel in Sundsvall. It wasn't anything serious.'

'Are you still a couple?'

Anders braced himself against the bathroom door and quickly stood up. Sofia took a step back.

'We were never a fucking couple. She was married and I was married. It was a sexual relationship and nothing more. In the beginning it was fun and flattering. We could talk to each other and that sort of thing, but eventually it got to be too much. She came up to the house every time I was there. One time she was already sitting in the living room and waiting for me. She had lit a fire in the fireplace and poured wine. As if she lived there. I told her it was over, but she refused to accept that.'

'When was that?'

'About a year ago. Sometime before Christmas. She had more to lose by getting divorced than I did, so I took a chance and threatened to tell her husband. Then she stopped.'

Anders closed his eyes and took a deep breath.

Sofia saw a dark look in Kaj's eyes.

'And it didn't occur to you to mention this to us when your daughters disappeared?'

Anders shook his head, staring blankly into space, sapped of all energy.

'I didn't think she was that fucking sick in the head.'

Sofia put her hand on Anders's arm, and he let her do it.

'Do you know where she might be?'

95

Kaj hurried down the hospital hallway with Anders. He had told them that Jelena Hagelin's ex-husband inherited an old farm from his parents outside Husum, north of Örnsköldsvik. A desolate two-storey house that had been empty for more than ten years, the perfect place to hold two people hostage without anyone hearing or seeing anything. Anders had insisted on coming when they went to arrest Jelena. In a different situation that would have been out of the question, but if his daughters were found alive, they needed to have a parent there.

The regional SWAT team had already been assembled for yet another raid. This time, nothing could go wrong. Sofia thought about the adrenaline-fuelled special operations assets and tactical units she had met over her years in the profession. A raid without an arrest was the definition of anticlimax to them. Please let them find Ellie and Madeleine this time, alive.

Sofia was slowly making her way down the hospital hallway when her cell phone rang.

'It's that lady from Drömme again, Judith Nordin,' Eva said tiredly when she answered. 'I'll put her through.'

Sofia was about to protest, but somewhere deep inside her something told her this could be important.

There was a click and then she heard Judith's determined voice.

'You haven't gotten back to me about Ingegerd's daughter.'

'I haven't received a concrete answer on that yet. At any rate, the home-help service was paused a while ago. That's all

I know. We're in the middle of a very demanding investigation right now. I haven't had time to look into it any further.'

'What are you talking about?' Judith sounded upset. 'The home-help service hasn't been paused at all. They were last there yesterday.'

There it was. The thought she had pushed aside to focus on the hunt for Jelena, Ellie, and Madeleine. The home-help service. Hadn't Nina Sandberg said that Ingegerd Westin was on her Sunnansjö area route?

'Do you usually chat with the home-help personnel who look after Ingegerd?'

'Yes, why?' Judith sounded offended. 'That's not a crime, is it. We run into each other sometimes when I'm pulling my trash bins down to the main road. I'm not spying on her, if that's what you're implying.'

'No, I didn't think you were,' Sofia reassured her. 'Do you know if it's usually a woman with dark hair who's there? Thin, quite pretty.' She could feel it viscerally, that this was right.

'Yes,' Judith said immediately. 'She has a funny first name, Elina or something like that.'

'Jelena? Is she the one you've seen at the house this last week?'

'Yes, but...' Judith fell silent. 'Wait a minute.'

'Judith?'

'Wait, I said,' Judith hissed. Sofia could hear her moving around in her house and then opening the front door. 'There's someone standing in the bedroom window.'

'What did you say?' Sofia pressed the cell phone closer to her ear. 'Someone is standing at your window?'

Judith muttered something inaudible. There was a rustling. It sounded as if she were putting on a jacket.

'I can't hear you,' Sofia said.

'In Ingegerd's window.'

'Someone is standing outside Ingegerd's window?'

There was a scratching sound over the phone and Sofia heard a zipper being zipped up and then the front door being closed.

'Inside. There's a little girl up in Ingegerd's bedroom window.'

96

The gun feels heavy in my hand. The carved wooden stock is worn smooth from many years of use. Ingegerd said that Ruben belonged to a shooting club for his whole life. He even competed. She told me that before she had her stroke, before all of this, back when she still trusted me.

The girl is sitting with the crocheted teddy bear clutched tight to her chest and watching the movie I put on.

I walk over to the bed and caress her cheek with my free hand. She doesn't react. She's still drowsy from the nasal spray.

My tears begin to flow. This was not how it was supposed to be.

But everything went wrong.

I sit down on the edge of the bed and turn the safety off on the gun. She won't have time to feel anything.

My hand shakes as I aim the barrel at the back of her head and turn my face away.

She hugs the bear tighter.

97

Fredrik stopped just outside the elevators in the psychiatric ward and took a deep breath. He saw Jonna in the lounge which was right across from Ida's room. It was time to grab the bull by the horns. He could not avoid them any longer. Jonna stood with her back to him, talking to her parents. He tried to convince himself that this would go well.

Ida's mother was the first to notice him as he walked up. She was in her sixties, with short hair and wearing a purple wool coat. Next to her stood a stocky, muscular man in a checked shirt with a down jacket under his arm. Ida had said that her father had been a boxer in his youth.

Fredrik held out his hand to greet Ida's mother, but she took two steps towards him and held out her arms. He fell into the hug as if it were the most natural thing in the world, leaning his cheek against her snow-dampened coat. She smelled of perfume and wet dog at the same time.

'I'm sorry. I'm so terribly sorry. I...' He pulled free and looked down at the floor.

'No one has control over things like this other than the person themselves.' Her voice was gentle, and she had a thick northern Swedish dialect. She grasped his hand and pulled him towards her husband.

Ida's father reached out with his big hand and Fredrik shook it after he wiped his own hand off on his jeans.

'Björn. And this here is Lotta.' Ida's father pointed to his wife and then smiled, a warm, inviting smile. 'Come have a seat.' He gestured towards the seating area by the TV.

'How are you doing?' Lotta looked at him and Fredrik felt something inside him melt. Her round cheeks were rosy from the cold and everything about her radiated motherliness.

'Good, given the circumstances. It's all been a bit much this week.' He realised how pathetic that sounded. They had nearly lost their only daughter, and here he was complaining.

'We understand that your friend Philip is having a hard time right now.'

Fredrik looked at Lotta in surprise.

'Did Ida tell you that?'

'Ida tells us everything.' She glanced at her daughter's hospital room, and he saw her eyes well up.

'Have you been in there today?' Fredrik asked.

'No,' Jonna said, shaking her head. 'Ida was in the shower when we got here. She's going to come out here to the lounge when she's done.'

A nurse came by and showed there where they could get coffee. Björn stood up and set his jacket down next to him.

'Milk and sugar?'

'Just milk,' Fredrik replied. Björn patted him on the shoulder and disappeared off down the hallway with Jonna next to him.

After they left, Lotta turned to him, reached out her hand, and put it on his.

'You mustn't think that this is your fault, Fredrik.'

'But if I hadn't…' The shame made it hard for him to talk.

But Lotta didn't let him interrupt her.

'It's not your fault. Ida has struggled with depression for many years.'

Fredrik looked up at her.

'This isn't the first time we've been here,' she said, continuing to look into his eyes. 'Some people come down with physical illnesses and others bear the burden of the invisible, mental illnesses. We've made the choice not to hide it from other people.'

Fredrik ran his hand over his stubble to hide his tears which were welling up. Lotta's words hit him right in the heart. Ida wasn't the only person close to him impacted by mental illness. He thought about Philip, sitting alone and isolated on Ulvön Island, with only his own thoughts and his anxiety for company. Not to mention himself. Sometimes he felt like his whole life was just one big mess of anxiety. Maybe Lotta was right. Could being open about one's difficulties be the key to faring better?

Björn and Jonna came back with a tray of disposable coffee cups. Just as they sat down on the sofa, the door to Ida's room opened. Her long hair was still wet and had left dark stains on her light pink sweatshirt. She was wearing plaid pyjama pants and the fluffy wool slippers she had bought at the Christmas market at Skansen. She still looked pale, but her gaze seemed steady as she approached them. Lotta, Björn, and Jonna stood up and Ida hugged them one by one. Fredrik sat with his elbows on his knees, looking down at the floor. It wasn't until Ida touched his shoulder that he dared to look up. They looked at each other for a long time and neither of them said anything. Eventually, Björn cleared his throat and put his hand on his wife's shoulder.

'Well, maybe we should go grab some coffee then,' he nodded towards the hallway.

Fredrik glanced at the full, steaming paper cups that were already on the coffee table.

Ida smiled.

98

It's quiet in the basement. I've knocked and hollered down a few times, but I no longer get any response. Maybe she's dead. I should go down and check, but I don't dare. It doesn't really matter.

The girl is sitting in the bed next to me watching Winnie the Pooh. *I couldn't do it. But I can't take her back either. She's mine now. My daughter, Ellie.*

She asks for her mother sometimes.

You mother has entrusted you to me to take care of, I tell her. We're going to be together now. She doesn't respond but also doesn't ask any more.

She gets to be awake for a while. I need to change her clothes and clean her up before we leave. I bought a cute, pink dress with matching tights and a white down jacket with snowpants to go with it. I packed a bag with several changes of clothes for me. I have my passport, but nothing for her. I'll have to figure that out when I get to the boarder. Or maybe try to buy a passport on my way through Stockholm or Malmö. What little jewellery I have, I'm bringing. A few pieces of Ingegerd's, too, but not all. I would never take them all. We just need to get home and then it will all work out. I'll tell my mother and father that she's mine. They can watch her during the day while I get a job as a cashier or working in some factory.

It is never going to be Anders and me. I understand that now. It wouldn't have mattered if everything had worked out. If I had cleared Amanda out of the way and pretended to find Ellie for him. He still wouldn't have been grateful. He has just thrown away all the love I've given him. I'll give it to her now, to Ellie.

I kiss her on the head and go downstairs to pack up her things. Ingegerd whimpers from her room, but I don't have time to turn her now.

You can have your wife, Anders, keep cheating on her with other women, but I'm going to have the girl.

She won't need to grow up with someone like you.

99

Sofia did her best to run across the hospital parking lot towards the car, but the baby protested wildly by kicking and pushing its head into her abdomen. Every step sent a shooting pain down into her legs. She crumpled herself into the driver's seat as fast as she could and started the engine. For the tenth time, she tried calling Judith, but there was no answer. Her heart was hammering from the run and her mind was racing. Could it be Ellie that Judith had seen in Ingegerd Westin's window? Or had she been mistaken despite the binoculars? Ingegerd's house must be several hundred meters away from Judith's. But she had genuinely sounded convinced and there had been no stopping Judith. The sound of the front door banging shut and footsteps in the snow was the last thing Sofia had heard before she had realised their call had ended.

The thought of Ellie made Sofia press harder on the gas pedal. She was driving well over the speed limit, despite the treacherous winter conditions. The sun sat low in the sky, blinding her, but even so she sped up a bit. As she crossed the bridge over Mo River, she had to slam on the brakes to avoid a Saab that suddenly veered into the passing lane. She was in her personal car so she couldn't turn on the blue flashers or make an announcement over the radio. Nor did she have her service weapon available should she need it.

What was Jelena's plan, actually? Did she want revenge because Anders had dumped her, or was she trying to get his family out of the way? Sofia couldn't help but think about that awful case in Arboga in which a woman had broken in and attacked a mother and killed her two children with a hammer. All so that she could have the man she considered to be hers to herself. Is that what had happened here? Or was this about something else?

As Sofia drove, she tried dialling Kaj's number. When she finally succeeded in hitting the right buttons, it rang but no one answered. The same was true for Marie and Vera. Sofia looked at the time. Twenty minutes had elapsed since the SWAT team and the intervention unit along with Marie and Vera had left police headquarters to drive out to Husum. Kaj and Anders had joined them straight from the hospital. By now, they should at least be close if they had been driving with their lights on. She tried Anna Sondell's number, but the prosecutor didn't answer either.

As she turned onto Sidensjövägen, heading towards Drömme, her phone finally rang.

'Karim, I'm glad you called.'

'I'm just on my way in to take over for Marie, but I'm late and I can't get hold of her. You sound short of breath. Did something happen?'

Sofia gasped for breath.

'I'm on my way out to Drömme.'

'Why?'

'Judith Nordin called.' She tugged on the seatbelt to get some air. 'She says she saw a girl in one of the windows of Ingegerd Westin's house. According to her, Ingegerd doesn't have any kids or grandkids, but Ingegerd's home-help visits were paused because supposedly her daughter was going to care for her. I think that's where Jelena Hagelin is holding Ellie and Madeleine.'

'Who's Judith Nordin?' Karim asked.

Only then did Sofia realise that Karim was not aware of her inquiries into Judith and Ingegerd Westin. He didn't seem to know anything about what Nina Sandeberg had revealed about Jelena Hagelin. Their chain of information seemed to have been broken in the rush.

Karim sounded confused.

'Is Jelena the one who helped Amanda Svensson?'

'I don't think that's how it happened, but I'll explain it later. I'm almost there.'

'Sofia,' Karim's voice was sharp. 'Don't do anything stupid now. I'll call Kaj and Vera and tell them what's going on.'

She slowed down as she started to approach Ingegerd Westin's house. From a distance, everything looked exactly like it had the last time she was there. Sofia drove up to the house very slowly and stopped the car in the driveway. When she turned off the ignition, she discovered that the front door was open. Her hand reflexively went to her thigh, where her gun had been during all the years she had worked in the field. There was no visible movement in the windows, either downstairs or upstairs. Without a sound, she opened her car door and got out.

'Karim, send reinforcements to Drömme 440 in Sidensjö.'

When she saw that there was someone lying inside the open door, she added, 'And an ambulance.'

100

'I love you.' Those were the first words that came out of Fredrik's mouth once Ida's family was out of earshot. 'I love you, and you have to forgive me.'

Ida looked into his eyes. There was no reproach in her dark brown eyes. She sat down next to him on the sofa in the lounge and took his hand.

'Ida, I didn't mean to…' He couldn't express what he was feeling. Shame, but also an absolutely terrible horror at the thought of how the whole thing could have ended. Ida squeezed his hand. Her lips were dry and cracked. She was swallowing with difficulty. Jonna had explained that Ida had been intubated to help her breathe. The tube had been removed, but it probably hurt her to talk. Fredrik handed her one of the coffee cups. She took a sip and grimaced.

'I'm not accusing you of anything, Fredrik.' She cleared her throat. 'This was my choice.'

'But if I hadn't said such stupid things…'

It was a statement more than a question, but Ida shook her head.

'This wasn't the first time.'

Fredrik looked at Ida.

'How many times?' he asked.

'Several.'

They were quiet for a moment.

'But never again?'

'Never again,' she said with a smile and squeezed his hand harder.

This was the person he was going to spend his life with. He was sure of it now. Ida also carried a darkness within her. They would understand each other on a completely different level from other people. They would help each other move forwards. He glanced down the hallway, not wanting to be caught by Ida's parents and sister asking her if she wanted to be his wife. He hadn't had time to buy a ring but remembered the safe deposit box he still had down in the basement of Handelsbanken over by Östermalmstorg. His grandmother's beautiful gold wedding rings were there. One was set with three diamonds. His grandmother had worn them her whole life, even though she had already been widowed by the age of fifty. There had never been any talk of remarriage for Greta Fröding.

But he didn't care about the ring now. He couldn't think of a better opportunity to propose to Ida. Well, actually he could think of thousands of better times and places, but he didn't want to wait.

He stroked the back of her hand. It was so soft. Despite the dark circles under her eyes, she was prettier now that she had ever been. Fredrik took a breath, steeling himself to be brave enough to say what he wanted to say.

But Ida beat him to it.

'Did you read my letter?'

101

'Hello?' Sofia called, her hand reaching for her gun again, but it still wasn't there. 'Ingegerd?'

Sofia heard whimpering from inside the house and stopped in the driveway to listen. She felt naked without her gun and looked around for something to defend herself with. There was a shovel next to the garage door. She grabbed it and then moved stealthily towards the front door. She knew that she should wait for the reinforcements, but saving lives came before everything. If she waited for the others, it might already be too late.

She rounded the mailbox and tilted her head back to look up at the upstairs windows. There was no sign of any little girl.

'Hello,' she called again. 'I'm from the police. Is there anyone here?'

She heard the whimpering from inside the house again.

Sofia continued towards the front door. Even before she stepped up onto the first of the front steps, she could see that it was Judith lying inside the front door. Her grey hair had come loose from its bun, and several strands were splayed out over the threshold. She was lying on her back with her eyes closed. Sofia took the steps two at a time and pushed open the door to enter. As she leaned down and felt Judith's throat for a pulse, she peered into the house. A painting had fallen off the wall and the glass in another one had been smashed.

Judith's pulse was steady and fine. Sofia saw that she was bleeding from the back of her head and that she had big, red blotches in her hair.

'Judith,' she whispered, shaking her gently. 'Judith, is there anyone in the house?'

The old woman blinked a few times, moaned and clutched her head.

'Is there anyone here?'

Judith's eyes rolled backwards as if she were losing consciousness again.

Sofia looked up. She heard the whimpering again and realised that it was coming from the room at the far end of the long, narrow hallway.

'Hello?' she called out again and received yet another whimper in response. Louder this time. With the shovel in front of her, she proceeded into the house. Kitchen to the right, empty. Stairs leading upstairs to the left, empty. Next to the staircase, a door that she suspected went down to the basement, locked. Living room and dining room, also to the right. Outside the dining room, she saw the deck. It was empty. There was only one room left downstairs now. Through the open door at the far end of the long, narrow hallway, she could see the end of what looked like a hospital bed. A pair of naked feet stuck out from under the covers, and she could see that the toes were moving.

Sofia steeled herself, raised the shovel and got ready. She counted her breaths, trying to calm herself down. Then she rushed into the room with the shovel held high.

The look in the eyes of the terrified old woman in the bed made her stop short. There was a wheelchair next to the bed. Sofia lowered the shovel and walked over to the woman.

'Ingegerd?'

She nodded.

'Is there anyone else here, Ingegerd?'

Her lips moved, but no comprehensible words came out. Sofia saw that her mouth was drooping on one side and suspected she had had a stroke. One of her hands move slowly from the covers and slid down alongside her body. The index finger curled into a claw. Ingegerd tapped on the mattress and looked urgently at Sofia.

'In the basement?'

Ingegerd nodded again.

102

Ida looked expectantly at Fredrik.

'Yes, I read the letter,' he said.

'And?'

'I don't know what to say.'

That was true. What Ida had done for him was more than he could take in. It wasn't just that she had believed him when he said Niklas had survived. She had actually looked for him.

'You tried to find Niklas, didn't you?'

Ida smiled.

'Yes, but not everything is in there.'

The backs of his hands immediately began to itch. He scratched impatiently, trying to keep his breathing calm. Actually, he didn't want to know what she had discovered. He was all too aware that the odds Niklas had survived were minimal.

Ida grabbed his hand, and his sense that he was about to receive bad news intensified. Was he up to hearing the truth? To having to accept once and for all that Niklas was dead and that he had completely failed to protect his little brother?

Ida told him about the detective work she had done that fall trying to find Niklas. Fredrik listened intently and didn't ask any questions. He let her describe her research at her own pace.

It had not been easy to obtain information about what had happened when the MS Estonia sank. How to sort through the blurry memories of a disaster where no one had had time to document events properly? It had happened long before the digital age they lived in now. Nothing happened now without being filmed and posted on the internet. He had contemplated that many times. What would it have been like if the Estonia had sunk today? Would there have been cell phone videos from inside the ferry? Final messages somehow uploaded to the cloud somewhere for family members to watch. The promises to always love and never forget as the masses of water filled the vessel. It was such a horrific thought that he felt sick. How many people had lain there, injured or unable to make their way out, and just waited for their cold death by drowning? His mother and father were two of them. Fredrik rubbed his face to shake off his terrible thoughts. He was grateful that nothing had been documented. The memories of what had happened that night were enough.

Ida explained that it had started with the idea that she would do a little poking around, which had then grown into an obsession. She had talked to journalists, authors and rescue personnel, but most of all Swedish, Finnish and Estonian survivors. They all had their own version of what had happened and gave different answers to questions about whether it could be possible for a person to have survived and then disappeared.

Fredrik sat completely silent. She hurried past certain things, and he realised that she was doing that so he wouldn't have to relive it all yet again.

Ida leaned forward and drank from the coffee, which was getting cold sitting on the table.

'I got hold of two people who had been on the passenger ship, the MS Isabella. One was a crew member. He was adamant that everyone who had been rescued had been counted, identified and brought ashore when the boat reached port in Turku. The other was a cook. He had done his military service as a paramedic. He said there were about fifteen people – staff members, performers, bartenders, well, everyone who could still stand and had not succumbed to seasickness – who helped receive the injured and frozen survivors. A temporary emergency room had been set up in the bar in the bow, where blankets from the whole ferry were brought to warm up those who had been plucked out of the sea. The staff had massaged the survivors all night to bring up their body temperatures.'

Fredrik tried to imagine what it had been like. Had Niklas been there? Wrapped in blankets and cared for by someone who had given him something warm to drink and eat?

'The cook said that they had picked people up directly from the Estonia's car deck, too, but no survivors. How they could do that in full-on stormy conditions and with several meter high waves is beyond me,' Ida said. 'What heroes.'

Fredrik nodded. He would never forget the rescue swimmer who had lifted him out of the raft that was full of freezing cold seawater. The rescue swimmer had held onto him so hard that he hadn't even been afraid as he was lifted straight up into the air towards the waiting helicopter.

'Anyway,' Ida continued. 'He was very sure that he had received a very young boy who had been picked up by one of the MS Isabella's lifeboats. He had even tried to get in touch with him several years later but had been told then that no one under the age of ten had survived the disaster.'

Fredrik leaned forwards over his knees so he wouldn't start to hyperventilate. He could not process what Ida was saying. He had been trying lately to come to grips with the idea that the dream he had nurtured for so long that Niklas could have survived had been just that. A dream. A dangerous fantasy that prevented him from moving on with his life. He had argued with Sofia about it, his conviction that his little brother had survived was one of the reasons they had gone their separate ways. And now Ida was telling him that in spite of everything there was a possibility.

She set the coffee cup down on the table and squeezed his hand again.

'He was one hundred percent sure that the little boy he had taken care of had said he was from Stockholm.'

103

Sofia felt around the doorframe in the hopes of finding a nail with the key to the basement door hanging on it, but there was none. She scanned the hallway. There was a varnished pine dresser behind her. She pulled out the top two drawers and swept her hand around through the crumpled scarves and mittens without finding anything. The bottom drawer was full of padlocks, bike locks, reflectors, matchboxes and hats. She yanked it out and emptied the contents onto the floor. As she spread everything out to get a better look, she heard the sirens from police cars in the distance. She looked over at Judith, who was still lying on the carpet near the front door. She had begun to move and was clutching the back of her head again.

There was no key in the last drawer either. Her eyes fell on the shovel which was leaning against the door frame outside Ingegerd's room. Without a further thought, she retrieved it and turned towards the door to the basement. It was a typical thin, hollow, 90s-style door. If she hadn't been pregnant, she surely could have kicked a hole in it, but her belly was too much in the way for her to be able to put enough strength into it. Instead, she raised the shoved and aimed a swing at the middle of the door. The shovel blade went right through, cutting open a gash in the white surface. She pulled the shovel back out again and kept swinging. Soon she had made a hole big enough that she could get one leg through. A few more times and she would be able to get her whole body through.

Winded, Sofia dropped the shovel on the floor and took a few panting breaths with her hand on her belly before she called down the pitch-black stairs into the basement.

'Police, is anyone there?'

Not a sound to be heard.

She reached her hand through the hole and tried to find the light switch. Then she remembered that she had seen a flashlight in the bottom dresser drawer and turned around to grab it from the pile of things on the floor behind her. After turning the batteries a few times, it came on.

The sirens sounded closer now. She carefully squeezed through the hole in the door and shone the flashlight down the stairs. The first thing that struck her was the stench. Faeces, urine and dirt. She pulled up her sweater and pressed it to her nose. But she did not smell that corpse smell.

'Hello?' she called again and leaned down to try to shine the flashlight out into the room below her. 'Madeleine? Ellie?'

The beam of light fell on a concrete floor. She caught a glimpse of a few simple wooden shelves that had overwintering flowers and jars of juice and jam. There were some broken terra cotta pots underneath.

She took a few steps down the stairs and then stepped out onto the hard, concrete floor. Straight ahead there was a chest freezer and to the left of that, under the stairs themselves, were some blankets crumpled up into a nest. She needed to take only one more step to discover the feet sticking out from the blankets. She caught a glimpse of drainpipe jeans and socks that had once been white.

'Madeleine.' Sofia walked quickly over to the body that was curled up in a foetal position. 'Madeleine. It's the police. Can you hear me?' She cautiously tugged at the blanket. The stench that rose up was nauseating. She let the light from the flashlight fall on Madeleine's body. The jeans were stained and her hands tied with a zip tie behind her back.

Sofia shook her gently but could feel through the thin T-shirt that her body was stiff. The light from the flashlight reached

Madeleine's face the same moment that she heard Vera call her name from the hallway upstairs.

The eyes were open and the face frozen in terror.

Madeleine Svensson was dead.

104

Sofia moved as quickly as she could up the basement stairs. She wanted to get away from the stench and the horrified look in the dead young woman's eyes. Where was Ellie? Had she met the same fate?

When Sofia got back up into the hallway, she saw the ambulance personnel. Judith lay with a neck collar around her neck, holding a compress to her head wound while the two paramedics lifted her onto the gurney. The house had not been secured yet and they actually should have stayed outside, but Sofia knew that the mission to save lives was so firmly ingrained in the paramedics that they sometimes pushed the limits.

Several people in black helmets with raised weapons moved from room to room downstairs. For each room, a loud 'clear' could be heard before they moved on to the next one.

Vera and Kaj stood in the front doorway waiting for the house to be secured. Sofia had time to make eye contact with Vera before she grabbed the railing of the staircase that led upstairs and heaved herself up the first step.

'Ellie? It's the police. Answer me if you can hear me.'

Several members of the SWAT team were heading towards her now and Vera set off down the long, narrow hallway.

'You stop right there.' The man who had come up alongside her was physically imposing. His voice was sharp and not to be contradicted.

She turned around and looked at Vera.

'Madeleine is in the basement, dead. I think Ellie is still in the house.'

The man pushed his way past her and several of his colleagues followed with their guns raised. Vera followed a few paces behind them. Sofia followed her, even though Vera waved her hand for Sofia to stay downstairs. The upstairs hallway was dark. The doors to the adjoining rooms were closed, and the wall-to-wall carpet and the yellowed pine walls swallowed what little light came from downstairs.

The SWAT officers proceeded, pushing open the first door. It led into a bathroom with orange waterproof carpeting on the walls and the floor.

The bathtub was empty and so was the shower.

'Clear.'

The next door was opened. An office. It was also empty.

'Clear.'

The man who had stopped Sofia on the stairs took a few steps back away from the last door and raised his gun. Another stepped forward and pressed the door handle down. When the door swung open, he stopped short. He lowered the gun and stepped aside so that Sofia could see the unmade double bed in the middle of the room. A quiet 'clear' could be heard from behind her. Several officers were on their way up the stairs but stopped when they saw their colleague's raised hand.

There in the bed lay Ellie, curled up with a teddy bear in her arms. When she saw them, she sat up and took her thumb out of her mouth. Her movements were unsteady.

'I want my mom.'

—

Twenty minutes later, Sofia stood in the driveway with a blanket around her, talking to the paramedics who were loading Judith into one of the ambulances. Her head was bandaged and she had a neck brace on, but she was conscious.

'I said that the police were on their way,' Judith croaked, with a joyless smile. 'She knocked me over when I tried to stop her at the front door.'

Sofia patted Judith's arm and praised her for her courage. Then the doors were closed, and the ambulance drove away. Marie came over and put her arm around Sofia.

'What a terrible tragedy.'

Anders sat in the back seat of a police car with his youngest daughter in his lap. They were both wrapped in blankets and Anders was crying quietly, his cheek resting against Ellie's hair. Apart from the psychological stress the girl had been put through, she seemed to be doing relatively well, but she looked thin and haggard. They had found bottles of formula in the kitchen and Dexdor, a nasal spray sedative. There had been several empty bottles in the bedroom where Ellie had been kept. There had also been a number of suitcases packed with both children's and adult clothing as well as money, jewellery and Jelena's passport. It seemed as if she had planned to run away with the girl.

Sofia disentangled herself from Marie's arms and walked over to the police car. She gently knocked on the window and Anders nodded that she could open the door. Ellie had a crocheted teddy bear with button eyes under her arm which Sofia suspected Ingegerd had made many years ago. Maybe in the hopes of being able to give it to her own child someday, a child that never came to be.

'I'm sorry,' she said, leaning into the back seat. He nodded again but didn't say anything.

'We're going to need to ask Ellie some questions later.' The girl reacted when she heard her name and snuggled closer to her father. Anders didn't respond.

'Do you have any idea where Jelena might have gone?'

He shook his head and buried his face in his daughter's hair.

'I want Mom. We need to go to Mom right now.'

Sofia stretched into the car and gave Anders a light hug, with Ellie between them. He hugged her back with his free hand and then she closed the car door and the car drove away. Ellie would be taken to Örnsköldsvik Hospital for further medical evaluation.

The personnel from the other ambulance stuck their heads out the open front door and waved to Vera and Kaj who stood talking to Johan, who had been called to the scene to perform the forensic investigation. They were preparing to remove Madeleine's body and wanted to make sure that the car with Ellie and Anders had left first. Vera waved back that they had left, and the gurney with the woman in rigor mortis in the foetal position was carried out to the waiting ambulance.

Ingegerd had also been taken to the hospital for examination. Sofia hoped she would never need to return to the home where she had been held prisoner for more than a week with a person dying in the basement, a child held captive upstairs and a madwoman for a caretaker. She must have heard Madeleine's desperate cries for help without being able to do anything.

Vera came over to Sofia. For a moment it looked as if she was going to hug her, but she made do with briefly putting her hand on Sofia's shoulder.

'Without you we might not have found Ellie in time. Who knows what that fucking lunatic might have done?'

Kaj, Marie and Johan came over to them. They stood together, the four of them, and watched as the doors of the ambulance containing Madeleine's body were closed before it pulled away through the snowy landscape.

'Now we just need to get that psych case, too,' Vera said, crossing her arms in front of her broad chest.

The fatigue hit Sofia now with full force, and she was afraid she would fall asleep standing there.

'You'll have to do that part without me.' She pulled her jacket closed as best she could over her big belly. 'I'm going on maternity leave now.'

105

Everything has been taken away from me, everything. They have ripped the child that should have been mine out of my arms. I will never get to see her again. The bond we created will not be kept alive. She won't remember me. Will never feel the love I could have given her.

We were so close.

That fucking neighbour. She wanted to come in, she said. Check on Ingegerd and go upstairs. Refused to accept my no. The police were on their way, she said. If you had only been quiet, my little child. Then she would have turned around and left. I can still hear your heartrending scream. Deep down I know it was me you were calling for. I was going to be your mother.

The last thing I had left has been taken from me.
And I know exactly whose fault that is.

106

Sofia looked out at the dark water. The sun had set a long time ago. She had gone straight from Ingegerd's house back to her flat in Örnsköldsvik, packed her things and set her sights on the Köpmanholm dock and the last boat of the day to Ulvön Island. She wanted nothing more than to forget the remembered images of the dead Madeleine Svensson and the thoughts of what might have happened to Ellie if Judith hadn't seen her there in the window.

The icebreaker had been through, so the hovercraft had been replaced by the far more comfortable MF Ulvön ferry.

It was palpable that the islanders could sense the scent of spring in the air. A lot of the cargo on the aft deck consisted of potting soil, planks and exterior paint. There was still snow on all the flowerbeds, but the sun would soon thaw out her island. She would get to enjoy the spring with her newborn baby.

Sofia took a seat in the cabin and greeted some neighbours who were also on their way out. During the winter half of the year, there were rarely or never any tourists on the boat and the commuters knew each other well.

'I heard on the radio just now that you found the girl. So nice that that's over. But it sounds like there was someone dead there, too. You don't suppose I might dare to ask who?'

Sofia shook her head and took a cinnamon roll out of the bag the woman held out to her.

'And no one was arrested? Although obviously you can't say anything.'

Sofia took a bite of the cinnamon roll, smiled and looked at the woman.

'No.'

They changed the subject, and the woman pointed to her belly.

'Not long now, is it?'

'Less than four weeks and I'm going to spend them lying on my back.'

The woman laughed and put the bag of cinnamon rolls back in her backpack and got out a book instead. The conversation lapsed. The ferry between Köpmanholmen in Örnsköldsvik and Ulvöhamn took one and a half hours. No one expected to chat the whole way. Some knitted, others looked at their cell phones or seized the opportunity to nap for a bit.

Sofia sat looking out at the large ice floes being pushed out of the way by the ferry. The noise was deafening as they scraped against the metal hull. She thought about Philip. How would he react when he found out what had happened to Madeleine? She had called Fredrik and he had immediately gotten into the car to drive up. They had agreed it would be best if Sofia told Philip face to face. Just to be on the safe side, she had called Tord and asked him to pick her up and come to the house with her. Not that she was afraid of Philip or his reaction, but because it was nice to have someone along who could support her when she needed to explain the terrible thing that had happened.

Tord was standing on the dock waiting for her when the ferry docked at Fjären. Over the years there had been a shift, and more year-round residents lived on the north side of the island now than down in the harbour. The ferry would remain in Ulvöhman overnight if the icebreaker had gone, but during the winter few people got off there.

Several of the passengers stopped to chat with Tord, the island's unofficial leader. Sofia's red Golf was parked a short distance from the dock.

'How are you doing?' he asked when they got into the car. People on the island did not worry about seatbelts and even though she should know better as a police officer and mother-to-be, Sofia enjoyed the feeling of not having her stomach constricted.

'I feel better now. Things have been really rough at work the last few days.'

Tord reached out his hand and patted her on the belly.

'You shouldn't be out chasing criminals so close to your due date. After all, you have the girl to think about.'

Sofia smiled, leaned back and closed her eyes as Tord started the car. They backed out of the parking lot, continued onto the forest road and away from the dock and the lit-up ferry.

Without seeing the thin woman standing still on the upper deck, following them with her eyes.

107

It was dark in the house when Sofia and Tord stepped inside. Only the little lamps in the kitchen windows were on. The clock over the cabinet by the door showed quarter past eight. Sofia took a few steps into the hall and then proceeded into the kitchen. The TV was on in the living room and Philip was sitting on the sofa. As they started turning on the lights, he didn't take his eyes off the show that was on.

'We're here,' she called out, but he didn't respond.

Tord carried in a few bags of food that he had bought down at the shop, and Sofia went straight to the laundry room to change out of her tight maternity jeans into sweatpants and ragg wool socks. She immediately felt the tension in her body begin to ease. The investigation had taken more out of her than she had wanted to admit at first. All their theories about threatening construction workers, financial difficulties, divorce and custody disputes had ultimately been scrapped for a much simpler one: that Jelena had done all of this out this out of her love for Anders. It was hard to comprehend how a person could be so twisted. Sofia shook her head to clear away the thoughts. It was over now, and she could stay in this house until the baby was born. Margit had assured Sofia that first-time childbirths took their time so she would have enough time to make it out to help even if she wasn't on the island when Sofia went into labour. Sofia's midwife at the maternity centre had grumbled about her decision to give birth at home, but Sofia had been adamant about how she wanted it to go right from the beginning.

She stood still in the laundry room and took a deep breath before going in to talk to Philip. She felt that familiar anxiety that came with imparting bad news. Informing someone of a death was the worst of all. Her first week as a cadet, she had been forced to visit a family who had fled Afghanistan in a refugee centre outside Gustavsberg. The youngest child was still breastfeeding. The Swedish Migration Agency had denied the family a residence permit, and, learning that, the father had gone straight out and thrown himself in front of a train. Sofia had brought an interpreter with her, but the women had become so upset that the interpreter had also started crying. Even though she had informed many people of the deaths of close family members since then, she would never forget that time.

She felt so sad to have to tell Philip about Madeleine. In such a short time, she had come to care about Philip. She didn't know if that was because he had simply been left in her care or because he was a link to Fredrik. But he had come to mean something to her.

She took a deep breath and went out into the living room. Tord left what he was doing in the kitchen and followed. He sat down at the dining table, which they never used for anything other than drying mushrooms and berries. Sofia sat down next to Philip on the sofa. He scooted over to make room for her, but did not make eye contact. It was as if he could tell she was bringing bad news.

'Philip.' She put her hand on his leg. His eyes were still locked on the television set. Sofia could see his chest trembling as he inhaled and his eyes filling with tears.

He already knew.

Sofia leaned over and put her arms around him, tried to pull him as close to her as her belly would allow. He resisted at first but then allowed himself to be hugged and broke into loud sobs. Tord watched them with compassion but made no attempt to go over to them. They sat like that for a long time.

Once Philip had cried himself out and broke away from the hug, he finally looked at Sofia. The grief in his eyes was immeasurable.

'Did she suffer? Did Madeleine suffer before she died?'

She considered telling him the truth for a moment. But immediately realised that she wanted to spare him from the image of his girlfriend, alone and at the mercy of a crazy person who let her die of thirst in the dark in a basement. She knew the autopsy would take a few days, but it wasn't a wild guess that Madeleine had died of dehydration. Sofia had heard of people surviving nine days without water, but they were the exceptions, and Anders had said that Madeleine had been born with a heart condition. Maybe that had hastened her death. If only they had arrived sooner, maybe Madeleine would have survived. The fear of death she must have felt was unimaginable. Sofia didn't want Philip to need to remember the young woman that way.

'No, Philip,' she finally said. 'She didn't.'

108

Sofia stood at the counter, drying the last of the teacups. Tord had made sandwiches, and they had eaten them in silence with Philip.

She had encouraged him to go lie down, but he didn't want to. Instead, he sat in front of the TV and watched nature show after nature show. Fredrik had texted that he was on the ferry. He must have been going well over the speed limit to make the last ferry departure, but all she felt right now about that was gratitude.

Sofia heard Tord's cargo moped start up out in the driveway. He was going home to sleep and would come back in the morning. He had ordered a good month's worth of food which would be delivered to the Ulvö dock with the first boat in the morning. The shop in the village sold only the basics and Sofia suspected that Tord had bought pallets of diapers and wet wipes from the mainland. They had decided that he would move into the guest room and then they would spend the final weeks before the baby's birth assembling the crib, test-driving the stroller and the other things that expectant parents usually did. Sofia was infinitely more eager to do this with Tord than with Kaj. Although she probably wouldn't be able to keep Kaj away from the island. Of course he had as much right to the baby as she did, but she wished he would wait until it was born before he started parenting. After all, they were not a couple.

Her back started protesting the uncomfortable position. She rested her elbows on the counter and was trying to stretch her muscles when something outside the window caught her attention.

Someone was standing down on the boathouse dock.

109

The wind is blowing hard off the sea. My hands and feet are so cold that I can't feel them anymore and it stings my cheeks.

But it doesn't matter.

Nothing matters anymore.

The cold doesn't bother me. The fire raging inside me is enough to keep me warm. And the gun in my jacket pocket gives me courage.

From the boathouse, I see the lamps in the kitchen and her silhouette as she moves around the house. That big belly and that waddling gait.

Will I ever get to experience the feeling of carrying a baby in my belly?

Maybe not.

But she will never get to experience the feeling of holding her baby in her arms.

110

Sofia hurriedly grabbed the cardigan which was hanging over the back of the sofa. Philip looked up at her, his eyes red from crying, as she went by.

'Are you going out?'

Sofia pulled on the cardigan.

'I'm just going out to get some air.'

Philip didn't ask any more questions, and she proceeded to the front door to get a pair of boots. As she reached for a hat from the hat shelf, she felt her insides suddenly implode. Like when an aquarium full of water breaks. She stood there with the knit hat in her hand. Something was running down her legs. A strange silence spread through her body.

Half-crouched, Sofia went into the bathroom and when she sat down, the water gushed out. Her water must have broken, and she was gripped by fear. The baby was coming, even though it wasn't due for several weeks. A pain shot through her that was worse than anything she had experienced in her entire life. A cramp seemed to cleave her from within and she did not succeed in stopping the scream from finding its way out of her throat.

'Are you okay?' Philip asked from the other side of the bathroom door.

'My water broke,' she called out as calmly as she could. 'Call Tord. And the midwife. The number is on the fridge.'

She heard Philip hurry off just as the next contraction came. It was even stronger than the first one and for a second she nearly blacked out.

'Philip! Hurry, it's urgent.'

She held onto the shower wall and waited for the contraction to end. It was immediately followed by another and then another. In between the contractions, the pain went away completely which gave her a brief breather, but the fear that set in at the first sensation of a fresh contraction paralyzed her. She had believed that she had a good tolerance for pain, but apparently she hadn't experienced enough of it to understand what pain really was.

She tried to pull up her pants but could not stand up. She yelled again to Philip but received no response. It must have been several minutes since she sent him to call. Long enough for him to find the midwife's number and come back. Or had he shut down and was back sitting in front of the TV again?

'Philip!' She yelled as loudly as she could. No answer. With tremendous effort, she got up into a standing position and got her pants on. She waited for the next contraction and let it subside before she reached for the door and unlocked it. There was no one out there. The TV was off and there wasn't a sound in the house. She went into the kitchen and saw Philip standing with the cell phone pressed to his chest and the slip of paper with the midwife's number in his hand.

'Philip?' she said in a quiet voice, before yet another contraction swept over her. 'It's fine, Philip. It's completely natural. I can handle this.' She didn't know if she believed herself. 'Did you call the midwife?'

He was staring as if turned to stone at the glass door in the living room that led to the deck.

'Philip?' The next contraction had begun, and she wanted to know that help was on the way. She took a few steps closer to pull the slip of paper out of his hand. Philip's eyes were glued to the snow-covered deck.

When she looked up, she discovered what he was looking at.

Under the outside light stood Jelena Hagelin.

111

'Run!'

Out on the deck, she saw Jelena tugging and pulling on the patio door. She was holding a gun in one hand. For a second, their eyes met. Then Jelena turned around and ran towards the front of the house.

Sofia grabbed Philip's arm. He nearly lost his balance and stumbled along after her towards the bathroom.

It was no longer possible for Sofia to resist the pain making its way up through her insides. She leaned forward over her knees and screamed at the top of her lungs with her hand pressed to the underside of her belly. Outside she could hear Jelena's footsteps on the gravel path. They were getting closer, and Sofia rushed to the front door and locked it.

'You have to help me,' she yelled over her shoulder, but received no response. Jelena threw her full weight against the door, shrieking with a brutal fury. Sofia turned around and looked at Philip, who looked terrified.

'Upstairs, the big bedroom,' she moaned, pointing up the stairs. 'My dad's gun safe.' She reached for the bowl on the cabinet next to the front door. Her hand trembled as she gave Philip the key. He took it and stood there in the front hall. Jelena kept tugging on the handle and kicking the door. It was quiet for a second, then the pane of frosted glass exploded, and Jelena's hand appeared among the shards of glass still hanging from the frame. She was groping around for the deadbolt but couldn't reach it.

'Philip!'

He disappeared up the stairs and came right back with Sten's old double-barrel shotgun and a box of cartridges. Sofia waved for him to hurry into the bathroom. She followed, hunched over with her hand under her belly, and then slammed the door shut and locked it behind them. Jelena was not at the front door anymore. Maybe she was looking for another way into the house. Sofia loaded two cartridges into the gun. She aimed at the bathroom door to be prepared if Jelena made it inside, but then the next contraction paralyzed her and she dropped the gun on the tile floor. The pain had moved from her diaphragm and pelvis to the birth canal. She could feel the burning from the baby's head as it tried to come out.

'My pants,' she gasped, kicking her legs. Philip looked at her in horror but then crawled over on all fours and helped her get them off.

'What should I do?' His eyes were suddenly clear and steady. He pulled down some towels from the towel warmer rack and spread them underneath her as she lay down.

'I don't know,' Sofia whimpered, looking into his eyes as the next bearing-down contraction made her body shake. The midwife had said that this would take hours, maybe multiple days since it was her first baby. She had assured her that the women who gave birth in cars and elevators were third- and fourth-time mothers. Why was the baby coming now and why was it happening so fast? Was something wrong? At the same time, her body was screaming that this was right. That it was ready, and that she had a job to do.

It did occur to her that a stranger was seeing her almost completely naked, but her relief at having Philip there quickly took the upper hand.

'I see the head,' he whispered. 'I think you should push now.' He pressed his hands against her shins so she could brace herself. Sofia felt a primal strength fill her. All the pain and fear vanished and the only thing that mattered now was getting the baby out. But as soon as the contraction ended, her strength evaporated. She leaned her head dully on the towel.

'I can't do this,' she cried. It was too hard, she wasn't going to be able to do it.

Philip grasped her arm and squeezed it hard.

'You can definitely do this. When the next contraction comes, just push as hard as you can.'

Just then they heard a bang and the sound of glass shattering from the living room.

Jelena had made it into the house.

Philip leaned with his full weight on Sofia's bent legs. The pain was increasing, but her strength was back. She took a deep breath and pressed her chin to her chest and pushed with all her might. She saw Sten's face plainly and clearly in front of her. He was smiling. He was going to be a grandfather. She pushed even harder, felt the baby's head burning like fire as it crowned. I'm dying now, she had time to think before the pain finally eased and she felt the baby slide out of her. Philip caught the bloody little body in a towel. Sofia caught a hint of a smile on his face before he handed the baby to her. Relief at hearing the robust cry washed over her. She tried to prop herself up on her elbow, saw the umbilical cord that still connected her to her baby. The bathroom floor was covered in blood and her body was shivering from the cold. She couldn't do any more. With the towel-wrapped bundle in her arms, she lay her head down on the cold tile floor and closed her eyes. She was so tired. All the energy she had just had had run out of her. All she wanted to do now was sleep. For a second, she let herself be lulled into unconsciousness.

'Sofia?' Philip shook her arm hard. Jelena's footsteps could be heard outside the bathroom door. She opened her eyes but saw only white dots. Philip kept pulling on her arm, but she waved him away, unable to take in what was going on.

The bathroom lock rattled. She recognised the sound. How many times had she used a knife to open a lock from the outside in the course of her work? Hundreds of times. The familiar squeak of the bathroom door being flung wide open made Sofia close her eyes. She heard Jelena turn the safety off on her gun. She realised it was over now but was far too exhausted to react. She pressed the baby tighter to her chest, trying to give it all the love she could before it would be too late.

A hundredth of a second of silence.

Then came a deafening bang that made Sofia jump and the baby in her arms begin crying loudly. Something fell to the floor in the front hall and Sofia cautiously opened her eyes. Jelena was lying on her back out there.

On the bathroom floor next to Sofia sat Philip holding Sten's shotgun.

112

The ambulance helicopter had landed in the snow below Sofia's house. Fredrik heard another one approaching from the sea as he ran up the path towards the house. The deck door was open, the glass smashed. As he climbed up the front steps, he encountered two ambulance drivers who brusquely shooed him aside to get past with a stretcher between them. On the stretcher lay a woman in her forties with dark hair and an oxygen mask over her face. Her eyes were barely open, but as the ambulance drivers passed him, her eyes met his. He shivered.

The pane of glass in the front door had been smashed, too. As he stepped into the front hall, he realised there was blood everywhere.

'Hello?' He called into the house, stepping over the broken glass.

'In here,' he heard a voice.

When he came into the living room, he saw Tord sitting on the sofa with his arm around Sofia, who was wrapped in a white robe. A woman in her fifties wearing a track suit sat on the coffee table in front of her straightening a towel around something in Sofia's lap.

Fredrik realised right away that it was the baby, even though it wasn't due for several weeks. The look on Sofia's face when she looked at the little bundle said it all. The overwhelming love he saw in her eyes made him feel warm inside.

Philip stood next to the sofa. His light grey shirt was bloody up to the elbows and there were large bloodstains on his jeans.

In his wildest imagination, Fredrik couldn't envision what had happened here.

'Oh, my God, are you injured?'

Philip shook his head.

'Was she the one who...' He nodded towards the front door as his words faded away.

'Jelena Hagelin,' Sofia replied briefly without taking her eyes off the baby in her arms.

Fredrik looked at Philip again. His eyes were alert, but full of grief. When their eyes met, his face crumpled into sobs. In two steps, Fredrik was over there, hugging him. They held each other hard for a long time and Philip sobbed silently against his shoulder.

'I'm so sorry, Philip, about Madeleine. I don't know what to say...'

Philip pulled free and wiped his nose with his hand. He had blood around his fingernails.

'Come, Fredrik,' Tord said, and Philip nodded that it was okay.

Fredrik sat down next to Sofia on the sofa. She looked into his eyes, lifted the towel that was covering the back of the baby's head, and held the baby up to him. Underneath the towel, a thick, coal-black head of hair was visible, and he could make out a scrunched, red face and an almost heart-shaped, red mouth. Carefully, she lifted the baby over into his embrace and his arms reflexively accepted it, even though he didn't know what to do with it. The woman sitting on the coffee table, whom Fredrik understood was the island midwife, adjusted the baby's head with a practiced hand so it was well supported.

'I was the one who... I helped.' Philip looked both proud and embarrassed, all while tears kept pouring down his cheeks. Fredrik looked at him in wonder.

'How did you know what to do?'

Philip shrugged.

'I've seen it in movies, I guess.'

The baby moved in Fredrik's arms, opened its eyes, and tried to look at him.

Fredrik looked at Sofia and then at the baby again.

'Is it a boy or a girl?'

Only then did he notice the colour of the baby's eyes. They were dark brown, almost black, exactly like his own. There was something familiar about the nose and the chin, too.

Sofia caressed the baby's head and looked at him.

'It's a girl,' Tord replied, beaming.

Six Weeks Later

113

Sofia pushed down on the stroller handle to bring the front wheels up so she could get over the snowbank that remained in front of the entrance to the police station. She wished she didn't have to go inside, but she had promised Kaj she would come by to show Astrid off after her visit to the daycare centre.

She looked at her daughter, who lay bundled with only her little button nose visible over the sheepskin lining of the stroller's bassinet. Mette had knit the hat out of pink and white yarn. Sofia hated it but had put it on for Kaj's sake.

He was so proud. He changed diapers, rocked her, and carried her. When it was time for her to sleep, he bundled her into her bassinet and walked with her for hours. Mette had been up twice, and Sofia had tried to keep a low profile. Humouring her talk of baby swim lessons, yoga for newborns, and pelvic floor exercises. Sofia was left alone with Astrid only when she was breastfeeding. Usually, she pretended that the breastfeeding was difficult so she could be alone. Her daughter ate greedily and quickly emptied the breast, but Sofia would let her lie there for a whole hour just to have her to herself without Kaj looming over her shoulder. They still had not discussed what their living arrangements would look like. So far, Kaj and Mette had slept in the flat in Örnsköldsvik and Sofia in the house on Ulvön. Kaj had continued to work remotely from the Örnsköldsvik Police Station to be close to her and Astrid. He didn't seem to be in any rush to return to his regular workplace in the Kungsholmen police building in Stockholm.

When Sofia rolled the stroller into the lobby, Eva stuck her head out and lit up immediately.

'Ah, I finally get to see the little beauty!'

She soon came jogging out the door of the cubicle that contained her reception desk. Before Sofia had time to react, Eva had slipped her hand down into the stroller and pulled the sheepskin cover off Astrid. The sudden move startled the baby, and she immediately began to cry.

'Oh, honey,' Eva crooned. 'Did I scare you?'

She picked up Astrid, who loudly protested the unexpected handling. The fact that the whole world was now talking about a virus that people were succumbing to left and right did not seem to concern Eva in the slightest. Rather, she nuzzled her nose right in under Astrid's chin and inhaled deeply.

'Oh, they smell so wonderful when they're newborns,' she exclaimed, ignoring Astrid's protests. 'They like it when you're a bit firm with them.' She gave Astrid's butt a few hard pats. Sofia's daughter now sounded like a fire alarm and several people who were sitting in the waiting room raised their eyebrows in disapproval.

'I think she's hungry.' Sofia reached for her daughter and took her into her arms. 'Could you help me out by keeping the stroller down here in the lobby while I take her upstairs?'

Eva nodded, pleased to have been given an assignment related to the baby. She handed Sofia the diaper bag.

'Kaj and Vera just got back from lunch.'

Sofia smiled gratefully and rocked Astrid to calm her down. Before she swiped her access card to open the door, she took a deep breath. She would stay for half an hour at the most.

—

Forty-five minutes later, she was still sitting in Kaj's borrowed office with a steady stream of visitors who all had to look at Astrid. Most of them kept their distance, but Karim could not help himself. After carefully sanitising his hands and stating several times that he was healthy as could be, he picked Astrid up. She allowed herself to be held without protest. Karim's eyes welled up as he gazed at Sofia.

'She looks just like my girls when they were little.'

Sofia smiled but avoided Kaj's gaze. Astrid truly did look like she could be Karim's daughter. Her thick, dark hair and olive skin bore no resemblance to either Kaj's or her own colouring. A fact that Kaj seemed completely oblivious to.

Karim rocked Astrid in his arms and spoke softly to her in Persian. He disappeared out into the hallway and continued strolling back and forth with her out there. It was as if he were made to take care of children, Sofia thought. Although perhaps that wasn't so odd given that his wife was a midwife and they had four daughters of their own.

'Do you want to see the video?' Kaj asked after casting a wary eye out into the hallway.

'What video?'

'Of Jelena Hagelin's interrogation.'

Sofia had completely forgotten that the preparations for Jelena's trial were underway. Anna Sondell was prosecuting her for kidnapping, manslaughter and attempted murder. They had all the evidence they needed for her to receive a long prison sentence. Her DNA had been found underneath Madeleine Svensson's fingernails, on the competition pistol that had been stolen from Ingegerd Westin's house, and on the letter from the crashed car. In addition, they had Sofia's and Philip's testimony about her attempt to murder them.

Jelena had already undergone a section 7 exam and was awaiting a forensic psychiatric exam.

Amanda Svensson had been awakened from the induced coma, removed from the respirator and, according to the doctors, the prognosis for her recovery was good. Ellie and Anders had been at her bedside when she woke up. Amanda had picked Jelena out in a photo line-up on her first attempt and described how she had held a gun to her and forced her to write the letter and then drive off the edge of the embankment.

Kaj located the video of the interrogation session on his computer and hit play. The screen filled with an image of Jelena Hagelin in a hospital bed. Vera sat on one side of the bed and Kaj on the other. Only his back was visible. One of Jelena's arms was bandaged from the shoulder to the elbow. The shots Philip had fired had hit her arm and shoulder, which was the only reason she was alive today.

'How is Ellie doing?' was the first thing Jelena asked after Kaj had stated the date and time and that Vera was also present.

Neither he nor Vera responded.

'You know why we're here, right?' Vera asked.

Jelena nodded.

'You are a suspect in the death of Madeleine Svensson, the kidnapping of Ellie Svensson, and the attempted murder of Amanda Svensson. Among other things.'

Jelena nodded, seemingly unmoved. Either she was heavily medicated or she didn't really feel any guilt about what she had done, Sofia thought.

They had found hundreds of pictures of Anders Svensson on Jelena's computer and in her cabinet in her office. Some were taken during the time when they were together, but most of them were copied from his Facebook page. There were also pictures that had been taken in secret through the windows of the vacation house. Pictures in which Anders was asleep, sitting on the deck drinking his morning coffee or fishing at the lake. Jelena had followed his every move over the last year. She even had pictures from his home in Stockholm. But she had not been content merely to photograph and stalk the object of her love. She had also spent many nights alone in the house in Sunnansjö, sleeping in Anders's bed, wearing his clothes and taking care of the house while waiting for him to return. She had admitted to all of it, and it was also corroborated by Johan's crime scene analysis.

'Why did you kidnap Ellie and Madeleine?'

Jelena stared blankly straight ahead for a long time.

'It just happened.'

'Just happened?' Vera repeated.

'I was driving by on my way to Dagny's. Then I saw the light was on in the windows. I just wanted to look at him.'

She looked at Vera as if she thought Vera would understand.

'You can't see the house from the road,' Vera pointed out.

Jelena shrugged, but then her face contorted into a wince and she clutched her wounded arm.

'She was there when I got there,' she said, her brow furrowed in pain.

'Madeleine was?'

'Yes.'

'What happened?'

'I thought... I thought he was cheating on me with someone else. It was like my head was on fire. After all I had done for him.'

'So you knocked Madeleine out with the fire extinguisher?'

Jelena nodded.

'But I didn't want to just leave her there. I felt sorry for Anders, who would have to see all that blood.'

Sofia shivered watching the computer screen. How warped could a person's idea of love be?

'So I put her in the car and then I drove to Ingegerd's. I had planned to dump her in the Mo River, but she woke up and started screaming when I opened the trunk. She kicked me in the face and tried to get away. So I hit her again, with the tire iron. As I went to try to pull her out, a car drove by, so I was forced to leave her in the trunk.'

'Why did you go to Ingegerd's house?'

'Ingegerd needs to be moved several times a day. Also at night. She can't just lie there in wet diapers, you know?'

Jelena stated this as if it were extremely obvious. As if Kaj and Vera were the heartless ones who didn't understand that an elderly person required care. As if that had absolutely nothing to do with the fact that she had used Ingegerd's basement as a dungeon and let a person die of thirst down there.

Jelena shook her head.

'I didn't know where to take her. Then I remembered that Ingegerd has a basement and that she could lie down there while I figured it out.'

Jelena looked troubled.

'But when she woke up, she was insane. Over and over again she screamed that I should let her go and that she was Anders's daughter and that I would get money from him if I let her go. I must have sat on the other side of that basement door for a whole hour listening. I didn't know what to do with her. At first I didn't believe her. That she was his daughter, I mean,' she added as if that were an important detail. 'Then she told me to go get her phone.'

'So you went back to Sunnansjö to get it?'

Jelena nodded.

'How did you get in?'

'With the spare key that used to hang in the woodshed during the renovation. I had made a copy of it.'

'What happened then?'

'I read the text where it said that Anders was going to bring Amanda and...' Her eyes filled with tears. 'And Ellie. That's when I realised how I could get him back.'

Jelena turned to Vera and looked directly into the camera for a second. Her eyes were cold. 'I would take Ellie, hold her for a few days, and then I would find her. Anders would be so grateful. And if Amanda just disappeared, then he would start loving me again.'

Kaj took his eyes off the screen and looked at Sofia. She was shaking her head. The interrogation video kept playing.

'You were going to take Amanda's place?' Vera asked.

Jelena squeezed her eyes shut.

'I would have been a far better mother to Ellie.'

'And Madeleine?'

Jelena looked down at the hospital blanket.

'She screamed non-stop. Every time I tried to go down there with food or water, she screamed and tried to attack me. Plus, she had seen my face. I didn't know what to do.'

'So you let her die?' Kaj asked.

'Please, don't tell Anders.' Jelena looked pleadingly at Kaj.

How could a person be as horrifically detached from reality as Jelena was, Sofia wondered.

'Did you arrange Amanda's attempted suicide in your car?'

'In Dagny's car,' Jelena clarified.

'How?'

'She got to choose,' Jelena said. 'A gunshot or driving over the edge of the embankment. She chose the embankment.'

'So you threatened to shoot her if she didn't drive over the edge?'

Jelena nodded.

'But she survived?' Kaj said, looking at Jelena.

'Yes.'

'How did you feel then?' Vera asked.

'I was angry, of course. It was like it was all for nothing.' Her voice was a monotone devoid of any emotion. Only when they discussed Ellie did Jelena seem to possess any emotions.

'But not everything, right? What about Ellie?'

Tears once again filled Jelena's eyes, but she didn't bother to wipe them away.

'After everything had gone wrong, I just wanted to have her. Nothing else. Not Anders. She could become my daughter. I could…'

Jelena drew a ragged breath which was followed by a wave of hoarse sobs. She covered her face with her hands and her crying intensified.

'Ellie, my little Ellie.'

Over and over again, she moaned Ellie's name.

Kaj paused the video.

'It keeps going pretty much like this. It feels like we have quite a clear motive.'

Sofia nodded.

Karim came back into the room with Astrid in his arms. She was sound asleep.

Sofia turned her back to Jelena's face, puffy from crying, on the screen. She didn't want to see or hear any more. Karim reluctantly handed her Astrid.

'You have to promise to bring her in again soon,' he said.

Sofia gazed at her daughter. The round face and the perfect mouth. Her soul ached with love for this little miracle. In a way, she could understand Jelena. If the love she felt for Anders was even close to the love Sofia felt for Astrid... No, it was not the same thing. A mother's love was pure. Light. The love Jelena wanted to give Anders was anything but that. It had been born in darkness.

Epilogue

Fredrik raised his hand to shield himself from the dazzling April sunshine. His eyes, red from crying, stung and he had forgotten to bring his sunglasses. Apart from his own car, the parking lot was empty. He locked it and stepped up onto the sidewalk. Philip had already gotten out and was standing there looking at two people who were talking to each other over by the kiosk-like flower shop. They were standing unusually far apart, even though they seemed to know each other. Everyone was affected by the pandemic that had gripped the world the last couple of months. People were locked in their homes waiting for the contagion to creep in beneath their doors and strike them dead. Every day, Fredrik followed the developments on TV and was horrified at the panic that prevailed. People were hoarding canned goods and toilet paper, doomsayers were predicting mass mortalities and preaching that the pandemic was the scourge of God upon us. Others were taking it in stride and carried on with life as usual. He was somewhere in between, in between all of it, it felt like. As if he were hovering, vibrating between two magnets without being able to be pulled in one or the other direction. Between the desire to fight and the desire to give up, between his love for Ida and his love for Sofia. Most of all, between a desire to move on and his conviction that he and Sofia now shared a bond that could never be broken. Astrid was his daughter. It didn't matter that Sofia refused to talk to him about it. Anyone with eyes in their head could see that she was his child. And he wasn't planning to just let himself be pushed aside. As soon as everything with the funeral was over, he would request a paternity test. It didn't matter what Kaj had to say about the matter.

The church bells started ringing and Fredrik gestured to Philip.

'It's starting soon,' Fredrik said. 'We have to go in.'

Philip didn't say anything, but he looked up and nodded. He looked briefly into Fredrik's eyes and then took his hand, an unusual gesture from someone who viscerally disliked physical contact. Fredrik squeezed it back, grateful for the closeness at this moment. He pulled his open jacket around himself more tightly with his free hand. It was still cold out and the trees around the cemetery were almost bare. Only the tall thuja hedge boasted fresh, evergreen needles.

A pastor dressed in white met them in the doorway of the church. She was in her fifties but had already gone completely grey. She had grey hair, a grey face and grey eyes. Since shaking hands was no longer an option, she nodded compassionately, first to Philip and then to Fredrik, and invited them to enter the church.

They were the last to arrive. They followed the pastor down the stairs to the cloakroom, hung up their jackets and then entered the nave. The pews were full from the first to the last. Fredrik felt Philip stiffen when he saw the white coffin overflowing with yellow and white flowers. Once again, he grasped Philip's hand, not caring what it looked like. A few people turned around when they came in, nodded awkwardly in greeting, and then went back to browsing through the hymnals, reading the program or fiddling with their white roses, which were to be placed on the coffin as a final farewell. Anything to avoid having to make eye contact with the other mourners.

The family sat at the very front. The ushers had done their best to make sure that everyone practiced social distancing, but the pandemic and the fear of contagion seemed to have been forgotten for the moment.

They looked for a seat in the back, but Fredrik quickly noticed the waving hand inviting them to come sit in one of the front pews as a part of the family. He dragged Philip with him down the aisle and sat down at the far end of the second row. The man who had waved nodded to them as they sat down. Fredrik realised that the four-year-old girl sitting next to him with a crocheted teddy bear in her lap must be Ellie. Next to her sat a young woman with a black silk scarf tied around her head. An angry red scar ran across one side of her face.

The pastor cleared her throat and looked at the congregation.

'We are gathered here today to say a final farewell to Madeleine Svensson.'

Acknowledgements

I want to start by thanking my editor, Petra König-Kämpe, and my publisher, Karin Linge Nordh, for being unflaggingly in my editorial corner of the ring for this second round of the Ulvön Island series. I also want to thank the whole gang at Bazar for a fantastic job with the launch. Thanks also to Karin Wahlén at Kult PR and my superhero agent, Judith Toth at Nordin Agency. You are a fabulous group of women, and it is a pleasure getting to work with you all!

Writing a murder mystery is not a one-man job. It would be foolish to claim otherwise. Many people have shared their time and helped me with facts to make this fictional story as credible as possible. For this, I am more grateful than I have the words to express. I hope that I haven't forgotten anyone and, if I have, I apologise most humbly.

Thank you to Mia Nilö, licensed speech therapist, Elina Einarsson, anaesthesiologist at Örnsköldsvik Hospital, Joakim Meidell, internal medicine resident at Örnsköldsvik Hospital, and Cecilia Nordius, registered nurse, for your help with questions about jaw injuries, overdoses and sedation.

I would also like to thank Linn Johansson, construction engineer, for your help with questions about the construction industry and its regulations, and Jennie Westerlind, former caregiver with Örnsköldsvik's municipal home-help services.

Thanks as well to Marinette Wallin for driving me back and forth across Ulvön Island, by land and by sea, in pursuit of information and for sharing all your wisdom. Thanks also to

Ulrika Gidlund for the many delightful Ulvön stories and to Johan Norgren, skipper of the M/F Ulvön.

A big thanks to Gitte Tinglöf Källman, musician, who took part in the rescue work on the MS Isabella on 28 September, 1994, for her vivid description of the terrifying night the Estonia sank.

For help with the police world, I'd like to thank the crime scene investigators of Police Region North's Forensic Unit 3, Anna Jinghede, forensic dentist, PhD student and police/crime scene investigator at Police Region Bergslagen, Kjerstin Svedberg, retired head of Norra Ångermanland Local Police District, Kicki Svedberg, former associate judge of appeal for the Swedish National Courts Administration, Rickard Hagström, inspector in Norra Ångermanland, Börje Öhman, former head of communications with the police and chief of the county criminal police for the Swedish Police Authority in Sundsvall, Michael Lundberg, inspector/on-call investigation leader with Jämtland Police District's Investigation Section, Niklas Stjernlöf, inspector/on-call investigation leader for Jämtland Police District's On-Call Investigation I, as well as Anders Jarlkell, inspector with Police Region Stockholm. Many thanks also to Krille Hållberg at Missing People in Västernorrland.

Last but not least, I would like to thank my family for all your support, my future husband for all your love and my beloved children Selma, Nils and August for putting up with having a mother who is an author. Thank you for giving me a reason to keep breathing when life becomes overwhelming.

Any errors there may be are my own, and all similarities to existing people are coincidental. The region around Örnsköldsvik and Ulvön Island, however, have been reproduced insofar as possible just as they look in real life.

Do you love crime fiction and are always on the lookout for brilliant authors?

Canelo Crime is home to some of the most exciting novels around. Thousands of readers are already enjoying our compulsive stories. Are you ready to find your new favourite writer?

Find out more and sign up to our newsletter at canelocrime.com